BLACK
GIRLS
MUST
DIE
EXHAUSTED

BLACK GIRLS MUST DIE EXHAUSTED

A Novel

JAYNE ALLEN

HARPER

An Imprint of HarperCollinsPublishers

BLACK GIRLS MUST DIE EXHAUSTED. Copyright © 2021 by Jaunique Sealey. All rights reserved. Printed in the United States of America. No part of this book may be used or reproduced in any manner whatsoever without written permission except in the case of brief quotations embodied in critical articles and reviews. For information, address HarperCollins Publishers, 195 Broadway, New York, NY 10007.

HarperCollins books may be purchased for educational, business, or sales promotional use. For information, please email the Special Markets Department at SPsales@harpercollins.com.

Originally published in 2018 by Quality Black Books.

Designed by Jamie Lynn Kerner

Library of Congress Cataloging-in-Publication Data has been applied for.

ISBN 978-0-06-313790-5 (pbk.)
ISBN 978-0-06-314299-2 (library edition)
ISBN 978-0-06-316138-2 (international edition)

21 22 23 24 25 LSC 10 9 8 7 6 5 4 3 2 1

NOTE TO READER

Dear Reader,

It's not often that a book becomes as much about what happens outside of its pages as inside of them. *Black Girls Must Die Exhausted* has been birthed by readers into an ever-evolving collaboration of culture, community, fellowship, healing, and important conversations that we're all just beginning to learn how to hold space for. And now you become a part of the story.

I want to personally welcome you into this world. As the characters begin to take shape for you and fill out in your mind, as they become friends and maybe even family, as you possibly even feel compelled to talk back to the pages, just know that you're becoming part of a much larger family, the community of *BGMDE* readers. We are all right here with you.

I originally wrote *Black Girls Must Die Exhausted* to show that—when you strip away the divides, barriers, categories, and all of the various ways we've learned to separate ourselves, one from another—at our foundation, love is the language that we all speak and the very lifeblood of our existence. Love comes in many forms—self-love, love between friends, familial love, and romantic love among them.

In a gorgeously complex life full of challenges, it is tempting to think that struggle somehow makes us unworthy in some way, rather than qualifying us for something greater. We tend to believe that the scars that come when we scrape against the pains of life are anything but the beauty marks that fortify us.

If you understand that every day is a great triumph, a victory over all of the forces that would try to tear you down, then you understand how very important it is to celebrate everything that gives us the courage to keep daring for our greatest selves.

This book itself *is* my *love letter*—to you, to Black women, to women, and to all those who understand the beauty that comes through struggle and the benefit of doing their own work to heal, to understand, to grow, and, most importantly, to love more fully.

If you are looking for ways to support this work and to encourage more works like it, please consider first writing a review. Please also consider spreading the word, following us on Instagram and Twitter, and joining the mailing list. The easiest way to create change is to do the thing closest at hand. If you're new to writing reviews, or would like some guidance, please feel free to visit JayneAllen.com for more information and third-party resources on how to become a powerful, credible, and effective objective reviewer.

There is a need for more diverse voices in literature with the freedom and leeway to write undiluted perspectives for more diverse audiences. I want to thank HarperCollins for providing that leeway and serving as a conduit between an overlooked audience of readers and the books they'd like to see more of. We don't just need more diverse books, we need more diverse perspectives with the expectation and acknowledgment of a more diverse audience. With your help, the tides are shifting.

Thank you for joining the adventure, one book at a time.

With abounding love,
Jayne Allen

BLACK GIRLS MUST DIE EXHAUSTED

1

THE DAY I TURNED THIRTY, I OFFICIALLY DEPARTED MY CHILD-hood. Not the pigtail braids, devil-may-care, "don't get your Sunday church clothes dirty" whirlwind of playtime whimsy. And not the extraordinarily fun bad-decision-making adolescence of my college years. If my childhood was an ignorance of consequence, then the onset of adulthood was a head-on collision straight into the meaning of *everything*. Thirty was the end of the dress rehearsal. I was *officially* grown. And to me, that meant a checklist.

Education?

Check.

Good job?

Check.

Reliable transportation?

Check.

Down payment for some property?

Check.

Dating options limited to marriage material?

Check, check, and check.

I had that checklist *on lock*. But then, at some point, once you get into it, your thirties throw some major curveballs your way, and you realize that real life, not just adulthood, is what happens between the lines of that checklist. You learn that life isn't really about checklist-type problems. And that's when you have to find out who you *really* are, because one minute you had all the answers, and the next you've got none at all. So, of course, just when I started to gain a comfortable rhythm with regular life concerns, my body went ahead and did the unthinkable.

"It's bad," I heard the doctor say. "I wish I had better news. The reality is, Tabitha, you're only thirty-three, but without taking significant steps in the next six months, you may never be able to have a family."

I had already left her office, but her voice still trailed me to my car, and stayed with me on my drive to work, echoing in my mind on continuous loop. The only merciful interruption was the real-time computer-generated interjections of my navigation app, steering me around the stubborn Los Angeles traffic. Even worse than getting bad news was that it was going to make me late. In my profession, late was tragic; but on the day of our weekly newsroom meeting, late could mean you just lost the assignment that would've made your career. And for my place in line I had already fought, cried, bled, and eaten far more than my fair share of ramen noodles.

My mind was racing, so I'm sure it paraphrased, honing in on what was really the most important consequence to a person like me. In reality, the doctor could have been diplomatic. Maybe she said, "You'll never be able to have *biological* children," or something like "You won't be able to *use your own eggs* to have children." Whatever she said sounded nothing like hope. My own version of family included becoming a wife *and* mother. In a life of careful planning, this reality was always a foregone conclusion—the one puzzle piece that was supposed to fall into place on its own. This was the quiet assurance I gave myself, that I'd eventually fill the gap in my life I'd learned to ignore but could never manage to completely forget.

This morning's news placed that all in jeopardy. I learned that I have something called *premature ovarian failure*. Gotta love that kind of name, right? Rather than a much more friendly "disorder," the word "failure" is already wrapped right in. So there's just no sugarcoating this kind of bad. You know what this type of "failure" is caused by? *Stress.* The crazy thing is, if you asked me just an hour ago, before that appointment, I would have *sworn* that I was just fine.

"Stressed? I'm not stressed," I insisted. Well, really, I protested, but my doctor was unconvinced.

Instead, she informed me that studies held all the unfamiliar warnings I wish I'd heard before. "It could be little things that you just aren't noticing," Dr. Ellis said. "Something happens that seems small at the time, or you've become desensitized, but it all adds up. Either way, the test results don't lie."

But to me, those were just numbers and words meant for someone else but mistakenly delivered to me—because I did not *feel* stressed. At least, not before leaving the doctor's office. I was even unfazed navigating the infuriating molasses maze of morning traffic. I could proudly say I barely cursed, never had an episode of road rage, held the door open for people, smiled at strangers, and I always made time to put on lipstick. What was there to be stressed about? Before today, everything was going according to plan—I was dating a "paper perfect" man, suitable for marriage and tall enough for kids; I was up for a promotion; and I had just met my savings goal for a down payment for my very own first dream house. Sure, my family-making hormones were starting to bubble, but I thought I had *time*. I focused on my career, my friends, spending Saturdays with my grandmother, and loving on Marc, who hadn't quite mentioned marriage but who I was sure would eventually. *No need to rush, Tabitha.* That's what I'd tell myself in every one of those moments when even the slightest hint of "where is this going?" started to rise in my belly. Who needs to be pushy about things when you have time, right? With today's news, I was just starting to discover how very wrong I was.

In my well-ordered world of focused professional upward mobility, crossed-off checklists, and comfortable semi-serious dating, I thought I had prepared for everything. So, how was it being ripped apart at the seams by one little doctor visit that was supposed to be routine? I had only gone in for a very simple follow-up to review the results of my regular blood tests. I should have known it was a problem when Dr. Ellis insisted on seeing me in person, rather than just sending an email. Evidently, my fertility numbers matched those of a woman about to receive her AARP card.

"Your body is working too hard to produce an egg each month," she said. "It seems like there's been an imbalance going on for some time. The good news is that we caught it while there's still time to pursue options in front of you."

Options? In my mind, having a family was never an *option*. Options were for things like the shoes you pack on vacation, or where you decide to meet your friends for dinner. But I've always known what I wanted, at least since I was nine years old, because once you're made aware of what you don't have, it becomes the thing you dream of.

Crap. Distraction caused me to miss my turn, prompting the tinny-voiced navigator to reroute me, matching my thoughts of the moment. How did I get here? It's not like I *forgot* that I was single or *forgot* to have children. Not possible. It hummed in the background on every night out with my girls, every trip to the supermarket, and every solo tax return. And once I turned thirty, no matter my accomplishments, educational or professional, there was no chance of escaping the question "So, how come you're not *married yet*?" I could almost see it written in cursive on perplexed faces, along the wrinkled expression lines crossing well-meaning foreheads. In the eyes of the even more curious, "What's wrong with her?" twinkled in Morse code. It felt as if people thought that my degrees came with a free Mrs. option that I didn't elect at graduation. It just wasn't that easy.

All along, I'd done my share of dating. Dating for me was always for the family you hoped to make, even at some level when I was "just having fun" in my twenties. So, of course, in my thirties, I was dating with the care, intensity, and dedication of a second job. Unfortunately, up to this point, dating itself hadn't yet made for any *relationship* that I was sure should or could turn into a long-term expectation—not even with Marc. It just seemed that once thirty hit, all the folks for whom marriage meant something, especially the men who considered having a wife and family as an accomplishment in its own right, had already taken their nearest best option to the altar. The men who were left and still single, well, they considered it an accomplishment that they had neither wife nor child, and never got "caught up" or "caught slippin'," which likened falling in love to unprotected casual sex. They treated love like a disease you catch, and if real adult commitment was the incurable version of it, then for them family was basically death. And goodness knows, I wasn't trying to kill anybody—what I wanted was that same-page kind of love, the connection between two people that gave each of them a lot more answers than questions.

So, in spite of my very best efforts *and* stilettos, I'd been as single as a wrapped tampon. Except, for the past year and a half, I was better classified as not exactly single-single. I would have to admit: it took me a while to get centered on what seemed to be more of the right type of dating track for my type of goals. When I started dating, I beelined for the boys with hot bodies, actor dreams, and table-waiting futures. Coming back to LA from grad school, I realized that I should probably find another responsible "adult" with whom I could at least pretend to build a fairy tale. What I got was a doctor who was too busy for me, an artist manager from the music industry who wined and dined me for a month and then ghosted, and a seemingly mature single dad in his late thirties who gave me the key to his apartment on our second date and then asked for it back when his mother came to visit two months later. Then, in between, there were the "deceptives" and "time wasters," who wanted extensive emotional attachment but in the end could only commit to being friends.

LA guys were a special breed, and not just because people came here to chase after neon-vivid dreams of wealth and fame. So, when I met Marc, who seemed in every way an educated, handsome, professional guy with a healthy amount of swagger *and* decency, I wasn't trying to stray too far to the left or the right. At the beginning, I felt lucky. But as time progressed, lucky turned into love, for the both of us, in spite of our schedules. Even when my visibility at the news station increased, bringing with it tempting offers of more time and attention, I ignored them, because they weren't men of Marc's caliber. Plus, he had my heart. He made me smile and laugh, and when we were together I felt like the most beautiful and sexiest woman for miles. He just had that way about him, that same way that made me feel so lucky in the beginning.

Our relationship had long-term potential, although with a heavy emphasis on *potential*. It wasn't lost on me that we still only spent weekends together and I hadn't met his family or shared a holiday. Yes, I knew I didn't have forever, but I thought I was doing the right thing—find the right guy, and then give him the time and space he needed to make some moves toward a future together. In the year and a half we'd been dating, he never once brought up marriage, so I didn't either. And neither one of us brought up the topic of kids, other than at first to discuss birth control measures. He'd sometimes acknowledge that someday they would be very nice to have, and I'd agree but never push, no matter how badly I wanted to. Knowing that Marc wanted to be a father was enough for my checklist. I thought I could just wait him out until we got to the right place in our relationship. I was just always so sure that there was time. Today, the shock was still settling in my stomach that there was not. The doctor told me that all I had was six months, *at best*.

I felt my palms hit against the steering wheel, as frustration animated my insides. What a waste of diligence spent not getting pregnant, only to find myself in a situation where, when I'd hope to be able to, I possibly couldn't. *Ugh!* The idea of the clock running out on my fertility felt like every bad date, every tough breakup, and every guy that I turned down in high school had all turned into big, permanent cracks in my life's sidewalk. I hated the idea that maybe these people had taken something from me that I could never get back. Dr. Ellis had said "options," but I couldn't help but to think, what really were my *options*? Up to then, the only options I'd been concerned with were the stories I'd pitch in the news-room, restaurants for dates with Marc, and maybe my dream of which little house I'd buy. Now my newsroom pitches would become do-or-die opportunities to get my next pro-motion, dates with Marc would turn into critical conversa-tions, and my little house would evaporate into an expensive egg-freezing procedure that I couldn't even afford. But this car ride from the doctor's office was no good time to get started on that. I was already late for work and frazzled.

What I really needed to do was steal the time at red lights to repurpose my visor as a makeshift vanity and slap a bare-bones makeup "beat" on my face. It was too much of a trick to control a steering wheel with one hand and contour with the other, especially since my hands were still shaking. My reflection looked back at me with a grimace. I was definitely without my usual "pretty." I was a television reporter and yet not a "classic" beauty. So, success for me meant there was the fifty percent premium on standards to meet, my hair to straighten, and masks of makeup and appropriateness to wear over my brown skin. I managed it all with the compo-sure that you'd expect of a professional and, most of the time, without a second thought. Was *this* stressful? The need to conform to a standard that I couldn't naturally meet? Well, today it was. Today, my mind let well-settled ideas unspool themselves from my usual tightly wound spindle of coping. Today was the first time in a long time that my appearance felt like a burden I wanted to just let go of. Even as I fought to resume my makeup routine, my mind perched on the verge of becoming an unraveled mess, struggling to find order in the loosely connected thoughts plucked from forgotten memories and the life plans that might no longer apply.

At a time like this, I wanted to call my mother. Well, I wanted to be able to, but the kind of empathy that this situation required was not in her wheelhouse. I was supposed to deliver grandbabies, at least two, and she always told me that she was hoping for three, so that she'd always have a little one to shop for. My mom talked about grandkids all the time, even though she lived on the full other side of the continent in Washington, DC. This conversation was her version of a calendar reminder for a recurring meeting or appointment. We'd speak on the phone about all things unrelated, catching up on life in our respective worlds, and suddenly, like a ping, the topic would pop up and insert itself into polite conversation like, "So, how are things going with Marc, and when can I expect to meet my grandchildren?" It didn't help that I was an only child, at least on my mother's side, and her only hope of becoming a grandmother. I guess all along I felt like I somehow owed her that, especially since I couldn't go back and fix the past. *Crap.* The robotic voice warned me of a traffic slowdown on my route, and I was still twenty minutes out from work according to the navigation ETA. I was close enough to take a shortcut through my old neighborhood and save myself at least five minutes on the way to the station. I decided to take the turnoff.

I last lived here, in View Park, with my parents. It was a neighborhood of Black professionals set off on the southwest side of Los Angeles. We weren't living large, but we were living "Black folks" fancy. This wasn't all the way ritzy, like the really rich entertainment types in Bel Air and Malibu, but was especially *comfortable*. Even more than the LA mega-mansions and the Hollywood Hills contemporary showplaces, *these* were still the kinds of homes I dreamed about most often. Most were ranch layouts of varying sizes, but some were towering estates spanning what seemed like a full block. Lawns were always immaculately manicured, and palm trees lined most of the streets, some of which gave the perfect view all the way to downtown. We owned our home with a palm tree *and* a lemon tree out front, and I had my own room. I hated the color, but my mother picked out what it was *supposed* to be—a pale Pepto Bismol pink "for princesses." I certainly didn't think of myself as a princess growing up—sometimes, I thought of myself as a teacher or a doctor, someone with a career, someone who put both feet on the ground every morning, got dressed, and fought her own battles. My mom learned her fairy tales from her mother and Walt Disney, but I learned mine from Oprah.

Back then, my friends and my school were all within walking distance and so, in the evenings, with just a short walk and no bus ride, I was able to get my homework done quickly and indulge in one of my favorite hobbies. I was probably a little too old for it then, but I still absolutely loved to play with my collection of Barbie dolls. Their pink world, I didn't mind. Pink just was never the right color for my reality. For those dolls, I had everything, the dream house, the Corvette, you name it. With them, and *their* pink, anything

was possible from one day to the next. I used their thin Barbie bodies to make my own role models who lived the way
I wanted to, with their own cars and their own houses that
could be decorated as they saw fit. It was a space that I could
control amid the perfectly organized, designed, and imple-
mented perfection that surrounded me in every other aspect
of our lives as a family. My mother married my father almost
directly after college and, as far as I knew, her career focus
was my dad, building a perfect life for him and playing the
role she had always believed she was best suited for—a beautiful, supportive homemaker and, eventually, mother.

On our very last evening as a family, nine-year-old me
played in my fantasies, sitting on the floor of my bedroom in
clothes still wrinkled and dirty from school recess. Suddenly,
I was startled by what sounded like a roiling, piercing wail
from my mother that came from the kitchen. I had heard
the back door close and thought nothing of it because it was
the time my dad usually came home. Or the time he used to
return, before he started spending nights away on work trips
that had been coming up with increasing frequency. Scared
for my mother, I rushed into the kitchen to see her sitting at
the table with her head in her hands and my dad standing
near the door with his jacket over his arm and the strangest
look on his face. They seemed lost in their own moment—my
mother sobbing and my father standing there, until I finally
managed to get some kind of sound out of my mouth and
they noticed me.

"Wha . . . what's wrong, Mommy?" I asked. My mother,
upon hearing my small voice, took in a sharp breath. I think
she had forgotten that I was in the house. She turned and
looked at me—the memory of her usually immaculate makeup

running down her eyes would today make me think of a Picasso painting or some real-life version of an Edvard Munch distortion.

Her glistening eyes found mine and she said in a frighteningly serious tone, "Your father is leaving us for his *other* family." And there it was, as she turned back to sobbing, this time collapsing on the table.

"Oh my God, Jeanie, I can't believe that you would say that to her!" my dad shrieked, throwing his briefcase against the kitchen floor. I stood still like a prey animal while my immature mind processed what I had heard. *What? My dad, leaving? What other family? Leaving? Where's he going?*

"Daddy, you're leaving?" was all I could muster, an echo of what I had heard. "When?" I started to cry-talk, questioning with escalating panic and increasing volume. My father came over to me, kneeled down, and looked me in my eyes.

"I'll never leave *you*, Tabby. There're some things your mother and I need to discuss. Can you go to your room and I'll come see you in a bit? I promise I won't leave. I promise. Okay?" Something about his reassurance bought a temporary calm that allowed me to break from the sight of my sobbing mother, walk back into my room, and close the door. I didn't want to hear any more of whatever was going on in the kitchen. I tried to resume my scene—my blond Barbie had been teaching her friends about something we had learned in school that week—but suddenly those dolls didn't seem that interesting anymore. In that instant, their world felt as fake and plastic as their slippery rubber legs. I put them away and tried to keep to my routine, washing up, putting on my night clothes, and eventually getting into my bed. I lay on my back with my hands folded across the top of my entirely flat chest, staring at the ceiling, waiting who knows how long until my door eventually opened and my dad came in. He walked across my pink shag carpeting to my pink princess bed and finally sat on the edge. It was the next conversation that turned that day into my very first "D" day—I learned there was a woman named Diane and there would be a divorce and that my dad was eventually not going to be living with me and my mother anymore. So indeed, there was another "D" discovered on that day: *deception.*

The concept of an "affair," and the fact that my dad had one, was something I'd learn on a different night—one of many to follow in which my mother sought comfort in glass after glass of wine that loosened her lips to release truths I would have rather not known. But there was one thing my mother did not speak of, and neither did my father. It was only when I finally did meet her, and laid my own eyes on her face—smiling to excess, white teeth, rose-colored lips, brown hair, and bright blue eyes—that I realized Diane was white. It was the stereotypical insult added to injury for my mother. An actual white woman was something that she could imitate but never be.

The betrayal of Diane was a further sting to my mother because my father's mother, my grandmother, the other and original Tabitha Abigail Walker, was also white. When my mother and father got married, my mother was under the impression she would be my father's choice for his adult life. And not that there was any friction between my mother and my grandmother, but until I was born, Granny Tab was the only other woman that my mother had ever had to compete with for my father's attention. When I was younger, I remember Granny Tab's bright-blue eyes and her box-dye-brown hair that always bopped just above her shoulders in the perfect bob, and her schoolteacher glasses that sometimes hung on a metal chain around her neck and sometimes perched on the end of her thin English ski-slope nose. She spent her career as a teacher in the LA Unified School District and retired while I was in middle school. It was really Granny Tab who taught me how to read and write my name in cursive and helped me pass algebra. Growing up, I never used to think of my grandmother as "white." She was just my Granny Tab and "hey, Mrs. Walker!" to the rainbow of kids in her classroom when I visited. I knew she was from West Virginia, but she didn't talk about it much, and we didn't spend any time with her side of the family. From my understanding, things didn't go over so well when she married my grandfather, but he wasn't someone we talked about much either. All I knew about him was that he was a Black man from the same town as Granny Tab; they were married right after high school and then they divorced when my dad was little, only for my grandfather to disappear completely shortly after. Sometimes I wondered what could have happened to make someone as warm as Granny Tab turn away and never look back at parts of her family. Those thoughts never lasted long, because she radiated enough love on her own to make up for all the missing folks from her side. So, for her, "family" was the family she chose, the family she made (minus the family she unmade), and the family my dad made after that. Up until Diane, my dad's end of things was mostly Black—my mom and me. He and my mother met at Howard University, for goodness' sake.

Even with a white grandmother, "whiteness" never played any role in my identity. As far as I was concerned, there was no difference between what my dad was and what my mom was, and by extension, no difference between either of them and me. Thinking about it, I suppose she *could* have, but Granny Tab never "wore" her whiteness as if it were a badge or some kind of cape, or default setting relative to my "Blackness" or "brownness," so to speak. She just simply was, and I was, and together, we all just *were*. I would have never dared utter the words "mixed" or "biracial" if someone asked me my cultural, racial, or ethnic identity. And that wouldn't be because I was making some kind of political statement or a choice of one thing over another. It just would be most accurate to say that it never occurred to me that I had a choice of it at all. Ever since I was a little girl, my grandmother had always been my much older "twin," my adult best friend and the reason I was proud to be named Tabitha Walker. But once the Diane thing had happened, all kinds of lines that had never existed before started to pencil themselves into our lives, and all kinds of questions that we'd never thought to ask needed answers.

My father's abandonment grew its own roots in my mind, eventually grafting on to other teenage insecurities, making ugly knots of angst that I channeled into excelling in my studies. My mother had fewer options—she'd become a planet spiraled off into space without the rotational gravity of the sun. When stability was lacking, in the midst of all of the tumult and my mother's challenging window of self-doubt and confusion, Granny Tab was always a safe haven for me. If things got too heated or too cool at home, she was a short bus ride away. On the worst days, especially when I was younger, I would go straight to Granny Tab's house and climb into bed with her, bury my head in her shoulder crook, and cry. If I didn't have to go to work, that's exactly what I'd do today.

She'd wrap her arms around me with no words, just holding the space for me and for us. She was strong in that way, the quiet way, the way of just being there and not needing to fix what couldn't be fixed by anything other than tears and time.

The blaring sound of a horn behind me pulled me out of my reverie and stopped my accompanying hypnotic mascara application at the green light in front of me. I was just five minutes from work now, but the flood of difficult memories and the swirling in my mind had taken my attention off the flow of cars ahead. I dropped my hand holding the wand to my lap and held the bottom of the steering wheel while I screwed the tube back into a single piece. Pulling my thoughts and my eyes back to my reflection in the mirror, I could see that I was just one lipstick application away from being presentable—except my lipstick wasn't in my makeup bag. *Crap.* It was in my purse—on the seat.

The sudden acceleration of my car combined simultaneously with a clumsy reach for my purse, catapulting it onto the floor, open side down. Out of the side of my eye, I saw the contents scatter in a Rorschach pattern all over the passenger-side floor. I allowed myself a quick glance down and then swiftly brought my eyes back to the road and eventually to the rearview mirror. I saw the lights before I heard the siren. *That can't be for me . . .* I thought to myself. But, there it was, the patrol car, behind me, definitely behind me.

No. No. No. No. No. Not today, Lord. I had no idea why he would be stopping me. And in this current climate, wearing brown skin, nothing about seeing the black-and-white pattern of a police cruiser made me feel safe. Nothing at all. Now, more than ever, it made me feel like my life was in danger.

Immediately, my heart started racing, creating a throbbing in my ears and lending a hollowness to the sounds all around me. I turned down the radio and looked for a place to pull over to the right side of the street. I couldn't help that my hands were gripping the steering wheel so tightly that my knuckles looked almost white underneath the usual golden brown of my skin. My breath was shallow and quick, even though I tried to slow it down to avoid full-on panic. *Dammit.* My purse and all of its contents were on the floor—including my wallet. At some point, if he asked for my ID, I was going to have to reach for it. *Oh my God. I don't want to reach . . . for anything.*

My cell phone was on the passenger-side floor as well. *I can't even record this. Who will be my witness? What if he thinks I'm reaching for a gun and it's just my cell phone? I've never even held a gun . . . never . . . not even a toy gun like Tamir Rice, but he still got shot, didn't he?* Of my greatest concerns in the moment, I couldn't control who he saw or what he thought when he looked at me. There was no good way to explain I had parents and friends and a whole office of people who were waiting for me. As disjointed and dysfunctional as they might be, I did have a family. I had some kind of a family. I hoped he understood that whether or not I showed up for work, or for dinner, would matter to someone. It would. I'd be missed—I knew that much. I couldn't explain to him that . . . *Oh my God, he's coming.* I looked up from the array of lipsticks and loose change scattered around my upside-down purse on the floor and into the rearview mirror and saw that the officer was walking toward me. He was tall, with a solid build. He had close-cropped blond hair and he was wearing mirrored sunglasses that looked cold and invincible. His hands were at his utility belt as he approached—the belt that carried his weapons, so many weapons. I could only pray he didn't use any of them on me today. I had no idea why he would, which was just as scary as the fact that, based on everything I'd seen, I also couldn't name why he wouldn't. I just wanted to get to work.

I saw him approach the driver's side of my car and I was exceedingly careful not to move one inch from the ten and two position on my steering wheel. He motioned for me to roll down the window. I whispered silent prayers as I slowly moved my left hand to the window controls. The window obeyed and descended into the door.

"Ma'am, can I please see your license and registration?" the officer asked. I hesitated, near tears. *Try to hold it together, Tabby. But you can't reach, not for anything. You already know what they do to Black people who reach.* I was petrified. Everything was on the floor, everything. What if he thought . . .

"Ma'am, license and registration," he repeated, a little more insistent this time. I struggled to manage my breath and to find words at the same time.

"I . . . I . . . can't . . . I can't—I don't want to reach . . . It's on the floor . . . I'm sorry, I'm just really scared right now," I blurted. The words all came out of me in a blustering hurry of word dribble. My mind was racing, my heart was racing, and my hands were wrapped around the steering wheel tightly enough to form calluses. I didn't want to die and suddenly I found myself in a situation where I had no idea how to stay alive. The widely played video of Philando Castile ran through my mind . . . the sound of the gunshots ringing as he reached for his wallet, obeying the officer's command, echoed as a warning that the wrong breath, the wrong move, the wrong anything could end me in a cloud of unwarranted bullets.

"Oh, for Christ's sake. Ma'am. Can you please step out of the car?" The officer looked at me with shifting intensity. *Oh Lord. Oh my God. This is how it starts.* I remembered the video of Breaion King's traffic stop, where the police threw her tiny doll-like body onto the ground with the shattering force of unexplainable rage. I tensed and held on tighter to the steering wheel. *Oh my God. He's going to hurt me.* I felt the stinging in the back of my throat as tears of helplessness threatened and pushed against my eyes. I tried to fight them back. I tried to breathe. I tried to remain calm and maintain clear thinking. My life depended on it. My life depended on everything that I would say and do next.

"P-p-please . . ." I struggled with this simple word as my trembling doubled in intensity and moved up to my neck and crept into my jaw. "I'm . . . I'm on the news—I'm on TV. I'm just trying to get to work. I don't want you to hurt me. I just want to go to work," I pleaded. It felt as if I were begging for my life. I thought of my grandmother—my mother—even my father. But none of them could protect me from this moment.

"Ma'am. Get. Out. Of. The. Car. I am not going to hurt you. Do it slow and do it now. Unlock the door. Unlock the door. I am going to open it. You're going to get out. Okay? Do that now." I felt his growing impatience. *Dear God. Please help. Please help me now. Please please please help me. Please. I'm going to unlock this door, God. Please be with me. Please.* Saying nothing, I managed to nod my head and slowly, slowly reached my left hand down to unlock my car door. The officer took the outside handle and pulled the door open. "Now unbuckle your seat belt and step outside please. Just here. Step outside of the car." I replaced my left hand on the steering wheel and peeled off my right hand to slowly reach for the seat belt release. There I was again, reaching.

"I'm just going to put my hand down to unbuckle," I said. "I don't have anything anywhere on me. I'm on television. I'm a reporter. I'm on television . . . I . . ." I forced the words out with heavy labor. Anything more than a whisper felt like I was going to unleash the scream of terror that was building inside of me. And I wanted to scream. I wanted to scream so badly with my entire soul—*LEAVE ME ALONE! LEAVE ME ALONE! WHY WON'T YOU LEAVE ME ALOOONNNE!* But I said nothing. I held it in. I held my breath and unlatched my seat belt and let it release across my body. And slowly I turned and pulled my shaking frame upward and outside of the physical protection of my car to face the officer. *Oh God, please help me.* I closed my eyes and lingered in one final prayer that I released to float out on my exhaled breath.

The officer stood in front of me briefly—I could tell he was considering me, even from behind the emotionless stare of his mirrored aviator sunglasses. He took in a breath and his rigid posture softened a bit.

"I can't believe it has come to this," he said, his hand reaching up for his sunglasses.

"What?" I said, frightened about what that could mean for me in the next moments. The officer shook his head and pulled off his sunglasses. Officer Mallory. M-A-L-L-O-R-Y. I tried to commit that to memory and looked for the badge number. 13247. Mallory—13247. *Okay, got it. Oh no, I forgot the numbers.* He looked at me with blue eyes squinting to adjust to the light. He leaned forward just slightly to repeat himself.

"I just said, I can't believe that it has come to this. *This*. Look at you—why are you so afraid?" he asked with seeming earnestness. "I'm *not* going to hurt you. Listen," he said and hesitated. "I'm going to touch you. Is that okay? I'm not going to hurt you."

I paused, confused about what he was asking me to allow. I was not certain that I had any true agency or choice in the moment. I nodded my head, saving my energy in case I would need to scream. He slowly lifted his hands up, placing them gently on my shoulders. I caught the glint of a gold wedding band on his left hand. Maybe he had a family—a daughter. Maybe he could understand what it was like as a parent to think about his innocent daughter not making it back home. "What is your name?" he asked.

"Tabitha," I said, struggling with even my most familiar words against the violent trembling in my body. I felt unsteady in my heels. Strangely, his hands stabilized me slightly. "Tabitha Abigail Walker. I'm a reporter on KVTV news. I'm just trying to get to work . . ." I said, trying to make a case for my safety—to make him understand that mine was not a name that would just disappear. If that registered with him, I didn't notice. He continued just as before.

"Ms. Walker. Seeing you . . . like . . . I . . . I just can't believe this. Look . . ." he said, searching for his words as he sought out direct eye contact. He moved his head until his eyes met mine directly. "I'm a third-generation cop, okay? Third generation. My grandfather was a cop—and my dad. They're the reason I put this uniform on every day. Every single day. To them . . . to *me*, this uniform means service. It means honor. It means everything opposite of whatever it is that's making you stand here in front of me like *this*." He paused again, and then continued. "And don't think I don't know—I *do* know . . . I've read the stories—seen the videos too. The same ones you have. But that's *not* what this uniform means to *me*. Okay? That's not what it means. Do you understand that?"

I struggled to take in his words. All I could do was look him in his eyes and let the tears fall from mine.

The air hung heavy between us for a moment and neither of us spoke. I couldn't say anything, even as some of the tension started to drift out of my body. There are just some moments when words cannot perform their duty. There are just some thoughts that are bigger than words. It was in this space that we stood, in consideration of each other until we could find the next space of our shared reality. It was my turn to speak.

"I'm sorry . . . I've just seen so much . . . I didn't mean. . . . it's not disrespect . . . I'm just . . . afraid . . . I know I maybe shouldn't be this afraid . . . but I am," I tried to explain. His words had touched me because I could see them echoed in his eyes. I wanted to believe him, so I allowed his reassurance to calm my racing thoughts. "What happens now?" I asked.

He took another long breath and dropped one hand from my shoulder but kept his eyes locked with mine.

"I pulled you over because you were driving erratically. You missed a light back there and it seemed like you might have been on your phone." He broke eye contact with me and glanced over into my open car. He returned to meet my stare. "From the looks of things, you probably weren't, but you also weren't paying attention. I want to let you go—but I need to make sure that you're going to be safe driving. You said you're heading to work. Just take some time and collect yourself before you get back on the road. Can we agree on that?" He paused to search my eyes for a response.

"Y-yess . . . yes. I can do that," I managed to respond, grateful to not have to fully explain the distractions of my morning.

"Okay. I'm going to let you go," he said with a lingering pause, signaling that he was considering his next words carefully. "I can't pretend to know what's going on in your mind. I have no idea. But we're not all like what you guys are seeing and hearing about," he finished, then turned and walked away, heading back to his patrol car. I stood still, considering the moment and his final words to me.

"Neither are we," I said quietly. "Neither are we."

I turned slowly back toward my own car and allowed myself to drop into my seat, closing the door after me. With my hands back on ten and two on the steering wheel, I let my face drop onto the center of it. The cascade of tears came with heavy sobs as the entire weight of the morning's events released itself from my body with the force of a thunderstorm. It shouldn't be this way—nothing should be this way. I should have more eggs. I shouldn't have to be this scared. I should have been at work already.

I am Tabitha Abigail Walker, a Black girl in contemporary America, and I am personally and emotionally spent. It's not even eleven a.m. and I already feel as exhausted as my egg supply.

2

I WOULD GUESS THAT ON SOME DAYS—AND MAYBE FOR SOME, EV-
ery day—people other than me could be found walking into
their workplace pretending to be someone they're not. Somehow someone's composure on the outside, even if assembled
in the privacy of a personal world of chaos, manages to hide
the storm-ravaged landscape on the inside. Today was my first
time feeling acutely aware of that disconnect. I felt as held together as an overstuffed packing box sealed with Scotch tape.
After the episode with the police and my fateful appointment
with the doctor, I should have taken myself straight home to
nose-dive into an entire bottle of wine. Instead, here I was,
taking deep breaths in my car in the office parking lot. I told
myself that as soon as all the shaking and sniffling stopped,
I would go in. I had no idea how I'd managed it, with the
traffic and especially with the police stop, but I was at work
and parked only ten minutes late to the newsroom meeting.
If I could force a quick recovery, I'd make it in time to pitch a
story, or at least get staffed on a good story team.

Ordinarily, I loved our weekly newsroom meeting, where
we discussed the stories we would cover and staffed the lon-

ger assignments to tackle in teams. I always tried to propose topics that had at least some connection to LA's Black and minority communities. Most of the time they got shot down, or twisted into an unrecognizable "broader" version that missed my point. Maybe the truth of it was that I needed to start thinking less passionately and more strategically, especially since I was up for my next promotion. With time on my side, and a built-up confidence from enough success along my path, I had been choosing to be more authentic than ambitious. I felt like I could reach my Oprah dreams my own way. But if my plans for a beautiful "everything I ever wanted" life with Marc didn't work out, I'd have to fall back on my relationship with my career, and *we* needed to make more money. My dream-home down payment was already going to be a hundred percent of my savings, but at least with a house, I would have something to show for it. If Marc wasn't ready to move forward, the only option Dr. Ellis gave me was to freeze my eggs.

"Freeze my eggs?" I asked her with wide eyes. She spoke about it like it was the most natural thing in the world and gave me a referral card for a reproductive specialist—well, actually, an *infertility* specialist. "Isn't it expensive?" I asked, already knowing it was by the ritzy high-rise concierge doctor zip code on the card. *Egg freezing?* It honestly didn't even sound right, at least not for me. First, however much it cost, I knew I couldn't afford it on my reporter's salary. Second, how could I even know if it would really work? And when would I have the time? I dreaded the thought of having to make that phone call to yet another doctor, to have a *procedure.* I'd never gone to the doctor for more than a checkup and antibiotics. But, realistically, could I count on Marc being down to move forward so quickly? If he wasn't, then I needed a raise, so *I needed that promotion*. As helpless as I was, as helpless as I felt, the only thing I could do today in the form of any kind of rescue was to pull it together and perform well in that newsroom meeting. I promised myself that as soon as it was over, I'd make a beeline to my phone to set up happy hour drinks with my two best friends, Alexis and Laila. They'd help me figure out what to do about my eggs and maybe, even more importantly, how to tell Marc. The card that Dr. Ellis gave me for Dr. Young sat at the top of my purse, mocking me. Daring me to call and risk even worse news. It hurt my head to even think about scheduling that follow-up, so it would have to wait, even though I didn't even have a day to waste.

Finally satisfied with the touch-up on my makeup, I closed my car visor and exited my car for the third time that day, hoping for a better result than the previous two times. I smoothed down my skirt with clammy hands as I walked through the doorway under that KVTV sign that I first crossed two years ago. Back then, as a new hire, I was ecstatic to have a reporter position in Southern California and specifically in Los Angeles. Not only was LA a major market, and my hometown, but it was a place where exciting things happened with a steady stream of interesting news to cover. I'd heard stories from so many of my friends from grad school who decided to go into local television news only to find themselves feeling painted into some obscure corner of America. Now could really be my time to try to advance in the ranks. I had paid my dues, worked the weekends, and missed the birthday parties, vacations, and lazy Sunday brunches with my friends. My next step was most immediately to senior reporter, then, ultimately, an anchor role—weekend would be a start, midday would be amazing, and weekday evening anchor, six p.m., that was the Holy Grail. That was the time slot that all of my professional dreams and financial aspirations were made of. I let my imagining embolden and fill me up, where the events of this morning had deflated my spirit. I kept up my internal pep talk all the way to the meeting room.

If I could land the role of senior reporter, it would mean that, rather than just basic day-to-day assignments, I would get a team of people to help me research more in-depth investigations and longer-term reporting assignments. It also meant I'd get more of a say in the topics that I covered and how they were presented to the viewers. It was important to be represented in the newsroom, that was for certain, and that's why I usually pushed myself so hard in those weekly meetings. Communities that were underrepresented in the newsroom were underrepresented in the news. And sometimes the news was as important as life and death. Like today, what if Officer Mallory hadn't been so honorable? It was some person's journalistic work that even made him aware of why someone like me might be afraid. That's why I was never any good at solely focusing on my own professional ambitions, even if I wanted to and even if it was in my better interests. There were no African Americans, male or female, leading any of the reporting teams at KVTV. A pity, because our perspectives held value, especially about the goings-on in LA. Still, even without my own cultural representation in the news team leadership, I didn't believe that meant it *couldn't* happen. So, I made it my responsibility each week to try to be heard, even if I sat around a table full of cutthroat competitors, like my colleague Scott Stone, who was up for the same promotion as I was. He always gave me the impression that he'd step over anyone to get there—and I was the one person in his way. Now that I knew just how badly I needed this promotion, maybe I needed to start following his lead.

Scott Stone had fewer years in news than I did, but he was the epitome of ambition and confidence. He always contributed ideas, always gunned for the best assignments, and didn't ever take anyone else into account. If I slipped, even a little, he'd be there to take the food right off of my plate. So he was the other reason that, in spite of puffy eyes and completely melted mascara that made me look like a raccoon on its worst day, with my mind consumed by spiraling thoughts of failing fertility proclamations and worst-case scenario flashbacks of a terrifying police interaction, I still managed to woman up before I put my hand on the doorknob to walk in the conference room. Deep breath, straightened shoulders, plastered smile—a perfect performance of graceful composure. I knew I had to. If I didn't, he'd use the opportunity to throw me under the bus. So, with a shield of concealer and a fresh coat of lipstick, I marched my way into the newsroom meeting only fifteen minutes behind schedule. It was no surprise that Scott was the one talking, but I shored up my bravest face.

Our boss and the executive news director, Chris Perkins, was an old-school news guy. Over his multidecade career, he had made his rounds at several stations and was known in the industry for being tough but fair. He had shepherded some of the best careers in the business. Plus, he got ratings. He was deathly pale, pudgy, balding, and short, but he had a commanding presence and could certainly run a meeting. The glassed-in conference room, with its light-gray conference table and standard-issue pockmarked acoustic tile on the ceiling, would always seem to buzz with new life as every corner and crevice filled with the energy of reporters, anchors, and news staff researchers brashly discussing "what next?" On the best day, it was like the most spirited family conversation around a holiday dinner table—except spanning all the topics you should avoid if you wanted to keep the peace: politics, religion, you name it. I'd normally spend days preparing for these meetings with the focus of a theatrical opening night. I relished what details I could—what to wear, what to say, how to say it, not too much, not too little—because the moment I walked in that door, everyone and everything else felt entirely out of my control.

Sitting around the table, we'd review ratings and discuss new stories. Reporters like Scott and me who were up for promotion to the more senior positions would try even harder now to get placed on support teams for the best assignments. The visibility and ultimately good ratings were known to be positive tick marks in your column for the one-up. So, for all of these reasons, it was critical for me to be there—my absence would be like the sky opening up and the heavens above smiling down directly on Scott.

I walked in the room with my hurried "sorry I'm late, guys," and headed toward an open seat in the ring of chairs encircling those at the table. Scott, of course, didn't stop talking, but everyone else shifted their eyes to study me as I crossed the room. I was *never* late, and I was never not perfectly presentable. I realized that today my cream silk blouse was wrinkled and not even close to being neatly tucked into the back of my black pencil skirt. My concealer was doing its best work, though, hiding those bags and circles under my still-bloodshot eyes. My only pair of red-bottomed black stiletto pumps dug their way across the office carpet as I made my way to my intended chair. From the usual agenda, we had already gone over the ratings, and it looked like we were well into brainstorming with a list of team stories on the board. Everyone got an opportunity to pitch, and then the best of those made the board to be assigned by Chris to a senior reporter and a team. We sometimes informally called this portion of the meeting the "gauntlet" because it could get pretty brutal. An open session like this meant that everyone was allowed to speak freely without the constraints of regular meeting decorum. Chris seemed to feel it fostered better creative energy that way. All I felt was embarrassment for being late and anxiety about doing well.

Because I was up for the senior reporter role, my contributions to this portion of the newsroom meeting were all that much more important. Chris told me in my last review that to be successful on the news team, he expected my ideas and team assignments to reflect my insight and skill for identifying news, but at the same time we needed to connect to our audience and, most importantly, draw ratings. Our news team was competitive all the way around—*everyone* was trying to move up in some way.

I took a look at the whiteboard. The topics had already been thrown out and assignments were being made. I was disappointed to know for certain that I'd have no choice but to hold on to my ideas until the next meeting. I still had a chance to get placed on a good story, so I studied what was left closely:

LA Mayor Race

School Lunches—Nutrition Concerns

New Football Stadium—Progress and Displacement

LA Real Estate Trends—Who's Buying and Is It Enough
to Avoid Another Crash?

What Does Silicon Beach Offer to LA's Women and
Minority Population?

The Newest Developments in Cosmetic Surgery

Assignments had already been made for school lunches
and local politics. That was fine with me, because I really
wanted to investigate the story of how a changing LA was
making real estate unaffordable for the minority communities being pushed out of their homes by one or another type
of development. The new football stadium was a prime example. It was great for the new residents of Inglewood and those
who could afford to grow along with the increasing economic
base. But what was happening to the longtime residents who
weren't beneficiaries of the economic boon? Yep, this new
stadium was a story I could really sink my teeth into, and it
was just coming up for discussion as I walked in the door.
Even though Scott was talking, there was still time for me to
get staffed on the team.

Chris, standing at our whiteboard, addressed those of us
in the room, congregated like petals around the long oval
conference table. "So right now, we have Marlee as senior reporter, plus Andrew, and that leaves room for one more on
the reporting team for the stadium topic. Who's in?" I shot
my hand up almost as soon as my butt hit my seat—I'm sure
it looked like I was half standing, like kids in a classroom

ooh-Ooh-OOH!-ing for the teacher to call on them when they were certain they had the right answer. I wanted *that* assignment. As I felt myself catch Chris's eye, out of the corner of my peripheral vision I also caught the one and only Scott Stone looking at me with a half smile as he slowly and casually raised his hand as well. *Of course.*

Chris continued, "Okay, Scott, Tabitha—make your pitch for the spot. What's your perspective on the topic?" *Oh crap.* Sometimes Chris would do this Thunderdome-style runoff when more than one person was vying for the last open position on a reporting team—he said it built and showed enthusiasm for the news that we covered. Ordinarily, I'd be all over it, but after the morning I'd had, I was kind of spent. No matter how I felt, I still wasn't going to just hand it over to Scott without any effort.

"I think that this is a great opportunity," I offered, "to wrap in some of the surrounding Los Angeles neighborhoods that have been traditionally minority dominant, and see how the character is changing. What is the new stadium bringing, and maybe more importantly, what, or *who*, is it leaving behind?" I smiled for emphasis, pleased with myself.

"I think the story could be bigger," Scott interrupted as I had barely finished. My lips now drawn into a tight line, I turned to look at him and felt my eyes narrow in his direction. He didn't notice and kept command of the room. "I mean, I would go into the history of football in Los Angeles, the original Rams, the role that the Coliseum itself played in them leaving—you know, how the dangerous area around it really hurt home game attendance, and now the hope that's returned with the possibility of a new championship. This city is ready to win—especially after that painful loss in the 1990 AFC game." The room groaned in sympathy with Scott's sports trivia that went way over my head. *What AFC game? What about people's actual homes, Scott?*

"Well, Scott," I quickly interjected, "that *dangerous* area was actually people's homes and neighborhoods, and the danger was often a matter of perception, not actually—"

Chris interrupted before I could really get going.

"Tabby, it seems like you're pretty passionate about the real estate angle. Why don't you take the next story and, Scott, we'll give you the Rams Stadium. Let's pull some of the sports history into it." I was seething, but it seemed pretty clear to me that Chris had made a proclamation without room to protest. I knew I could learn the football trivia if that was the direction he wanted to go in, but I wasn't going to be able to spew it in the next two minutes, and certainly not enough to run the circles I needed to around "Golden Boy" over there. How was this going to help me get a promotion? I thought about raising my voice to object anyway but couldn't find the courage or the energy. With the room seemingly settled, Chris crossed off the stadium topic and moved into discussion of Los Angeles real estate.

When the meeting finally ended, I took myself into the ladies' room again to check on my makeup job and to get a small breather alone without having to head straight to my office cubicle. If I could make my way to senior reporter, I would also have an office where I could close my door for at least a little bit of privacy. Until then, this was my sole escape to try to regroup before heading back into a fishbowl. I placed my hands on the rim of the sink that sat just beneath my hip level and used the leverage to push myself forward so I could inspect the bags under my eyes. Just as I did so, the door opened, ushering through Lisa Sinclair, our midday anchor.

Lisa was everything that you'd expect of a Southern California television personality. She was lithe and statuesque, blond and beautiful, with unnaturally perfect teeth that were set in a perfect mouth under a surgically tweaked nose. She came from a St. Louis station a couple of years ago and fit the part so well that they canceled the other interviews on her first camera test. She and I had not spent much time talking except a hello in passing in the halls. This was the worst time for that to change. On any other day, she'd be a great ally and mentor, but today I wasn't thinking clearly and needed to get the hell out of there as quickly as possible.

Lisa walked in and looked at me. She came over to the mirror to fix her hair and touch up her lipstick, which happened to be the exact perfect color. Who ever finds their *exactly perfect* shade of lipstick . . . "Tough meeting in there today," she said, interrupting my thoughts.

I thought for a moment more, looking for a politically correct answer to hide my true thinking: *Yeah, I hate that jerk Scott Stone.* "Not so tough, just the usual," I said, blinking to avoid rolling my eyes.

"Well, I couldn't help but notice how Scott slimed his way onto your story. That sucked," Lisa offered. I responded with a slight smile at the possibility that she could see through him as well.

"Yeah, but he does that all the time. Like I said, the usual," I said passively.

Lisa finished the last flourished swipe of her lipstick and turned to face me. "Look, this place isn't easy—not for any of us. It's definitely a battle to get your voice heard—especially as a woman. I remember before I made anchor, as a senior reporter—I had to always fight the guys for the better stories—and if it involved sports, well, you could forget it." I nodded and she continued. "I've been talking to a few of the other women, and we've been putting together a women's issues group for the station. It's partly for support, but really to amplify our voices here and to get our concerns on the table. Do you know that our healthcare plan . . ."

Our healthcare plan? I could see her preparing to go into a rant of her concerns. I just wasn't in the mood and I was already late to my desk. I needed to find an escape.

"Yes!" I said hurriedly. "Our healthcare, whew—really bad—could be so much better." I moved to place myself on the other side of Lisa to reach for the door handle. "Lisa, I would really love to hear about this, but I have to meet with the senior reporter on my news team. Maybe we could talk later?" I said sheepishly as I pushed my way out of the door, knowing I was being awkward, but saving a larger embarrassment. "Keep me posted on the developments?" I didn't wait for an answer. I just left Lisa Sinclair standing there, like a perfect statue with her beautifully decorated mouth slightly agape in bewilderment as I made my exit. *Crap.* She had the security of an anchor position and seniority that I didn't. What she brought up sounded like an unnecessary distraction, and I just needed to focus on getting that promotion. Why couldn't she be offering something that wouldn't jeopardize that for me? Like being my mentor or something easy? Maybe she could afford to make waves with her women's issue group focused on our healthcare plan, but I needed a raise. I needed Scott Stone to stop stealing my spot. I needed to stop my ovaries from quitting on me, and I needed to learn how to feel safe in my own city. My mind drifted back to the morning's traffic stop. I pulled out my phone on the way to my desk and sent a text to Laila and Alexis.

Me:

Drinks tonight—Post & Beam?

Alexis:

Yes! Robert has the boys tonight—6?

Laila:

6 is good—I need a damn drink after today.

Me:

Me too—last nerve officially just severed.

Alexis:

LOLz—I'll buy the first round!

And just like that, I had something to look forward to. At least I'd see my girls. Six p.m. couldn't come soon enough.

EVENING ANNOUNCED ITSELF WITH A SPECTACULAR ORANGE-AND-pink wash of sunset. The soft pastel color made me think of a pencil-top eraser, the old-school delete button. This is what I needed happy hour to be. I hoped it would at least blur the fresh sting of a very tough day. As I walked through the doorway of Post & Beam, I immediately felt the sense of being at home. The place brought to mind the familiarity of *Cheers* mixed with the contemporary, yet warm, clean, and neutral décor of an urban trendy restaurant. The open kitchen and glowing pizza oven in the center made it feel like a hearth of soulful offerings, Southern comforts, and general good vibes. I can't remember a time being there that I didn't see the owner walking around with greetings for everyone. Sometimes, when he recognized me or one of my friends and we chatted with him a bit, he'd comp our first round of drinks.

It was one of the first new restaurants to open at the Baldwin Hills Crenshaw Plaza, which sat at the entrance of both the Baldwin Hills and View Park neighborhoods. In the fifties, these communities were predominately Jewish, but with the real estate patterns and agent-driven "white flight," these palm tree–lined enclaves became tony hosts to Black professionals and celebrities. Living here was a true sign of having "made it," especially if you lived among the "Dons"— the high-up streets in Baldwin Hills with near three-sixty-degree views of Los Angeles. And in nearby View Park, there were still million-dollar-plus homes that sat on top of their side of the hill, with everything you could imagine in fancier parts north, like tennis courts, pools, and even household staff. The renewed interest in View Park/Baldwin Hills brought increased opportunities for new businesses, like our beloved Post & Beam, but nobody could say they weren't worried about losing some of the rich history and character of the area as well. Coming back was like revisiting my best memories—when I was a kid and everything seemed good and easy and on its way up.

Gentrification was changing the neighborhood, certainly. Each time I went back, I saw fewer and fewer of the people I knew from my time growing up there before my parents divorced. Alexis had been my neighbor down the street, and that's how we originally met. She still lived there, in a house a few blocks from her parents, married to Robert, her high school boyfriend. Robert, after a wild ride through high

school and college, became a proud, card-carrying member
of the married-man club when he and Alexis were still in
their twenties. As a complete departure from his younger self,
he became one of those men who considered marriage and
family an accomplishment worth having on his way to the
new promised land of old-man Kangol hats, jazz festivals,
and Social Security checks. His parents were still married, as
were Alexis's, and hers still lived in the same house down the
street from my old one. We had been friends since our earliest memories and still had pictures of us together from times
we were too young to recall. When we were younger, we were
always thick as thieves and never had any problems until
Robert came sniffing around at the end of middle school.
Where I was the studious one, getting straight A's and act-
ing like a debutante even before I was one, Alexis filled out
early, leading into her nickname, "Sexy Lexi," which is what
all the boys, and I do mean *all* of them, started calling her.
She was the first to develop breasts and a plump booty. She
had all the curves that I could only imagine while my body
stayed straight up and down, front and back as flat as a pine
board. When my mom moved away, and I went to stay several
miles away with Granny Tab in the Fairfax district, Lexi and
I didn't get to spend as much time with each other, and we
wound up at different high schools. Robert took the opportunity to fill in for my absence. He was a popular athlete,
and before long he got "Sexy Lexi" to wear his cheap little
gold chain with the fake-ass diamond nameplate on it that
his parents bought him at his insistence to legitimize his rap
career, which lasted five minutes and never went much past
our neighborhood. Robert always swore up and down I didn't
like him. Honestly, it wasn't that I didn't *like* him, it's just that

after a certain point of drying Lexi's tears, it seemed clear to me that Lexi could do better. But, evidently, she didn't want to. She loved herself some Robert. They made me godmother to their boys, first Rob Jr. and then little Lexington. I hate to pick favorites, but that little boy Lexington, with his big brown eyes, hair of vibrant, densely packed curls, and mischievous snaggletooth smile would have you looking in your purse for candy that wasn't there. If she weren't married to Rob, Lexi would be living a version of my dream family life. She had a stable, helpful husband, two kids, and still-married parents who lived just down the street.

I was the first to arrive, so I secured a place at a communal table for Alexis and Laila. I figured that Alexis would arrive first and Laila would come at her standard fifteen minutes late. Laila Joon was always late, but always worth waiting for. Laila was from the Bay Area, and I met her in undergrad at USC's journalism program. I was focused on broadcast news, and Laila had intentions to be a syndicated newspaper columnist. She was all the way Oakland with her "hella" slang and long mane of bohemian dreadlocks. She never minced words but was still as mysterious and enchanting as her name, Laila, which was pronounced Lah-E-Laa, a version of the Arabic word for night. Her mother, who came from a Black Muslim family, gave her the name to mark that side of her heritage, as she would carry the Korean last name of her father, Joon. She looked Black, she looked Asian, and the combination brought questions encountered with unrelenting frequency. She never failed to look at people with extreme side-eye when they inevitably asked her, "What are you?" Laila, who as a writer was quick-witted and basically fearless, once said to that question, "I'm mixed . . ." to an unsuspecting inquirer who pushed their luck, pressing for the *with what?* follow-up. Laila said defiantly, "I'm mixed with Black and mind your business." What I loved about Laila beyond her fearlessness was her ability to always be herself, even when it wasn't comfortable or popular. Laila was the one who convinced me to apply for the job at KVTV and spent every weekend with me practicing my interview until I was as sharp and polished as a brand-new razor. With Alexis married with kids, Laila became my wingwoman when I moved back to LA after grad school. We navigated the wilds of the Los Angeles nightlife together as single girlfriends. This made tonight a rare occasion, with the three of us, because it was usually beyond difficult to get Alexis out at all.

To my surprise, after ten minutes of waiting, with no sign of either one of my friends at the door, Alexis finally appeared, walking in right along with Laila. They rushed me at the table, wrapping me with our customary big hugs and cheek kisses.

"Girl!" Laila said with her usual frenetic energy. "You sent the Bat-Signal and it wasn't even lunchtime yet! I knew some *bulllll-shiiiiit* must have gone down today. Where's our waiter—I need a drink ASAP." Signaling for the waiter with a raised arm, she turned back to look at me. "Um, hm, I see you. You couldn't even wait for a sista, you've already been sippin'!" she said with her big wide grin.

"How you doin', girl?" Alexis asked with her motherly sincerity. Even though I'd known her practically forever, I still couldn't believe how much she'd changed from the "Sexy Lexi" that she was in high school. Her figure eight curves from back then had rounded out significantly, more so with each of her two children. She was still beautiful and brown, and carried herself with the confidence of a longhaired siren, but you could see life lived and the obligations of family in her appearance. Laila, on the other hand, still had the physique of a track star. She was naturally beautiful, with freckles and honey-colored skin that always seemed to carry a glow of the California sunshine with it. This day, she had pulled her shoulder-length dreads up into a wide bun around the crown of her head.

"Girl, you won't believe . . ." I started in, ready to tell them everything.

"Wait, just one second, Tab," said Alexis, settling her wide and supple hips onto the stool in front of me. "Let me just text Rob and the boys and let them know what time I'm coming home. I know they're going to ask me to bring dinner—they act like they don't know how to use an oven or a stove . . ."

"Or Postmates—or Uber Eats—doesn't Rob know how to use his phone?" Laila challenged. Alexis just threw her a look.

"You would think . . ." she murmured, instantly immersed in her phone, while her fingers danced quickly across the screen. "Okay. That's done. Tab! What happened?" said Alexis, throwing the entire weight of her attention back to me.

"What didn't happen today. First, y'all, do you know anything about 'ovarian reserve'? Evidently, I have, like, none— my ovaries are just like, 'yeah, girl, we out,'" I said, weakly making my very best attempt at humor.

"Whaaaat? What does that mean?" asked Alexis.

"Wait, so you ain't got no eggs?" spouted Laila.

"Shhhsssshh!" I tried to bring the volume down to keep my personal issue out of ear-hustling distance of the couple at the far end of the shared table. "Basically, yes, that's my situation. The doctor told me today. I have six months to do something drastic, and if I don't—I have basically zero shot of having my own biological child . . . or family."

"Girrlll, your mother is going to freak. Did you tell her?" asked Alexis. She knew my mother well, and she was right.

"Nope, not yet. You're the first people I've told," I said, lifting my drink to my lips. I should have known to order whisky instead of wine.

"Well, what are you gonna do? What about Marc?" Alexis inquired.

"I'm going to talk to him about it, I guess . . . when I see him. It's a pretty heavy topic, don't you think? I mean, we've talked about kids in the long run, but not like this . . ."

"Talk to him? What you need to do is talk less, and have more sex. Are you still taking birth control?" asked Laila in her typical practical fashion.

"Yes, of course I am!"

"Well, people forget all the time. That's all I'm gonna say," Laila said, waving down the waiter. "Ask Alexis." I turned and looked at Alexis with a look of surprise. Maybe there was something I didn't know. Alexis looked a little like a deer in headlights. Her mouth dropped open, but she composed herself quickly to explain.

"Well . . . ob-vi-ous-ly, that's *not* how the boys got here— but Rob and I did have a little scare before he proposed . . . thankfully, it brought us closer. I think it made him take our relationship more seriously after that—can you use your big mouth to order a Pinot Noir for me, Laila? Much appreciated." Alexis turned away from Laila and then leaned in closer to me from across the table to continue. "Laila's not wrong, though," she whispered. "Just something to think about." She patted my hand as if to seal in a secret.

I don't know if I was more shocked that my two best friends were trying to convince me to consider the unthinkable, or that Alexis had shared something with Laila that even I didn't know about her and Rob. Legitimately, that had me more perplexed than potentially making a Maury Povich controversy out of my current relationship. I kind of felt like I had been cheated on. *Were they hanging out without me?* I couldn't imagine what Alexis and Laila would have in common without me in the middle. And to think that they had some kind of secret back-channel sisterhood was beyond my comprehension. *Petty thinking? Probably.* With a slight tinge of internal guilt, I made a mental note to ask about it later.

"Okay, so tricking Marc into a baby was not on my list of optionnnnsss . . . but thank you *both* very much for the advice," I said, rolling my eyes. "Although, let the record show that Alexis is the only one of the three of us who has actually used her uterus."

"Oh, don't think I didn't try, girl, in college, I definitely did. But those basketball players at USC had it strapped up tight! No NBA baby for me!" Laila screeched, causing us all to drop our heads with laughter. "Not that that's what I really wanted—because of course I wanted to wind up at a dead-end job at a newspaper. It's what every girl dreams of . . ." As Laila finished, the drinks came for her and Alexis and another for me. Just in time.

"Laila," I said, laughing, "you don't have a dead-end job! You're killing it at the paper—I need to learn from you how to make some moves." She shifted and took a drink, raising her eyebrows. I continued. "Anyway, if Marc's not down, I really have just one option, and that's to freeze my eggs. Which *kills* me to think about—I had just saved enough for a down payment."

"Oh no!" Alexis said, reaching for my hand again. "You'd have to lose your down payment for a house? I'm so sorry, Tab—that's awful! And I'm not just saying that as your Realtor—you've been saving forever! I know how much having the house has meant to you. Maybe you'll get that promotion?"

"Oh, that," I said. "Yeah, the promotion that Golden Boy Scott is constantly undercutting me for. He just stole another story from me today in our newsroom meeting. I wanted to cover the Rams Stadium and thanks to him wound up covering LA real estate. Which I can't even afford now, by the way."

"That snake!" hissed Laila.

"Seriously!" I said, glad to finally have an ally. "And then after the newsroom meeting, Lisa, the new midday anchor, came up to me talking about joining some women's issues group at work! I'm thinking to myself, *my* issue is this promotion. Okay? Oh, and now my lemon law ovaries. You gonna help with that? Because if not, I want no part . . . especially now."

"Well, maybe it can help in some way?" offered Alexis. "I joined a women's issues group at work, and it became like a little bit of a support group. And then we began to present our recommendations to management once a quarter. I can't say that it's changed much of anything, but I do feel like it's brought us closer together in the office."

Laila snickered and then continued after Alexis. "At the paper," she said, "they made a Black woman the head of diversity and inclusion. Somehow, though, all that came of it was a designated inclusive bathroom, a monthly ethnic cultural menu option in the cafeteria, and then still only two Black women on staff and only one in the newsroom."

I shook my head. "We're just always caught right in the middle carrying a double, even *triple*, burden," I said. "And never knowing which issue is *the* issue that's going to get *us* what *we* need. How can you fight other people's battles when it seems like nobody is fighting yours?"

"I will say that I do feel like I'm constantly asked to pick feminism, or any other 'ism,' over racism," added Alexis. "Almost like every time I bring up an issue involving racism, I get some kind of sexism example thrown back in my face."

"That's 'cause we're 'post-racial' now, Lexi," said Laila, throwing up air quotes. "Supposedly, it's all in your head."

"Sometimes I do feel like I'm going crazy," I said. "I got pulled over by the police today—and almost had a meltdown."

"Oh no! Tabby!" said Alexis, showing panic in her face. "Are you okay? What happened?"

"I want to say nothing happened," I said, trying to explain the moment that I still hadn't processed into my own understanding. "He let me go—but, I don't know . . . He told me his whole family had been cops and . . . and . . . I guess, basically that it hurt him to see me that scared."

"I would assume he has a television and the internet . . . and eyes," said Laila. "He can't be completely oblivious to what's happening to Black people out here."

"Well, that's kind of it—he said that he *did* know," I said, trying to explain something unexplainable. "He just felt bad about it and he wanted me to see him differently. I was basically hysterical, y'all."

"Well, I'm just glad that you're okay and that you were able to walk away without it escalating for no reason," said Alexis. "Remember the cops used to pull my cousins over all the time in LA when we were in high school? For no reason at all and throw them on the curb. As if criminals only have brown skin. They were straight-A nerdy boys with glasses! They never should have had to go through that!"

"That's why alcohol should be under PTSD coverage on our insurance!" said Laila, taking a drink. "And I'm taking my medicine right now. Believe me. Doctor's orders." I laughed along with Alexis. Laila, who was now looking down at an empty glass, even had to laugh at herself. "Waiter, let me get one more dose before happy hour is over!"

I stayed at Post & Beam until I felt the weight of my worries lift a little from my shoulders. I might have started my day in tears, but at least it ended in laughter. When I got home, I thought about my house hunting with Alexis coming to an end, and Laila's words echoed in my mind. Dr. Young's card still sat at the top of my purse, and Marc's unanswered text lit up on my phone. I'd have to deal with both tomorrow. I still wasn't sure what I would say to Marc or how I could explain my situation, let alone ask him if he wanted more of a life with me. Once I had showered and changed to nightclothes, there was just one thing left to do. I held my birth control case over the sink and looked at it long and hard. I mean, *people forget all the time, right?* So, I closed the case and put it back on the counter, turned off the light, and went to bed.

3

THE PAST WEEK WASN'T MY FINEST HOUR ON A NUMBER OF LEVELS. It was so rough I gave myself a pat on the back just for making it to my regular Saturday morning workout with Laila. If all went according to plan, I'd give my normally straight-pressed naturally curly (actually, pretty nappy) hair a full "sweating out" before I dropped my freshly showered self in Denisha's salon chair for my standing appointment. Of course, as usual, Alexis was a promised plus-one, but a no-show at the gym. One thing she would not miss, however, was her hair appointment, usually scheduled just about the same time as mine. Today, I would not miss it either, because tonight, after a week of conversations with Marc, imitating normalcy and specifically avoiding the news from my doctor or the topic of my future, we were finally going to see each other. Was it *our* future? *What would he say?* I didn't want to lose him, that was certain, but there was no way to avoid any of the conversations that I knew we needed to have. The thought of all the dating rules I *knew* I'd be breaking caused a rise of panic in my throat throughout the day. My chest felt like it was tightly bound, much worse than wearing two pairs of Spanx, or even three, as Alexis said she considered doing after her second son was born. If she'd just come to the gym sometimes, maybe Alexis wouldn't need three pairs of Spanx, or be so hard on herself, but there's no good way of telling that to your best friend.

Alexis and I had both moved on from the trappings of our old lives in our old neighborhood, but still came right back to Denisha on Slauson, who had been doing our hair since high school. It wasn't the fanciest place—in fact the dingy and cracked linoleum tiles on the floor were well past their replacement date even before I left for college. The bars on the door and colorfully painted front windows gave both a sense of security and a reminder that you were in a neighborhood that required you to "stay woke." I couldn't recall anything ever happening more than the usual revolving stream of peddlers of bootleg movies and fake designer bags. Once, a guy came in selling fresh frozen seafood out of his truck. Denisha swore that he had the best crab legs she had ever tasted. Sometimes it's like that in the hood—unexpected treasures could be hiding right behind unassuming facades. Or danger could be lurking there too. I needed to get my hair done, and Denisha's reliability was worth the risk.

As my profile on the TV station started to rise, it was funny to come into the salon and be treated like a homegrown celebrity. I couldn't say that I wanted the attention, especially walking in there looking like I did after the gym, but I couldn't help but embrace their sense of pride and celebration in feeling like one among them had "made it" beyond the invisibility inherited in our community. I was always surprised to get questions about obscure stories I covered and to get pitches for new things that were happening in the surrounding and still largely Black neighborhoods. Denisha once wanted me to cover the growing petty burglaries happening in the area. Her theory was that as marijuana became legal, the gangs were starting to push their young members to commit other types of crimes for valuables. With California's Three Strikes laws, the older gang members strategized to save themselves from permanent bids at the expense of younger kids whose records could be expunged once they turned eighteen. I thought it was a good idea to at least investigate, and pitched it in one of our newsroom meetings. Guess who shot it down? Scott Stone. Rather than argue with him in front of the entire staff, I let it go. I wanted to push it but had nobody to back me up. I knew there must be a time coming to fight these battles, and I could if I got promoted. Then they'd be *my* stories, no matter what Scott Stone had to say, or anyone else for that matter. Then ratings would decide. And based on the conversations at the hair salon, Black people were definitely watching our news coverage and wanted to see more about the lives they experienced. It's always been a fine line to walk knowing that sometimes I might be the only one in the room with the platform to amplify the stories that shape the lives of forgotten people. Their world was a cultural oasis suffocating in the midst of the changing landscape of growing Los Angeles.

I had to take Denisha with a grain of salt too—on some occasions, she'd say the wildest stuff imaginable. Once, she told me she was convinced there were aliens. "And they're on TV just like you!" she said. I asked her how she knew which were the aliens, and she said, "Well, from what I can tell, they have bigger eyes and they don't blink as much." All I could do was laugh.

"Hey, girl, how you doin'?" Denisha asked as she dropped a plastic cape around my shoulders. "What are we doin' today? The same? I swear, you need to let me give you a cut and some highlights—it would look so good on TV!" She was always trying to get me to change my hair. I've been wearing the same style for years—a conservative cut with long layers and my natural dark brown color, sparse grays covered, pressed straight and loosely curled. Standard-issue news reporter, thank you very much.

"Just the same ol' same ol'," I told Denisha breezily. We'd had the conversation about changing my hair enough that she knew it was pointless to push the issue. My evening with Marc crossed my mind and made me reconsider. I turned back to look at Denisha. "Actually, a little sexier than the same ol', today," I said with a sly smile. Denisha gave me a knowing look.

"Ummmm-hum, I got ya, girl," she said, winking at me. "Head over to the shampoo bowl."

Walking over to the shampoo bowl, my eyes caught on a woman at another salon station getting a shaping of her short natural hairstyle. Now, *that* I did envy. It would be a dream to be able to just wash my hair and let that be it—even if with a few styling products. Just being able to feel good wearing my hair as it grew out of my scalp, I imagined, would be so freeing. I was snapped out of my reverie by a commanding voice.

"This bowl right here." Denisha's shampoo girl, who seemed to change every week almost, was directing me to sit for my shampoo. She might have been harsh in tone, but she gave my scalp a scrubbing for the gods and brought me back to Denisha's chair.

"So, when is Mrs. Thing coming in today?" Denisha asked.

She was talking about Alexis. The girls in the salon liked to tease her because she seemed to incessantly talk about "her *husband* this" and "her *husband* that" and "Rob and the boys"—admittedly, it could be obnoxious. But Lexi was like that. She went all in on the husband-and-kids fairy tale and viewed it as an accomplishment that she found a "good one." Who could fault her? Denisha was single, as were virtually all of the other stylists in the salon. And I had Marc—going on a year and a half . . . and . . . well, clearly not the most ideal situation. When everyone around you was single and looking, I could see how being married would feel significant. So I gave Alexis a pass—but in that salon, that's about as much leeway as she'd get.

"Well, you know she didn't make it to the gym this morning," I said. "So I guess she should be here for her regular eleven a.m."

"I don't know why that girl won't work out!" exclaimed an exasperated Denisha. "With all this high blood pressure and diabetes happening around here. We need to do better. I've started working out. I walk every day," she said proudly, holding a curling iron over my head.

"Yeah, now you just have to stop eating those cheddar biscuits!" said the stylist from across the room.

"Girl, you know I need to have my cheddar biscuits!" said Denisha, laughing. "And my Long Island iced tea. Look here, I've got a snatched waist and I'm cute in the face—my man is *not* complaining." On that, I'm sure Denisha was right. She may not have had a husband, but she always had a man, or more than one. She used to tell me that she had a boyfriend *and* a "toy-friend" for her in-between needs. If she didn't do my hair, I swear I'd still come just for the comic relief. "Well, speak of the devil!" Denisha said, announcing Lexi's arrival. Lexi blew in the door, breathing heavy, holding her handbag in one hand and the hand of her youngest son, Lexington, in the other.

"Now, you sit right there and *do not move*. You hear me?" Alexis commanded her four-year-old. "Mommy is going to get her hair done—you play on your iPad. Okay? And do not leave this seat." She pointed at him, giving a lingering look until he nodded his head in acknowledgment. Then she turned to me. "Hey, girl! Don't leave before we chat—I have to tell you something." She left me mildly bewildered, wondering why she couldn't just text me. I waved a frantic hello to little Lexington.

"Girl, you better sit still before I burn you with this iron!" Denisha warned. I moved back into position in the chair, stiff as a board. I knew when to follow directions—a curling iron burn was a weeklong blemish I didn't need, especially on my forehead.

As I was finishing up with Denisha, Alexis came back from the shampoo bowl escorted by shampoo girl #102. "So, what did you need to tell me?" I asked. Alexis pulled me off to the side out of Denisha's hearing range.

"Just that Rob is planning a birthday party for me in three weeks," Alexis said. "He wants it to be a surprise, so I'm supposed to act like I don't know. But, girl, I don't trust him with all the details. So when he calls you—just act like I haven't said anything. But try to get some recon," she whispered. "I know I'm going to have to—"

"If you don't let that man do this thing!" I said, cutting her off. "Lexi, I'm not going to tell you anything—but you know I'll be there!" I gave her a quick hug, rushed over to

Lexington and then out the door before she could protest. "Bye! I'll call you!" I said as I made the telephone motion with my hand and exited to the echoing farewell following me out of the salon.

Once in my car, I got ready to do what I had been dreading. Even before I spoke to Marc, I was going to have to break my news on a stage with a much brighter spotlight. The tightness in my chest felt multiplied by a sharp pang in my gut. *You can do this, Tabby*, I thought to myself. *You can do this*. I pulled up my hands-free phone settings and said, "Dial . . . Mom."

4

"Tabby Cat! I thought you'd be calling just about now." My mother's voice cheerfully danced its way through my car's sound system. "The general and I just came back from a lovely afternoon walk. Didn't we, sweetheart? Yes. Tabby, Nate says to tell you hi!" When my mother told me she met General Nathaniel Williams a year after she and my father divorced, I breathed a sigh of relief. He seemed perfect for her. He had translated his career in the military to a defense contracting business that was very lucrative, and built a beautiful home in Potomac, Maryland. A while after they met, my mother's long-distance visits with him gradually increased in frequency and duration until one day, just before the end of my eighth-grade year, she asked me to sit down for what I could tell would be a serious conversation in our living room. The general had asked her to marry him, and my mother wanted to say yes. To her credit, she left that gigantic diamond all the way in DC so that she could fly back and talk to me first before giving her answer. I was happy for her, but all I wanted to know was if I was going to have to move. It took two full weeks of negotiation, but eventually an arrangement was made. My mother would move to DC, but I would stay in LA. I would move in and live with Granny Tab for high school to graduation. There were tears upon tears, and wringing hands and furrowed brows. There were *I don't know*s, followed by *It doesn't feel right*s, but eventually she left and collected that ring. My mother was ecstatic about marrying General Nathaniel Williams, and certainly about the "Williams," because that meant that she could keep her monogrammed items with her new married name.

"Hi, Nate," I said dutifully through my car system.

"I feel like I haven't talked to you in forever!" my mother said, continuing with her familiar refrain. "You know, since we don't live close, we just have to talk more, right?"

"I know, Mom. It's just been . . . a busy week."

"Oh, let's see—what did you have this week . . ." My mom paused in her recalling of our last conversation. I halfway hoped she'd forget about the doctor and I could push off the inevitable for just a little longer. "Oh! That's right, the doctor's visit. How was that? Everything turn out okay?" *Crap.*

"Well, the good news is . . . I'm perfectly healthy," I started explaining. "And . . ." I paused, trying to find the least inciting words to describe the questionable fate of her grandchildren.

"And what, Tab?" my mother said, her voice clearly demonstrating concern. "Good news . . . you said there's good news . . . is there . . . *bad* news?"

"Well, it depends on what you mean by *bad*." *Ugh, mistake. Better words, Tabby,* I told myself. *Find better words.* "There were just some routine tests, but . . . well, as it turns out, it was good for me to learn that I have fewer eggs at my age than other people . . . in time to do something about it, I mean." I could feel myself starting to sweat. "I just have to freeze my eggs, in the next few months, that's all." There, with that, everything was said. I could only hope I'd earned a transition off this topic.

"*Freeze your eggs?!* And do what with them?" my mother shrieked, her tone becoming increasingly shrill. "Tabby, that's expensive—and it doesn't even work!"

"Mom, it *does* work!" I could feel my temples start to throb midsentence. "At least, that's what the doctor said. Plus, it's just to have options, okay? I guess I have to do it to maintain my options in the future." I tried my best to stay as calm as possible, even though I felt the panic start to rise again in my chest.

"I don't understand you girls," my mom replied. "You get all deep in your careers, miss the marriage window, and then have to resort to all kinds of unproven unnecessary procedures—*expensive* procedures! Doctors will tell you anything these days . . ."

I could feel my blood pressure going up.

"Mom!" I tried to hold back from shouting. "Stop. It's fine. I'll be fine. It's not about my career—it's about . . ."

"Is it Marc? Is he pressuring you to do this? I honestly don't know what you two are waiting on."

What *we* were waiting on? Hearing what my mother said, I couldn't help but laugh and feel like crying. I reminded myself that she meant well and took a deep breath.

"Nooooo . . . it's not coming from Marc," I said with a fully fake half laugh. "And I don't know when or if Marc wants to get married. He hasn't asked me. You know you'd be the first to know if he did!" I could swear that my mom's timer on my romantic relationships registered by the millisecond.

"Well, Tabby, maybe if you put less focus on your career for a second and more focus on him, he would!"

My breath caught in my throat. *Was she right? Was that it? Was my career really stalling my relationship?* I couldn't imagine how. Marc always told me how he liked that I was independent and had my own ambitions. Sure, we didn't see each other much during the week, but we certainly made the most of the weekends. Plus, there were far fewer times that he wanted to see me that I was unavailable than the other way around.

"Marc likes that I work, Mom," I said, sounding only partially defensive. "And I like it too." I let those words hang in the air. The weight of memories that my mother and I shared from the "dark years" after my parents' split wove its way into the space between us—even miles apart. The silence spoke volumes of words far too painful for either of us to voice ourselves.

"Well, just don't let him drag his feet, Tabby." My mother eventually broke the stalemate. "You let him know that you're ready. And that's coming from the general." She always brought Nate into it to emphasize a point.

"I got it, Mom, nothing to worry about." I was glad to see the turn for my destination ahead. It was the perfect excuse to end the inquiry. "Okay, I've gotta go—I'm at Granny Tab's."

"That's so good that you make it every week to see her!" My mother's cheerful tone instantly returned. She was right, I did go every week to see my grandmother, no matter what else I had going on. I just made the time. After a hip injury and a congestive heart failure condition, she had to leave her apartment for an assisted living facility. She chose one in

Glendale near her best friend, Ms. Gretchen. After meeting Ms. Gretchen, I understood why Granny Tab would want to stay close—she reminded me of a much older Laila. My mom continued, "Tell her hello for me and let me know how she's adjusting. Let's talk sooner than soon!"

I breathed a deep sigh of relief after we said our goodbyes. I loved my mom, but her world and my world were universes apart. There was no way to make her understand that the expectations she was taught in her generation didn't seem to exist anywhere anymore. Other than Alexis, I couldn't think of *any* of my friends who were married, let alone had kids. We *did* want to focus on our careers first—that seemed like the obvious route. No man these days was looking to take care of a woman. Working women were the new housewives, as far as we all knew. And single was becoming the new married.

I really loved pulling up on Crestmire, my grandmother's fancy assisted living residence. The outside had the look of a ritzy New England seaside inn, right in the middle of Glendale, California. You could have easily mistaken it for a high-end apartment building for a bunch of young successful professionals. That is, until you walked inside. And there, everywhere, were gray-haired people, sitting in chairs, walking with walkers, playing cards and board games at tables, all with the quiet hum of chatter in the background.

I stopped at the front desk to check in. I hadn't expected to see a new face. I wondered if that meant I would have to explain. "I'm here to see Mrs. Walker—Mrs. Tabitha Walker," I said to the aide seated behind the curved wood station.

She looked at me for a moment with a look of slight confusion. "And you are . . . ?" she asked, searching my now frowning brown face for an explanation.

"I'm Tabitha Walker—Tabby, her granddaughter. I'm named after her." I forced a smile to show my trustworthiness, observing the look of bewilderment on the face in front of me. I assumed that she had seen my grandmother and was having trouble putting two and two together.

"Um . . . um . . . Okay, just sign in here," she said, pushing the book toward me. "Unit 1265," she said as I started to turn in the direction of my grandmother's hallway.

"I know!" I called back to her. "I'm here every Saturday!" It felt ridiculous to me, but I couldn't blame her for being slightly befuddled. That questioning look, the moments of confusion when it came to me and my grandmother, it's what we'd dealt with practically my entire life. We did as much as we could to try to find some kind of humor in it, at least most of the time.

I walked into my grandmother's unit and was happy to see that the curtains had been opened and that bright sunlight was tiptoeing through the abbreviated apartment space. I knocked on the door as I pushed it open farther.

"Granny Tab?" I called out, hoping not to startle her.

"I'm in the bedroom, sweetie! Coming right out!" echoed back the voice of my grandmother.

I made my way into the living room area. Familiar furniture greeted me from my grandmother's old place in the Fairfax district where I used to live with her. Moving here, she had to downsize and get rid of a lot of things. Here, at least she kept the brown chenille fabric sofa that had hosted so many memories of my youth, not to mention my very first make-out session as a teenager. *This sofa has seen better days* . . . I thought, sitting down on my usual side of it, my hips fitting neatly into the corner like a hug. I ran my hand across the adjacent cushion, feeling the soft texture underneath my palm. In spite of love and care, the worn areas showed, but the couch still worked "for what it was made for," as my grandmother would say about so many things, including herself. She came to assisted living last year after she fell. On top of the resulting hip injury, congestive heart failure caused her to become dizzy from time to time, so she agreed with my dad and me that it was time for her to let go of just a small bit of her independence so she wouldn't be living alone. She refused my offer to move into my loft in Downtown LA, and instead chose to move to Crestmire with Ms. Gretchen.

Granny Tab and Ms. Gretchen knew each other from teaching in the LA Unified School District. Sometimes Ms. Gretchen would be around when I visited, sitting at Granny Tab's kitchen table, pretending not to listen to our conversation, but interjecting all the while. She was a spitfire kind of woman, and at ninety-two years old, she had more energy than Granny Tab and me combined. I looked up just in time to see my grandmother emerging in one of her many flower-print dress and cardigan sweater combinations. The oranges in the print of this one reminded me of wildflowers and set off the blue of her eyes.

"So good to see you today, Two!" my grandmother said as she made her way through the compact apartment space to the kitchenette. Among my other nicknames, Two was a special one used only between my dad, my grandmother, and me these days. I'm told it came about when I was somewhere around two years old and just learning to form coherent phrases. The story was that once I realized that my grandmother's name was Tabitha and that mine was also Tabitha,

I ran around in my diapers for a week proclaiming, "I'm Tabitha Too! I'm Tabitha Too!" In this limited circle, the "Too" stuck as "Two," and Tabitha became "Tabby" to most others.

"Looks like you're moving around pretty well, Granny Tab," I said in the most encouraging tone that I could muster.

"Oh, not so bad for an old woman past her prime." My grandmother gave a wink as she tinkered with her whistling teapot and pulled down two mugs from the cabinet. We would be having Lipton tea today—it was the only thing that my grandmother drank in the mornings and into the early afternoon. She told me that when she was little, Lipton tea was a luxury her family couldn't afford, growing up poor in the hills of West Virginia. So, once he started making money, my grandfather would buy it for her along with some fancy teacups when he could, as promises of a better life to come. She always said that tea made her think of possibilities and new beginnings. Given my situation, I'd better have two cups today. I got up to help her bring our mugs over to the small kitchen table, where we sat with our hands around the steaming cylinders. "So, how are things at work? Did you get your promotion yet?" she asked.

"Not yet," I said. "There's an unofficial competition between me and—you know that reporter, Scott Stone?" She nodded. "Well, he keeps cutting me off in meetings and warping my ideas. I've got to find a way to move past him."

"I know you will, Two," she said, putting her pale hand covered with cascading wrinkles on top of my brown one. "You're strong. Like me. I know you'll figure out a way. And if not, he better watch out—I'll crack his cranium!" my grandmother said, cracking herself up while shaking a feeble fist in the air. We both laughed.

"Well, I need that promotion, so I'm going to get it." I said the words as reassuringly as I could. "As it turns out, I have to do a procedure where they take out some of my eggs and freeze them for later. That's going to take some money."

"Well, why don't you ask your dad to help you?" Granny Tab asked sincerely.

"No way," I said. "I don't want to feel obligated to him, and especially not to Diane. Nope, no way." An involuntary shake of my head followed for emphasis, causing my freshly styled curls to bounce against my shoulders. They'd never offered anything up before, no help with school, nothing. From comments made after their girls were born, it seemed pretty clear to me how their resources were directed. I spared Granny Tab that, holding it in to myself as I did with as much as I could these days.

"I know the situation didn't start out the best, Two, but I really wish you'd give it a chance," my grandmother said, searching my eyes. "Go have dinner with your dad sometimes. They're all picking me up tonight—the girls too. Diane always tries to make a meal as big as Christmas!" This issue was a sore spot, and just about the only topic where my grandmother and I didn't see eye to eye. She'd long ago forgiven Diane for the affair, especially after the arrival of more grandchildren. It wasn't that I never felt pangs of guilt for not knowing them well or seeing my half sisters grow up, but the price of having to put up with Diane was too much to bear. Even after all this time, I still remembered the incident at their wedding as clear as if it had happened yesterday.

I was thirteen years old then, and attending my father's wedding as a guest, not as any part of the ceremony, and barely an acknowledgment. Just before the reception, Diane took time away from her obsession with pictures and guests and gloating through her walk of victory in the irony of a white wedding dress to pull me aside, delivering the only words she had for me.

"Well, I guess you'll have to stop calling Paul '*my* dad' after today," she said glibly, not even registering any recognition of the look of appalled shock that I was only thinly concealing. "Now he's going to be Tanner's dad too!"

Bitch, I remember thinking—that was my name for Diane in my mind. And not "bitch" like the friendly and fierce way exchanged between me and my girlfriends. When I got back home, I hesitated to even tell my mother what happened, but I did.

"That *biiitchhhh!*" my mom hissed the next morning while she made us breakfast, breaking wide from her usual composure. "She has got *some nerve* telling *my child* what to do, and what to say to her *own father.*" I caught my breath as her hand hovered over the knife drawer, letting her fingers encircle the drawer handle to pull it toward her. From the inside, her hand returned to the counter gripping the end of a spatula that she slammed down on the counter, making a hard plastic clack for emphasis. "Next time you see her, you tell Diane that *your* momma said . . ." She whipped her head around from scrambling eggs to look me directly in my eyes. Hers were pitch-black and now dancing with fire. Suddenly, abruptly, she caught herself in the moment, and paused. I could almost see her mind change its course as her body straightened upward at least an inch. "Never mind," she continued, almost cheerfully, "I'll tell her myself."

Then she turned to me fully and pointed right at me with the orange spatula, as if there was a target for her right between my eyes. "And don't you *dare* let that"—she paused so she could emphasize the *w* in her next phrase—"whh-oman tell you what to do, beyond what *your* father says is respectful. You hear me?"

For a second, I just knew that she was going to say "white woman," bringing up the injury that hung silently in the air, but she didn't. I nodded quickly to signify that I understood, and with that, the conversation was over. I knew better than to push that kind of issue with my mother, *or* to ask her what she was really going to do. For weeks after that moment, I actually waited for the news about Diane's mysterious and untimely demise. In the end, on the few and far between times that I did see them, first the three of them (Diane was intact), then four, and eventually the five *other* Walkers, I continued to reference my dad as *my* dad, just like I had always done, and there was no one that said anything else to me about it ever again. Since not much had changed about Diane, as she had often been similarly insensitive even in later years, I just decided that it was who she was, at least to me, and chose to cope best by keeping my distance.

"Maybe, one of these days," I said finally, snapping my mind back to Granny Tab's suggestion of joining them for dinner. "But tonight I can't. Tonight, I have a date—with Marc," I said with a teasing smile.

"Oh yes, your beau Marc," Granny Tab teased back. "Well, now I know why your hair looks so pretty! Now you just need to put on your leep-stick!" I laughed. She was making another reference to the younger me who would always ask if I could put on her red "leep-stick." She was the keeper of all my memories.

We were startled out of our reverie by the simultaneous sound of a knock on the door and the door swinging open. There was Ms. Gretchen, in all of her blond glory, ninety-two years young in a bubblegum-pink leisure suit, wearing matching Nike Air Max sneakers.

"Tabitha," she said, addressing my grandmother. "I need you to come and tell this new girl about me going to the mall. She's trying to stop me, honey!" Ms. Gretchen's voice reverberated with good-natured intensity. "Hey, Tab! Looking good, girl!" she said, turning her attention to me. "I'm going to have to catch up with you next time—I have things to do! Come on, Tabitha!" She grabbed my grandmother's hand. Granny Tab smiled and started the process of getting up so she could accompany her friend. "Now, I'm gonna try to walk real slow wit'cha, but you got to try to speed it up. My Uber is coming, and I can't afford to have my rating go down!" *Good Lord, what is this ninety-two-year-old woman doing worried about her Uber rating?* I thought.

"I'm coming, Gretchen, good Lord," my grandmother said, letting herself be pulled toward the door by the insistent force of nature otherwise known as her best friend. I followed them down the hall.

"Now, Tabitha," Ms. Gretchen said as they walked down the hallway, "you have *got* to tell this girl that I have all the same privileges to leave as I would in my own house. Now, see, she's new. But I don't have time today! I have an Uber waiting and a nail appointment!"

"There was a new person at the desk in front," I offered in their slow-moving direction. "I don't think that she believed I was your granddaughter."

"Well, now," interrupted Ms. Gretchen, "*that's* not 'cause she's new, Tabby, that's 'cause she's ignorant. But she's gonna learn today!"

The three of us arrived at the front desk like some kind of misfit gang. Ms. Gretchen approached the front desk aide.

"Now see, I brought two people to tell you. You better call someone. I've got sense enough to know I can't predict the weather, but what I do know is that I'm not going to miss my nail appointment foolin' with you!"

"Now, Leslie," said my grandmother, trying to be diplomatic in reading the now bewildered aide's nametag, "Gretchen does have privileges—you should call one of the nurses . . ." Sure enough, almost on cue, and likely because of the growing commotion, a familiar face in a doctor's coat appeared.

"Well, good afternoon, Ms. Potts and Ms. Walker—hello, Tabby, visiting with your grandmother today, I see? How nice." Dr. Johnson was here every Saturday, and I saw her often. The poor aide at the front desk now looked totally confused.

"I'm glad you showed up, Dr. Johnson," said Ms. Gretchen. "Could you *please* explain to Leslie—who's *new*—that I *shall not* miss my nail appointment today? My Uber is outside to take me to the mall."

"Ms. Gretchen, Leslie is right that our residents are not supposed to leave the premises without an escort for safety . . ." Dr. Johnson started. "But," she continued with a wink, "we know you have a few special exemptions. You're clear to go." Dr. Johnson turned to address the now fully overwhelmed aide, who was looking from one to the other of us with her mouth open. "Leslie, just make a note on the log.

She'll be back in a couple of hours." Dr. Johnson turned to Ms. Gretchen, who was already halfway out of the front door. "A couple of hours, right, Ms. Gretchen?"

"Sure thing, Doc!" And with that she disappeared into the light of the outside and into the passenger-side back door of an Uber that sure enough had been idling there during the entire episode. Her departure left the other four of us to momentarily regroup, and then my grandmother and I headed back to her place to make the most of my remaining time to visit. After all, while she had plans in Calabasas with my dad this evening, I had plans with Marc, who I had yet to see after my news from the doctor. I still had no idea what I was going to tell him . . . and what I wasn't.

5

SATURDAY HAD ALREADY STARTED TO FEEL LONG EVEN BEFORE I put the last touches of my makeup on preparing for my date night with Marc. The conversation with my mother weighed on my mind. I eventually succeeded in shutting her down when we spoke, but somehow she managed in just a few words to plant a seed of self-doubt. True, Marc and I had been dating for a year and a half, but on many weeks, our times spent together would look much like this one. Texts and a few calls during the workdays and then a formal Saturday date that would lead into Sunday. It certainly didn't have the momentum of a relationship that appeared to be moving forward. I couldn't help but wonder if my work schedule *was* partially to blame.

When we first started dating, Marc made it incredibly clear to me that he didn't want a woman to make him the center of her life, and he liked that I had my own career and goals. "I wouldn't mind being Steadman someday," he said when we discussed my career as a journalist, and he never complained about the lack of time spent together. Sometimes, it seemed like Marc relished having the freedom and leeway apart from me. But that wasn't bringing us any closer together either. I was just always taught that the man was supposed to take the lead, and as a woman, you were supposed to let him. There was never any idea of a joint negotiation of a future, but I was going to have to try to start one tonight—with no playbook and no idea of how receptive, or not, he would be.

Knowing that I could be inviting disaster, I tried to calm my nervous thoughts as I finished getting ready. I loved him, that was for sure—just not in a completely innocent, silly high school "first love" kind of way. It was smart to love Marc. He was the type you could love and not feel guilty about it. Seeing him still gave me butterflies, talking to him made me feel special, and I could certainly see having his baby, or babies, even now—and I wouldn't even mind if that meant maternity leave and time away from the station. In light of my mother's commentary, it felt reassuring to know that I *was* willing to make some sacrifices. Just that I hadn't been asked to—not by Marc and not by life circumstances, at least not before. This was the week that all that changed.

The ping coming from my phone was Marc, letting me know he was downstairs in his car at the front of my building. I took one last look at myself in the mirror, even turning to see how my exercise was paying off—I looked good, very good, and I needed to. Tonight, Marc was going to get an earful.

"Hey, babe!" I said breezily as I swooped into Marc's idling new Porsche Panamera. I made it a point to close the door gently because, no matter what he said, or what was supposed to be, I was positive that if he had to choose between me and this car, I would be the first to go. I had seen far too many times the cringe on his face when the door closed too forcefully, and this was when he still "drove American," as he liked to say.

"Whassup, Tab, damn you smell good, girl!" Marc said as he looked me up and down in his casually seductive way, biting his firm and generous lower lip. Marc was sexy. Very sexy. He wasn't the tallest, but he kept his body fit and well maintained. His flawless chocolate-brown skin was the perfect canvas for his thick black eyebrows, well-trimmed five o'clock shadow, and strong Jamaican features. In my mind, he was my own version of Kofi Siriboe, *with* a business degree from Stanford and a very successful career as a commercial real estate broker. He sent a charge through my body as he grabbed my hand. That and the regular butterflies brought a blushing and flirtatious smile to my face.

"We still have some time before our reservation. We can hit a bar on the way, or just have drinks at the restaurant. Up to you," he offered. Another thing I loved about Marc: maybe he couldn't make relationship decisions, but he sure knew how to make good reservations—and wine selections. I was never disappointed with his choices on date night. I was hoping this trend would extend to the more serious topics that we'd have to soon discuss, so I opted to just go straight to the restaurant.

On this night, Marc decided to take me to the Little Door, arguably the most romantic hidden gem of a restaurant in all of LA. The French cuisine was served in a cozy courtyard under gently flowering trees and a woven net of tea lights complementing the stars above in the open night sky. It was worth taking a little bit of a drive from Downtown LA, where I lived. I didn't mind—to be honest, it was nice to sit and be driven around for a change, through LA traffic, in this very nice car. His was a far cry from the near-dilapidated Honda Civic that I had driven for ten years and was still recovering from. Marc-land could be a very nice escape, if that's what I wanted. But now I needed more than an escape, I needed a partnership. I waited as long as I could, past drinks at the bar, past small talk through appetizers, even past our entrees, until I brought up the events of the week.

"So, I didn't get to tell you." I started telling Marc the story. "I got pulled over by the police, randomly! I was basically in tears and almost convinced that I was going to die—my wallet and everything fell on the floor . . . and you saw what they did to Philando Castile just for reaching for an ID . . ." I was dead serious, but Marc had started laughing at me.

"Tabby, you're an attractive Black woman," he said. "It's not *you* who has the problem with the cops. They're not looking to tag you. You were in no danger at all."

I looked at him with skepticism. *What's the difference between being in danger and feeling like your life is on the line? That's what I wanted to know. What exempts me from the seemingly senseless violence? Just because I'm a woman? Well, what about Sandra Bland? Maybe because I'm on television?* I had plenty of questions in mind, but I let him continue.

He took a bite of his food and then leaned back in his chair, his handsome face showing he was considering what he had just said. "Plus," he continued, "if you're really worried, then you need to head over to the USC bookstore, just like I did as soon as I got the Porsche, and get a license plate." Wha—? Oh, I had forgotten. Classic Marc. Classic too smart for his own good, overthinking Marc. As soon as he got his fancy car, he went over to the University of Southern California bookstore and bought a "USC Law" trim to go around his license plate. This was notable because Marc went neither to law school nor USC. He said he did it "so the police will think twice before they stop *my* ass." When I asked him why he picked fake USC over fake UCLA credentials, he said, "Because UCLA is the state school and USC is the private one— I'd rather have them assume I come with money and will sue their ass if they fuck with me." It was just that kind of crazy thinking that made me love him.

"Oh yeah, I forgot about your USC Law 'decorative' license plate trim," I said, throwing up air quotes and breaking into a laugh.

"See, you got jokes," he said with a smile. "You can play around if you want to, but you realize only one of us tonight has a story about a run-in with the po-po's." His face registered a self-satisfied grin. My posture softened slightly, acknowledging that he did have a point. We shared another laugh, and then, I cleared my throat. The conversation was about to get serious. My palms started to sweat. I sat up straight again.

"Well . . . I think I was also doubly upset because . . ." I paused, searching for the next words while trying my best not to chicken out. "I . . . heard from my doctor that morning too. Not good news . . . My biological clock is ticking, babe, like faster than it's supposed to." Reflexively, I reached for my wine and studied his reaction as I drank. The smile he was wearing vanished almost immediately.

"What does that mean?" he asked as he leaned forward, his brow crinkled with concern.

"I guess it means that I have way fewer eggs than I'm supposed to at my age. I have to do something in the next six months, or I lose a lot of options," I said quickly. With that,

Marc leaned back in his chair, and I was a little relieved to see that he seemed much more comfortable than I expected.

"Oh, okay," he said, his hand coming up to rub his chin. "You can freeze them or something, right?" I took in a breath sharply. I wish that hadn't been his first response.

"Yes, I could do that," I said. "But it's expensive, and you know I've been trying to buy a house. It would be my entire down payment."

"Doesn't your insurance cover something like that?" he asked. I thought about it quickly and realized, *It doesn't.* That was the short answer, but it had never occurred to me that could even be an option. I mean, *whose insurance covers egg freezing?*

"No, definitely not. It would be out of pocket, totally," I said.

"Well, that's crazy," Marc said. "All the tech companies are covering it. Google, Facebook, seems like everywhere. The girls in my b-school class talk about it all the time. Some even factored that into how they picked their job at graduation. I thought it was almost a standard benefit by now." His words surprised me. My mind quickly drifted to Lisa at work. I wondered if this was one of the issues that group she was pushing was going to address. Probably not; she already had a kid *and* a husband.

"Yeah, sadly, I don't have it like that at the news station . . . Listen," I said, grabbing his hand, hoping mine hadn't gone too clammy. "I was thinking . . . about us . . . and I wanted to know what you were thinking, really . . . about where we are, you know, with . . . with *our relationship.*" I managed to force the words out, again studying him for a reaction. He pulled his hand back from mine slowly and brought it to the stem of his wineglass. He took a long drink. A real long drink. *Shit. ShitShitShit*. Then, he took a deep breath before continuing.

"Well, we're not at the point of having a kid together, if that's what you're asking. I mean, I want to have kids eventually, but I want to do it right, and I need to be at another stage in my career," he said, looking at me with the hope that the conversation was over. *Not yet*.

"But . . ." I said slowly, as I searched for the next words to get the answers I needed, ". . . do you want to have kids with me? Even if it's eventually?" *Damn*. That still wasn't what I wanted to ask. I tried to stop myself from talking in circles and find a way to get to the point. "What I'm trying to say is . . . do you see long-term potential for us . . . in the short term?" There, maybe that was it. My stomach tightened, and I felt my palms start to moisten again. I couldn't help but think that I was probably ruining this romantic night under beautiful stars, and quite possibly my relationship alongside it. I heard Marc drag in a long breath. He reached back out for my hand.

"Tab, I love you. I'm sure of that. But we're still getting to know each other. I can't say that we're ready to make big moves in the next few months, but I could see a future for us down the road." Marc's voice sounded full of sincerity. "Even with some kids," he added with a big smile, clearly trying to lighten the mood. It wasn't the answer I was hoping for, but it would have to do for now.

We had enough wine at dinner to make short order of things once we got back to my loft. My heels were off as soon as we hit the door. Marc grabbed me around the waist and put his warm lips onto mine. We always got this part right. The downtown lights danced through my wall of windows as he led me past the sofa and directly to the bed. My feet nestled in the off-white fur of my bedside rug, and I felt my dress drop to the floor around my ankles. His kisses dropped lower too, first to cover my neck, which was pulsating with the quickened pace of my heartbeat. Then down to my breasts, rising to meet his mouth with every one of the shortening breaths I was taking. I felt my strapless bra fall to the ground near my feet with a silent announcement.

Marc cupped his hands around the curvature of my back and brought me around to lay me on the bed. I lay back and watched the twinkling lights while he went to work exciting my body past the point of no return. I was so turned on, I forgot about the pills—*my pill* . . . I hadn't taken it yet today, and only twice this week.

"Marc . . . baby, my pill, I haven't taken it today . . . I . . ." I got lost in some maneuver he was executing with his tongue against my sensitized body. "Maybe we should . . ." I tried to offer up everything I didn't want him to accept in that moment. *Maybe we should stop?! Say it!* My mind screamed. But I didn't let the words travel to my lips. I tried. I really did, before we both lost ourselves in wave after wave of pleasure that seemed to come from all directions. It felt right, even if it was wrong. So, so very wrong.

6

"BEEETCH, YOU OUT HERE TRYING TO HAVE AN NBA BABY!" LAILA shouted over the champagne flute at her lips at our Sunday late-afternoon brunch table, cracking herself up at me and my indiscretions of the previous night. "I mean," she continued, partially slurring her words, "Marc ain't no NBA player, but he got an NBA car! With his fine ass!" she added with a grasp of the air with her non-champagne-holding empty hand for emphasis. Clearly, she was already tipsy. I knew I shouldn't encourage her, but we were having fun. I hoped that no one within earshot would recognize me from the station.

"An NBA car *and* a Stanford business degree," I added, feeling only a slight tinge of reluctance about objectifying my own man. We clinked glasses on that, and I washed down any lingering pain of superficiality-induced guilt with more pink champagne. "We would make the perfect couple . . . if we . . . well, if he would just cooperate."

"What are you going to do if you're actually pregnant?" Laila hissed. I looked up to think and blinked at the bright California sunshine. We picked the trendy rooftop restaurant at the NoMad hotel. Just like Saturday morning workouts,

Alexis couldn't join, so it was just the two of us. After waking up with Marc and sharing a cup of coffee in my kitchenette and a long goodbye kiss with him, I had Laila as my date for brunch to start the afternoon. Marc had work to do, and I had bad decisions to analyze.

"I don't know!" I said. I *really* didn't. Honestly, I hadn't thought the scenario all the way through. "I'm thinking about Plan B."

"What the hell kind of Plan B would you have if you're pregnant?" Laila spat back at me. "Sounds like you're already on Plan B, and C, and D . . . definitely Plan D," she said, exaggerating the *D* and cracking herself up all over again. This girl.

"Plan B, like brand name 'Plan B,'" I said. "The morning-after pill, silly."

"Oh! Thaaat Plan B!" Laila said. "Wait, wait, let me pull myself into serious professional journalist mode. I need to ask you reporter questions—like I'm dealing with a hostile information source . . . Ms. Tabitha Walker, what is it that you *want* to happen?" *Damn, Laila!* She always knew how to get to the core of what I didn't want to confront.

"What I want to happen, Marc took off the table last night," I said. "I wanted him to want to live an adult life . . . with me . . . and maybe a plus-one." I paused to think a bit before continuing, "I can't force decisions on him that he's clearly not prepared to make. If we did wind up pregnant, it would solve a lot of problems for me, but probably create even more—especially with a man who is unwilling . . . I mean, with all that said, I guess . . . I guess I really have no choice but to take the morning-after pill? Right? Like, what other options . . ."

"Sounds like CVS to me!" Laila interrupted. "You can go get the Plan B and a bottle of wine to wash it down with— perfect combination . . . beetch!" she screeched, doubling over with laughter this time. *Now we were in unfamiliar territory for me.*

"So what do you do? How do you get it?" I asked her. I had no recollection at all of ever seeing it on any of the shelves, come to think of it.

"Just go to the pharmacy and ask for it."

"Just like that? Is it covered by insurance? Don't I need a prescription?" I asked, perplexed.

"Covered by insurance?" Laila spat out the words, laughing at me again. "Girl, hell no! It's not Viagra. This is for women after the Viagra actually works. And since it's *just* for women, you *know* it's not covered by insurance! But you don't need a prescription for it. I guess they make you go up and ask for it to keep people from thinking they're candy," she said, rolling her eyes.

"Well, I'd rather pay for Plan B out of pocket than egg freezing!" I said, suddenly remembering part of my conversation from the night before. "Marc told me that a bunch of other employers in California cover egg freezing! That's so far from my reality at the station."

"Egg freezing? Girl, that's like twenty K. If my eggs expire, that's just gonna have to be it for me. There's no way that I could afford that working at the paper. Not even if my name was on the masthead . . ."

"And to think that Viagra has become a standard benefit," I mused.

"When men start caring about some shit, it'll happen!"

Laila said confidently. "Let enough men have to start paying for IVF, keeping them from buying their midlife crisis sports cars. You'll see some changes then, I bet!" I laughed at the sober truth coming from her very tipsy tongue.

"Maybe so, but until then, an 'oopsie baby' is not the ideal way to go about saving my bank account. Ugh!" I exclaimed through my gritted teeth in exasperation. "I still can't believe that I got myself into this situation!"

"Don't feel bad," Laila said with a dismissive wave of her hand in my direction. "You aren't the only one playing fast and loose with the D . . . Me and Mr. Big . . ." She cut herself off with a sly grin.

"Wait, you have a Mr. Big? Who?"

"Yeah, girl, a Mr. Biiiiig. Big hands, big bank account, big personality, *big* . . ." she said with emphasis as she snickered down into her drink.

"Oooh, Laila! You're getting some! Haha! I knew you had that glow-up look happening. Details, please!" I leaned forward, not wanting to miss a word. Laila was a true Gemini. She only told you what she wanted you to know, and meanwhile, she'd be living some entirely separate life that you'd only find out about when she was ready to share.

"Well, that part is all good, and then there's a part that's complicated . . . I just met him at the recent NABJ conference—the one that *you* were too *busy* to go to. He's on ESPN and," she continued dreamily, "it was sparks right away. From our first conversation to the first night we spent. Everything . . . it just happened . . . and we really should have . . . should be, strapping up . . . especially because . . . because, well, let's just say he has . . . a situation."

"Laila, I know 'a situation' does not mean what I think it means. Your ass is crazy, but I know you're not out here being stupid . . . Tell me you're not . . ."

"Okay, fine," Laila said, bringing her champagne glass to her lips. "I'll tell you no lies . . ." And with that she took a sip, turning to pretend-watch the people next to us.

"What?!"

"I told you! I met him at the conference. He wasn't wearing a ring. I had no idea—I didn't think to ask, and things just went so fast. Whisky and weed, girl, it's like a roofie. We had this whirlwind night of passion and conversation and then next thing I know I wake up in a hotel room with this man and . . . well, before I knew anything . . . we were doing it again!" Laila said, throwing her hands in the air.

"All night?" I asked, admittedly now more intrigued by the stamina than the circumstances.

"And all morning . . ." Laila said. "And it's been like that ever since we met . . ."

I leaned forward, further intrigued. I had never been in this kind of situation before. "So, how did you find out that he's married?" I asked.

"Eventually, I asked. Without the ring, it didn't occur to me, but I *am* an investigative journalist—so even if I didn't want to see the signs, eventually I would have anyway."

"Oh my God, Laila! So you're *dating* a married man?" I made a mental note to dial back on my tone. I could tell even from my end that I was coming across as a little judgy—and knowing Laila, that would be the first way to make her shut down on me entirely and tell me absolutely nothing, all over again. Given my history with Diane, as I listened, I found myself struggling with finding a way to be supportive.

I wondered briefly if my dad had been wearing *his* ring when they met.

"Well, he says that he's on the fence," Laila said eventually, snapping me out of my own thoughts. "Things haven't been good between him and his wife for a minute now. He's really high profile and doesn't want to risk the divorce just yet. I think he just needs some time . . . He doesn't have sex with her anymore," she added. I didn't know what to say. I wanted my friend to take the chances she needed to find her own happiness, but I couldn't help but feel worried about everything I was hearing.

"At the end of the day, we don't know what *any* of these dudes out here are *really* doing." Thinking briefly about Marc's reluctance, I added, "Yours *or* mine."

"Yeah," said Laila, pensively. "We do need to do a better job of protecting ourselves."

"Girl, we *definitely* do." Even with that, I somehow didn't feel convinced that either one of us would suddenly start making the right decisions. For a moment, both of us were lost in our own thoughts.

"Let's order another bottle!" Laila said, interrupting the silence. "If you're pregnant, let's toast to Plan B!"

The reality of her statement hit me hard with a pang in my gut. *If I'm pregnant?* Holy shit. I raised my hand for the waiter. We did need another bottle.

Walking back home after brunch, admittedly failing the straight-line test, I decided to make a stop at the drugstore on the corner. I contemplated going somewhere much farther out of the way, where I wouldn't have to see the same pharmacist again, but there was no way I could even think about slipping behind the wheel.

I thought about what Laila said. I couldn't believe that she was dating a married man. Didn't that make her a *mistress*? Just like what Diane had been before my dad decided for whatever reason to leave my mother and me, marry her, and make *her* the foundation of his new and improved family. The look on my father's face that day in the kitchen flashed in my mind. My childhood mind only registered his reaction to my mother's crying as *upset*; but as an adult, looking back, I could see it as much more complex and disturbing. My best adult description was a mixture of mortified helplessness and *indifference*. It's the latter part, the *indifference*, that even over the years, still haunts me the most.

I shook myself back to the present as the automated door swung open in front of me revealing familiar rows of sundries. I wasn't ready to make such a heavy decision about Plan B, or to have an embarrassing conversation with the pharmacist, so I decided to take the long way to the back of the store and stroll the brightly colored cosmetics aisle. I was grateful that nobody else was there. I walked slowly, letting my fingers linger across the lipsticks, trying to remember the first shade I wore when Granny Tab finally allowed me to put on a "girlish" blush in public during sophomore year of high school. I moved forward and examined the nail polish, letting my mind wander through thoughts, trying to ignore my biggest question: *Do I want to take a chance?* Marc was clear on his point of view, but weren't we both responsible for the decisions we made? What if I just didn't want to take the Plan B pill? And that was the truth of it, wasn't it—*I didn't want to take it. I really didn't want to.* Overhead, I heard the metallic robotic announcement, "Assistance needed in the cosmetics section." I turned to look around me, to the right and to the left, and still, I was the only person in the aisle. I hadn't pushed any buttons, so I wondered what could have possibly prompted the announcement. Now certainly wasn't the time I was interested in dealing with the randomness of a drugstore sales associate. And almost as a response to my question, into my field of peripheral vision came the dark uniform of the store security guard sliding in place at the entrance of the cosmetics aisle, trying to pretend he wasn't looking in my direction. All I could do was laugh silently to myself. To think, here I am, trying to make a major life decision, and all they see is a shoplifter casing the store for cheap cosmetics.

Just out of spite, I ran my hand slowly across the rest of the section as I made my way back to the pharmacy. When I got there, five people were waiting in line to speak to the pharmacist. I took my place at the end. I thought about the moment with the security guard, and my conversation with Laila, and my encounter with Officer Mallory. And all of a sudden, I felt tired—too tired to wait. I decided that I was going to do what I wanted most. I was going to go home. I made a pivot toward the front of the store and headed toward the door. It just so happened that I found myself passing through well-stocked shelves of wine to either side. I reached out and grabbed the closest one that looked like a bottle of Sauvignon Blanc, paid for it at the counter, and gave the security guard at the entrance a long look. "When I'm not stealing mascara, I'm buying wine," I said as I walked out of the door. Turns out, *bullshit* also washes down well with a bottle of drugstore vino.

7

IT'S AMAZING WHAT A BUSY TIME AT WORK CAN MAKE YOU FORGET about. In my case, I forgot about the Plan B that turned into plan "bottle of wine" for just about two weeks until the *buy tampons!* calendar reminder popped up on my computer screen at work. *Had it really been two weeks?* It had. My Los Angeles real estate assignment from the newsroom had taken over the spare room in my brain and what would have been left of my time with friends, including Marc. I remembered what my mother said about priorities, but given what Marc said about our future, my priority would have to be my promotion. The only date I didn't cancel was my standing appointment with Denisha. No way I was not getting my hair done for the week.

With our piece on real estate trends starting to come together, I was looking forward to getting back to my regular pace. I guess I had truly welcomed the distraction of being fully immersed in research, team meetings, and writing copy, which allowed me to avoid thinking about the possibility of being pregnant. *Pregnant.* Just a brief mental taste of the idea brought a warm smile to my face—followed by a swift smack of reality. Marc didn't want this. Hell, I don't even know if I wanted this right now. The flash of a future filled with years of resentment and custody battles, childhood trauma and unhealthy adversity brought me face-to-face with consequences I hadn't even begun to consider. I pulled out my phone to text Laila.

Me:
Dude, it's been 2 weeks.

Laila:
What's been 2 wks?

Me:
Plan B

Laila:
Which Plan B?

Me:
Bottle, not pill.

Laila:
Oh shit!
Laila:
R U pregnant?

Me:
How would I know? Should I take a test?

Laila:
Did you miss ur period?

Me:
Not yet—supposed to come tmrw.

Laila:
Tests don't work until you miss. Just wait.

Me:
Should I say something to Marc?

Laila:

Hell no! Just wait.

Me:

What r u doing tonight?

Laila:

Seeing Mr. Big . . . U?

Me:

Working . . . as usual. See u this wknd?

Laila:

Maybe! Not if tonight goes right tho! Toodles!

In some ways, I admired Laila for always being . . . Laila. I figured she was right, however—it was too early to test, too early to panic, and definitely too early to bring it up to Marc. Even without a day to spare, all I could do was wait.

8

SATURDAY CAME AROUND, AND BY THEN IT WAS PRETTY CLEAR
there was no need for any escalation of my premature panic.
The bloating and light cramping started as a telltale Paul
Revere–style warning that *Your period is coming! Your period
is coming!* I needed to prepare the fort with the necessary mu-
nitions to be ready for a sudden bloody attack. I played no
games and went the tampon route before I left for Denisha's
to get my hair done. Before I even got to Granny Tab's place,
it was already time to swap out for a freshie. Part of me was
relieved, but just part.

These two weeks allowed me to live in denial that my
fertility options maybe weren't dwindling with each passing
day. I didn't want to give up my hard-earned down payment
that I planned to use for a house, and I couldn't put any more
pressure on Marc, who made it clear he wasn't into my idea
of timing for a family. I wasn't ready to lose him, not at all,
so now wasn't the time to push the issue. I had been hoping
for a simple solution that I could have mistakenly stumbled
upon, that would have just not-so-innocently placed us where
I happened to want to be. And we would have been equal

culprits. I guess if I were further honest, I would say that I tried on the idea of being pregnant more than once in these past couple of weeks. It began as just a tiny idea that I let slip between my ears and sit there like a little bird on a perch. I started to like the song that it was singing to me, something sweet, joyous, and hopeful. Not to say that by my period coming, I felt like all hope was gone, just that things were going to be a little tougher than I'd prepared for. For the first time, I was facing a circumstance knowing for certain that no matter what, I would have to sacrifice something I held dearly, and there was just no getting around it.

Walking into Crestmire, thankfully this time with no friction at the front desk check-in, I happened to see my grandmother and her right arm, Ms. Gretchen, at a table chatting over what looked like a game of Uno and some ice cream. It was so funny to me that these folks who had lived so much life now found themselves doing many of the same things we used to do as kids, when we had lived no life at all. Either this was some kind of shameful tragedy, or evidence that we work our whole adulthood just to get back to who we could have been in the first place.

It was Ms. Gretchen who actually saw me first and started her frantic gestures of waving me over, with the curls of her shoulder-length blond, highlighted hair bouncing in rhythm. Granny Tab had stopped dyeing her hair a long time ago and resigned herself to what seemed like the inevitable takeover of gray, like weeds in any garden. I suppose at some point she had rightfully grown tired of fighting against the badges of old age and seemed eventually to embrace it with a calm grace. Ms. Gretchen, on the other hand, fought like hell. She always had her hair colored, curled, and coiffed to precision, and her nails were manicured, polished, and long. Usually, Crestmire didn't let the residents keep their nails too long because of the "hazards." Spats could get nasty. Once, I honestly thought that someone was going to lose an eyeball over a botched bingo seating assignment. You're serious about what you're serious about, even if it's a chair. In spite of that, Ms. Gretchen always got her exemptions through.

"Tabby! You take this seat right here," Ms. Gretchen offered. "I'm going to go get you some ice cream. You want some ice cream? Of course you do. I'll be right back." And with that she bounded off with the energy of someone half her age toward the kitchen, giving my grandmother and me the opportunity to give hugs and for her to clear the cards up.

"How are you today, Granny Tab?" I asked.

"Same ol' same ol'!" she said cheerfully. "When you get to be my age, so many things are changing that the same is good sometimes! How are you, Two?"

I debated how I was going to answer that question. There was no denying that I needed to call the infertility specialist and make an appointment. But I was procrastinating because I was scared. I was scared for more bad news and scared to be on my own with something so significant that could affect the rest of my life. These were the things I didn't want to burden my grandmother with, but I wanted to tell the truth. "I'm good, Granny Tab! Still fighting for that promotion at work! And . . . and I need to go ahead and make an appointment with the infertility specialist. If I don't, well . . . I have to, that's just it, because I know I want to be able to have kids someday."

"Oh yes, you *definitely* want to be able to have kids!" Granny Tab said. "And I hope that I'll get to meet them—either here, or before they get here if I'm up there." She pointed to the sky with an upward roll of her eyes and a quick tilt of her head. She sometimes talked about death like that, as if it were a comfortable old friend who had invited her to one day visit his summer home.

"You will definitely be around to meet my kids, Granny Tab!" I said. "You're gonna be living with me, remember?" I teased her and pinched her playfully on her arm. Crestmire was nice, but I always thought of it as a temporary necessity. Granny Tab swore up and down she liked it here just fine. She said that it was as good as, if not better, than her Fairfax district place that she had lived in since forever. It was the fall at the Fairfax place about a year ago that led to the discovery of Stage 2 congestive heart failure. She could still get around on her own, but none of us, herself included, wanted to take any chances. So for now, here we were. My goal, though, was always to move Granny Tab into *my* house, and one day it would be the two of us again, just like it was in high school. She resisted, insisting that would make her a burden, which she never wanted to be. We settled on her taking on the role of nanny, and that seemed to be a scenario that made her comfortable, optimistic even, for a life after Crestmire. The thought of telling her that things might be different stung my insides.

"Oh yes! That's right, sweetheart," Granny Tab said. "Well, you could just get pregnant, couldn't you? There are all kinds of newfangled stuff these days, and girls don't even have to get married anymore. You see, I didn't have that option back with your dad. Of course, I was much younger than you when I got pregnant, and there were a lot of other . . . circumstances." She paused, getting lost in an arriving memory. I let her continue. Granny Tab didn't talk about her life back in West Virginia often, so when she did, I didn't dare interrupt. She continued with her reverie, smiling at me. "I know I've told you how I met your grandfather. Honey, the times were so different back then. It was totally forbidden, you see, for the races to come together at all. In West Virginia, we were well entrenched in segregation. So, when I saw your grandfather down on Main Street and he smiled at me, that great big handsome smile, I knew it was trouble. He took a risk, just with that. He wasn't supposed to, you know—as a Black man, he wasn't supposed to look at, let alone *smile*, at a white woman. But he did." A wide smile broke out on my grandmother's face, so big that it made her pause. I saw the blush come to her cheeks almost as if she were back in that very moment, feeling the same temptation from a taboo gesture. She brought her hand, which had been resting on the table, up to her face and leaned forward to continue like she was telling me a secret. "I'd see him around, here and there, and he'd always sneak me that same smile. It became like a secret that we shared, just the two of us. And oh boy, I was mischievous too! My best friend, Evelyn, was a colored girl who managed to live next to us—next door. That's the word we all used back then, *colored*, I still remember her that way. Our schools were segregated, but our neighborhoods weren't. In high school, she would sneak me to the colored dance parties with her, and I'd be the only white girl there! I had such a good time, Two, and I learned all the dances! And your grandfather . . . oooh, he was the best dancer of everybody. Just the best—and we just danced and danced— handsome devil," she said with a giggle that she invited me to share in. "And then when I fell pregnant with your father, I was only nineteen. I couldn't tell anybody—my daddy would have killed all three of us, I just knew it. Daddy wasn't a bad man so much, but he was as prejudiced as they come, just like everybody back then—didn't know any better. And Evelyn got to go off to college, but I had to come out to California. Your granddaddy joined the service out here so that we could live together and raise your father. It was one place where we could be, you know, be Black and white together. It wasn't so much legal in many places back then."

"Got to give him credit for that!" Ms. Gretchen said, rejoining us with ice cream that she handed to me as she sat. "As my daddy always said, 'a man that ain't got no plan for you ain't your man.' That's how it was back then, the men had responsibilities and they knew when it was their turn to step up."

"Amen to that, Ms. Gretchen!" I said, laughing and taking the ice cream. I wanted to hear more about Granny Tab's life, but Ms. Gretchen had broken the spell. "I wish that were coming from the men I know!" I joked. "Looks like I'm gonna need to have a baby soon, or probably more likely, freeze my eggs."

"Honey, hush! Well, what about that nice young man you've been seeing? What's his name, Mike?"

"Marc," I said. "Yes, I've been dating Marc about a year and a half now."

"And what's he waiting for?"

"I can't say, Ms. Gretchen. I'm ready, but he says he's not. Not yet." I attempted to be lighthearted, but the gravity of those words made me look down at the table, avoiding the assessment reading in Ms. Gretchen's eyes. I felt a warm flush rising in my cheeks.

"Well," Granny Tab interjected quickly, "you two are still young . . . it's better to do it the right way from the beginning than have to undo it down the road. You can't undo a baby . . . or who you have one with," she said, drifting off again. That last statement triggered my curiosity. *Was she talking about her own experience?* Neither Granny Tab nor my father spoke much about my grandfather. It was so infrequent that he seemed more like an apparition of several generations back than a person who was once in my near-immediate family. I knew they had split sometime when my dad was young, but it always seemed strange that he would just disappear. Still, no one spoke of it, and I knew better than to ask.

"You can't undo a baby, but you *can* undo a marriage!" Ms. Gretchen sang back to us both. "I've done it twice. Both two sorry-soul good-for-nothings—weight on my shoulders. Good riddance!" she said, waving her hands in the air. "There's no reason that Marc shouldn't be trying to marry you, honey!"

I laughed. "You would think, Ms. Gretchen. But he's on his own schedule, I guess." Hearing my own words made them harder to deny.

"You guess?" Ms. Gretchen said, raising a penciled-in eyebrow. "You should *know*, honey. And he should *let you know*. Like I told you, my daddy said to me as soon as my little boobies started to sprout and those boys came sniffin' around, 'Now, Gretchen, a man that ain't got no plan for you ain't no man at all. And he's definitely not *your* man, you hear? Real men got plans for the things important to them. If he ain't got no plan for *you*, then you ain't what's important.' And I never forgot that. I might have married the *wrong* men, but I didn't *ever* have trouble getting asked."

I couldn't help but realize that Ms. Gretchen had a point. Marc and I hadn't spoken much over the past couple of weeks, but I was going to see him in just a few hours. Although, I would say, if I had known his true plans for us then, sitting at the table with Granny Tab and Ms. Gretchen, maybe I would have skipped that dinner.

9

I DON'T KNOW WHY I WAS SO NERVOUS GETTING READY FOR MY date with Marc. The scare had passed and, unless I planned to bring up "planning" of any sort, the evening would be just as routine as any other. What I needed was for it to not be routine. I needed him to see me as more than just an option, a possibility for his future. Was Marc stringing me along? Wasting my *time* even? I pushed the thought of Ms. Gretchen's words to the back of my mind, but they had been haunting me from the moment she said them: "a man that ain't got no plan for you . . ." But, Marc *was* my man. He was my man who I loved, who I was attracted to and the person I knew I could spend the rest of my days making a marriage and family with. *Could that be enough for him?* I spent a little extra time on everything, an extra touch of eyeliner, a little bit tighter dress, and the sexier stilettos that were a little less comfortable but more undeniable. Marc might not have had a plan for me, but I'd be the one with plans for that evening. It had been a long two weeks since we had last seen each other, so I was eager to reconnect beyond the phone calls, text messages, and occasional naughty video chats that had kept us integrated into each other's lives.

Instead of picking me up, Marc wanted to meet directly at a restaurant, not too far from my place downtown. Perch, which sat high up atop one of the office buildings, had a great patio for open-air dining and an upstairs for dancing. This was exactly the kind of evening I'd hoped we'd be having and a welcome departure from my thoughts of babies and promotions and down payments that I could likely kiss goodbye. What I needed, and what Marc and I needed, was to have fun. When I walked in, I saw him sitting at the bar. He seemed nervous, playing with the calluses on his hands, his thumb rubbing against each of them, one at a time. I guessed he also had a rough couple of weeks at work. I gave him a huge smile and headed in his direction. He stood up and wrapped me with his arms in a way that I welcomed like water falling on a neglected fern.

"Wow, Tab, you look great!" he said, pulling away from me slightly awkwardly. I tried to linger close to him a little longer, telling him he not only looked good but also smelled great. And he certainly did. We made small talk together until our table was ready. Once we were seated and our meals had arrived, I told him about Lisa's continual insistence that I prioritize the women's issues group over my own concerns. And I told him about Alexis's birthday dinner that was coming up, extending their invitation to him. At that, his brow furrowed, and he reached for my hand.

"Tab, um, about that . . . I just don't think it's a good idea that I go."

"What?" I shot back in shock. "Babe, why not?" I asked with the full innocent ignorance of a deer caught in the headlights of a trailer truck. My mind started reeling, and I could feel my chest tightening.

"Look, I've been doing a lot of thinking about our last conversation. And I'm just on the fence about everything. I'm not ready. I don't think I can be ready anytime soon . . . and . . . I don't want you to miss out on your life and the milestones that are important to you." My breath stopped in my throat. And all of a sudden I lost my appetite. In spite of the sick feeling creeping into my stomach, I allowed myself to reach instinctively for my glass of wine. My other hand, I pulled away from his.

"Marc, what does that even mean? Are you talking about wanting a baby?" My thoughts went back to the nine-year-old me standing in the kitchen with my parents, learning of their split. I felt the same helplessness and hoped that my voice could hide the whine I felt mounting inside. *Why? Where are you going?* I wanted to ask. Instead, I tried to maintain my composure, to be an adult. Maybe he was saying something different. I searched his face before continuing, with the tinge and cadence of desperation creeping into my words, "I told you I do . . . but, eventually! It doesn't have to be today, babe—where's this coming from?"

"Tabby, I just don't know if I see a future for us." *I think my heart just stopped.* "It's been a year and a half—we haven't gotten any closer." I stopped breathing. "We still see each other what, once, twice per week?" My mouth dropped open. "I'm not a central part of your life any more than you are in mine." He reached for my hand again while I sat frozen and wide-eyed like a statue. "I love you, but I don't know that I'm in love with you . . . I don't know that I *can* be. Maybe I can't be with anyone."

I sat in stunned silence and finally turned my head to look off into the distance for a moment of privacy to process. I could hear my breath start to stagger, which meant the tears were on their way. All I could think of was escape.

"Could you excuse me for just one second?" I said to him. "I'll be right back. I need to . . . go . . . I need to go to the rest-room," I said as I stood. While my normal composure was breaking, I wasn't going to give him, and especially not the rest of the restaurant, the spectacle of me crying. *What in the entire fuck just happened?* I didn't understand. Marc and I had an honest talk two weeks ago. I told him my situation and my preference, but I hadn't applied any pressure. *Maybe he didn't understand, and some clarity from me could help ease his concerns?* That's what I wanted to believe. *Yes, that's it. This is just a misunderstanding.* With my tears dried by wash-room paper towels, I let hope flood into me on my return to the table.

"Is this something that we can talk about?" I asked as Marc returned to his seat after helping me with mine. *Still a perfect gentleman . . . on paper.*

"Sure, we can always talk about it," Marc said. "But I'm not sure that would change anything about how I feel. It's been on my mind for a while." *For how long, Marc? How long?* "And then, when you said the thing about the eggs and the babies, it's like it accelerated all my thoughts."

I blinked at him, still absorbing the shock of the situation. I struggled to keep my mouth from dropping open again. I couldn't believe he was doing this.

He continued, "I mean, I'm just at the start of my career and, please don't take this the wrong way, but . . . I've got a lot of options . . . I'm getting more attention than I ever imag-

ined and . . . I'm just not sure. I'm not sure about anything. I
don't even know if I want to get married."

This I couldn't even process. We had reached a place beyond my comprehension. I had done everything but *beg* him
for our relationship.

"Marc, *where* is all of this coming from?" I asked, feeling the heat rising in my face. "We've always said that one
day we'd both like to have a family. *One day.* Are you saying
you want to date other women? You want to fuck them? Is
that what you want?" I could hear my voice getting shriller,
louder, but there was nothing that I could do to control my
rising panic and mounting anger. I never spoke to Marc this
way, but this was past my limits.

"Tabby, I don't know what I want. That's just it. I don't
know. And I think that right now, you need someone who
knows. And . . . I just can't be that guy."

"Marc, I didn't say that."

"Yes, you did."

"I didn't. I didn't. That's not what I meant—it's just . . . I
have to decide about, you know, *this*," I said, gesturing with
my hands toward the direction of my womb. Marc said nothing, other than letting out an exasperated sigh. He took a sip
from his wineglass, avoiding eye contact.

"Is there someone else?" I asked.

"No, Tabby. No. Not someone else. I'm not a cheater."

Then what are you, motherfucker? I wanted to ask. The air
between us was pregnant in the way that I was not, heavy
with the words spoken and the weight of those unspoken. I
just couldn't imagine letting it end this way.

"Marc, I *love* you. I'm in love with you. I've given you eighteen months of my life—of my thirties! There's not someone

else I want to be with. What's so wrong with *us*?" I pleaded, with increasing awareness of my surroundings and the fact that I'd been emotionally ambushed.

"I love you, too, Tabby. I just . . ."

Ms. Gretchen's words echoed in my mind, playing over Marc's hollow ones. *If a man has no plans for you . . . then . . . he's not your man . . .* I watched Marc's mouth move but heard nothing that mattered. Looking at him now was like looking at a complete stranger who I'd only seen for the very first time tonight. I noticed the small scar underneath his right eye, partially covered by his long black bottom eyelashes. I saw a little sparse patch in his beard and the gray hairs crowding in like white-headed dandelions in an otherwise carefully manicured lawn. I looked up at the thinning spot at the top of his otherwise immaculately cut hair, with a fresh edge up. *Someone else's man,* my mind kept telling me. *He loves me? He doesn't love me. Not possible.* Love wouldn't bum-rush someone in the middle of an otherwise comfortable relationship. *Love* doesn't do *that.* I'm not saying that I needed Marc to be the man of my dreams, or ride in on his white horse to save my fertility options, but he could have at least given me some warning. Then again, maybe *that* was why—why the distance during the week, and why he wanted to meet me here tonight instead of picking me up. I bet there was even a reason why he wore the stupid outfit he wore. Why he picked *that* shirt and those jeans. It all hit me, these realizations like repeated gut punches. There was a word for what this was, I just couldn't think of it.

After I checked out mentally on the conversation, Marc made no effort to reel me back in. He hadn't come to negotiate. He'd come to execute. When the conversation reached a lull of nothing else to say, he asked me if I wanted to order dessert—as if I could possibly still have an appetite. I told him no and that I really was ready to leave. He offered me a ride home, which I accepted only to ride in silence the few blocks back to my place. I guess I entertained the extra time with him just to see if he was going to change his mind, or tell me that this was his very dumb idea of a joke. That moment never came. He walked me to my door and told me he'd call me next week to check on me. I gave him a closed-mouthed feeble laugh, while *I can't believe you, asshole* burned through my eyes. When he went in for a hug goodbye, I limply brought my arms around him and placed my palms weakly on his shoulders. I didn't want him pressed against me—I didn't want to feel his body, I didn't want to want him. Not anymore.

I got upstairs and melted onto my bed with all of my clothes still on. I didn't even have the energy to take them off, not even my shoes. I placed myself in the fetal position, curling my body around my womb, the place where all of this began. I closed my eyes, too spent to think, too shell-shocked to allow tears, too numb to process. All I could think of was the Sunday dinner at my dad's house that I had unwittingly agreed to attend because my grandmother asked me to. There was no way I'd do that now. I reached over for my phone, which was lying next to me on my bed, to compose a text.

Me:

I'm not going to be able to make it to dinner tomorrow. Sorry, emergency.

To my surprise, my dad responded almost right away. I had no idea he was still awake.

Dad:

Everything OK?

If I had a different dad, or maybe if there had never been a Diane, I'd have answered that question differently. I'd be a girl who'd call her dad in tears about the boy who broke his baby girl's heart. And he'd console her and tell her how special she was no matter what that boy said or thought and that she could always count on her dad no matter what. That could have been, but it wasn't. Not for my dad and me.

Me:

Yes, fine. Just something got sprung on me at the last minute.

Dad:

The girls would have really liked to see you.

Diane's kids.

Dad:

Me too.

Me:

Next time, promise.

Me:

Love you.

Dad:

Love you, Two

And as I drifted off into a forced and restless sleep, the word that had escaped me at the restaurant dawned on me. It was the exact word I was looking for as Marc performed a

JAYNE ALLEN   103

calculated and surgical extraction of my beating heart from my chest. The word that floated around in my mind like an amorphous fog clouding all of my other thoughts. That word took form and revealed itself just then. It was *betrayal*.

It was early Sunday morning, and I gripped my steering wheel tightly. I just had to get to one place. I had woken up from a terrible bad dream that Marc had broken up with me. Except it wasn't a dream. It wasn't a dream at all. I had no desire to talk to anyone, not my mom, not Laila, not Alexis. Just to get to the one place that had always been my respite and shelter when the storm hit. This time, *home* wasn't on Fairfax, home was at Crestmire.

I drove like a zombie who only knew the basic rules of the road. My hair was pulled neatly under a baseball cap, but I still had on my dress from the night before, only I had replaced my heels with UGGs and dropped a Burberry trench across my shoulders. As crazy as I'm sure I looked, I felt so much worse. I did everything I could to keep the events of that dinner from replaying on loop in my mind; it was my only defense to avoid the self-inflicted emotional torture.

When I got to Crestmire, I waved myself past the front desk. I wasn't sure if visiting hours had started, or even if there were visiting hours. I barely had the energy to mutter "Tabitha Walker" in passing. Perhaps the aide at the desk recognized me, or perhaps, mercifully, she recognized the desperation of heartbreak the way that only a woman can see in another person. I was thankful she didn't stop me as I headed straight for Granny Tab's unit. The door was unlocked, as was customary for nighttime. I knocked on the door three times and opened it, letting my voice announce my presence. I headed my slumped frame into Granny Tab's bedroom to find her groggily just lifting her head up to focus her half-sleeping eyes on me.

"What are you doing here this early, Two? Is everything okay?" she asked.

I could barely hold back the tears to answer. I spoke and crossed the floor over to her at the same time. "No, no, it's not okay. It's *not* okay. It's *not* okay." And that is all I could muster. It was all I had in words to describe what had happened to me. It was the only way I could describe what Marc did to a year and a half of *my* life without my input or consent. What it felt like to be not consulted in the disposal of a relationship that we both were in. "It's not okay" was the only rebuke I had for a man who had treated me like a car that you could trade in for a better one, just like when he swapped his BMW for that Porsche he drives now. "It's not okay" were my only words. And it was all I needed. Granny Tab, lying on her side, scooted back from the edge of the bed toward the middle and opened out her arms, with the top one holding the blanket and sheet she was lying under askew. I dropped my baseball cap on the floor, along with my trench, stepped out of my UGGs, and lay directly next to Granny Tab. My head found its place in the soft part between her neck and bosom as her arms closed around me. And there, for the first time since I can remember, the first time since I was a little girl, I lay with her and cried.

10

THE KNOCK ON MY DOOR, ALTHOUGH EXPECTED, STARTLED ME
still because I had allowed myself to get lost in my new-
found identity as a recent dumpee, following my "911 bring
wine" text to Laila about forty-five minutes prior. Between
us, a "911" text meant get over here faster than the police in
a white neighborhood and bring a bottle of wine, because
we're going to need it. It didn't require any follow-up "are you
okay?" question because, with a 911 text, you already knew
the answer. It also didn't require a "what happened?" reply
because you knew that's what the wine you were bringing
was for. Once, Laila sent me a 911 text that said, "911 bring
wine—2 bottles." That was when we were in senior year in
undergrad. Somewhere near the bottom of the first bottle, I
learned that Laila's professor had invited her for a threesome
with his wife at some LA swinger sex party. We drank the
entire second bottle to try to forget what we talked about over
the first one. Laila never reported him or made any kind of
fuss about it—it had been the end of the semester and she
had received an A in his class. We knew it was inappropriate,
but what recourse was there when everything turned out all

right? It just became another scar on our liver and $4 dent in our bank account—we were only drinking "Two-Buck Chuck" back then, a wine since replaced by the demands of our much more sophisticated palates, refined over many trips to Napa, Sonoma, and Santa Barbara.

I still hadn't changed out of my dress from the night before. I left a small lagoon's worth of tears at Crestmire. Back home, I was finally able to rehydrate and continue crying on my sofa. My 911 to Laila was a last-ditch effort to avoid calling in sick to work the following day. I must have been quite a sight, with my usually immaculately coiffed one-day-post-appointment hair all disheveled, sweated out from not being wrapped the night before, a fluffy pink terry cloth robe swinging open over a very nice, very expensive dress and UGGs—of course I was still wearing the UGGs. Laila took one look into my bleary eyes, with blood vessels streaking across my sclera like red lightning, and engulfed me with a big hug. The wine bottle she was holding in her left hand made a slight thwack against my right shoulder blade.

"Girl, I got the 911!" Laila said, ushering us both inside and heading straight for my kitchen area. "How bad is it? What happened?" she asked as she opened the wine bottle and pulled two glasses out for us.

"Marc . . . He . . . broke up with me last night." I poured the words out with a fresh glut of tears, collapsing again on my sofa with my face in my hands. I had put a box of tissues near my feet earlier and used one to swipe at my running nose.

Laila finished filling our glasses and made her way quickly to sit next to me, pulling me into her so my head could rest on her shoulder. "I don't know what to say, Tab. I'm so sorry." She rubbed the top of my arm for comfort. "Do you want me to go key his car?" she asked, trying to feign seriousness. "Because, I will—just say the word and I will light that Porsche right up!"

I couldn't help but laugh. "That car is too important to him to scratch. It's probably like a voodoo doll—you scratch the car, and he'd start bleeding," I said, reaching deep inside myself to try to continue the humor. Although part of me wasn't joking. "Laila, he just kept saying that he couldn't be what I wanted and that he wasn't even willing to try. And I'm thinking, what the *fuck* have I been doing for the past year and a half with my life? With my time? *Wasting* it with his ass?" That was all I could get out before the tears started to fall again, triggered with just the thought of Marc's coldness—his ability to "cancel" our relationship like it was an unwanted magazine subscription.

"Fuck him. For real, girl. Fuck *him*!" Laila said with full animation. "If he doesn't know what he's got and how amazing you are, then fuck him. He doesn't deserve you. You can find so much better." I wished so hard that I could believe Laila when she said that. But it just seemed like our go-to consolation every time a relationship didn't work out. Sitting here, in my thirties, with the clock speeding down on my fertility, it sure didn't seem as true as it did a few years ago. The reality was that I couldn't just say "fuck him" and walk away. I had invested valuable time—relationships pass in dog years when you're in your thirties, and you can't give up valuable real estate in your childbearing window without needing a return of some sort.

"I guess what hurts the most," I said, "is that he could just let me go, just like that. Like it was nothing. Like *I* was nothing."

"Tabby, I'll tell you what my dad told me," Laila said. "He said, 'a man can only value you as much as he values himself.' You can't let this get to you—you're amazing."

I wanted to hear her. I wanted to be as strong as she thought I was. I wanted to believe her description of me over Marc's actions. I just couldn't. I felt so weak and helpless sitting there, weighed down by my own self-pity, with hope floating away from me like a lost red balloon released by a child's clumsy hand. Even the lowest part of the string was out of my reach. Marc valued his car, and he valued his job, and he certainly valued his degrees; he seemed to value his family and his boys—friends he kept from undergrad and grad school. So, I didn't buy it that he was incapable of valuing someone. Just why couldn't he value, or why didn't he value, *me?*

"Or maybe it's just me, Laila."

"It's not you. It's him. Fuck him. I'm seriously going to go toilet paper his house. I'm going right now." Laila made the move to get up from the sofa. I halfway believed her.

"He lives in a condo building, Laila." I chuckled in spite of myself.

"Well, then, I'm going to go to his building and send a toilet paper roll up by the concierge. And I'll tell him to say Ms. Joon said, 'This is for you, because you're a piece of *shit!*'"

We both broke into laughter and by that time, the wine had started to soak in, releasing some of the sadness sitting on my diaphragm. Suddenly, I could breathe again, and at least the pilot light was back on in my spirit. I pushed the heavy thoughts of Marc, and especially what that meant for my future, as far back in my mind as I could to change the subject.

"What's up with your new guy?" I asked.

"Oh, Laurence?" Laila said coyly, blushing in a rare way.

"Oh, Laurence?" I mocked her playfully. She knew better than to pretend. "Girl, yes. The man that you told me about who we're going to pretend isn't married for the purposes of this conversation, although we both know that he is."

"Well, we know *now*," Laila said. "He didn't have his ring on when we met, girl, remember?"

"Um-hum."

"He's fine, though. It's a strange thing to say, but it's actually going well. It's almost like he's not married. You know? He calls me all the time, he's so supportive, attentive, wants to see me—so, I know the deal, but . . ." The smile that had been hiding in Laila's eyes spread to her lips and broke its way out between the glint of her Invisaligned teeth.

"You like him," I accused.

"Yeah," Laila said softly. "I do." We both sat for a moment in contemplative silence, understanding the weight of her words and not understanding them all at the same time. "Well, are you going to tell Alexis?" Laila said, shifting her body.

"Alexis?" I echoed, thinking. "No, I don't want to tell her now. I'll just wait until her birthday party. I bet she'll figure it out when she doesn't see Marc with me."

"You're not going to tell her? Oh, I know why."

"Yeah, *Mrs. Thing.* I know she loves me, but sometimes it does feel like she's looking for my relationships to fail, so that she can wave that ring in my face."

"Girl, in all of our faces! Lexi's my girl, but she puts way too much on the fact that she's married."

"She's been like that since high school. When I went to the magnet school and she went to the regular high school with all the neighborhood kids. It was like that became her *thing*, you know? Being in a relationship. She always had a man and I didn't and I guess that became her own version of a superpower. Unfortunately, it was pretty much Rob the whole time, even when he was doggin' her ass out."

"I didn't know him back then—he seems pretty mellow, and Lexi is always saying how great he is and how happy he is to be working steady now. I understand, though, he's got a lot of *ain't shit*-ness to make up for," Laila said.

"You said it. I've known them too long. That's part of it. You know they're going to make that birthday party torture. We had to RSVP our plus-ones by name."

"Girl, at least you *got* a plus one," Laila said, snorting with light disgust. "She didn't even extend one to me."

"Well *now*, I wish that were my situation," I said, exhaling heavily.

"That party is a full week away!" Laila said. "You'll have forgotten all about Marc by then and found somebody new on Tinder."

"What do I look like being on the news *and* being on Tinder? Girl, bye. I'm going to go and I'm going to do what I do best . . . drink." On that note, we clinked our wineglasses and left the rest of the unanswered questions lying at the bottom of an empty bottle. The untouched card for Dr. Young sat on my table as a reminder that while Marc had considered his options, I needed to focus on my own—before they went away.

11

I WAS ALREADY TWO DRINKS IN, HEADING WEST ON THE 10 FREE-
way on my way to Alexis's birthday party. An internet search
confirmed my suspicion that two drinks before driving was
just about the legal limit. After making it through the first
full week following my breakup with Marc, I wasn't trying to
risk another cop car pullover. From the very first minutes of
Monday morning, my only goal this past week had been to
get to Friday. Not my only goal, actually; my other goal was
to make an appointment with a reproductive endocrinologist
who could help me freeze my eggs and liberate tens of thou-
sands of dollars from my bank account. I got one of those
goals done; it was Friday, I had made it here, and nobody had
died yet. I knew I needed to stop dragging my feet on the egg
freezing, stop hoping for minor miracles, and just make the
call. *Why not just stop dragging my feet?*

If Lexi were not my best friend, and if I thought she might
ever forgive me for missing her birthday party, I would have
tried to skip this evening. My pregaming had me anesthetized enough to move past the lethargy of going someplace I
did not want to be, but it couldn't erase not wanting to be an

audience member for Rob's surprise extravaganza. Rob's history had been spotty at best for years, so Lexi's nervousness
at Denisha's salon showed up again in my own muted appre-
hension. Although she would never say it, her birthday dinner party being thrown by Rob was a "thing." And based on
what I knew about him, that "thing," whatever it was going
to be, was more about Rob and less about Alexis, even on her
birthday. It wasn't one of the fives—thirty-five, or "Oh Lordy,
forty"—so I hoped that's why they were so stingy with the
guest list, and not just that Rob was in over his head. The dinner was being held at Fig & Olive, a gorgeous Mediterranean
type of place in the section of chic restaurants and boutiques
on La Cienega, in the part of West Hollywood that borders
Beverly Hills. The white plastered exterior, resembling a
modern villa with generous patios, gave a sexy contrast with
the black iron window framing and the terracotta-tiled floor
in the interior. Fresh flowers, the dimmed lighting in subtle chandeliers, and low-sitting table candles did the rest to
bring the romantic idea of Casablanca to the end of just a
short drive across the city. Marc and I had come here on one
of our first dates, I remembered with a pang. We hadn't slept
together yet then, and I thought he was using this restaurant to close the deal that he couldn't. I still made him wait,
although just until the very next date—I didn't want him to
think he had won. I was grateful for that now, as I stepped out
of my car at valet. At least tonight I wouldn't have to manage
through the memory of a milestone moment sitting next to
an empty chair. I already missed him enough as it was, and
although I hated to admit it, I started using his old T-shirt as a
pillow cover just to smell him before sleeping.

Sliding out of my car at the restaurant, I knew I looked

good, and on this night my iridescent sequin T-shirt dress ended on my thigh just shy of where modesty would have required. My legs felt strong and shapely underneath me, and the stilettos I was wearing pushed my calves into perfect lines, allowing me to stride, gazelle-like and very confident, into the restaurant. Behind me flowed an invisible cloud of white flowers and the faintest sandalwood. I needed a pick-me-up after Marc's disposal. I might not be seeing him tonight, but I looked and smelled as if I were, and as if my intention was to be certain that he realized his mistake, even if I was the only person who noticed.

"Tabby!" Alexis was the first of the birthday group to see me as I walked through the door into the private rear patio area where her dinner would be held. Rob certainly had gone all out—flowers decorated nearly every open surface, and elegant ivory and gold balloons were stationed in the corners. It almost looked like a small wedding reception. "Oh my God, you look amazing!" Alexis said, embracing me with outstretched arms. She pulled back and looked to each of my sides and behind me. "Where's Marc?" I smiled, thinking to myself, *Well that only took her ninety seconds to ask.*

"Marc's not coming, Lexi," I told her calmly, trying to decide on one of the explanations that I had just spent an hour in my bathroom mirror rehearsing. "He . . . he and I . . ." I had to pause, having trouble deciding whether or not I was going to just say it. "We . . . broke up," I said, and watched her face fall—the exact reaction I had attempted to avoid. "But I'm fine! Totally fine!" I added quickly. "It's for the best, pretty mutual, you know?" I said, nodding my head in sync with my words to make them truer.

"Well, girl, you look fine! You look damn fine!" Lexi said,

looking me up and down like a dude would. "I'm so sorry, though. I know how much he means to you . . . I mean *meant*." She hugged me. "Maybe it's just temporary. And in the meantime, there might be some cute friends of Rob who show up by themselves—you never know! I think I have someone to introduce you to—a doctor," she said, smiling, as someone I didn't recognize started to pull her away.

"Go! Go! Say hi to your guests!" I said, probably overdoing the cheer factor and waving her on. "I'm going to find Laila, and we'll talk later!" I tried to seal it with the biggest smile that I could manufacture, like the glint from my teeth would hypnotize her into forgetting that I had just told her that I broke up with my boyfriend of the past year and a half.

Lexi freed her arm from her captor, dropping her head to the side a bit with pursed lips, looking at me. "Girl, *you know* Laila's not here yet." *Of course*, I thought. "I saved you two seats together on that end." Lexi pointed me in the direction of the left side of the room. "Rob and I will sit in the middle, and you and, now, Laila will be just across. And as soon as Todd gets here, I am making an introduction!" Alexis said with a wink.

"Todd?"

"Girl, Rob's friend, the doctor!" The thought of someone new made my palms start to sweat.

"Lexi, I'm not sure I'm ready . . . it just hap—"

Lexi cut me off. "Tab, don't be silly, you look great, and he's quality—I promise. Just be open—for me? It is my birthday . . ." Lexi said, batting her fake eyelashes in my direction. I did look the part, and there was no sense in wasting a sexy dress and heels. Lexi had a point.

"Okay."

"You'll meet him . . . with an open mind?" Lexi asked, raising her eyebrow.

"I'll meet him—with a mind as open as I can make it."

I knew what I needed to say next to give her fullest satisfaction. I didn't expect to say the words, but it was her birthday, and the coast seemed clear.

"Rob did a great job with this! I'm really impressed!" I said, forcing the last words out. To that, Lexi's face lit up like a town-square Christmas tree. She beamed.

"He did! Didn't he, girl!" Lexi threw her hand up to slap me five. Which I did, and finally she let herself be pulled to talk to another group of people. I sat down, checking my phone, by habit, but found no new messages there, so I settled for making small talk with the people around me until Laila came. She finally breezed in just as we were making our dinner orders.

"Hey, Laila!" I said with a teasing smile. She knew what I was saying.

"Girl, traffic. You know. Why they had to have this shit all the way up in West Hollywood . . . there is . . ." Laila stopped suddenly, catching herself. The people in the corner of our table were staring, some with their mouths slightly agape, like they were waiting for her to say the unimaginable. I could observe the quick switch in her demeanor, and she straightened herself, pulled off a Kool-Aid smile, and brought her voice up a few octaves. "Hi, I'm Laila," she repeated a few times very professionally as she shook hands with our dining companions. She got settled in, and we started our usual recap in low whispers passed to each other in a subtle way that journalists know how to do without actually being heard.

"Well, I have to say this is a lot better than what I thought it would be," I said.

"The night's still young," Laila said, giving the side-eye to Rob and Lexi, sitting across from us and deeply engaged in conversation with guests next to them. They looked like young lovers, with Rob's arm around Lexi and her laughing like she used to in high school, even before he gave her that STD junior year. I've seriously known them way too long. "Did you tell her?" Laila asked, breaking into my thoughts.

"Oh, about Marc?" *Of course about Marc.* "Yeah, kind of, but we didn't dwell. I told her I was fine enough times that she moved on. She's already trying to hook me up with one of Rob's friends."

"She needs to try to hook *me* up with one of Rob's friends. Lexi never offers any of Rob's friends to me, and I'd be way more open to one of them than you ever would . . . with your stuck-up ass." Laila snickered into her wineglass.

"Me stuck-up? Oh, come on. You're the one dating a Mr. Big," I said, in a forceful whisper.

"That's just because he came on to me and I didn't know he was married," Laila said. "I'd be perfectly content with someone with less ambition and a reliable . . ." Laila shifted her eyes down to her lap.

"Wait, now his *dick* doesn't work?" I whispered, a little too loudly. Some of the people next to us turned quickly and then tried to pretend they weren't listening.

"It works . . ." said Laila, reluctantly. "Most of the time. But he's almost fifty! So, there are moments. That's why he said he didn't want to use the condoms."

"You're talking about me and an NBA baby! You need to quit playing."

Laila giggled coyly in response, shrugging her shoulders with her palms splayed upward. Beyond her, I saw Lexi heading in our direction, leading a thin, half-balding, copper-complexioned man with glasses. He wasn't much taller than Lexi, which meant that he was barely taller than me, and likely not in heels. I held my breath, hoping that this wasn't *Dr. Todd* as she waved me to come over to them. I excused myself from the table and stood up. Laila and I exchanged glances. When she saw Alexis, I knew she understood where I was headed and why.

"Tabby, I want to introduce you to Rob's friend, Dr. Bryant," Alexis said with a huge grin and twinkle in her eye.

"It's a pleasure to meet you, Tabby. Call me Todd, please," he said with a nice smile. "Alexis is trying to make me feel like I'm working." He held his hand out to shake mine. *Hmm . . . straight teeth, but isn't he shorter than me?* I couldn't tell. I tried to squash the voice inside that kept pointing out his height. And the one making side-by-side comparisons to Marc.

"I'm going to let you two talk—I've got to get back to Rob," Lexi said, excusing herself. I felt myself blushing, and without words to really say during an awkward introduction to a stranger. Something about him was kind of handsome. Maybe his smile?

"So, Tabby, I won't keep you long from dinner, but when Alexis told me about her friend and then pointed to you, I *knew* I had to at least take the opportunity and say hello." He smiled at me—a big smile. *Hmmm . . . kind of disarming, friendly even.* I smiled back, still feeling shy. "Well, to say hello *and* to ask if perhaps I could call you sometime? Take you out?" The normal post-breakup Tabitha would have made some kind of excuse, but "ovarian failure" Tabitha knew better. I managed to find my voice.

"Okay, Todd, that would be . . . nice," I said. And: *How tall are you? Do you want to have kids?* My mind raced with a million questions I didn't ask. Instead, I gave him my phone number. I would just have to find out later. Especially about the height.

"I'll text you mine so you have it," he said. I nodded. With that we headed in our opposite directions, me back to my seat with Laila for twenty questions, and him back to the end of the table near where Rob was sitting.

"So, what's up with him?" Laila asked, just as I sat down. Before I could answer, we heard the sound of metal clanging against a wineglass. I turned, and it was Rob, standing up with a glass of champagne, looking like he was getting ready to make a toast.

"Everybody!" Rob said, clanging on the glass again. "Hey, everybody . . . I just need a few minutes of your time, and then I can let you all get back to ordering your desserts." Rob was beaming, and his chest stuck out strong and proud. He had started working out pretty intensely about a year ago and had turned his jelly-filled moobs into what looked like a much harder wall of muscle underneath his shirt. His Rolex glinted under the lights, and just above that, the wedding ring on his finger. He continued speaking. "Thank you all so much for coming out tonight to help me celebrate this beautiful woman right here." He turned to Alexis. "Alexis, when I asked you about the tenth anniversary of your twenty-fourth birthday, you said, 'Oh, I'm fine, I don't need to do anything.'" Rob made a pretty good imitation of Lexi's soft singsong voice. It made everyone laugh. "So, it was up to me to try to give you an evening that you *deserve*. And with these wonderful people here tonight, who love you just slightly *less* than me and the boys do"—he turned to address the rest of the table of groaning guests—"I said just slightly less, folks . . . just *slightly* less." And he turned back to Lexi. "'Cause me and our boys, we love you so much, Mama. You're everything to us." He took a lingering look at Lexi and then turned back to the crowd. "And I'm not going to keep folks long, because we need to make good use of this night that we have a babysitter, but I just want to let Alexis know a few more things. Baby, you were there for me when I didn't have nothin' . . . and you believed in me. You pushed and even while pushing, you held us down. You gave me our boys, and you made my life one that I wake up every morning so, so thankful to be living . . . with you. I love you, baby." Rob leaned in to kiss Alexis. She dabbed her tears gently like she didn't want to wipe her eyelashes off.

"I love you too, babe," Alexis said to him softly, almost with a whimper.

"Can everyone lift their glasses, please?" Rob paused, looking around the table to give folks time to find some kind of libation to raise. "To Alexis, my very own, *oh so* Sexy Lexi, happy birthday. You mean so much to so many people, and we all love you more than it will *ever* be possible to express in words."

He signaled the table by raising his glass, and we all mirrored his actions. The sound of glasses clinking and "happy birthday" from the collective group filled our small room. Todd and I caught eyes for a moment and exchanged a smile. *Could this work? Maybe?* Rob quieted everyone again.

"And for my last act . . ." Rob said, reaching into his pocket to pull out a small white box with a red bow on it. "This is your gift. You deserve this, baby, you held me down, it's my turn now." And with that, he handed the box to Lexi, who could barely take it from him with shaking hands and a mess of tears. She lifted the top to reveal a black plastic rectangle sitting in the middle of a square wad of cotton.

"Oh my God, Rob! You got me the Mercedes?!" Alexis screamed, seeming to forget everyone else in the room but Rob for a moment. "Oh my God! Where . . . where is it?" she said, looking around, as if it were somewhere in the room with us by some impossible magic.

Laila tapped me. "See, not even *ten* yet. And look what's *already* happened." We shared the same knowing look, and I tried not to roll my eyes. I was happy for Alexis but couldn't get with the whole display of it all. I couldn't shake the feeling I was watching a performance of what happiness was supposed to look like. *Maybe I've known them too long*, I thought again to myself.

"It's right outside, babe!" Rob said, commanding the attention of the room to himself again. "Everyone, if you'd like to accompany me and my lovely wife outside, we can see her christen her new toy and come back and enjoy dessert."

"Do we have to?" Laila whined, looking at me. "I mean, like oh my God, really? What is this, *My Super Sweet 16*? Talk about dreams deferred . . . Jesus . . . some bullshit . . . this nig . . ." Laila muttered some more things under her breath that I couldn't even understand with all of the commotion moving toward the door.

"Yes, Laila, we have to. But we don't have to enjoy it. We just have to go support your friend."

"My friend?" Laila hissed. "Mrs. Thing is *your* friend. For real. Your friend who hooks you up with *doctors*. Clearly, I just inherited her ass." We both laughed and headed out to the front of the restaurant, where sure enough, a sparkling white brand-new four-door Mercedes was out front with the headlights on and a big red bow on the hood matching the one on the box. Alexis was doing a little dance on her way to getting in the car that made her ample butt and boobs pull her body in different directions. I was glad that she was happy, even if it felt like a show. Standing outside, I felt my handbag vibrate. Todd must have sent me his number. "Well, I guess the doctor wastes no time," I said under my breath, pulling my phone out. What I saw on the screen made me freeze in the moment, the shock traveling in waves from my hand all the way down to my toes. It *was* a text message, but from Marc.

Marc:

WYD?

I turned to Laila and elbowed her vigorously.

"What?!" she snapped back at me, turning to face me quickly.

"Marc just sent me a text message."

"He did? What does it say?"

"Look." I handed her my phone. And she widened her eyes as she looked at the screen.

"Oh hell no. Tab, I know you're not going to answer this. You can't."

I laughed it off. "Of course I'm not going to answer it!" I tried to sound as definitive as possible, like my mind was all made up. "After what he did? No way! I'm just going to let it sit there . . . And, I mean, 'What are you doing?' Seriously? Nah, I'm done," I said, convincing myself enough to put my phone back in my purse.

"You sure?" Laila asked.

"Yeah. I'm sure," I said. But, then again, this wouldn't be the first time I'd lied tonight.

1 2

BETWEEN MY RECEIPT OF MARC'S TEXT THE PREVIOUS NIGHT AND my ride to Crestmire, somehow I managed to leave my fingers off of the send button for any of the fifteen different and widely ranging replies I composed. If I had sent them all, he'd literally have been fucking *himself* in my apartment then having a glass of wine and a cry while we talked things through. I hadn't gotten a message yet from Dr. Todd, a fact that I surprised myself by noticing. In meeting him, I didn't recall even a hint of the butterflies I felt when I met Marc, or that instant physical chemistry that these days had me sleeping with a pillow between my legs. But there was a certain something there. Something that made the corners of my lips turn upward thinking about him and something that made me just a little bit hopeful.

Walking through my grandmother's door, I was thankful to be in a better place than previously and also that Granny Tab hadn't let my tears throw her into a lingering refrain of concern and worry. I cried, let it out, we talked, and other than the regular *how're you*s, she didn't make a point of bringing it up again. My mom, if she had so much as heard me cry like I did that morning, would have probably booked a plane ticket and tried to have me involuntarily committed. I came inside and greeted Ms. Gretchen, also, because the two of them were huddled at the small table in Granny Tab's kitchenette. Ms. Gretchen was showing my grandmother makeup and hair tutorials on YouTube with her smartphone. Now I knew exactly how Ms. Gretchen knew more than I did about winged eyeliner and highlighter palettes.

"Come sit down, Two! Gretchen is just showing me how to 'freshen up my look' for this so-called Senior Prom coming up." Seeing the confusion on my face, she went on to explain, "Evidently they do this every year here, just a night for us old biddies to get dressed up and move around."

"And to get laid!" Ms. Gretchen said.

"Gretchen!" My grandmother turned to look at her, eyes wide, her cheeks turning bright red.

"Tabitha!" Ms. Gretchen said mockingly, looking back at her. "Look, I'm old. Ain't nothin' embarrassing to me anymore. I can't help it if I've still got it," she said with a smile. My grandmother turned to me and rolled her eyes.

"I just don't know what to do with you sometimes, Gretchen. Good Lord."

"You need to come with me and get your nails and hair done sometimes, Tabitha. You're old and you let your hair go gray, but you ain't dead yet. Don't cheat yourself, treat yourself. I know I do," Ms. Gretchen said with a flip of her loosely curled blond hair over her shoulder. She was well maintained, anyone would have to give her that. Although the thought of her maintenance happening because she was still getting "tune-ups" at Crestmire was more information than I was prepared for.

"Enough about us, Gretchen," my grandmother said, turning her attention to me. "How are you doing, Two? What's new with you? Did you get your promotion yet?"

"No, not yet," I said. "It was Lexi's birthday party last night. Rob threw it for her at a fancy restaurant. And he bought her a Mercedes as a present."

"Oh, that's nice!" my grandmother said, unfazed by my description of Rob's grand gestures. "Did you see Marc there?" I felt a pang. I was surprised she asked about him directly after what happened.

"Um, no, Granny Tab, Marc didn't come. He didn't come because . . . we're still broken up. I think it's official."

"Now, what's that?" Ms. Gretchen said, showing shock through an otherwise knowing look. "Wasn't this the young man you were just talking about? What happened, honey?"

"Well . . ." I said slowly, carefully choosing my words. "Based on what he said, he wasn't ready for a real commitment, and the fact that I started thinking about kids got him all riled up and scared. So, he broke up with me last weekend."

Ms. Gretchen shook her head. "Kids are exactly what you *should* be thinking about right now, if you want 'em! Him too! Girl, he sounds crazy. Good riddance," she said with a swat of her hand.

Granny Tab shot her eyes at Gretchen and then back to me, brimming with concern. "Well, Tabby, I know that you liked him very much. I was hoping that things might have changed over the week. He hasn't reached out to you?"

"Actually, he has. Last night, he did," I said, letting my eyes drop away from hers.

"Well, are you going to talk to him?" Granny Tab asked.

"Maybe you should just talk with him and hear him out. If he's just scared, maybe he's thought it through and changed his mind."

"That's not what his message said," I answered quickly.

"What did it say, then?" she asked. I was embarrassed by the truth, which I knew would sound so much worse when spoken aloud.

"It said, 'What are you doing?'" I tried to get it out quickly. I couldn't even look her in the eyes.

"What are you doing?" My grandmother echoed, puzzled.

"Tabitha, that's what these young boys do in their text messages when they get lonely and want some female attention. It's just plain lazy, if you ask me," Ms. Gretchen surprised me by chiming in. *What did she know about the "WYD?" text?*

"Unfortunately," I muttered. She was right, though. I had really wanted him to say more. After what happened, I needed him to show me that he was reaching out on more than just a passing whim. That's why I didn't want to get my hopes up. "Yeah, it's really too bad. I thought that we . . . that he—"

Ms. Gretchen interrupted me. "Don't linger too long on this, baby. Not too much longer." She leaned back, signaling she was about to go into one of her stories. "Let me tell you a little something. I'm long on stories, but I'm short on advice. In life, I've only got one rule, well, other than the Golden Rule, of course, but *this* is *my* golden rule. I'm gonna tell you. When I first came here, to Crestmire, and I was looking at all the places like this, you know what they all had? Every single one had rocking chairs. I don't know why folks think that old people like to rock, rock, rock so much. I personally prefer a different type of rocking, but that's not my point." She paused, grinning mischievously. "I didn't believe that these folks liked these rocking chairs so much until I got here, to Crestmire. And, honey! You remember Clara, she seems like such a nice quiet lady with those big funny black glasses—make her eyes look like bugs when she's hunched over, squinting trying to work those puzzles she likes! Well, Clara and Margaret almost got into a fistfight in the room one day over that last rocking chair by the window. The one that looks out at the big willow tree outside?" Ms. Gretchen paused to wait for my grandmother and me both to nod in recognition. "I can't remember which one got it. But, anyway, when they get in that chair, what do they do? They look out and start to rockin' themselves, and let their eyes close, like they're going to sleep, and some of them do. But some don't. Some aren't sleeping, Tabby. You know what they're doing?" I shook my head no. "They're thinking."

Ms. Gretchen paused for effect, looking from me to my grandmother and back again before continuing. "They're using what's left of their dusty minds, goin' over life regrets. But they're not wishin' they had spent one less dollar, or spent one more day with some jackass that did them dirty. No, honey. They're sitting there trying to remember the good stuff. The big good stuff they got to do, just praying that there's enough of it. The stuff that even when your memory fades the details, that it's still gonna matter to ya', and maybe make you smile. That's what *your* time is for now, my dear, 'cause you won't always have the chance. And if this boy isn't going to matter, then you need to forget about him and move on. Time becomes more valuable when you realize it's running out." She shifted forward and made a motion to stand up. "And I have a nail appointment to get to. No new girl to make me late today! See you two later." And out the door she breezed, with her smartphone in hand, still cued up on a makeup tutorial.

"Gretchen and her stories," my grandmother said with a half laugh. "I do remember that fight, though—between Clara and Margaret. I thought Margaret was going to knock Clara's glasses clear off!"

"Well, who got the chair?" I asked.

My grandmother breathed a slight chuckle trying to re-member. After a moment, seeming to be in her own thoughts, she said, "Doesn't matter, I guess. I think Clara, but all the days here sometimes drift together. In my mind, I can see both of them sitting in that chair after it was all over. Not sure why it was so important then. Funny the things people think are worth fighting over."

"Well, looks like there's going to be a lot of excitement with this Senior Prom!" I said, trying to shift the mood. "We've got to get you all made up and fabulous. Can't just let Ms. Gretchen steal the show . . . and take all the . . . rocking chairs!" I said to my grandmother with a wink.

"Now, isn't that right!" Granny Tab said with a chuckle. "I think I might be excited!"

I stayed longer at Crestmire than usual because I didn't want to have to head back and face my first free Saturday night alone with the temptation of Marc's unanswered text message or the taunting of the silence from Todd. On the ride home, Ms. Gretchen's words swirled in my mind along-side ideas of how I would make my grandmother look and feel her most beautiful for the Senior Prom coming up. I also tried to think of my own rocking chair moments . . . and I tried my hardest to find Marc in any of them. Meanwhile, his unanswered message burned a hole in my purse like an unspent dollar in the pocket of a kid in a candy store.

Once I got home, sitting on my sofa, Saturday night got to me. My thoughts swirled with wasted time, failing fertility, Marc, and now Todd. Why wasn't I responding to Marc? Was it a waste of my time if I had nothing else to do? With a plan that seemed to make perfect sense, I picked up my phone to compose a message to him. Only, I already had a message, from a number I didn't recognize.

Unknown Number:
Tabby, please forgive the delay.

Unknown Number:
Made a big mistake in saving your number and had to get it again from Alexis.

Unknown Number:
Sorry—should have said it's Todd. Todd Bryant.

Unknown Number:
Last minute I know, but I'm off tomorrow. Could I interest you in brunch?

Yes, you could, Dr. Todd. Yes, you could.

TODD AND I AGREED TO MEET DOWNTOWN AT A CUTE LITTLE French restaurant on Spring Street. I made it a point to wear flats, just in case.

When I got there, Todd was already seated, wearing a nice blue checked button-down shirt, jeans and leather driving shoes. His hair was cut down a little lower than when we first met, so the bald circle up top wasn't as noticeable. I felt myself smiling as he waved me over.

"Tabby!" he said, standing up as I reached the table. He awkwardly extended his hand again but seemed to change his mind at the last minute, turning our greeting into an equally awkward hug instead.

"Hi, Todd, good to see you," I said with the most flirtation I could muster. I was waiting for the butterflies but reminded myself I couldn't keep comparing everyone to Marc. We started with small talk through our order, and I learned that he was just finishing the last year of his psychiatry residency and that he was planning to practice in LA once finished, joining his uncle's practice to eventually take it over. He confessed that he hadn't been a KVTV viewer, but after we met, made it a point to catch enough of the news airings to watch my reporting.

"I'm impressed. You're really talented and relatable," he said. "I'm sure there are a ton of brothas in LA who could be sitting in my place. So I know I'm lucky to get you at such short notice." *Ha. If you only knew, Todd. If you only knew.* I just smiled back at him, trying to keep the trauma of Marc from surfacing in my eyes. "So, how does a girl like you wind up single?" *Oh Lord, this question.* I took a minute to think before I answered.

"I guess I'm newly single," I said. "If that's what you mean? Or did you want to know why I'm not married?" *Hell, I'd like to know that answer myself.*

"Either, or neither, actually," Todd said. "I'm just questioning my luck—silly thing to do," he said, rubbing his forehead with his hand. "I'm a little out of practice with this dating thing," he said finally. "I've been so focused on my residency, I kind of put that part of my life on hold." My eyebrows rose involuntarily. Another guy who wasn't ready and wasn't where he so-called wanted to be. I stiffened defensively.

"So, what are you looking for?" I asked, surprising myself with my directness.

"Maybe not anything specific," Todd said. "I didn't really have dating on my radar until Alexis mentioned you." *Oh no,* I thought. Todd was starting to sound more and more like Marc by the minute. I felt myself leaning back. He leaned in toward me to continue. "But you're worth a new plan."

13

"How's the real estate story going?" Scott asked me in the office kitchen as I waited for my dark roast to brew from the fancy coffee machine. My brunch date with Todd lasted well into early Sunday evening and ended with a few too many drinks and a promise to speak later in the week. Scott was the last person I wanted killing my vibe. If I wasn't so tired on this morning, I would have just left the cup sitting there and let the next person take it or take responsibility for throwing it away. Knowing Scott, though, he'd find some way to use even that against me.

"It's going super well, actually," I replied. "I've uncovered some really interesting connections between racial migration patterns and some of the pricing phenomena we're seeing today," I said, knowing for a fact that bringing up anything racial with Scott would be the quickest way to cause his disappearance.

"Ah, cool, cool," he said absentmindedly while he searched our office fridge for skim milk for his own cup. "Well, good luck with that," he said as he poured the blue-tinged thin liquid into his coffee. "Looking forward to seeing what your team puts together. I'm loving working on the Rams," he said with a smile as he walked out and passed me with a slight shoulder check. I whipped my head around to see if he turned back. *Did he do that on purpose?* I didn't have time to think through the answer because my coffee finished. I poured in my half-and-half and headed back to my desk.

A reminder had popped up on my computer screen, screaming at me, *Call Reproductive Endocrinologist and Make Appt.—TODAY!!!* I slowly shook my head at the thought that I still hadn't called. The mental image of my ovaries withering in real time brought a new sense of urgency. I couldn't afford to spend any longer avoiding the inevitable. I made myself a mental note to reinforce the written one and pulled out my cell phone. *Shit.* Another message from Marc.

Marc:
Good morning. Hope that you have a great day!
Marc:
Is it strange to say I miss you?

See now, dammit! It was so much easier to ignore an effortless "WYD?" text than this. Truthfully, even though my date with Todd went well, I still missed Marc, and I wanted to tell him as much. But the memory of being broken up with in an emotional ambush had a chilling effect, reminding me why I'd decided to ignore him. It was because he couldn't be trusted. And because he couldn't be trusted and I still loved him, I couldn't be trusted. *What if he wants to get back together, just to keep me in a never-ending series of dates? What happened to wanting to build a life with someone? To wanting to move forward?* Ms. Gretchen's words echoed in my mind

again. "If a man ain't got no plans for you . . ." *Dammit, Marc!*
Why can't you just be better? I thought to myself as I closed
out his text message. I scrolled through my contacts to the
reproductive endocrinologist's office recommended by my
doctor and hit the button to dial.

"Los Angeles Reproduction and Fertility Center, how may
I help you today?" A chirping voice burst through the phone.

"Hi, I would like to make an appointment, please," I said
quietly, trying to maintain some privacy in my cubicle in the
middle of the office.

"Okay! We can get you set up! Are you a new patient?"

"Yes, um, well, I would be new. I mean, once I become a
patient, then, I'd be a new one," I stammered. I had no idea
at all why I was so nervous. Maybe it was the idea of making one phone call and blowing my entire long-earned house
down payment.

"No problem. We'll just have to set you up for a consultation appointment with Dr. Young. That visit might be covered by insurance if you have infertility coverage. If not, the
initial consultation fee of three hundred and fifty dollars will
be due at your appointment. What's your insurance? Do you
know if you have infertility coverage? Quite a few plans don't.
If you do, you're lucky!" she said, way too cheerily. *Crap. Three
hundred and fifty dollars?* I didn't know if we did have infertility coverage. I'd only been concerned with the stuff to not
get pregnant, like birth control pills. *Infertility coverage?* Who
would think about that at my age? For whatever reason, Lisa
popped into my mind. She had mentioned our insurance
coverage as one of her women's issues gripes. I wondered if
she knew.

"I'm sorry, I don't know if it's covered, I'll have to check."

"It's fine. We'll ask you to send us a completed set of new patient forms and a copy of your insurance card before your appointment. We'll check for you and let you know if you'll have to pay." *I hope not!* I thought to myself, *$350 is a lot of money!* Just the consultation fee alone would have eliminated this option for me only a few years ago. I couldn't even begin to imagine how so many women were even able to make these kinds of financial sacrifices.

"When is the next available appointment?" I asked. Now that I had finally made the call that I put off for over a month, I could barely wait to get in to see the doctor. Again, I thought about my shrinking ovaries.

"Now, let me check. We can get you in to see Dr. Young . . ." The slow enunciation of her words coordinated with the typing that I could hear coming from her end of the phone. Anxiety started to clench in my jaw. "Ah, okay, the first available appointment is on the sixth—a month and a half from now."

What?

"You don't have anything . . . sooner?" I asked, thinking of my egg supply and my doctor's warning. I had already procrastinated dealing with Marc and my own dragging feet. I was worried that in a month and a half, I might not have any eggs left.

"Nope, this is it. Very busy office we have. A lot of mamas- and papas-to-be coming in!" she said again, singing her song of hope with an extra side of hope, drenched in hope sauce.

"Okay, I'll book it," I said, hoping I hadn't completely screwed up waiting so long. If I had just made the call on the first day with Dr. Ellis, my appointment would be coming up already. Now I'd have to wait even longer. She didn't say I had up to six months, she said that six months would be the end.

At least I had an appointment, but now with new worries. *Do we have infertility insurance coverage?* I thought again to ask Lisa, but hesitated to walk over to her open door, especially after our embarrassing first run-in in the ladies' restroom. *Maybe this is the kind of stuff they talk about in that group.* I'm sure it mattered, but I just needed to secure this promotion and then I could think about joining all the groups I wanted. The announcement had to be coming any day now. I could feel it. I'd have to make sure that LA real estate story came out well, because Scott Stone had already put me on notice that this was a battlefield and he wasn't giving up anything without a fight.

14

"HEY, TABBY CAT!" MY MOM ANNOUNCED THROUGH THE PHONE. She was the only person on earth who called me that.

"Hi, Mom!" I was happy to speak to her and only hoped she wasn't going to ask me to come visit again. I loved her place in Washington, DC, a seven-thousand-square-foot McMansion that she shared with only the general, but it was so far from LA and I couldn't afford to take the time off.

"How are you, and how is Marc?"

"Mom, I told you we broke up!"

"Yes, but people break up and get back together all the time. Your father and I broke up at least six times before we got married. They just can't figure out what they want until they don't have it. That's all. He hasn't called?" *Should I tell her about Todd? That we've seen each other twice now?*

I took a deep sigh. "He has," I said. "Well, actually, he's been texting."

"And you didn't write back to him?"

"No, not yet. I . . . I don't think I'm going to. I don't want to. I just keep thinking, what do I get out of it, you know?"

And I'm seeing someone else, I wanted to say. *Someone who knows what he wants!*

"Tabby, that is ridiculous. You should text that boy back! He's handsome and well educated, makes good money, and treats you nice. A lot of women would be right behind you to scoop him up!"

"Yeah, he treated me real nice, Mom, breaking up with me as soon as I told him that I had a fertility issue."

"Tab, people make mistakes. You know that."

"And then people have to live with the regret from their mistakes. I can't be the one always bearing the burden of it!" I said, not really sure why I was starting to yell. Once I felt the anger rising, I took a deep breath and closed my eyes to avoid a screaming match with my mother, which I knew I could never win. Everyone knows that no matter how old you get, you cannot raise your voice at the Black woman that birthed you and expect to live much longer.

"Don't be so dramatic, Tabby. He's a nice boy. You're over-reacting! And down the road from this, you're going to be the one with the regrets. I'm telling you."

"Tell that to my ovaries," I mumbled.

"Your ovaries? Tabby, you're not still planning on spending all that money to freeze your eggs, are you? What are you going to do after that? Make a baby with some stranger who dropped his sperm off to buy a burrito?"

"Or to buy books . . . for school. It could have been books for school, not just a burrito, Mom." I was already feeling defensive and spent. I *definitely* wasn't going to tell her about Todd. No sense in adding fuel to this fire.

"Same difference. You don't want that. And I don't need

to have any frozen Popsicle grandbabies. You need to just go ahead and call Marc back. Maybe he's got a new perspective by now. He probably just needed a little time to come up with a plan."

"Granny Tab's friend Ms. Gretchen said that a man who doesn't have a plan for you isn't your man."

"Well, he might have a plan by now. But you wouldn't know, would you?" *Damn. My mom had a point.* She really had a way of making points that were hard to argue with, even if you felt deep down in the roots of your soul they were wrong. She had really missed her calling. She would have made a great lawyer. She continued with a new subject, knowing she had already managed to draw first blood. "Granny Tab! I miss her! How is she? Is she adjusting well to her new place?"

"She's good. I still visit her every Saturday. At least I try to. She's all excited for this 'Senior Prom' that they're having at Crestmire where she lives. I told her that I'd come and help her get ready. Ms. Gretchen even taught her how to watch makeup tutorials."

"Well, I'm so glad. You two have always been like Frick and Frack." My mother laughed. "And you know, speaking of visiting, when are you coming to see me? I have your room suite ready and everything. It's the same shade of soft, delicate pink, just like your old room in View Park." *Ugh. I hated that room.*

My mother and I continued for another hour while I cooked dinner and poured a glass of wine for myself. When we finished, I still had some work to do and sat at my computer. Out of curiosity and a little procrastination, I pulled up a web page and searched for "frozen sperm," which brought up a number of cryobank options. I picked the first one to see if I could distinguish between the "book" donors and the "burrito" donors. Just then, a ping on my phone announced a text message. Gauging the time, I figured I knew who it was, but it wasn't Todd.

Marc:
I miss you, Tab.
Marc:
Can we talk?
Marc:
Please?

With a slight tinge of guilt, I thought back to my mother's words. Maybe Marc *did* have a plan. Maybe he had changed his mind? I was enjoying the new idea of Todd, but my feelings for Marc were worth a shot. Plus, if he had changed his mind, trying to figure things out with Marc was better than the books vs. burritos challenge I was facing. At least, that's what my mother would want me to think. And although I knew I'd already lost the battle not to respond, I had not figured out what I was going to say. I started typing anyway.

Me:
You hurt me.

I deleted it.

Me:
Talk about what? You broke up with me.

I deleted it.

Me:

We can talk, but I'm seeing someone.

I deleted it. No sense in being petty.

Me:

Yes.

There, that was it. Simple enough. To the point, and it put the ball back in his court. Plus, I didn't know what else to say.

Marc:

Can we go to dinner? Sat night?

Crap. I had plans with Todd on Saturday night. I'm sure he'd understand if I canceled. I at least needed to give Marc a chance.

Me:

OK. Where?

Marc:

I'll figure it out and send you details. I can pick you up.

Me:

Are you sure? I can drive.

Marc:

I'm sure.

Me:

OK.

Why I put the period at the end of "OK," I'm not sure. But it was intentional. Maybe it stopped me from seeming too eager to forgive and forget. I wanted to pretend like I wasn't happy that I'd be seeing Marc. I wanted to hate him forever, but that only lasted two days—the hating him part. For the rest of the time, I'd just been confused, and still sad. At least now there was hope. And if there wasn't, one way or another, Todd or not, there was still a date with a doctor in my future.

1 5

LET'S BE HONEST, I WAS GIDDY. I WAS CLOUD NINE, ICE CAPADES, closing song of a Disney film kind of giddy, and I couldn't hide it. Once I made plans with Marc—once I finally crossed that bridge on the inside, giving myself permission to want him again, it seemed like ages to Saturday. And there's nothing like having a backup option, just in case. At least, I hoped I still had a backup after canceling on Todd. I made an excuse about having to work and he asked me to call him when I was free again for a "proper date" as he put it. I couldn't even think about that, though. I was so preoccupied with my still slightly guilty reunion with Marc. Finally making my way into Denisha's salon chair, it started to feel real for me. I gave Denisha instructions to give me the "sexy" version of my usual hairstyle she'd whipped up before. Once I left Denisha's chair, Marc wouldn't stand a chance.

"Girl, I'm gonna get you hooked up!" Denisha said with her hot comb in hand. It always concerned me when she got too excited when it was time to press my hair.

"Thanks, D! So, we never did get to discuss Alexis's party," I said, intentionally probing for the commentary that only Denisha could provide. I could hear the tea brewing in Denisha's mind.

"Oh, *Mrs.* Thing, um-hum. I heard that her *huz-band* bought her a new Mercedes. She pulled up in the whip last week—it's . . . nice . . ." I waited for the continuation. It wasn't like Denisha to just leave something hanging in the air like that unaddressed. "Of course, I don't trust *no nigga* when they do shit like that. You know, doin' too muhh-ch." She snorted in what seemed like mild disgust. "*Uuah*," she gave as her final dismissive critique. I smiled to myself remembering Laila's reaction at the unveiling of the car at Fig & Olive. Display on display on display. Of course, Lexi would say just the opposite. Sometimes, it seemed like she almost *needed* to sense that others were jealous, like it was the air she breathed. "Matter of fact, your girl was supposed to already be here. It ain't like her to be . . ." Denisha lifted her wrist to her eye level *with* the hot comb in her hand, causing me to flinch again. "Damn, she almost an hour late!"

"Really?" I said, feeling my brow furrow. That sounded very much unlike Lexi. "You want me to send her a text and see where she is?" I asked.

"Nah, I ain't trippin'. I've got one ahead of her anyway after you." And with that, Denisha went back to the thermal attack on my edges and I went back to fantasizing about my upcoming evening with Marc. When Alexis finally did show up, nearly a half hour later, I almost didn't recognize her—other than her signature bubble butt bouncing in her Lululemon workout pants. She had a baseball cap on, and when she looked up at me, walking in the door . . . there's no way to describe it other than to say, she looked *bad*. Really bad. Her bloodshot eyes had dark-colored swollen bags underneath, visible even from across the room. Even as I felt the anger welling up inside of me, thinking who might have done this to her, I realized that these bags weren't the bruising you'd get from a punch to your face, but more like a gut punch to your spirit. She'd clearly been crying—so much so that she wasn't sleeping. It was all there and obvious, in spite of a feeble attempt to cover it up with a cap and concealer.

"Lexi?" I said as she walked in, using only her name to ask all of my many questions in the way that only best friends could understand. *What happened? Why didn't you call me? What's wrong with my friend? Who do I need to kill and why?*

"Hey, Tab. Hey, Denisha. Sorry I'm late," Lexi mumbled, walking over to the seating area. *Was she mad at me? Did I do something? Maybe someone overheard me and Laila at her birthday party?* I just sat there for a minute, mostly in shock. I was in complete mystery about what just happened. There's no way my friend of basically my entire life would look like someone had run over her with her own new car and not tell me about it. And then, my eye caught something that made me take a sharp inhale. *Oh my God.* Denisha must have seen it too, because I heard her gasp behind me. As Lexi turned to sit down and place her oversize Gucci bag in the seat next to her, as obvious as daylight, Lexi wasn't wearing her wedding ring.

What the hell? If anyone knew Alexis Templeton-Carter, they would know that she did not go anywhere without her 1.5-carat diamond engagement ring from Tiffany's. The only explanation could be that she lost it. *Perhaps that's why she's so upset! She must have lost her engagement ring and wedding band somewhere . . . wait—and wedding band?* Oh no. With Lexi on the other side of the salon and with Denisha still attached to my head, by way of a hot curling iron this time, I decided to send a text.

Me:
Lexi, what's wrong?

I waited for Alexis to use that bare hand to reach into her purse and to pull out her phone, but even after five minutes, it didn't happen. So I decided to switch tactics. "Lexi!" I shouted across the salon. Anywhere else, I would have been embarrassed, but here, it was right in line with the rest of the commotion coming from all directions. "Lexi!" I shouted her name a second time. This time she looked up. I waved my phone at her. "Get your phone. I'm texting you!" Lexi looked like a deer in headlights for a second, frozen. Eventually, after a long pause of just looking at me, strangely, as if she were actually deciding whether or not she was going to do it, she finally pulled her phone out of her purse, read the screen, and then started typing.

Alexis:
I don't know if I can talk about it.

Me:
What? Is Rob in jail?

Alexis:
No! It's bad, though.

Me:
Aren't we best friends? WTF?

Alexis:
Seriously, Tab. Really bad. Haven't slept in days. The boys are with my parents.

Me:

Abt 2 get out of this chair if u don't tell me.

Alexis:

Tell you later. After I leave here.

Alexis:

Don't want all these folks in my business.

Well, that's a first.

Me:

Did you lose your wedding ring?

Silence. It was a strange experience to be looking right at Alexis, watching her not respond to the question I asked. To see her just sitting there, holding her phone in her hand, fingers hovering over the keys. She didn't look up at me. Then, finally, I saw her fingers move.

Alexis:

No.

Alexis:

Well, yes, but no.

What the what?

Alexis:

Can you meet me after my hair appointment? Starbucks on Crenshaw? I have to pick the boys up from my parents right after, but will have a few mins to talk.

Me:

Yes. Just text me when you're leaving. I'll meet you.

Alexis:

OK.

There is no way that this is what I think it is. No fuck-ing way.

16

TIME SPENT WITH DENISHA IS NOT SHORT. I KNEW BETTER THAN to head straight to Starbucks when Lexi hadn't even made it to the shampoo bowl by the time I left, let alone to the stylist's chair. This was going to cut it close, with me still needing to stop by Crestmire and then get ready for my date. *My date.* Just the thought brought a warm flush to my cheeks. It's hard not to let optimism in when it's banging on the windows and doors of your personal resignation, even in the middle of your best friend's life crisis.

When Lexi gave me the signal that she was leaving the salon, I wrapped up my browsing at Target, bought my few items, and headed east to make it to Starbucks in time to meet her. If things hadn't seemed so dire earlier, I would have settled for a rain check. But, instead, I was already seated with a green tea when she walked in the door. The cap was off, her hair was down, but she kept her sunglasses on, even as she walked toward the corner table that I had reserved for us. When she sat down, they were still there.

"You gonna take the glasses off?" I asked her as gently as I could.

"You know I *hate* the idea of wearing sunglasses indoors," Lexi said softly without making a single motion toward removing them. "But, I can't—I look so bad . . ." Lexi brought her hand up to the side of her sunglasses almost to reinforce them on her face. She was right, she did look bad. Although the glasses felt like an awkward wall between us, I understood in that moment it was the privacy she needed. Closer up, I was able to see that my eyes were not deceiving me. Lexi was not wearing her ring. The thin tan line encircling her fourth finger confirmed its absence.

"Don't worry, it's fine," I said, touching her hand, like she had done mine so many times before. And then, almost as if by unspoken instruction, I stood up and walked over to her side of the table and wrapped my arms around her as best I could. I felt her body shudder next to mine, and her head dropped against my shoulder. I could sense heat and then wetness spread along my collarbone as her tears fell on my T-shirt. I'd seen Lexi cry before, but not recently, not the "adult" Lexi with kids and a family and her smiling face on bus stop benches advertising her real estate agency. That Lexi always had a perfect smile to go with her perfect life.

"I'm sorry, I'm a mess. I'm a complete mess." Lexi brought her hands to her temples. "And I have to go soon to pick up the boys. I just wanted to get my hair done, so I could feel at least a little bit like myself."

"What *happened*, Lexi?" I whispered, maintaining contact with her arm as I pulled my chair over closer to her so I could sit.

"It's so hard for me to say, Tab," she said, still softly crying and wiping away tears. I handed her one of the napkins from my tea. She took a deep breath before continuing, "Rob and I . . . are . . . we're separated."

"What? Why? What happened?"

"He was cheating on me," Lexi whimpered. "This whole time. This *whole* time."

"Wha . . . oh my God. Lexi. I'm so sorry. Cheating with who? How did you find out?"

"I'm embarrassed to even say," Alexis admitted. I told her to hold on one second so I could get her more napkins. There was no good way to discreetly cry in a Starbucks, but at least there were plenty of paper products. I handed her a fat stack, and she continued, dropping an already balled-up wad on the table and picking up a new set. "Some girl he met shopping. She works at Nordstrom, in the men's section." She paused again to wipe the tears and slow down her breathing. "Could you get me some water, please? I'm sorry, I'm really sorry."

"Stop apologizing, Lexi. You don't owe anyone an apology. Definitely not me. I'll be right back." I dashed off and by the time I had returned to hand her the cup, Lexi seemed calmer and the tears had taken a break.

"Thank you. Sorry . . . I . . . ." She just shook her head, seeming to realize that she was full of apologies that didn't make sense in this particular situation. "After my birthday party, we posted the pictures and the videos, you know, of the car and dinner and everything on Instagram. He was tagged, I was tagged, just normal." I nodded. "The next day, I saw a comment from someone I didn't know. All it said was 'Read my DM—something you need to know.' So I checked my inbox and sure enough, this person had sent me this long message saying that she had been seeing Rob and that he had played her and that she . . ."

"Oh Lord, she didn't say she was pregnant, did she?"

"Girl, *no*, thank God we're not living *that* cliché. No, just that she was sorry to tell me like this, but she felt I would want to know what my husband was out here doing."

"Are you serious? Man, I'm so disappointed in Rob," I said with *ultimate* restraint. I picked those words very, very carefully. I had learned over the years that while I was always a hundred percent on Lexi's side, no matter what happened, some part of Lexi was always on Rob's. No matter *what* happened.

"Me too, Tab. At first, I didn't even believe it at all. I thought that it was just some hatin'-ass bitch, jealous of my birthday pics and of course my new Mercedes. So I didn't even mention it to Rob at first . . . but, I know he saw that comment on Instagram and didn't mention it or ask me about it. So, something kept telling me that I had to at least bring it up with him. You know, people are crazy, but they're not *that* crazy. Like there must have been some reason for that woman to go through all the trouble to look me up, right?"

"That's a good point, Lex. People always want to say that women are crazy, but, nine times out of ten, there's a reason with a man's name."

"I asked Rob about it. And at first he denied it. But I know when he's lying. I've seen him do enough of it. He was showing *all* of the signs."

"Did he do that thing where he scratches the right side of his throat with his right-hand middle finger? He always used to do that in high school," I said, referencing too many memories to count. Rob *always* used to lie when he got caught, even about little stuff. Except he was terrible at it, so Lexi and I always knew what was up. I wasn't surprised that he hadn't stopped making stupid mistakes at the expense of my friend, but I was surprised he hadn't become a better liar over time; Lord knows he'd had enough practice.

"Yeah, girl, that and then some. So, I knew. And he knew that I knew. So, he admitted it."

"He *did?*" My eyebrows rose almost high enough to meet my hairline.

"He told me that there had been something going on . . . and that it went too far. He was feeling down on his luck because my career was growing and his was stagnated. Well, at least it was before he got this new job. He said that once he got the medical device sales job, he got busier and it all just died out on its own."

"Busier? That's why it ended?"

"Hmmm . . . yeah, he said *busier.* You'd think he'd say, because he has two kids and a crazy wife who would divorce his ass. So, I told him that he had to get out. He took a bag of his stuff and is staying with his boy Darrell in the guesthouse. He's been gone since Wednesday."

"Whaaaaat? Lexi, this is awful. So you already decided to take your ring off and everything? Are you guys getting . . . divorced?"

"It wasn't so much a decision," Lexi said. I looked at her confused. "We were arguing in the garage, so the boys wouldn't hear. I got fed up, took my rings off, and threw them at him. I guess they're still somewhere in the garage. I just haven't felt like looking for them. Only a few people have seen me without—I told them I lost them down the drain washing dishes."

"Jesus. I'm so sorry, babe," I told Lexi as sincerely as I could. Secretly, I loved the idea of Rob getting hit in the head by Lexi's engagement ring. For the first time, I wished it were bigger than 1.5, emphasis on the extra .5, carats.

"Don't be," Lexi said. "I know you're not Rob's biggest fan, but—"

"That's not exactly true," I said, cutting her off. "I haven't been a fan of the things he's done while he's been with you, but it's never been personal. I'm just *your* biggest fan. Always have been, always will be."

"Aww, thanks, girl. I know you *luh* me," Alexis said, smiling for the first time all day.

"You know I do! So, do I have to kill Rob, or what? You know I'll grab Laila and we will *ride* on that nigga, for real." Alexis laughed at my terrible accent. I had to, too, even though I wasn't exactly kidding. Laila actually probably would kill him. I'd always been much more of a planner. I'd *have* him killed.

"Naahh, not yet. I haven't figured anything out. I've honestly just been processing it all. I keep thinking over every moment—trying to figure out what was real about any of our life. Where he was when he said he was one place or another—like, did he *really* spend the night at Darrell's that time? Was that *really* a job interview he was dressed up for, smelling good? All of it."

"Lexi, that's awful to have to think of it that way."

"It is, but I just need a baseline, you know? Because right now, all I feel is falling. And my heart *hurts*." And with that, she reached quickly for another piece of napkin to catch the tears dropping from underneath her glasses. We sat for a few minutes in silence, me reaching over to her, her dabbing her eyes and quietly sniffling. After a few more uncomfortable moments, she took a look at her phone on the table and reacted with a start. "Oh *shit*, I have to go! I have to pick the boys up from my parents."

"Are you going to be okay? Do you need me to drive you?"

"No, I'm okay . . . I'll *be* okay. I gotta go," Lexi said, standing up with her key in one hand and her latest balled-up wad of wet napkins in the other. "I'm going to call you this week. The house is so strange without Rob there."

"Okay, Lex, call me whenever. I'm around—whenever you need me, okay? No matter what time."

"Thanks, Tab," she said as she turned to walk toward the door.

"Love you, Lexi!" I called after her. But she was already too far gone to hear me, and honestly, I was glad she had to go, because I would have never left her. Even still, I had an evening to prepare for. Her relationship might have been in trouble, but after tonight, mine with Marc was certain to be back on track.

17

IF ON ANY DAY I WOULD SKIP GOING TO CRESTMIRE, TODAY WOULD have been it. But, instead, even though I was hours behind, I was still on the familiar road to Glendale. I went to see Granny Tab on Saturdays because I missed her and it gave us a chance to spend time together. I went *every* Saturday because of guilt. For everything I didn't do and everything I couldn't, this was the one thing I could and did do that lifted the weight off of my shoulders. I felt bad that she had to leave her apartment and live at Crestmire so that others could help take care of her, so I visited. I felt bad that I almost never accepted my dad's invitation to dinner so that Granny Tab could have all of her grandchildren together, so I visited. I felt bad that I couldn't tell her to just "move in with me" and solve all of her problems, like she did for me when my mom moved to DC, so, I visited. And today would be another day for my absolution.

Lexi's bombshell erased all thoughts of Marc as a traitor from my mind, at least for the short term. Her situation gave me an entirely new point of view about my own. At least Marc only broke up with me. Rob had been living a full-on secret life. I had to pretend for Lexi's sake that I was shocked, but in reality, I wasn't. This wasn't even close to the first time that Rob had cheated, or even for Lexi finding out in an embarrassing way. The first time was in high school. Lexi asked me to come meet her at her house one afternoon, in a panic. I had debate club, so couldn't get there until six p.m. When I walked in the door, Lexi whisked me upstairs to her room—her family had one of the few two-story homes in the neighborhood.

"What do you know about STDs?" Lexi asked me in a whisper after she closed the door.

"Uh, just what we learned in sex ed, silly—that you don't want one!" I said. I was still a virgin then, so to say this conversation was a theoretical one for me would have almost been an understatement.

"I think I have one. I think Rob gave me something," Lexi hissed.

"Oh my God, *what?*" I asked, moving slightly away from Lexi toward the door, because "something" could have been anything, and at that time, I had zero idea or experience with what you could catch and how you could catch it. I was so naïve at that time, I might have even thought that cold sores came from colds. The hurt registered on her face from my obvious retreat. I felt bad, so I reached out my arm to touch hers. "Whatever it is, I'll still be your friend," I said.

Lexi started to cry. "It's like, little things, crawling . . . down there . . . like little spiders."

"You have *spiders* in your . . ." I stopped and let my eyes indicate the rest of my sentence. We didn't really have great words for our genitals then. Mine were still mostly unknown to me at that age. I wasn't using them for much.

"I think it's called . . . crabs . . . that's what they look like. And it's itchy."

"So, wait, like *right now*, you have spiders down there? In your underwear? Won't they come out?" I asked, trying not to show Lexi my rising panic. "Well, did you ask Rob?"

"No, I'm afraid to ask him. What if it's from something else? Then he'll think I'm gross and break up with me."

"Lexi," I said, looking at her in my most serious fifteen-year-old best friend kind of way. "Have you been cheating on Rob?"

"No way! I haven't been with anybody but him!"

"Then it's his fault! You have to ask him!" I said, wanting to shake her, but not really touch her, because of the spiders.

"I can't. Tab, you have to help me."

And there it was. Classic Lexi, classic Rob. As it turned out, Lexi *did* have crabs and Rob *did* give them to her. She eventually learned through the grapevine that he'd been creeping with one of the cheerleaders at school who had been creeping with most of the football team. It could have been worse. Lexi dragged me with her to the clinic, where they explained everything and told her that her solution and relief was as close as the nearby drugstore. After that she shaved everything and made it a point to show me her completely bare *and* spider-free vagina when it was all done. She eventually did ask Rob about it, who lied, of course. She eventually found a bottle of the same drugstore stuff that she used in *his* room. She told me, but she never confronted him with it. She was afraid that he'd be mad at her for "going through his stuff."

All the other times, and there were several, Lexi would find out, Rob would lie, Lexi would find out again because Rob was a terrible liar, Lexi would get mad, Rob would apologize and buy Lexi something, and then Lexi would forgive him like nothing ever happened. Once, Rob spent all his money at the shopping mall jewelry store buying Lexi the smallest chip of a diamond the world has ever seen. It was about the size of a period at the end of a sentence in a book. Tiny. In fact, the gold prongs that held up this chip where the tiniest I've ever seen, but even *they* were bigger than that diamond. Still, you would have thought that he had bought her the Star of Africa the way she wore it back then.

So, to think that my Lexi had thrown her Tiffany's upgrade *and* kicked Rob out of the house, I had to smile. Maybe, after all these years, she had developed a backbone. *Eh, probably not.* If I were placing bets, I would have said he'd be back home in a week. Still, that smile lasted all the way into my parking spot at Crestmire.

I walked in to find my grandmother sitting in the common area with her feet propped up, watching TV next to Ms. Gretchen. I headed over to them with a widened smile and pulled up an empty chair.

"Hi, Two! I'm so happy to see you!" Granny Tab said with her usual enthusiasm.

"Hey there, honey!" Ms. Gretchen said, getting up to give me a hug. My grandmother didn't.

"Two, I would get up to hug you, but the doctor said I have to keep my feet propped up like this for a while. My ankles were swollen this morning. He wanted them to go down." My grandmother tried to make it sound like no big deal, but I felt a pang of alarm in my gut. She was here at Crestmire because of congestive heart failure. Any swelling was a bad sign that things were getting worse, not better as we were hoping.

"Well, you look pretty comfortable to me!" I said with the big smile that I forced to remain across my face.

Granny Tab laughed. "Well, that I am!" I studied her, looking for any other sign of possible frailty. It was what I worried about all the time. Aging could be cruel, and I wanted it to spare my grandmother.

"Tabitha's got us sitting here like bumps on a log!" Ms. Gretchen huffed. "Normally, I try to get us to walk around a bit. I do my exercise every day," she said proudly. "But the doc says we got to sit, so we're sittin'."

"You don't have to sit, Gretchen," my grandmother said.

"Yes I do." After that, Ms. Gretchen gave no further words. Sometimes they reminded me of Lexi and myself. Best friends don't need that many words.

"Guess what? I have a date tonight," I singsonged to my grandmother and Ms. Gretchen.

"With who? A new beau?" Granny Tab asked.

"Nope, with Marc," I said.

"Oh boy! I knew he'd come back around!" Granny Tab exclaimed. Ms. Gretchen just sat with her lips pursed, saying nothing.

"Well, we'll see. I'm going to at least give him a chance. He's been making a lot of effort to reach out, so I finally said yes."

"Oh, so he finally got his answer to 'what are you doing,' I see," Ms. Gretchen said.

"Well, Ms. Gretchen, he wore me down," I sheepishly admitted. I thought about telling them about Dr. Todd, but the fact that I canceled on him to see Marc tonight was not going to help my case. Granny Tab interrupted my thinking.

"That's just how your father was with your mother!"

Granny Tab said excitedly. "I'll never forget when he started talking about this woman he met at school when he called home. From the first time he saw her, he said, 'Mom, I think I just met my wife.' And he tried everything to get her to go out with him! But your mother, she was a princess if there ever was one, and your father, well, he was definitely more of a frog back then!" Granny Tab cracked herself up as she spoke. "My poor baby boy, having a white mom, being down there at Howard University, neither one of us really knew what it meant to be 'Black' so much. But God bless his heart, your dad kept trying to figure it out!" Granny Tab laughed again. "He would report back about everything that he'd learned about Black history and culture dating back to the Egyptians! And the professors he had! I was just fascinated. Who knew that being Black was so rich and involved? It was a journey for both of us. But when he met your mom . . . Two, all that mattered was having a big afro like the cool boys had. And so, when he told me that, I was here, well, on Fairfax, trying to read up in the magazines on how to make an afro and how to take care of one and trying to tell him, but I didn't know! His hair was so different from mine." Granny reached up to touch her thin gray hair. "Evidently, it was also different from what it was supposed to be to make it look like a Jackson 5 afro too!" We all chuckled. "But that's what he wanted, so he kept trying. That's what he thought would make your mom like him. If he had some big afro. But his hair just wouldn't do it!" Granny Tab's laughter started to become contagious, and Ms. Gretchen and I both cracked up at the thought of it.

"If his afro didn't work, Granny Tab, what happened to his hair?" I asked.

"Oh, Two, it was awful. He had tried to let it grow long,

and it wound up looking something like a poodle, I guess. He used hair spray, which was my recommendation. I always used Aqua Net when I wanted my hair to have volume. So, that's what he used. In retrospect, it was a terrible suggestion!" Granny Tab just erupted in laughter then, cracking herself up to the point of almost doubling over. I imagined my dad using Granny Tab's Aqua Net to try to move the needle on his appearance of "Blackness." He was already pretty light-skinned, so I guess if visible Blackness were any measure of popularity at Howard, he would have failed miserably. Based on what I experienced the times my parents took me back to the university campus for the Homecoming celebration, Howard was a rainbow of Black—a representation of the entire diaspora. I always remembered that as a lesson on Blackness. That it meant not a color, but a culture. So I guessed that if my dad was having trouble, it probably had to be his general lack of cool, which he still hadn't quite managed to fix.

"So, how did he get my mom to like him? Something must have worked, because here I am!" I said, half teasing.

"And here you are, Two! That's true. Well, your dad had always been a good student. I required that, no matter what else was going on. So he got a great internship at a bank in New York City the summer after his and your mom's junior year. Well, coming up on senior year, *all* the girls started thinking differently, looking less for just afros and paying more attention to what they heard about the guys with bright futures ahead of them."

"You mean the ones who were gonna make some money!" Ms. Gretchen said.

"I reckon so. Two, your father was one of those guys with

bad hair, but a brilliant brain underneath!" Granny Tab said proudly. "Once word got out that he was going to be a banker, all the girls started showing up, and your mom was one of them! Of course, she won out, but that was because she was who he wanted in the first place," Granny Tab said, smiling.

"Which would be the point that I would make. A man is gonna want who he wants in the first place. Unless he's an egomaniac or plain *crazy*," Ms. Gretchen said. "And a woman wants who she wants too. I met my first husband, Richard, in college." Ms. Gretchen started telling her story by leaning toward Granny Tab and me. "In me and your grandmother's time, college wasn't just a given for women. Women were sent to what they called 'finishing schools' where they were taught so-called 'domestic arts'—how to be a good wife kind of nonsense, because that was all they were ever gonna be. No need to spend money educating a woman who was gonna sit in the house all day—that was common thinking back then."

I heard Ms. Gretchen, but I couldn't imagine it, so all I could do was shake my head and let her continue.

"I was thinking about another kind of job in college—I knew I was going to be a teacher." Ms. Gretchen said *teacher* with so much pride, you'd think the word was *president*. "Back then, going to college was a privilege to us, especially if you didn't come from a wealthy family, so we dressed up for school. On the day I met Richard, I was wearing my pencil skirt, and my cropped cashmere sweater with the butterfly collar. Let me tell you I had the teeny-tiniest waist back then, and I loved to show it! Oh, and of course I had my red lipstick on—bright red like a fire hydrant. We'd sit in the student union and smoke cigarettes—now, I quit years ago, but back then, that's what we did. And I was sitting there between classes, and I saw him and he saw me—and there we were, looking at each other like we were hypnotized! And he came over with his tall and handsome self, finally, and I tried to play it all cool, smoking on my cigarette." Ms. Gretchen made a gesture to imitate the way she must have been holding her cigarette, pulling her hand up and down with the other hand on her hip. I could almost see the girl that she used to be back in those days. "Richard came over to me, and I said, maybe you and I should skip the next class and you buy me a Coca-Cola." Ms. Gretchen's words dripped with sass. "Well, you know old Richard, well, he was young *handsome* Richard then, and he said, 'Well, I can't miss class, but I'd very much like to take you to dinner.' And that was it, he passed my test. He was good in school and good looking too! I let that boy take me to dinner, and then the rest was history," Ms. Gretchen said with satisfaction.

"Well, you divorced Richard, Gretchen," my grandmother said.

"Yes, Tabitha, I did. But not until I got good and ready to," Ms. Gretchen said with indignation. "We had some wonderful years together, Richard and I, but at a certain point, you know you've gotta call it over when 'till death do us part' starts to sound like a plan, rather than a promise. We weren't gonna make it together. Some people just weren't meant to fit. And some people, some women, do just fine on their own. My life has been fabulous after my weight loss."

"What are you talking about, Gretchen? As long as I've known you, you've always been as thin as a rail!" Granny Tab said.

"I meant my husbands," Ms. Gretchen said, cutting her eyes back to the television.

18

MY HEAD SWIRLED ALL THE WAY HOME AS I RACED BACK, BEHIND schedule, to get ready to see Marc. I had overstayed at Crestmire. Hearing old stories from Granny Tab and Ms. Gretchen was a welcome distraction from Lexi's news and my mounting nervousness and expectations around seeing Marc again. We hadn't even spoken after the breakup. And the day I had just experienced brought up so many questions for me about love. First, my dad had pursued my mom to the ends of the earth, only to leave her inexplicably for another woman once they were married with a child. It didn't make sense. And then there was Lexi, who had been and done everything for Rob to support and encourage him, just like he said at her birthday. Well, he was out cheating on her with some random woman he shopped with. And it wasn't lost on me that Laila was being a "random woman" in someone else's family equation. And here I was, trying to hold on to Marc because of the slim chance he'd have a baby with me before either one of us really wanted to. Maybe Ms. Gretchen had the right idea, to just cut the deadweight and move on. What I really wished for the most was the newsroom script for my own life.

I would have liked much more clarity about everything before Marc picked me up. But my questions took more than the time available to contemplate. In honor of Ms. Gretchen's pencil skirt, I wore a form-fitting black halter-neck pencil dress that showed off the tone of my shoulders. Being on television kept me honest about going to the gym and watching my diet. On nights like this, I appreciated cashing in on the extra benefits.

Marc was exactly on time and sent me a text to let me know that he was downstairs. I was happier than I expected to be to see his shiny Porsche four door idling in front of my building. Under the city lights it almost looked like a superhero's car, capable of anything. Seeing me walk toward him in my stilettos, he pushed open his door to meet me, presumably to walk me to my side. A gust of air greeted me from the inside of the car. He smelled like cologne—not just any cologne, but the one I once told him was my favorite. I smiled softly as he lightly touched the small of my back to guide me into a hug.

"Hi," I said in my throatiest voice. I still didn't know if I wanted the prize tonight, but I definitely wanted to win the game.

"You look great," he said, finally pulling back after lingering a bit in our embrace. It had been weeks since we'd seen each other—since he had broken up with me.

"Thank you, so do you," I said, and then gasped. Marc had ushered me around to the passenger side of the car and, opening the door, I saw a bouquet of gorgeous yellow roses sitting on the seat. "Marc! These are for me?"

He smiled sheepishly. "Yeah, a little corny, but yellow is supposed to mean *I'm sorry*. And, I miss you," he said as he brought his body so close to mine that I could feel the heat of his breath, which smelled minty with maybe the slightest hint of cognac underneath. I started to feel enraptured, which triggered a tinge of panic in me. *Too soon,* my mind warned, causing me to step back from him a bit and use my momentum to reposition the flowers and sit in the car.

"They're beautiful. I appreciate it, Marc, really. Thank you." I looked him in his eyes as directly as I could, mustering all available resolve to not stand back up and suggest that we skip dinner entirely.

"Shall we go?" Marc said, taking a deep breath and putting his free hand in his pocket. I nodded. Marc closed the door, took the driver's seat, and set us off to our dinner destination.

"Where are we headed?" I asked.

"Tab, you know better than to ask me that. We're going to dinner."

"But where?" I teased, enjoying the levity of the interaction.

"You'll just have to see," he said, smiling his sexy smile at me. *Damn, he's fine. And he smells good.* Marc was being deliberate again tonight—he even had on a blazer over his button-down and jeans standard. And I noticed the leather driving shoes instead of his usual low-key sneakers.

It didn't take me long to wonder. We pulled up just a few minutes from my place at the US Bank Tower, a downtown landmark. There was really only one place he could be taking me, then. It was certainly one of the most romantic restaurants in all of Los Angeles, and it sat at the very top of the Tower. Sure enough, an elevator whisked us upward, opening its doors to reveal a modern décor with a clean elegance

that accented but didn't mask the centerpiece of the design—
three-sixty degrees of floor-to-ceiling unobstructed views
across all of Los Angeles. It was enough to erase the last bit
of contempt from my mind and push me into hopefulness
for the rest of the night. In my mind, Marc and I were already
back together. I reached for his hand to walk to the table. He
took it briefly, and then brought his arm around to place his
hand on my lower back again, ushering me in front of him to
follow the hostess. Once we were seated and while we waited
for our orders, we caught up on everything large and small
that happened since we hadn't spoken in what seemed like
so long.

"So, what's up with the promotion? When do you find
out?"

"It could be next week, that's what everyone thinks," I
said. "I'm so nervous. My real estate piece went over well,
but you know, Scott Stone still gets all the broader interest
assignments, like sports and stuff."

"Well, you know, you have to be ten times better to get
ahead. I know you've got what it takes, Tab. You'll get it,"
Marc said confidently. I appreciated his belief in me, but part
of me didn't feel like he understood what I was saying. I had
to work ten times harder to get ahead as a Black person, but
also ten times harder as a woman on top of it. That's just how
it was, and sometimes I wondered if I was enough to meet
the stakes.

"Yeah . . ." I said slowly. "Oh, and you'll never believe
this. Lexi and Rob are separated!" Marc and Rob had become
friendly over the time that we dated, as we had been out as
couples on several occasions, so I felt like he would understand at least a bit of the shock of the development.

"Really? Why?" Marc asked.

"Because he was cheating," I said. "Cheating and got caught."

"My man was cheating? *And* got caught? Damn, that's a tough one. So, what happened?" Marc asked. I wasn't exactly thrilled with his reaction.

"Well, the girl hit Lexi up on Instagram . . ."

"Instagram?" Marc asked with a screwed-up face. "Aw man, don't tell me he was with one of them . . . what do they call it? Insta-Hoes? Insta . . . thot?" Marc's face scrunched up as he searched for the word.

"No," I said, cutting him short. "It was some chick who works in a department store men's section where he shops, but she reached out on Instagram to Lexi after Lexi posted her birthday pics. You know, the party that I invited *you* to . . ." I said, raising my eyebrow for effect. Marc just kept the shocked look on his face, so I continued. "Anyway, Rob bought Lexi a Mercedes—so over-the-top—and they posted the pics and everything. Next thing, this girl was in Lexi's DMs."

"This sounds like a bad reality show, Tab."

"I know. And then Lexi confronted Rob about it, and he finally admitted it. He was having a full-on affair! Because he got discouraged about work."

"Well . . ." Marc said with his sexy thinking face. "I can understand, but I'm not saying that's the way to go, though." He studied me after he finished speaking.

"You can understand? Really? I can't. I mean, why would you jeopardize your entire family, and all that, just for some random woman you met shopping?" I studied Marc's face for a reaction. Not finding one, I continued. "Anyway, Lexi made him leave, so now he's staying at his friend's. I think they're gonna get back together, personally. I give it a few more weeks," I said, taking a sip after my self-satisfied proclamation.

"Sounds like times are rough on that brotha. I'm gonna have to reach out to him," Marc said.

"Reach out? You barely know him. Are you friends?"

"Nah, not exactly, but we chat from time to time. I mean, I can understand what circumstances might have put him out there like that. It's probably rough to be away from his family. That's all I'm saying. People aren't always as strong as you think—and aren't always doing things with bad intentions. Sometimes we just fuck up. That's real." Marc shrugged his shoulders.

"Humph." I took another sip of my drink. "You can reach out to him if you want to, but until Lexi rocks with him, he's dead to me."

"Girl code, right? I get it."

"Hell yeah, girl code!" I said. I had to admit, even if we were talking about somebody else's relationship, after all the tension in our own, it felt good to share a laugh.

Dinner was incredible. The wine made everything blur together—emotions, thoughts, even my words sometimes, as we worked our way through the bottle. I knew I made the right decision holding off on Todd. And except for the Todd news, I caught Marc up on the last two weeks, with the unguarded openness that we shared before he broke my confidence in him, and my heart. For those wonderful, delicious moments, I forgot all about my tears and why they had been shed.

"Tabby, I've been doing a lot of thinking these past couple

of weeks," Marc said as he reached across the table for my hand to hold. I gave it to him. "A lot of thinking." His thumb caressed the sensitive area just under my knuckles.

I looked around the room, distracted in my thinking. *Is this what I think it is?* It distracted me further. At this point, I was fully mesmerized.

"What I did, breaking up with you, wasn't fair." *Wait, is he going to . . . propose?* "And, when I thought about it, it didn't even really make sense."

I braced myself. I wanted to say something but everything in me told me to hold my tongue and try to make it through the next few minutes to see what he had in store. I looked around the room trying to remember the moment. I managed to keep quiet by taking a sip of wine with my free hand.

He continued. "So, not only did I want to apologize, but I wanted to explain some things. Some things about me and my family—I mean, you know some. But you don't know the whole story, and it matters."

Family? It matters? Marc and I can be a family. I started to imagine what Marc's and my kids might look like.

"Marc, you know that you can tell me anything," I said dreamily.

"I know, Tab—I've always gotten that sense from you, and I feel comfortable. I mean, as comfortable as you can feel about shit like this—stuff like this." Marc shifted a bit, but still didn't let go of my hand. "Tabby," he said, looking directly in my eyes, holding my gaze, "my . . . my father is an alcoholic."

I took a deep breath in. Now, *that* wasn't what I was expecting. "Oh?" I said. It was all I could muster and still hide the letdown. Marc didn't talk much about his family other

than at first to give the basic information, and the usual up-
dates as we continued dating. We hadn't progressed to spending the holidays together yet, and his family had not made
it from Florida to visit. This was not what I thought he'd be
telling me right now. It was almost like the needle skipped
on the evening. Still, he had a point to make, so I let him continue. Maybe this was his strange way of bringing us closer.

"My father is an alcoholic and his . . . *disease* has really
played a foundational role in my life. In who I am—how I
think about things. I'm really just starting to realize it."

"How so?"

"Well, for one, it's hard to say this as a man, but I'm constantly worried . . . I mean, I'll just say it, I'm afraid."

At this, I definitely was no longer thinking of children
with Marc. In fact, as he spoke, I started to realize that I was
watching Marc take on some of the characteristics of a child
himself.

"Of what, Marc? Does he get physical with you?"

"No, not that kind of fear. I'm afraid . . . that . . . in some
way, that I'm like him. That I'll wind up like him. Even right
now, Tabby—I'm counting the drinks that I've had. Do you
realize that? I'm actually counting. When we're out, I don't
stop drinking because I'm driving, I stop because I don't
want to wind up . . ."

"Like your dad," I said quietly, half in thought.

"Yeah," Marc said. "And when you brought up the idea of
having a family and making things more serious between
us, it just made me panic because, to me, family has meant
chaos . . . and abandonment . . . and pain, Tabby, lots of pain."

I felt my chest tighten, so I tightened my grasp of his
hand. My heart started to ache for him, and all I wanted to do

was take the pain away. Seeing the look on his face, I forgot about everything I thought I needed and wanted only to hold him with so much of my love that he wouldn't hurt anymore. I wished that just by my touch, I could *heal* him. Seeing his brokenness, I wished that maybe I could be, at least for him, the exactly right kind of enough to make him whole.

"Marc, I had no idea. I . . . don't know what to say . . ." I stumbled over my guilt-laden words. "Me bringing up my . . . *condition* wasn't to hurt you. I just, I just know that I love you and if I had my choice of it today, you'd be the person that I'd have children with . . . and a family." It was hard to choose words around the topic when he had already told me that basic elements of a human life—family, children, and even marriage—meant for him such destruction and negativity. *How do you even have a conversation from here?* My thoughts were racing, but my mind was a traffic jam of slow processing.

"I know you didn't know, Tabby, I haven't told many people," Marc said, gaze intent. "I just don't have high hopes, or good examples, for marriage."

His words were a stab in my gut. *How could I ever fix that?* My emotions continued to swirl in all directions as Marc continued, seemingly unaware of the turmoil he was causing. "I've watched my parents over the years. They've stayed together, but I have no idea why. They're both miserable, and my mom . . . well, I worry about my mom every day. Sometimes, I wish that she would just leave." I thought about Lexi and Rob, and I wondered just for a moment what Lexi would do if Rob were abusive to her. *Was cheating abuse?*

"Why *doesn't* she leave him?" I asked, not really wanting to know the answer.

"I don't know. I've tried every way to convince her—I've offered her to come live with me, she wouldn't have to work. Really, she doesn't have to work now. But she won't leave my dad. I know it. She's not ever going to leave . . . until it's the end of things."

"The end of things?"

"He's sick."

"Oh, Marc, I'm so sorry. All this—I had no idea."

"How would you know, Tab? I didn't tell you. And honestly, I didn't want you to ask. I was just enjoying our moments, pretending that we could exist in a world outside of everything like this, that you could be my escape. You wouldn't like it in my real world. I promise you wouldn't."

"How do you know that, babe?" I said softly, hearing myself slip back into my familiar endearment. After this sharing, I had never felt closer to Marc. Maybe I could be the one to take on his burdens, since I'd been carrying my own for so long. "My family is kind of messed up too. I mean, my dad walked out on me and my mom and married his *mistress*," I said. Marc was unfazed by what I shared.

"Yeah, but at least your dad was dependable to *you*," Marc said, fixed on delivering his message. "My dad was there, but I never knew which one I was going to get. Would he show up drunk to my graduation? He did, by the way. Both graduations—undergrad and b-school." His words caught in a jagged breath. He paused before continuing, "I've just spent my whole life walking on eggshells. Like I said, you wouldn't like my world, Tabby, I promise." Tears glistened in his eyes like . . . diamonds. He blinked them away before any fell.

I just wanted to be close to him, closer than we were, physically. I wanted to feel him inside me, to envelop his pain and absorb it and send it away through my body into somewhere else in the universe. In that moment, I was in love with him, and wanted him to take me home.

"Let's get out of here," I said.

IN FRONT OF MY BUILDING, WE SAT IN MARC'S CAR, ENGINE IDLING, conversation meandering around every topic but the one we needed to address.

"So . . ." Marc said awkwardly, signaling a turn to the more serious. "What do you want to do?"

"I want to go upstairs," I said as seductively as I could, biting my lip. Marc took my hand.

"I mean, about us."

"Can't we talk about it in the morning?" I asked.

"We could, but I'd rather talk about it now . . . so that we're on the same page before we go . . . up there." Marc motioned upward with his eyes, to the higher floors of my building. What I wanted was clear. What he wanted was not.

"Okay," I said, straightening up and trying to push the boozy cloudiness from my thinking. "I made an appointment last week . . . for egg freezing." I thought Marc would show more relief in hearing this.

"Yeah . . . about that. Tabby, I'm also not sure that I want to have kids. I need you to know that."

On those words, it was almost as if time itself stopped breathing. I could hear the idling of the engine and tried to focus on the soothing music on KJLH in the background. I figured that I must have misunderstood what Marc said. There's no way he would be telling me something like this now.

"There are a lot of things that I still need to figure out.

That's why I told you everything I told you tonight," Marc said, searching my face.

As much as I tried to push it down, I started to feel a flash of anger spark in my gut. "I'm sorry, *what?*" I said, looking at him with incredulity.

"I'm just being honest. I don't know if I want those things. That's why I tried to tell you everything at dinner. I *do* know that I want what we have, and that you're an amazing woman. I don't want to lose you, Tab. I don't." Marc looked at me sincerely and reached for my hand resting in my lap.

I didn't move. Instead, I sat for a few minutes in stunned disbelief. Anger again threatened my control. I could feel myself slipping.

"Marc, what are you doing right now?" I said finally, yanking my hand away. *Of course this is what he's doing. It was never about me, was it?* "I cannot believe that you are fucking tonight up like this with this bullshit!" I said, hearing my voice enter a new volume. *Marc doesn't care about me . . . He only cares about . . .*

"Calm down, Tabby! I'm just saying . . ." *All this time. All this time wasted.*

"What *are* you saying, Marc? That you want me to waste another year and a half of my life on your indecisive ass? Are you fucking kidding me right now?" I barely recognized my own voice, or the words forcing themselves out of my body.

"Tabby, do you have to drop *all* of those f-bombs?"

For a moment, I thought that I was going to black out. "Yes, the absolute *fuck* I *fucking* do! Because what *you* are saying right now is some motherfucking fuck shit, Marc. Seriously!"

"I'm on your side, Tabby," Marc said quietly.

I was not quiet. I had already been quiet. Too quiet. *All this time wasted.*

"You're on *my* side? How, Marc? How are *you* on *my* side?"

"I'm supportive, I'm here for you," Marc replied with quiet intensity.

"Supportive? You're supportive? Do you hear yourself? In what way?" I demanded.

"Like with your promotion, I've encouraged you, I—"

I cut Marc off at that point, feeling like my head was just one more word from launching into orbit. *The nerve.*

"You *encouraged* me with my *job*? Are you serious?! The *one thing* I *do* have under control? You think that my career success is due to your *encouragement*?! You think *encouragement* is what stands now between me and this motherfucking promotion that I've been working my *ass* off for, for the past year and a half?! Have you even listened to any fucking thing I have said to you in the past month?!" I was trying not to yell, I really was, but I was most definitely yelling by this point. I was done being polite. "I *told* you I wanted to have children. So, you *know* that, Marc. Now I have to spend my entire fucking savings to make sure that I can, because family might suck for you, but it's the *entire world* I *never* had. And now you're sitting here in my life, in this car, wasting days that I've *borrowed*, telling me that you don't know if you want to have kids? And you don't know if you *ever* want to get married? Are you fucking kidding me?!"

Marc, by this point, had ramped up also. His voice was elevated now and full of passion. "Tabby!" he said, gripping the steering wheel tighter than I had ever seen him do while driving, "I was just being honest with you! I still want to *be* with you, I just don't know if I want to get married to *anybody* or have kids, with *anybody*. But my mind could change! Why won't you fight for *us*?"

I felt my eyes widen in disbelief.

"*Fight?*" I repeated loudly and with increasing volume. "Fight who? Fight you? For *us*? What the fuck for, Marc? What am I fighting for?" I could hold nothing else back. The flood of rage overtook me, making me too angry to sob, like I wanted to. I hadn't meant to make Marc my enemy, but in that moment he was everything and everyone and no one, all at the same time. "I am *already* fighting, Marc!" I spat out his name in the exact same way I would say *motherfucker*, but used all the restraint that was left in my body to spare him the direct insult. I continued to yell, though, at full steam, with tears eventually releasing in streams down my face, mixing with my mascara. "I'm fighting for my promotion at work— I'm fighting my ovaries—who also don't know if they want to have children, by the way! I'm fighting stress and weight gain—'cause I have to look good, right?! Oh, I'm fighting my hair—I can't even wear it the natural way it grows! *And* I'm fighting for my *life*, it feels like, every time I get pulled over by the fucking police. So, *now* you want me to fight you too? 'Cause *you* can't make up *your* damn mind? Like you're some kind of *prize* at the end of an obstacle course?"

Marc said nothing. He only looked at me with his mouth slightly agape, as if I had been speaking in tongues.

Just then, Ms. Gretchen's voice flashed into my mind. *If a man doesn't have plans for you . . . life regrets . . .* "Oh hell no, Marc. Hell no! You know what?" I whipped around and turned to face him, my eyes squinty and blazing with anger, pointing my finger directly at his face. "You will *not* be one of my life regrets, Marc, you won't!" I reached for the door and opened it, throwing one of my legs out.

"Tabby, don't . . ." Marc said feebly.

"Don't *what*, Marc? Don't reclaim my time that you've been wasting? Is that what? Don't sit here while you pull my life into your inability to make commitments? Fuck you!" I screamed, slamming his very expensive, shiny car door for emphasis and clacking my heels as quickly as possible to the front door of my building. I waved to the doorman with my head down as I swept in through the lobby to the elevators as quickly as I could, pushing the up button more times than I knew I was supposed to. I got up to my apartment and, for the second time in these weeks, cried myself to sleep still wearing my dress and stilettos.

I did have one regret. I wish I had taken those flowers.

19

TO SAY THAT MY EVENING WITH MARC HAD BEEN A DISAPPOINT-
ment would be like saying, "Serena Williams plays tennis."
Of course Serena Williams plays tennis, but that's not what
has made her remarkable. What has made her *remarkable*
has been her focus, drive, and mastery of something that
nearly every able-bodied person can do, but where she stands
in a league of one. She elevated the pastime of tennis to a
place of mental transformation. Her good is so extreme, it
evolved the game into almost another sport entirely. If you
played against Serena Williams, you wouldn't be playing
tennis, you'd be playing *Serena*. And when you played Serena,
if the true Serena showed up, then only Serena could win.
That was my experience with Marc last night. By every assessment, I had been played.

Still, by Sunday afternoon I had already started to feel bad
about the argument, and by the evening I began to second-
guess myself on the resolution that seemed so clear at the
slam of the car door. *Was Marc himself worth waiting for?* It
was something I needed to figure out, but it was competing
with life events that were now more important than ever. The

promotion announcements at work were soon. Very soon. Word in the office on Friday was that Chris might even use the next newsroom meeting to do it. Where I would otherwise obsess over Marc and my phone, I had no room left in my mind—instead, I was obsessing about reaping season on a hard-worked-for promotion.

On Monday morning, I was a nervous wreck. So I did what any other nervous wreck would do in my situation, I pretended to be somebody else. I didn't walk into the office building as just a reporter, I came looking my absolute best, striding in as I imagined the Beyoncé version of me would with theme music, a DJ, and a personal fan in tow. I was strong, powerful, invincible, gorgeous, talented, articulate . . . and all of a sudden, I was listening to the needle rip on my song. Just as the elevator doors started to close, Scott Stone walked into my elevator for the morning ride up. Because, of *course* he would. *Crap.*

"Morning, Tabby." He turned and greeted me with his sunglasses still on.

"Morning, Scott," I replied curtly, barely turning.

"Seems like today's the day. How are you feeling?" *Asshole.* What am I supposed to say to that? *Yeah, I most definitely feel like I'm going to get this promotion over you today, can't wait!*

"I probably feel similarly to you," I said. "And mostly nervous, I definitely feel nervous."

"I don't feel nervous. Not at all. I feel pretty confident, actually," Scott said, taking his glasses off and securing them in the pocket of his blazer.

"Oh? Maybe you know something I don't, then?"

"Nothing official, but it's seemed pretty clear for a while now how this thing was going to go," he volleyed back, looking at me like I was a small lost child. "I mean, you didn't think you were going to get the senior reporter role in *this* round, did you?" I looked at him wide-eyed. How was it possible that everybody else in the office knew that Scott and I were *both* up for the senior reporter role, except Scott?

"I've got the seniority," I said. "And my reports rate well, so I've always seen the lane as wide open . . . even up to now . . . up until the announcement gets made." I got ready to step out of the elevator as the doors started to open. Scott followed me and then he paused to face me, as the doors closed behind us.

"But Tabby," Scott said quietly. "Honestly, don't you think your perspective is kind of . . . *limited*?" In spite of all of the muscles I regularly used in my face, my mouth dropped wide open on its own. "I mean, you can't cover sports, we know that, and you're always bringing up . . . *urban* issues, in areas that most of our viewers don't even care about."

I stood there in absolute disbelief as Scott brought his arm up to rest his hand on my shoulder and look me directly in my eyes, with the sincerity of a father, even though we were almost exactly the same age.

"Look, just something to think about. Make some adjust-ments, and you probably *will* be ready for next year." With that, he gave my shoulder a little rub and turned in the direc-tion of his cubicle. Watching him walk away allowed a few seconds to recover from the paralysis of shock. When I could move again, I headed to the kitchen to grab a coffee before going to my cubicle. Time to shake it off. We had a newsroom meeting to attend.

The air in the conference room seemed charged with a different kind of electricity. I tried to use it to stop the morning's conversation with Scott from affecting my mood. *Was Scott right, though?* My mind continued to echo his allegations. On the surface, maybe I couldn't cover sports with the dexterity of an ESPN reporter, but I certainly could do the research. In fact, I'd probably do a better job than some know-it-all who thought they already knew everything there was to be known. And my perspective wasn't *limited*; it was *augmented*. Of course I saw all of the "mainstream" issues that related to the broadest base of our viewership, but I also saw the things that were affecting minority communities as well. Not just Black people and not just *urban*, whatever that meant. Still, maybe Scott's perspective was how Chris saw me too. He gave Scott that Rams assignment over me, and he stuck me with LA real estate trends. And actually, I was able to turn that tinder-wood-dry, tired concept into an interesting story by bringing in the topic of gentrification. Out of the corner of my eye, I saw Chris enter the room.

"As many of you are suspecting"—Chris began talking as his pale, pudgy figure moved into position to start the meeting, holding a thin stack of papers—"we're going to start today's weekly with some announcements." Everybody shifted nervously. What remained of Beyoncé-me took a stage-left exit. "We're lucky. Meetings like this in our industry too often come with layoffs. We all need to be proud that we've got the best numbers in the Southland. So, you can congratulate yourselves for that." The room broke into a spirited round of applause with some hoots and whistles. Chris continued, "So we *are* going to announce a few promotions, and then it's right into regular programming for this meeting. Congratulate your colleagues when you see them after we finish or, better yet, after work. They're going to be even busier than they have been, starting today." Chris didn't even lift his wire-rimmed-glasses-clad face up from the papers he was reading.

"Happy hour on me!" Donald Hugh, the evening anchor, said.

"You heard Donald, drinks on him tonight," Chris said, all business. "Let's get to it. Joining the anchor team will be . . . Senior Reporter Julie Johnson. Congratulations, Julie, you are now our newest weekend anchor." I looked down the table at Julie's face. She was beaming, and her smile was wider than a tropical banana. People around her patted her shoulders, and she turned to acknowledge each one, making her look somewhat like a bobblehead.

Uh-oh, I thought. *A woman joining the anchor team.* That was a big deal. That probably meant that a man was going to get the senior reporter . . . *Crap.* "And our newest senior reporter is . . ." Chris paused, seeming to read something on the paper in front of him. "Tabitha Walker." *See, I knew that Scott . . . Wait . . . did I hear that correctly? Did he just say Tabitha Walker?* I looked around, and everyone was looking at me showing teeth, but for a second, the room went silent. All I could see were moving mouths. To know it was real, there was only one face I wanted to see, that I needed to see.

I turned to look at Scott. My victory was written in the redness of his face. His shoulders had dropped at least an inch, and he had the same open-mouthed look that I had in the elevator. The taste of victory crept into my mouth like sweet blackberry cobbler and vanilla bean ice cream. As I closed my eyes to savor the moment, memories flooded into my mind in lightning-quick flashes of every time that made me believe I wouldn't make it. Every bad story assignment, every side comment, and even the brief encounter on the elevator with Scott. It was all there, but transformed now on the inside of me into a burst of light-filled, uncontainable joy that threatened to spill out of every pore of my body. I had overcome to bask in the sunlight on the mountaintop.

A pat on the back brought me back into the present. I hadn't even realized my eyes were closed. "Congratulations, Tabitha, here's your letter from HR." Chris was standing right next to me, speaking over my shoulder. "You'll start as a reporting team lead as of today's meeting." He handed me the paper on the top of the stack. "Okay, folks, let's get to business. We've got news to cover."

By the time the meeting ended, I had my first team assignment as a senior reporter. Two of my former colleagues had been assigned to work with me, and for the first time ever, I would have final say over how the story ended up on television. As we all walked out, Chris stopped me near the door, in the hallway.

"Tabby, do you mind coming in to see me in my office?" *Oh boy, this can't be good.* He didn't ask anyone else for a follow-up meeting. *See, even when you win, you can't win.*

"Sure, Chris, right now?"

"Yes, now is great. Let's head down together."

Chris and I walked down the hallway in tandem, which I appreciated in some ways, and worried about in others. On the one hand, as I had just gotten promoted, I didn't want my leveling up to seem in any way different from any of the others. The last thing I wanted was for people to think that I was getting special treatment, or worse, that I had already messed up. On the flip side, seeing me walk with Chris made it seem to people in the office like we were in alignment and that I was important. I just hoped it wasn't any kind of attention that I didn't want. We reached Chris's office, and he offered me a seat in his guest chair. I took it, and he sat behind his expansive desk, covered with enough papers to look like a snowstorm hit.

"Congratulations, Tabby," Chris started. "I'm looking forward to seeing you expand into this new role."

"Thanks, Chris," I said. "It's nice to be recognized for the work I've been doing here. Viewer ratings have been strong on my stories, and I'm looking forward to—"

"You know," Chris interrupted, "conventional wisdom would have said that I should have given the position to Scott. You know that, right?" I shifted uncomfortably in my seat, remembering the conversation that Scott and I had on the elevator. *Oh, what? What the fuck you just say? I know you didn't just say what I thought you said.* I took a moment to summon my professionalism to filter my thoughts into better words.

"I'm sorry . . . Scott?" I said politely, adding an airy layer to my voice. "Maybe I am misunderstanding you. Are you now saying that I didn't deserve the promotion?" I asked, trying to maintain a respectful tone but beginning to bristle.

"No, no, not at all. You both *deserved* the promotion, Tabby. The decision didn't come down to who deserved it and who didn't. Though, on the basis of *effort*, one could conclude that Scott did deserve it more." *Wait, what? Did you just say Scott deserved it more? Then why didn't you give it to him, Chris?* I paused another second to find my filter again, before responding. I could not believe that Chris was doing this.

"Chris, with all due respect," I said, doing my best to keep my voice even, "what exactly are you getting at?"

"My point is, Tabby, that in every meeting, you let Scott outtalk you, outmaneuver you, and take the better assignments from you without fighting for them. You let him win."

"Then why do I have the senior reporter job and he doesn't?"

"Because if I had promoted him and then had this conversation with you, we'd be in a lawsuit," Chris said with full seriousness. "I could either put you in this position and encourage you to grow into it, or watch you continue to fade into the background. I chose to take a risk."

"Chris, it's still sounding to me like you're saying I don't *deserve* the senior reporter position."

"Okay, you don't," he said simply, causing my eyes to widen. "Not yet, but people get what they don't deserve all of the time. Don't get so hung up on things that don't matter," Chris said, putting both palms on his desk. "Listen, I haven't built the success I have in my career by following conventional wisdom, Tabby. I did it by relentlessly following my gut. You need to start doing the same."

I felt my face flush with both embarrassment and irritation. *I can't believe this guy is sitting in front of me telling me I don't deserve this promotion I worked my ass off for!*

"I'm sorry, Chris, can you help me understand, just so I'm clear on what you're saying—if I didn't *deserve* it, then why am I here?"

"Because we need your *perspective*, Tabby. I've listened to you in the newsroom weeklies. You find angles to everyday stories that nobody has even thought to look for. That they can't even see. And you do it effortlessly. News today, what's fresh—it's all about *perspective*," Chris said, becoming increasingly emphatic with his words.

"And what about Scott?" I asked.

"What about Scott?" Chris said. "He's probably gonna quit. I give him three months, tops. He'll find another job where he can be hired as a senior reporter right away, and we'll hire another Scott from the hundreds of reporters just like him whose resumes are sitting on my desk right now. Scott is replaceable, and we'll replace him."

Is Chris saying what I think he's saying? I decided to speak the unthinkable.

"So, are you saying that I got the promotion because I'm *Black*?" I asked directly but in full disbelief. I could feel the tears welling in my eyes as I fought back any deeper internalization of my own words. I let them hang in the air, and Chris did too for a moment before he answered. A moment that seemed like an eternity.

"I'm saying that you got the promotion because you're *unique*." Chris leaned forward to rest his elbows on his desk. "I believe that we have only just begun to see your perspective *and* potential. And if I had to pick, I'd rather know what's in the mind of a Tabitha Walker than a Scott Stone. Scott Stone, I already know. I've seen it a million times before, and so have our viewers." I was now more confused than ever.

"So what are you saying that I need to do?" I asked.

"Fight!" Chris said, pounding his desk with a fist for emphasis. *Oh no, there's that word again.* Chris continued. "Tabby, you need to fight to make your voice heard. You need to stand up for your point of view—for your stories, for your perspective. Not just in the weeklies, but every day, in every room and on every team you work on! I'm not saying it's an easy job, but easy doesn't keep us on top." The exertion had Chris almost panting by now.

"Chris," I said, standing up to leave. "I can understand and appreciate your believing in me, but I *earn* what I have. I always have. I don't want a position I don't deserve, and I definitely don't want people around here thinking I just got where I am because I'm Black. I've always worked twice as har—" I began my diatribe moving toward the door, writing my resignation letter in my mind as I spoke.

"Tabby, *no one* deserves a new role at the beginning," Chris said, putting his full girthy mass behind his words. "Why are you so hung up on that one *word*?" he asked, giving an extralong pause. I was speechless, without answers. "*Everyone* has to earn their way on the back end in some way." Chris was pointing forward at the air now. "And the people who make *those* kinds of judgments—that some promotion or whatnot happened just because you're Black, or just because you're a woman—they're *always* going to think that. But the fact is, that *you* got the promotion, Tabby, *you* did. So it's *your* position now—to either prove *them* right, or to prove *me* right. Entirely up to you." And with that he sat back down and pulled toward him a messy stack of the loose white papers that scattered his desk.

Well, damn. I guess we're done talking, now? I stood near the door, still with my hand on the knob to exit but frozen with indecision. *Do I stay in here or do I leave?*

Chris looked up at me over his glasses without moving his head. "Are we on the same page?" he asked. I thought about it for only a second.

"Same page," I said reluctantly.

20

IN ALL MY YEARS OF A CAREER, I NEVER HAD ANYTHING HAPPEN TO me like what happened in Chris's office. I didn't know whether to laugh or cry. All I did know is that I'd better figure out how to listen to his words or find a new job. And then came the blur of logistics. HR and then the office IT guy helped me get set up in my new office, which I was glad to settle into for some much-needed privacy to sort through my thoughts. Just as it occurred to me that I now had a door, and that I wanted it closed, I heard a knock on the frame. I looked up to see Lisa standing in the doorway, holding two coffees.

"Congratulations, girl! I knew you were gonna get it. Ms. Senior Reporter!" Lisa spoke loudly in the friendly and overenunciated way that only seasoned anchors used, even in their downtime. For some reason, her use of "girl" needled my ear, just slightly, as it lacked the warm comfort and true familiarity that it carried when spoken between me and my actual girlfriends. I reminded myself that Lisa was just trying to make nice and connect. I did have in mind that I'd entertain the women's group after I got my promotion, but this wasn't exactly my sense of timing. I sat silently hoping she wouldn't bring it up.

"Thanks, Lisa! Is that coffee for me?"

"Oh, yeah, sorry!" Lisa stiffly rushed her way across my office to drop one of the cups she was holding on my desk. "Here I am holding it and not even giving it to you," she said, laughing at herself. "I didn't know how you liked it, so I brought some sugar and cream." She emptied her pockets, spilling out a mess of little plastic creamers, paper sugar packets, wooden stirrers, and napkins. "I just drink mine black—bad for the teeth, but that's why I use the straw!" she said awkwardly, showing me her cup that, sure enough, had a black plastic soda straw sticking out of it. "They don't have these in the kitchen, so I bring my own. Let me know if you want one."

"Oh, thanks. Um, I'll just take my chances I think . . . with the cup."

"Yeah, your teeth, Tabby, they're really beautiful. This bleaching job, I have to keep it up—it's so expensive." She waved her free hand across her mouth to emphasize her immaculately white, perfectly aligned mouth full of teeth, flashing a very large, glistening diamond in the process.

"Thanks, I've been . . . thinking about getting mine done," I lied, wanting to make her feel better.

"Well, just let me know—I've got a great guy in Beverly Hills. He does everybody," Lisa said in a speed just before rambling. I couldn't figure out if she was nervous or just awkward in person. This was only the second time that we'd spoken, as my efforts to avoid her had been largely successful after that day in the bathroom. *Try to let your guard down a little,* I told myself. "Listen," Lisa continued, "I'd love to buy you a drink sometime to celebrate, or dinner even. Making it to senior reporter is a big deal! I remember when I got that promotion. I was as scared as I've ever been! Do you mind if I sit down?" *Oh no, she's going to stay.*

"I'm so sorry, Lisa! Where are my manners? I should have invited you to a chair. You'll have to excuse me while I'm still an office newbie!"

Lisa waved away my profuse over-apology and sat down. "Just let me know what night would be good for you. I'm usually free on Wednesdays and can sometimes get Thursdays with a little bit of notice . . . My husband has his writers' group on Thursday nights, but he's really great about staying home with our son."

"How old is your son? Your husband doesn't mind babysitting duty?" I asked.

"My son is five. He . . . he has special needs. He's on the spectrum. Bill and I decided that it would be better for him to quit his job for right now so that we could have one parent at home at all times. It seems like Charlie does a lot better that way," Lisa said, half glazing over while speaking. I wondered how much more there was to it. I thought about Rob, and reminded myself that every husband doesn't cheat just because his wife is the breadwinner.

"That sounds like a real partnership," I said wistfully.

"It is!" Lisa said, fidgeting with her cup. "It's not what we ever planned, and it's not easy, but we do what we need to do to make it work. Since Bill is at home, we decided that we wanted to try for a second, but nothing's happened so far," Lisa said, gesturing to her incredibly flat abdomen. "So it looks like we're going to need IVF." I perked up at the mention of IVF—I knew all too well how much that could cost.

"Oh, wow, that can get pretty expensive, right?"

"Oh, you have no idea!" Lisa said. "Honestly, we almost can't afford it. My salary is good, but it's the only one, and the costs for Charlie's treatments, you wouldn't believe. It's a huge sacrifice, but we don't have a lot of other options. We want him to have a sibling . . ." Lisa trailed off, looking down at her coffee. I sat for a minute in the space of silence between us, deciding if I was going to confide in her with my own struggle.

"Actually, I know the IVF costs all too well," I said after a pause. Lisa looked up at me with curious eyes. "I have an appointment coming up for egg freezing."

"Oh my God, I wish I had done that when I was younger!" Lisa exclaimed.

"Well, this isn't my choice," I said. "I basically have to, or biological children for me is entirely off the table. And I'm my mother's only child. You know how that goes." Lisa nodded in understanding. "I'm going to have to use all of my down payment money. I've been saving for years to buy a house. My best friend is a Realtor, and she had just started showing me around. I was really looking forward to it." My mind trailed off into thinking about how much I had started to enjoy going to the open houses with Lexi.

"Well, you know, this is one of the issues we need to bring up in this place!" Lisa said. *Damn, here we go.* "Our insurance plan really should cover things like this. And there are options for plans that do. Just that *our* employer doesn't make it a priority. But Google does, Facebook does, Apple does . . ." Lisa started naming an impressive list of companies on her fingers.

"You know my . . . frie . . . um, ex, told me about this

not that long ago." I hesitated over what to call Marc. He was definitely an ex now, that's for sure. I pushed down a pang of regret as I continued, "I forgot all about it after he told me, but you're right. No reason *not* to bring it up here." I thought about Chris's challenge to me about making my voice heard. I bet if I joined the women's issues group, he'd come to regret that mandate.

"See, people think that some of these things are about social comforts or just a *feeling* of equality," Lisa said, leaning forward as if sharing a secret. "That's important, but people also need to realize that these are hard-core financial concerns. Trust me, if men's sperm were on a timer, this would have been covered a long time ago!" Lisa said, cracking herself up. We both shared a laugh as she stood up to head for the door. "Let me know about drinks, okay?" she said, catching my nod of agreement as she headed out of the door of my brand-spanking-new office. Well, new to me. *My new office.* Damn, *I did it.* I made it to senior reporter.

For some reason, Marc's voice saying, "I know you've got what it takes, Tab. You'll get it," floated through my mind. I debated for a second sending him a text to tell him. *For what?* I was torn, but couldn't think of a good reason to do so, so I didn't. We weren't together anymore. And after Saturday, we probably weren't even on good enough terms to qualify as friends. Instead, I decided to text Lexi. I would call Laila and my mom later and tell Granny Tab in person.

Me:

Lexi, I got the promotion!!!

Lexi:

Yassssss Bisssshhh!!! I knew you would!

Me:

Wanna get drinks tonight?

Lexi:

YES! Please.

Me:

Oh shit! I forgot—I have a work happy hour. Can you go late?

Lexi:

Yes, Rob has boys tonight. Will keep me from going crazy.

Me:

OK, will tell Laila.

Lexi:

Can it just be us?

Lexi:

I understand if not.

I would have loved for the three of us to all get together, but understood Lexi not being ready for the details of her relationship to travel beyond the two of us. It was still fresh, and her emotions were still raw. *Kind of like my emotions about Marc.*

I pushed Marc out of my thinking again. He had wasted enough of my time.

Me:

Sure, Lexi, just the two of us.

21

LEXI AND I DECIDED TO KEEP TO OUR REGULAR SPOT AND MEET AT Post & Beam. Driving up, the restaurant looked exactly the same as it always did, but it was my life that looked completely different from the last time I'd been here. I saw Lexi's car in the parking lot and walked in the door to find her sitting at a table in the corner. She was sipping on a straw and holding a tall, thin glass filled with clear carbonation and garnished with a lime.

"Hey, girl!" I gave Lexi my customary hug as I sat down.

"Hey, girl," Lexi said, her voice heavy with what seemed like concern. "Oh shit. Congratulations, Tab! Let me give you a real hug!" She jumped up from her seat and grabbed me tightly. "You go, girl, making big moves!" she said, sitting back down again after having perked up. She still wasn't wearing her ring. I guess my glance was obvious; she followed it, looking down at her own hand. "Nope, still not on."

"You still haven't found it, Lexi?" I asked, almost in a panic for her.

"Girl, I found it." I let some silence pass, hoping she'd

elaborate. But all she did was pick up her glass again and take a sip.

"You're not drinking?" I asked.

"No, I am." She looked down at her drink after seeing what I guess was a puzzled look on my face. "Oh, this is vodka soda. I heard it has fewer calories . . . and is supposed to be better when you want to lose weight."

"Lexi, this is a hell of a time to go on a diet."

"I haven't been eating much, with all the stress of this craziness with Rob, so I figured, I need to make good use of it," she said, patting the area of her torso, just under her generous breast shelf. "Tab, I looked in the mirror the other day, and I could barely recognize myself! I mean, I went from Sexy Lexi, to Supersize Lexi. My ass is huge!" *Yeah, honestly it was.* I had noticed Lexi's expansion for a while, but in this moment struggled with whether I should lie and tell her that she looked great, or find another way to reinforce what might be a path to a healthier lifestyle. I settled for a compromise.

"People can't stay young forever, Lexi You have two kids. I hope you're not being too hard on yourself."

"That's just it, Tab. I haven't even been paying attention. This weight just crept up on me—just like the rest of my life, it feels like. For a while now, my existence has just been Rob, Rob Jr., Lexington, work, mortgage, get the boys to school, get them to their practices, try to pay attention to Rob, go see Rob's mama, go see my mama, get my hair done, and *maybe* catch up with you and Laila, and then, damn! What about me? Where have *I* been in all of this? It's like I've been absorbed by my own life—like there's no *me* anymore. Do you know what I mean?" Lexi asked, lifting her eyebrows and turning her head at an angle for emphasis.

I was speechless. The person in front of me seemed like a possession of Lexi's body. It was almost like I was talking to the middle school Lexi, the one before Rob, who told me everything and entrusted me with all of her secrets. I'd spent the last almost twenty years with the other Alexis, the one who was constantly balancing truths and fictions, mostly because of Rob, some because of insecurities, and eventually all at the expense of our closeness.

"Wow, Lexi, I had no idea you were feeling like that. It seemed like you were just in some sort of bliss," I said. It was true, she had made it seem like her life with Rob and the boys was the happiest place on earth.

"I don't think I've been feeling anything for a long, long time. It's like I've gone numb. Rob's . . . affair"—Lexi spat the word *affair* out like spoiled milk—"it was a wake-up call. I needed to wake up from whatever world I was living in."

"He's still at Darrell's?"

"Yeah, still at Darrell's and begging to come home every day." Lexi sounded dismissive. I was shocked. The Lexi I knew could be without Rob about as much as she could go without a critical appendage. I was completely thrown off by her nonchalant attitude.

"So, you're not trying to let him move back in?"

"Not anytime soon," Lexi said. "I still need time to sort out my thoughts. Right now, I feel like I bought a bag of bullshit. This is my chance to find out what I really have, you know? All my adult life, I have just been Mrs. Carter." *Well, Mrs. Thing, actually,* I thought. "And *this* is what I traded in my entire twenties for? Here I am at almost thirty-five, and

I don't know who I am other than Robert Carter's wife and mother of Rob Jr. and Lexington. And that's just pathetic." Lexi took another long sip of her drink, almost to the point that I could hear the exact mix of air versus liquid she managed to extract. "And Rob's ass is out here lying and cheating and shit. Can you imagine?" Lexi gave me that rhetorical-question quizzical look again. "So, to answer your question, hell naw, I'm not ready to let him move back in. I need some more time . . . and answers."

I did not expect this Lexi to show up, but I smiled a bit with what I could only identify as pride, seeing her stand up for herself. *Welcome back, old friend, welcome back.* Lexi's words were good enough to allow them to sit in the air while I waved down the waiter for my own drink and a refill for Lexi's diet concoction. My news had gotten lost in Lexi's personal drama, but that was understandable. Even if tonight wasn't much of a celebration of my accomplishments, hearing her sound this way was almost like its own reward.

"So, girl, tell me about today!" Lexi changed the subject, seemingly reading my mind. "You got the promotion—what was Scott Stone's reaction like?" Lexi giggled mischievously. I was relieved for my turn to dish. I needed to take a well-earned victory lap with my best friend.

"Girl, it was crazy!" I said. "First, of all people, I wound up riding in the elevator with him and his cocky ass. He's not so cocky now. He tried to play mind games, making me feel like I wasn't worthy, you know."

"No he didn't!" Lexi said in disbelief.

"Yes, girl, it was awful. By the time I got into the meeting, he almost had me convinced that I'd be working for him! When it came time, though, Chris said my name, not his!"

"Won't He do it!" Lexi said, giving me a high five.

"Come through, Jesus!" I said back to Lexi.

"And amen, girl! That is such a blessing. I am so happy for you!"

"Thank you! I'm still processing it all. And then, Chris, our news director, called me into his office. I thought that I was about to have a Me Too moment for real." Lexi's eyes got big. "But it seemed he was trying to encourage me, or give me guidance? I'm not even sure."

"Well, what did he say?"

"He basically said that Scott had outworked me, and that I needed to assert myself."

"Assert yourself? You know what the beginning of *assert* is, right?"

"Exactly! If I had asserted myself any more, then next thing I know, I'm too *aggressive*, right?"

"What'd Janelle Monáe say? Tightrope?"

"Exactly. But, then, get this—Chris said that I got the promotion because he believed more in *my* perspective and *my* potential and that *now* I was going to have to *prove* myself."

Lexi laughed halfheartedly. "Don't we always have to prove ourselves?" she said, as our drinks arrived on the table. We both laughed. "So, have you told Marc? Are you guys back on speaking terms? Or are you getting regular *doctor* visits by now?"

"No, *big* no, and my bad on Dr. Todd. I canceled our date on Saturday to go out with Marc. And that ended *badly*," I said, making the understatement of the year. "He sent me over the edge. Girl, Marc is on some bullshit. He had the nerve to spill his entire guts and *then* tell me after all this time that he doesn't think he wants to get married or have kids! I was like, 'Then what are we doing here?' Girl, you know that's over."

"You have *got* to be kidding me," Lexi said.

"Nope, serious."

"So, what about Todd?"

I sighed. "Girl, I don't know. I want to like him, but I've invested so much time into Marc. There's just something about him that does it for me, you know?"

"Well, from everything I heard, Todd is a great guy. Rob said you were gonna be too . . . Well, he didn't think you were gonna give him a chance."

"He said I was gonna be too what?"

"Girl, never mind what Rob said. He's having a whole secret life, with a wife and two kids at home. He obviously isn't the one to listen to. Do you. If you want to try to work things out with Marc, that's on you to figure out. If you want to see what's up with Todd, I did my part." With that Lexi threw her hands up with a shrug.

"Marc *is* trippin', though. I'm just confused."

"As you *should* be, Tab! But don't be stupid, you need to call Todd. He's a good guy. Marc, I swear. The *nerve* of him wasting your time like that. He *knows* you want to have a family! Honestly, that's one of the reasons that I'm still even thinking about what to do about Rob. I am *not* looking forward to dating. Men out here have seriously lost their minds! And plus, I wouldn't even know where to start looking." Lexi was right, but I didn't have any answers, just more questions. I knew I still wanted Marc to come to his senses. And I knew I wanted to want Todd, but how could I start on something new when my heart was firmly somewhere else?

"Well, it's probably too soon, for both of us. Just know, when you're ready, there are all kinds of apps. I'll show you. You'll have a date in no time . . . that is, if you want one, Sexy Lexi," I said with a sly smile.

"Ha. I probably need to lose a few pounds first," Lexi said with a self-conscious half laugh. "I may not be able to get back to Sexy Lexi, but I can at least be a MILF." At that, we both cracked up.

It felt good to have my friend back. I could still see the sadness behind her eyes, but I could also see something much brighter and more radiant that I hadn't seen in a long time. I hoped that thing, whatever it was, would latch on and grow. And if Lexi getting to a better version of herself meant that I was wrong about my guess on the timing of Rob's return, then I'd very happily stand corrected. It would be worth it.

I had sent a text to Laila earlier, letting her know about my promotion. Leaving Post & Beam, I was surprised not to hear back from her. As I thought about it, she hadn't been in touch as much as usual with no good explanation. I figured that she was spending more time with her Mr. Big, *someone else's husband*, my mind reminded me as I thought about it. Laila was playing with fire, and even on the day of my championship victory, that still had me worried. I sent her another text just as I left the restaurant, asking her to get in touch, and tried to push it out of my mind. If I didn't hear from her by the morning, I'd really have to give her a call.

22

I FINALLY REACHED LAILA, WHO NEVER PROPERLY EXPLAINED HER version of ghosting over the past week or so, but did agree to meet me at the gym for our regular Saturday morning work-out. This time, when Lexi said she would meet us there, I actually believed her. Laila was far less credulous. We stood waiting with ten minutes left before our boot camp class started.

"Do you actually think she's coming, Tab? Lexi hasn't made it here on any Saturday ever," Laila said.

"She said she was! I mean, when I saw her this past week, she was drinking a vodka soda. Have you ever seen Lexi drink a vodka soda?"

"Nah," Laila said. "But that's a pretty good point. Let's call her and find out, 'cause I'm about to go in and get my spot before somebody takes it." I took out my phone and dialed Lexi's number. She answered on the second ring, and sounded breathless. Laila and I both looked mortified, before we realized what was happening.

"Hello," she said, panting.

"Um, Lexi?" I said. "What are you doing? Should we call

you back? It sounds like you're in the middle of something . . . personal."

Lexi laughed, still out of air. "Girl," she breathed the word out. "Nah, I'm on the exercise bike at home. Can't . . . make. It. There. To. Day," she finally pushed out.

"At least you're getting your sweat on!" I said.

"Sounded like you were getting your *swerve* on!" Laila interjected from behind me. I tried not laugh into the phone.

"Told you . . . not playin'," Lexi panted. After two loud breaths, she continued, "Rob . . . had. Some. Thing. Come. Up. So. I have. The . . . Boys. See. You. At. Denisha." I was happy to hear across the line that Lexi was at least getting her own version of a workout in. She might not be doing boot camp with us, but clearly she meant what she said about getting her body back. I hung up with her and followed Laila, who had already left to go inside the classroom.

Boot camp was extra hard, and that day we focused on arms and abs, a painful workout. Laila, with her still lithe figure, usually would be a beast through these types of exercises, working up a sweat twice mine. But today she was taking it extra easy, just gliding through the movements and only halfway doing the crunches.

"Girl, why are you bullshitting?" I asked Laila. "You can't be trying not to mess up your hair!" I whispered, looking at her dreads. Usually Laila was my inspiration to work harder. Today, I was outpacing her so badly that . . . "What is wrong with you? Are you pregnant or something?" I joked with her. She looked back at me seriously.

"Maybe."

What? Oh hell no.

"Maybe?"

"Could be, but probably not. I'm just waiting," Laila said casually.

"Waiting on your period?"

"Something like that." *Something like that?* I hoped that Laila wasn't saying what I thought she was. The train of thought distracted me from my calorie burn, so I left it alone. I made it through the hour, drenched, and finally toweled off. My hair had turned into a puff, in spite of the ponytail that I pulled it into before class. At least I would be seeing Denisha in just a couple of hours. Laila stood next to me drinking out of her water bottle, with just a few small areas of sweat showing on her shirt.

"Girl, what is up with you?" I asked. Laila toweled off longer than necessary, but then finally answered.

"I don't think I'm pregnant, Tab," Laila said reluctantly. "But the reality is that I'm not doing what I need to be doing to be sure I'm not."

"Laila, he's married." I tried my best not to sound judgmental. "Please don't forget that. The other side of that shit is nothing nice. Trust me."

"I know," Laila said resignedly. "The whole thing is a mess, but I'm in it now, so I'm just trying to manage, day by day."

"What's there to manage?' I asked.

"My feelings, for one," Laila said. "By the time I found out he was married, it was too late to back out of how I was *feeling*. I keep trying, but it's not easy, Tab, it's really not."

I thought about this guy and the idea of him prancing around, not wearing his wedding ring, presenting as single, but not being available. It was so selfish, but so common. I tried to imagine my dad doing that, meeting Diane, and

Diane being innocent somehow. The picture didn't fit. I could see Rob doing that, though, a hundred percent. That sounded exactly like something Rob would do. I wondered if this is what his side-chick had been dealing with. She had to be pretty upset to reach out to Lexi on Instagram, of all places. I definitely didn't want Laila to have to deal with some crazed wife looking for her husband.

"But what about his family?" I asked.

"What about his family?" Laila answered quickly. "We don't talk about it and, real talk, his family is *his* responsibility, not mine," she said coarsely. "Look, I know it's not right, and not ideal, but I'm already on max with everything else I'm dealing with. Every time I think about breaking up with him, it makes me sad, just unbearably sad. So, I'm not thinking about that right now. I'm just going with the flow, taking it one day at a time. It'll work itself out." She bent down to stretch, as if to show clearly she was done with the topic. "Enough about Mr. Big, girl! That's not even fun to talk about. Tell me about your promotion! Congratulations!" She gave me a big hug.

"Ew! I'm so sweaty!" I said, trying to hug her back, but backing away at the same time.

"It's cool, we're heading to the showers. I can take a lil' bit of your funky sweat on me for five minutes. Plus, it makes me look like I worked harder," Laila said with a smile.

"The promotion was cool . . ." I said. I was kind of getting tired of telling the story, but I did want Laila's insight on the part that I still didn't understand. "It was cool until Chris told me that he promoted me over Scott just because of my potential and that I needed to earn my spot."

"Well, didn't you earn the spot by getting the promotion?" Laila said, looking genuinely confused.

"See, that's what I thought! But then he said that Scott had been working harder than me—overtalking me in meetings—and that I needed to be more assertive and make my voice heard."

"Damn. That's crazy. Seems like he's in your corner, though," Laila said, scratching her scalp between her dreads. "I wish I had had someone like that in my career, like ever. No one noticed what I did one way or another. I would kill for five minutes of solid feedback."

"I guess," I said uncomfortably, trying to process the new perspective. "Well, you, me, and Lexi need to get together and have a toast. Lots going on these days." I remembered my re-breakup with Marc and that Lexi had a whole life development that she hadn't yet filled Laila in on yet. I wanted to let her do that herself, rather than spill beans at the gym. At the same time, I didn't want to feel like I was lying to Laila. Lexi's split with Rob was something that Laila would probably expect to have been told before now.

Laila and I agreed to meet in the coming week as we headed to our cars in the parking lot. We hugged and then went our separate ways, just like we usually did. Just like normal. So, how could I have known what storm was brewing?

23

SOMETIMES I GOT FED UP MAKING MY WAY TO SEE DENISHA SATurday after Saturday, just to bring my hair into some "presentable" state, light-years away from its natural condition. My standing hair appointment was my most faithfully observed religion, and on this day, I contemplated becoming a heretic.

"Let's just cut it all off," I told Denisha, only half joking.

"Girl, all that long pretty hair you got?" Denisha said. "What you need to do is let me give you some highlights—it would look so pretty on television." And that was enough, just a simple reminder of why I was here, every week, without fail, in Denisha's chair. I couldn't "go natural," I couldn't wear braids, and I couldn't get locs like Laila, whose name was public but whose appearance was always safely concealed behind a computer screen. I envied her freedom and authenticity.

Just slightly over three hours later, I was on my way to Crestmire, with my hair "bouncing and behaving," as my mother liked to call it. Denisha had spent most of the time pitching me story ideas, most of which would have gotten me laughed right out of the newsroom. I was still trying to figure out my "perspective," as Chris called it. The biggest break in my routine came from Lexi, who showed up unusually giddy and finally admitted that she had a date. She installed a dating app on her phone for "practice," as she called it, and lucked upon meeting someone interesting right away. Lexi's new commitment to fitness and vodka sodas had started to pay off, and she was looking much more like MILF material. We talked about maybe going to a movie, but since she had now made other plans, my evening was free.

I found Granny Tab and Ms. Gretchen in Granny Tab's apartment this time. Ms. Gretchen moved about, flashing her neon-yellow nails while making tea for the two of them. Granny Tab was sitting on the sofa.

"Hey hey!" I called out as I came in the door. I was welcomed enthusiastically.

"Well now, Two, I've been dying to ask you! How was your date?!" Granny Tab asked me even before I fully extracted myself from my hug with her.

"Oh, Granny Tab, it didn't go that well."

"Well, that's too bad, sweetheart," Granny Tab said, disappointment on her face. "Didn't he say he wanted to get back together?"

"Yeah, on his terms," I muttered.

"And you told him to kick rocks!" Ms. Gretchen said. "Thatta girl!" She gave me a highlighter-colored thumbs-up from the kitchenette.

"Well, something like that," I said. "At first, he really started to open up to me. He shared about his family—his father . . ." I paused, considering whether I should keep Marc's confidence or tell it all. "His father . . . has a drinking problem. He said that his family was chaotic, in turmoil even, and that he . . . was scared to move forward with marriage or kids."

"Oh, dear," Granny Tab said.

"Well, just what does any of that have to do with you?" Ms. Gretchen said.

"I don't know, I guess for me not to take it personally? I thought that it was endear—" Ms. Gretchen cut me off.

"Disgusting is what it was. Using your compassion and humanity against you like that. Now, that is the lowest of the low."

"You think so?" I asked. "I mean, at first, I did feel like he was playing me. But, since we haven't been speaking, I've had some time to think, and I guess I thought it was endearing . . . well, at least the sharing part was."

"Endearing?" Ms. Gretchen said. "Plheh. It's a trap. They get you all open emotionally and then start asking you to make all kinds of compromises. Make you forget about what you really want. Good dick'll do that to you too if you don't watch out."

"Gretchen!"

"Tabitha!" Ms. Gretchen mocked my grandmother again in their familiar game of feigned indignation.

"Maybe he'll come around," Granny Tab said. "But probably no sense just waiting on him until he does, I agree with that. Don't keep all your eggs in one basket." I thought about Todd again. He hadn't called, and neither had I. Maybe I needed to change that. Granny Tab broke my thoughts. "So, what about this promotion? You said that you got it. I'm so proud of you!"

My spirit sank a bit. She was so excited that I was almost

too embarrassed to tell her the rest of the truth of what happened. But my grandmother was my safest place.

"I'm excited, but I'm still a little confused. It was almost like my boss said I got the promotion because I'm Black." My grandmother blinked her blue eyes at me in surprise.

"Well," Granny Tab said slowly, "from what I've seen in *my* lifetime, it's great that somebody would get something *good* on account of being Black."

"But, Granny Tab, if that's the case, it makes me feel like I'm not talented—or not good enough to make it on my own."

"Only a *fool* would think that anything they've done was on their own, Tabby," Ms. Gretchen said. "Nobody makes it on their own—at least, not anywhere worthwhile."

"Two, if only you knew how much things have changed. I don't know that you'd be thinking so much about these kinds of details that you can't control. You better just take the good that's coming to you," Granny Tab said, adjusting her position on the sofa and putting her feet up on the ottoman. *Oh no, swelling again.* She continued, "Remember my childhood friend, Evelyn? The one who lived next door and used to sneak me into dance parties? Well, she was the valedictorian of her high school, and you know what? She couldn't even go to the college that was right in our hometown. Nope, she had to go almost two hundred miles away to the colored school, West Virginia State. Was that what she *deserved*? I've told you, Two, I used to think to myself when I was growing up, *Black girls, they sure must die exhausted.* So many battles to fight, through segregation, Jim Crow, which I saw firsthand, up through Civil Rights, and today, even. I know it must feel like a lot," she said, concern in her wrinkled face.

"All this nonsense about being exhausted, Tabitha," Ms. Gretchen interjected. "I say don't ever die of exhaustion on somebody else's terms!" As if on cue, the teapot on the stove started to whistle. Ms. Gretchen pulled it off and set it aside. "Whatever life you can get your hands on, you've got to live it right out to the corners. When I die, I want to skid into heaven with the last wheel falling off," Ms. Gretchen said with a Cheshire cat smile. You couldn't help but laugh. She motioned me over. "Tabby, come take over for me with your grandmother's tea. You know this is my time to go run my errands. You go ahead and take my cup." She gave a wink while gathering her belongings. "Tabitha, I'll see you again this evening." Ms. Gretchen shot a beeline look to my grandmother, told me bye, and then bolted out of the door. I pulled out the Lipton tea bags, poured the hot water, and brought the two cups over to the sofa to sit next to my grandmother.

"That Gretchen, I tell ya'. She's always sayin' something, doing something. She's toooo much," Granny Tab said with a smile.

"Has she always been like this?" I asked.

"Always has been. I reckon she will be until the day she dies."

I thought about Alexis. I couldn't imagine us being separated like Granny Tab and her friend Evelyn were.

"Granny Tab, were you sad when your best friend had to go away for college?"

"I was, Two. It was *terrible*. I was just a mediocre student, but that was enough to get *me* into the local university right next to home. I never understood how someone so bright and intelligent as Evelyn would have had to go so far away, just on account of her skin color. That's why, when I fell pregnant with your father, I knew there was no way that I'd let anyone separate us. Not me from him, not your grandfather from us. No way."

"And that's how you wound up in California."

"Pretty much. Your grandfather joined the service. That was how he was able to secure some income for us straight-away. I was pregnant and nineteen and didn't have much education. And you know, at that time, it wasn't even legal for us to get married where we lived. That's why we had to get far away from West Virginia and not look back."

"Don't you miss your family?" I asked.

"I got my family sitting right here." She patted my leg. "What's there to miss?" *Family*. It's true that Granny Tab was my family. My closest family. It was strange to hear that, at one time, we were meant to be pushed apart by arbitrary designations.

"Granny Tab, can I ask you a silly question?" I asked, even though I already knew I could ask my grandmother anything. But this time, what I wanted to know felt foreign as a thought, and strange coming from my lips. "What does it feel like to be white?"

My grandmother absorbed my words, took a deep breath, took off her glasses, and squinted just a bit, which told me she was thinking.

"Hmmm. I've asked myself the same question on occasion, when I was reminded of it, most of the time by cruel people when I was with my son . . . your father," she said quickly, touching my knee. "I'd look at him sometimes, and look at me and wonder how we could live in a world that treated the two of us so differently, when he came from my own body. My skin color changed in the sun too, just like his, like yours—just not as dark, but believe me, I tried," she said with a smile, running her pale fingers soothingly across my golden-brown arm. "I'd try to think, was 'white' a hair texture? A state of mind? I never could put my finger on it. Maybe it was just what we were told it was supposed to be, 'cause I have never *felt* white." My grandmother shook her head softly before continuing. "So, the best I can tell you is that as I've experienced it, it's more of a what it's not than a what it is. I mean, I got reminded of being a woman all the time, but being white?" She brought her hand to her face and gently rubbed her cheek. "Sometimes, when there's no friction, no reminder of what you can't do, it feels like a hole that needs to be filled with something—so desperately. Filled so that there *is* a something. Your dad, then you . . . my grandchildren, you have been my greatest something. And I don't know that there is any more than that."

We sat still for a moment after that, both of us contemplating her words. It was some time before she spoke again. "I never thought to ask it of anyone, not even your dad, whose whole life I watched. Yours too. I guess I thought I understood from observation. And it never occurred to me how silly that might be not to ask, until just now. I reckon I should ask you, Two, what's it feel like to be Black? Do you consider yourself Black?"

I laughed a bit in answering. "I don't think I have much of a choice, Granny Tab," I said with a smile. "To consider myself Black or not Black, I mean. Society just looks at me and sees a Black woman, no matter what I have to say about it."

"I suppose you're right, Two," Granny Tab said pensively.

"How does it feel?" I continued, trying to think and still talk. I'd honestly never considered the question before, not while living it. "I can tell you that your thought, about it being exhausting, that sounds about right sometimes. A lot of times it *does* feel exhausting. Because everything bad in society is about you, but when it comes to the good, nothing is *for* you. I feel like I'm not enough and too much, all at the same time. And then, other times, being Black feels exhilarating—because *every* good thing that happens feels like a victory, even the small things. Because you're constantly reminded that you're an *other*, so you know whatever good happened *in spite of.* So there's celebration, there's joy." I paused, just to think. It felt so complicated. I pushed myself to find more, in the deeper parts, hidden in the folds of my spirit—the secrets. "And emptiness is there too—a different kind from what you described, though. A need for . . . validation, maybe to be seen, approved of, to matter as an individual, not just a monolith. And a desire to know that if I do follow *all* the rules, that I get the promise on the other side, just like anyone else. And by anyone else, I mean anyone else who is *white.*"

"It hurts my heart to think about it sometimes," Granny Tab said softly. "When your dad was just a little baby, I held him in my arms and I felt so powerless. I loved him so much and wanted the world to love him too. Why wouldn't they, I thought. I was naïve back then." She turned away pensively, letting the weight of a lifetime of memories press her shoulders into a slouch. She turned back to me with tears in her eyes. "I couldn't always protect him."

I wanted to move to hug her, but I had hot tea on my lap. She quickly wiped the tears away. "Could you get me a tissue, Two?" she asked before I could move toward her. "It seems that there's something in my eye."

I returned with the tissue in hand, gave it to her, and sat back down. The moment had allowed her to recompose herself. To think of it, the only time I had ever seen Granny Tab cry herself was when I left for college. She said the same thing then: "I guess I must have something in my eye." I smiled at the memory.

"Granny Tab," I said, "can I ask you another question?"

"Of course, sweetheart."

"If you could," I began, thinking while speaking strange-tasting words, "would you choose to be Black, like me and my dad?"

Granny Tab took another deep breath, so deep this time I could see her aged diaphragm struggle to expand that far, staggering her inhale at the end of it. She paused for a moment longer before beginning to speak.

"I don't suppose I would," she said. "I'm sure I wouldn't have lasted this long if I were." She paused to smile at me. "There's a world on the inside that I don't pretend to understand. I just remember drying tears and feeling the panic of wanting to protect those who I loved from a world that decided on hating them. I remember the fear, thinking I would be separated from your grandfather when it mattered most— when he was all that your dad and I had. That was *hard*. But I didn't have to *wear* it every day. I can't say that I could have," she said, searching my face. Her denim-colored eyes looked like tiny oceans as they filled with water. She dabbed them with another tissue, and only then did I even notice that she had taken my hand. "Two, you don't have to answer this if you don't want to, but I suppose I'll ask it all the same," she said, squeezing my hand. "If you could . . . have the choice to be white, to have the world see you as white, would you want that?" she asked.

As I thought about it, images flashed through my mind, of Officer Mallory, of Chris, of Diane, my mom, my dad, of Scott Stone and Lisa at work, of Marc and even Todd, and then Laila, Alexis, and my godson Lexington with his huge doe eyes. I took a moment to consider my next words. I spoke to myself as much as I did to my grandmother. "Somehow, being Black is not who I am, at least, not all that I am. But I know, at least in some way, it's *made* me who I am. So, I wouldn't trade, Granny Tab. I'd wanna stay who I am."

Granny Tab squeezed my hand again. My grandmother smiled her biggest smile. I smiled back at her. I didn't say it, but she'd made me who I was as well.

"You know, Tabby, I wanted to tell you. Gretchen, God bless her, she's always got something to say. I wish I had some of her spunk when I was younger." I smiled again to think of a young Granny Tab. Granny Tab met me with a look of seriousness that made me stiffen a bit in anticipation of what she was preparing to say. "But I need to tell you, I disagree with Gretchen about Marc. It's sometimes too easy to throw a person away, Tabby. Sometimes his fumbling around through bad decisions can make you forget that a man has his whole future ahead of him. People can change. Well, if he keeps trying. And that's the rare type, Two. Not the guy who's got it all figured out, but the one who keeps trying to sort out his mess."

"But, Granny Tab, don't you think he's wasting my time?

He said he doesn't want to get married, or have kids!" I whined back.

"Seems like he said he doesn't know yet," Granny Tab said. "I'm not saying that you should wait around. Maybe you're doing the right thing by moving on. Maybe you just need to date someone else for a while. Sometimes a man has to sit in his stink long enough, and you don't need to be there for that. Live your life, Two, but just give him the chance to come back around. That's all I'm saying. Your Marc seems like he could be the rare type."

"I'll think about it, Granny Tab, I really will," I said.

"Your dad is the rare type." Her words took me by surprise. *My dad?*

"I don't think so, Granny Tab," I said. "He's seemed pretty consistent to me."

"That's because you haven't given him a chance to show you," Granny Tab said. "Why don't you ever show up for dinner?"

"You know weekends were always my days with Marc," I said, more defensively than I would have liked to. "I couldn't," I said weakly.

"You can *now*," Granny Tab stressed. "Go tonight, for me." I thought about it. Normally, I would do anything for my grandmother. This was asking a lot. But she never asked me for anything, and she was right, I could. I guess I also wanted to talk to my dad and get his perspective on what Chris said. I'd have to deal with Diane, but the advice could be worth the pain and suffering this time.

"Okay," I told Granny Tab. "You're right—tonight I can. I'll go. Just for you." Granny Tab leaned forward and used both of her arms to wrap me in a hug. "Do you want to ride with me to Calabasas?" I asked. Granny Tab's face fell.

"I wish I could go tonight, sweetheart. I would just love to see all my babies together in the same place. But I promised Gretchen that I'd have dinner with her and watch Netflix."

"Granny, you and Ms. Gretchen are gonna Netflix and chill?" I asked with a light giggle.

"What's that?" Granny Tab asked.

"Never mind," I said, smiling. "Never mind."

24

THE ROBOTIC VOICE OF MY NAVIGATION APP ANNOUNCED THAT THE exit to my dad's Calabasas home was coming up in half a mile. The warm feeling of this being a good idea had already faded about fifteen miles back. Sheer dread had crept its way into my car and was now firmly strapped into the passenger seat, its clammy hand wrapped in a squeeze around my insides. I reached the guardhouse in front of gigantic gates walling off the entrance to the community. After this long of a drive, and the cost of living in this part of the LA suburbs, I couldn't imagine whom the gates were actually keeping out. The person who really needed a security gate was me, around my downtown condo building.

"Hi there," I said to the guard, rolling down my window. "I'm heading to the Walker residence."

"Your name, please?" he asked me politely, holding a clipboard.

"Tabitha Walker."

"Oh. Can you pass me your ID?" he asked. I handed it to him, and he compared it against the white sheet of paper on his clipboard.

"Just one second. I need to check a different list." He turned back into the little tan-colored Spanish-tile houselette and started flipping through a stack of notecard-size papers in a box, sitting on the desk. He must not have found what he was looking for because he flipped through twice and then walked back over to my window and handed me back my ID. "I'm sorry, ma'am, I'm going to have to call up to the house and get an okay from the Walkers. I don't have you on the pre-cleared list or the family list." *Of course you don't, I guess that figures.*

I told him that was fine and waited patiently while he dialed my father's house as I sat in my car studying the closed gates and their ornate wrought iron detailing, painted the same bisque color as the guardhouse. I overheard the faint sound of Diane's voice floating out of the space between the phone and his ear. Finally, the fancy iron gates opened their mouth to swallow me in.

Driving up to my father's house, I realized I had forgotten how nice it was, and how nice his neighborhood was in general. Or, maybe, I had just pushed it out of my mind. Expensive European sports cars dotted the street, serving as upscale graffiti in front of immaculate homes. My dad and Diane bought their place at the end of the cul-de-sac just before Dixie, their youngest daughter, was born. *My little sister.* Technically, Dixie *was* my little sister, as was Danielle, the older of the two. It was Danielle who opened the door. She was thirteen and almost as tall as me. I had her by less than a half an inch. She had the same long, flat and lean figure that I'd had at her age and, looking into her face, she could almost be my hazel-eyed, light-skinned twin. Even with those features, Danielle showed much more of our shared ethnicity than Dixie, who could have almost been cleaved from Diane as a clone. Dixie bounded down the steps into the foyer just as Danielle shouted, "Dad! Tabby's here!" Danielle looked back to me standing in the doorway. "Are you coming in?" she asked with the usual teenage sarcasm of thinking you're smarter than everyone, including your idiot big sister. *Big sister. I'm these girls' big sister.* "Dad's in his study. Mom is in the kitchen," Danielle said as she turned to walk across the marble toward the back part of the house.

"Is Tanner here this weekend?" I called after her. He was away for college, but on the off chance he decided to visit, I wasn't up for any surprises.

"He only comes home for holidays," Danielle called back without so much of a swivel back in my direction. My sigh of relief was cut short by another voice echoing into the foyer.

"Hi, Tabby!" Dixie called out as she bounded down the stairs toward me. Except for our nose, which we shared with our grandmother, absolutely no one would think that Dixie and I were related at all, let alone half sisters. In her appearance, all of the Caucasian genes from both sides converged into a bright-blue-eyed, straight-haired, sun-kissed brunette who wouldn't have even been questioned if she tried to go to Granny Tab's local university back in the day. She ran up to me, seemingly oblivious to the fact that we were almost strangers, with almost a year since we had last seen each other, and wrapped her gangly arms around me at my waist. Hugging her back, I pushed away a small pang of regret for not knowing her better. *Diane's fault*, my mind gave me as the perfect exit from that thinking.

"Hey, Dixie!" I said, hugging her back. "How are you? How's school?" It occurred to me I knew less of what to ask her than I would Rob Jr. or Lexington, who actually weren't that far off in age. Thankfully, my dad took me off the hook from having to come up with conversation with my little nine-year-old alien, filling the entryway with his booming voice.

"Tabby! I'm so glad you made it!" He seemed genuinely excited as he walked toward me from the direction of his study, his arms already extended to give me a big hug. "I'm so happy to see you, baby girl!" My dad squeezed me like I might change my mind at any moment and run back to my own comforts of Downtown LA.

"Hey, Dad!" I said. "Good to see you." It was nice to not have to say things I didn't mean. Even if I didn't exactly want to admit it, it *was* good to see him.

"It's *great* to see you!" he said with the ebullience of a master politician. "Come on, let's head back. Diane is in the kitchen." Ugh, *Diane.* As we walked back, following the same path Danielle took earlier, I tried to imagine my dad's neat head of dime-size curls and receding hairline embodied as an afro attempt, propped up by Aqua Net. I had to stifle my laughter. "What?" he asked, turning to look at me.

"Nothing . . . well, just that Granny Tab told me that you might have had an afro once," I told him.

"Oh Lord, not *that* disaster. I can't believe she told you that!"

"Dad, you had an afro?" Dixie said, looking up at him.

"That was a long time ago, Dixie—in college."

"Could I have an afro too, Dad?" asked Dixie innocently. My dad and I both shared a laugh between wiser adults. I waited to see how he was going to answer this question.

"Probably not, Dix," my dad said. "Your hair's not curly enough."

"Well, what if I want one?" Dixie said.

"You'll have to ask your mother," my dad bunted. "I don't know anything about styling women's hair." He placed his hand on top of her head, messing up the top of the thick layers hanging down her back.

"Mom!" Dixie yelled out, skipping ahead of us. "How do I get my hair in an afro?" My dad and I laughed.

"Oh boy," he said. "Now I'm going to have to rescue Diane."

We made our way into the expansive kitchen. Diane was moving frenetically between the center island and the stove top, setting things into serving trays and clanking, clacking, and shuffling in all manner of ways.

"Girls!" she said to Danielle and Dixie. "Go wash your hands and then come get the table set up." She wiped her hands on her apron and looked up at me, smiling wider than I remember being accustomed to. "Tabby! Hi! I'm so glad to see you! I heard that you might make it for dinner this time!" She came in for a hug. I hugged her back feebly.

"Hi, Diane. Yes, I'm glad I could make it too. It's been very busy at work . . . and stuff . . ." I said, searching my mind for better excuses.

"I understand. I heard you got a promotion! Congratulations! We're all so proud of you." She was beaming. News traveled fast among the Walkers. I imagined my mother in this moment, what she would say. I'm sure she'd tell Diane that she could save her pride for her own children. The thought made me smile a bit.

"Thanks, Diane. It was definitely a relief to finally find out." I was trying my best to be polite. She smiled, and then looked past me to my dad.

"Paul!" she said. "Can you help here? I need to get some of this stuff from the stove to the island to serve it."

"Whoa there, baby. I did my part—I've got the carne asada just right out there on the grill. How about I bring that in, and maybe Tabby can give you a hand with the oven," said my dad, the master of creating both awkward moments *and* awkward childhoods.

"Tabby, do you mind?" Diane asked.

"No, not at all," I said, heading over to help. *At least she asked nicely.* Soon enough we had all of the food set out and everyone circled the island, heaping a Mexican-inspired feast onto our plates.

The table conversation was polite but mostly empty. We didn't come near any of the subjects that my friends and I normally discussed, like politics or work or relationship issues. Most of the topics were brought up by the girls or had to do with the girls—what they were doing in school this week, when their next sports game was, and where they were thinking about going for a family vacation. I was just hoping for it all to wrap up soon enough, so that I could get to my real reason for coming—I needed to talk to my dad. As we all got up to clear the table, I maneuvered to his side, trying to create privacy in a room full of other people.

"Dad, could I talk to you for a minute? Alone?" I asked.

He looked around surprised, and then to me. "Sure, Tabby. Let's go to my study." He called out, "Girls, Tabby and I are gonna go to my study and chat for a bit. We'll be back."

"Can I come?" Dixie called out.

"You can come in in thirty minutes, Dix!" my dad said after she came up, giving him the doe-eyed treatment.

"But I want to talk to Tabby too!" Dixie said, walking away. Her words surprised me. *She wants to talk to me?* I was confused. I hadn't spent much time with the girls, even after Diane tried to guilt me while I was in college for not coming to see them, aka babysit. That guilting continued until it was time to go to grad school, and in part I was glad to be going out of state for two years of relief from the constant pressure of Diane's exigencies. They started extending the invitations to the weekend dinners a few years ago. Granny Tab would come almost every week, while I would make a few a year. It wasn't the girls' fault how their parents' relationship had started. Then again, it wasn't mine either. But, still, we all had no choice but to be a part of living out the consequences.

My dad closed the door behind us in his dark mahogany wood–accented study and motioned toward the brown distressed leather sofa that crinkled beneath us as we sat on its cushions.

"So, what's up?" My dad crossed his leg at the knee and stretched his arm comfortably across the back of the sofa.

I fumbled a bit for the most efficient words to tee up my question, but I found them soon enough. "I thought maybe you could help me understand something . . . about work," I said.

"Okay . . ."

"When I got the promotion—"

"Congratulations again, by the way. That is just so awesome!"

"Thank you," I said, probably a little too quick for wanting to get to the real issue. "So, right after I got the promotion, Chris, he's our news director—our boss—right after he announced it, he called me into his office."

"Hold up—I'm not going to have to get my gun, am I?" my dad said, half joking.

"No! No, nothing like that. Although even I wasn't exactly sure at first," I said, letting out a light laugh. "Chris called me into his office and told me that Scott Stone, my competition, had outworked me, but he gave me the promotion anyway." I watched my dad's eyebrows rise. "Right? And he said that he thought the station needed my *perspective*. Is that code for something racial?" I asked.

"Did you ask him?" my dad shot back at me.

"Actually, I did."

"And?"

"He said I got the job because I was 'unique.'"

"Unique, hmmm . . ."

"Yeah, unique. And then he said I didn't deserve the position, but he believed that I could work my way into deserving it, and he wanted me to start asserting myself more and fighting to make my perspective heard."

"That sounds like good advice."

"It does?"

"Sounds reasonable to me. The guy had his choice of who he wanted to promote, and he picked the person who he thought would make for the best stories and highest ratings. At the end of the day, ratings *are* what it's about, right? I don't think that somebody worried about ratings would be throwing someone in a prominent position on television just because they're Black, Tabby. Seems like it would be more so in spite of, no?" *In spite of . . .*

"So, you don't think it was just because I'm Black—like it could have been some kind of diversity thing, or something . . ."

"Tabby, if that's the case, that would be the dumbest

diversity initiative ever and you should find a new job, because that station is going under," my dad said with a half
flippant expression. "Nobody, and I mean *nobody*, in business
is risking their job *or* their company just to promote a Black
person. No way. If you got that promotion, it had to be ratings
driven. Plain and simple."

"I get it . . ." I said quietly, still processing the irrefutabil-
ity of his words.

"And, it sounds like this Chris, the news director, might
be a good mentor for you. He gave you solid advice."

I was silent for a while, debating if I should bring up Marc.
There was something even more pressing that I wanted to
know. I sat there for a few minutes hesitating over the abrupt
change of subject.

"I know this is a completely different subject, but . . . you
know when Granny Tab told me about your afro, she told me
that you did it to try to impress my mom . . ." I said, smiling.

"I don't know if that part is *completely* true. I was trying
to be cooool," my dad said in the most uncool dad kind of
way. I laughed.

"I need to ask you something else . . . It's pretty personal,"
I said.

"Whatever it is, I'll try to answer," my dad said earnestly.

"What made you stop trying . . . with my mom?"

My dad moved almost immediately from his relaxed posture to a stiffened position. He brought his hand to his chin,
rubbing it there while his eyes shifted to indicate he was
thinking. He let out a deep sigh.

"I wouldn't say that I or *we* stopped trying. It's just that
we reached the end of our . . . *capabilities*," he said slowly,

seeming to search for and select each word with full intention.

"But then, you had more capabilities with Diane?" I asked.

"At first, I might have thought that with Diane it was . . . easier. It felt easier at the beginning. But looking back today, we've had to deal with the exact same problems, just over a longer period of time. Your mom needed changes I wasn't ready to make. That I didn't know *how* to make."

"And Diane?"

"Diane . . . she . . . probably needed the same things. She just made me feel like . . . she made me feel like I couldn't fail her. Like no matter what I did, it wouldn't change her view of me. Does that make sense? I guess I needed that."

"Have . . . you ever cheated on Diane?"

My dad recoiled as if I had physically pushed him. He took in a sharp breath. The surprise on his face looked almost like he had been attacked. His eyes narrowed at me, and then softened. Then he looked worried. And then, he finally spoke.

"I . . . don't want to lie to you, Tabby." Those words hung in the air with no follow-up for too many critical seconds not to be a final answer. "Why do you ask that?" he said finally.

"Rob cheated on Lexi. She found out just after her birthday. Some girl he met shopping." I said it all in a deluge, sounding close to what I used to sound like as a little girl. "They're separated, and have been over a month now."

My dad's look of concern deepened. "And you want to know, what? Do all men cheat?"

"Marc and I broke up too," I said in response to his question. "Not cheating. At least, I don't think it was. He said he didn't know what he wanted for the future with me. Evidently, his dad is sick and his family is all screwed up. And I'm . . . I'm just confused. *Everything* that I was *so* sure of just isn't turning out to be what it seemed."

My dad shook his head, still saying nothing, wringing his hands now, and he leaned forward with his upper body supported by his tentpoled forearms anchored against his thighs. He took another deep breath and sat upright. "Tabby, I can't speak for all men. But what I will say for myself—what your mother needed from me was on the other side of some damage that she didn't cause."

"And what about Diane?"

"Diane didn't necessarily have different needs. But the timing was different. We almost split too. On several occasions." I looked at him with the surprise of what I had just heard. *They had?* "I guess part of why we stayed together through it all was because we both felt that we *had* to." I looked at him, waiting for him to continue. "And then one day, after the hell and fighting, and even packing up to go . . . you just know you're going to make it. I'm not happier in my relationship with Diane because I'm with someone other than your mom. I'm happier because *I'm* someone other than *who I was* when I was with your mom. Do you understand that?"

"Yeah," I said, my voice almost a whisper. "I get it."

"Tabby, no matter what it is, work, Marc, whatever, stop doubting yourself so much. Just stay true to who *you* are and what *you* want. Why compromise? Nothing is ever going to be worth it if you have to. Not on that level." He leaned over to give me a hug. It was a comfort that was easy to get lost in and a moment I wished wouldn't end. So I savored the small talk of catching up until almost exactly on cue, we could hear the knock of nine-year-old knuckles on the door.

"Can I come in now?" Dixie yelled. "You said thirty minutes!"

"So, you wanna take Dixie home with you?" my dad said, laughing.

"Come on in, Dixie!" I yelled at the door to my *little sister*.

25

THE FIRST OPPORTUNITY TO TRULY FEEL THANKFUL FOR MY NEW office came when my computer screamed at me *"Egg Freezing Consultation This Afternoon!!!"* with a calendar reminder in the center of the screen. My appointment date with Dr. Young had finally arrived. Not that I had forgotten in the least. When I thought about Marc, I thought about Dr. Young. When I thought about Dr. Todd, I thought about Dr. Young. When I was at work and meetings got boring, I thought about Dr. Young. Dr. Young was my insurance policy when men and time and my janky ovaries had failed me. In fact, without really knowing why, I had taken extra care in getting dressed this morning, all for this afternoon. I even wore red lipstick. I had been waiting on this appointment since that fateful day when I learned about the condition of my fertility, and the buzzer was running out on the clock.

Dr. Young's office was in a ritzy, high-end Century City medical building, complete with valet parking, which still didn't make me feel any better about the price tag for the egg-freezing procedure. For what I had heard of the costs, I expected a lot more handholding and a luxury office appointed with expensive Danish interior design elements. Instead, I arrived at a relatively lackluster lobby to check in with the front desk clerk, who seemed like she hadn't quite managed to fully wake herself for the day, even though it was late in the afternoon. Now I longed for the overly perky assistant whom I had spoken with on the phone.

"Ms. Walker, do you have your insurance card?" I handed it to her. "Thank you. I'll just need to make a copy. Looking at your new patient report, it appears that you have infertility diagnosis coverage, but not infertility treatment coverage. That means today's appointment will be covered, but any subsequent treatment you choose will be out of pocket." It felt to me that a statement like that would be followed by an "Okay?" type of question. Instead, the receptionist handed my insurance card off to another person and continued to look at her computer screen. I imagined the other side was continually running an escalating tally, like an out-of-control old-fashioned cash register.

"Do you have an estimate of what the out-of-pocket costs would be?" I asked.

"The doctor will go over your treatment plan during your appointment, and then the billing manager will discuss pricing with you just after," she said in a rehearsed and robotic tone while continuing to type. Again, I felt the absence of a missing "Okay?" at the end of her phrase, but I was starting to get the sense that this would be a theme. I followed her instructions to take a seat and used the opportunity to discreetly study my waiting room cohort while hiding my own face behind a magazine that I was only pretending to read. There were two hetero couples in the room, and then two women, each alone, like me, and a man sitting alone as well. I wondered for a second why the man sitting alone would be in an IVF clinic, and then I remembered that Dr. Young also collected male "contributions" at his office for sperm banks. I wondered briefly if the guy sitting there could be my baby daddy. He looked nothing like Marc, which maybe now was a good thing in my book. I studied his height, his physique, his eyes, his nose, and his mouth . . . ah, he wears glasses? Hmmm, does that mean my baby would have bad eyesight? *Books or burrito?* My mind wandered, thinking back to my conversation with my mother. It was impossible to tell based on the simple LA-type casual dress he wore, but my eyes landed on the book bag at his feet, which told a different story. *Ah, books!* I allowed the slight feeling of hopeful vindication to wash over me as I heard my name being called through a newly opened door near the receptionist's desk.

"This is your first time seeing Dr. Young?" the nurse asked, escorting me to my exam room.

"Yes, and I'm a little nervous," I said.

"Oh, don't be. You'll love Dr. Young. He's a real character," she said, following with a giggle. I removed everything of my wardrobe except for my red lipstick, replacing the clothes with paper garments that made for easy access to all of my so-called private regions. Dr. Young came in after a little wait, accompanied by another female nurse, a new face. He was a relatively short, late-middle-aged man with thinning hair and an obvious inky-black dye job. He wore his white doctor's coat over khakis and a button-down and sported wire-rimmed glasses.

"Ms. Walker . . . Tabitha, is it okay if I call you Tabitha?"

Dr. Young asked. *Finally, someone in here asks me if something is okay with me.* The sincerity reflected in Dr. Young's slightly accented English put me more at ease.

"Sure," I said.

"So, Tabitha, you're here to do egg freezing? Or you're here to get pregnant?" Dr. Young asked me life-altering questions as casually as someone taking a lunch order. *Whoa, Doc, hold on. I'm here for options, not insemination.*

"Just the egg-freezing option, please. I'm not ready to get pregnant just yet."

"Hmph," Dr. Young said, looking up at me over his glasses while he continued to study my chart. "Bad numbers. You need to start right now, do you know that?"

"Dr. Ellis said . . . I mean . . . yes, I was informed that I needed to take immediate action," I said, feeling a rising level of panic.

"We'll run some tests if we can today. You can start in two weeks with your next cycle. We're going to aim for twenty eggs total. So you . . . you're probably going to have to do two or three times." *Two or three times?* Again, this was a moment where I was expecting to hear "Okay?" at the end, but it never came.

"Um, Dr. Young, when do we discuss how much all of this costs?" I asked.

"The billing manager will discuss with you. My job is just to make babies," he said, smiling. "Are you currently using birth control?" *Shit.*

"Umm . . . no. Not currently."

"No birth control?" He looked up at me again over his glasses. I felt my face flush.

"No, no birth control. I was taking the pill and then I . . . stopped."

"You're using condoms then?" Dr. Young asked me.

"Um," I said, stalling for a better answer. "Um, some of the time?" I said, trying not to lie.

"You trying to get pregnant?" *Obviously . . . not?*

"Well, eventually, but not necessarily right now."

"Not right now? Then you must use birth control!" Dr. Young brought new animation into the room. "Do you know that fifty percent of pregnancies are unplanned?! How do you think they happened?" He looked at me, and I sat mouth agape, unsure if he wanted me to answer. I was just reclaiming control of my speech when he continued. "No birth control! No condoms!" he said with his arms in the air. "Anything can happen! If you use no birth control, no condoms, you walk down the street, the wind blows, and poof! You get pregnant! A bird poops on your shoulder and you get pregnant! You want to get pregnant walking down the street?" He said this with full passion this time, waving my chart in his free hand and a pen in the other.

I didn't know whether to laugh or cry, and I was completely unsure if he expected an answer. Given my compromised fertility, part of me felt oddly flattered by his sudden display of optimism. Or, maybe he just said this to everyone. After a long silence with him continuing to look at me, I assumed I was supposed to respond this time.

"Um, no, Dr. Young, not walking down the street," I said, watching the nurse behind him roll her eyes slightly and cover her mouth to stifle a laugh.

"Then you must use some form of birth control." He sternly turned his attention back to my chart. We stayed silent for the surprisingly brief exam and after as Dr. Young scribbled his notes in the file. "Okay, see you in two weeks," he finally said. "We get eggs now, make a baby later. But *you* don't make a baby. Use protection." And with that, he handed my chart to the nurse and walked out of the door. The nurse used that opportunity to release a light spray of laughter she had obviously been holding in. I sat in stunned silence, feeling a strange mix of emotion, like I had just been scolded by my father.

"Dr. Young, he's a character," the nurse said.

"So I've heard."

It was finally time to see the all-knowing billing manager to determine my financial fate.

"Dr. Young said that he wants to get you started right away. Do you have an idea of how you'll be financing?"

I had planned on draining the marrow out of my savings, but if there was another way, I wanted to know. "I was planning on using savings, but are there other options?" I asked.

"Well, some people use savings, or have family to help. Some people go into different kinds of debt, second mortgage on their home, credit card debt, personal loans . . ." the billing manager said, with complete disaffection for the major life events that she was describing.

"People have to mortgage their home?" I asked, feeling my eyes widen.

"Well, if that option is available to them, yes, sometimes," she said, entirely unmoved.

"Well . . . how much . . . does it cost?" I asked.

"Here's a list of our plans." She slid a photocopied piece of paper over to me. I studied it. It appeared that each round, taking into account medication and the cost of the procedure and office visits was a minimum of about $12,000. *Shit.* And evidently, with my numbers, the medications could run even more expensive than what I calculated. Two or three rounds? That was $36,000, or more! That meant that I was in for my savings and then some. The savings that I had worked for years to build. But I had no choice, and no time to think of missed vacations and meals with friends and wardrobes that I wore well past the point of replacement. "You make a deposit today of two thousand to make your appointment for two weeks from now." I was becoming used to the drill in this office. I reluctantly handed over my credit card and watched my dreams of a starter home being swiped away.

I made my appointment for two weeks later and left Dr. Young's office in a mix of relief and sadness. I had saved for years for a completely different purpose. Now my entire savings would go into a bank of an entirely different type. And, to top it all off, I needed to go buy condoms. These days, in my life, especially lately, you could never know which way the wind was gonna blow.

26

LEAVING MY APPOINTMENT, I DEBATED GOING BACK TO WORK, BUT this level of sticker shock needed special attention from my friends. Waiting for my car from valet, I shot out the Bat-Signal to Alexis and Laila.

Me:

Leaving Dr., about to be broke. Happy hour?

Lexi:

Oooh! Egg freezing appt? How did it go?

Me:

Terrible, need cheap drinks ASAP.

Laila:

Cheap works for me too. I'm game.

Laila responded? I was glad—she had been extra MIA lately.

Lexi:

Come to my open house? Lots of free drinks.

Me:

And random ppl?

Lexi:

> No, will be over early. Leftover wine is fair game.

Laila:

> Address?

    Laila's message sealed the deal. Driving over, I couldn't help but laugh at the irony, thinking that I had just received confirmation that I was going to have to empty my savings and here I was on the way to an open house. I wondered when I'd be able to again find myself in a position as a buyer. Los Angeles was expensive, and rent for my downtown loft wasn't cheap. Even with a promotion, my salary was just barely covering the gulf of my expenses. If Granny Tab weren't living at Crestmire, I'd think about living with her all over again. Unfortunately, she'd decided to sell the condo to pay for the cost of Crestmire, not wanting to lean on my dad and Diane in any way. Not that they ever offered to help.

    I pulled up at the address of Lexi's listing and sat in my car for just a moment, watching through the passenger-side window as stragglers toddled out of a stylized wooden door. Lexi specialized in rehabilitations and flips, and this was a property that I remembered she had been working on for a while. It was a house that looked just like one I would otherwise be in the market to buy. Perhaps, I'd even be at this open house—as a *buyer*, not an interloper to drink free booze at the end. The thin paper with pricing options for egg freezing lay on my front seat. Also fitting. It literally sat between me and what could have been the house of my dreams.

    After enough lamenting, and being satisfied that all of Lexi's home-purchasing visitors had departed, I hopped out of my car and went inside. She had done an incredible job with the redesign. Dark hardwood panels greeted my feet on the floor, and a bright, airy modern interior welcomed me inside. I could see Lexi moving around in the kitchen through the expertly staged living room area that I walked into.

"Hey, Lexi!" I called out to her. It looked like I had timed it correctly. The place was empty.

"Hey, Tab, come on back to the kitchen. I'm just cleaning up. Pour yourself a glass of wine."

"Lexi, this place looks great! Now that I officially can't afford it . . ." I said.

"Tabby, you know there will be other houses!" Lexi said, waving her hand with a broad sweep around the kitchen. "You don't want to miss out on having kids. I'm telling you. I would give up everything I've ever owned for Rob Jr. and Lexington."

"Wouldn't it be nice to have both, though! I'm just saying. Here I am drinking free wine and living a fantasy that this isn't about to be someone else's kitchen."

"It's as real as you make it, Tabby . . . at least tonight!" Lexi said, laughing. We made a hollow tink against each other's plastic wineglasses. My eyes shifted down to Lexi's hand. *Still no ring.* The tan line was even starting to fade into the color of her surrounding skin.

"How was your date?" I asked, taking a seat on the stool and the marble-top kitchen island. Lexi started to answer but was interrupted by the door opening and Laila announcing herself. We paused long enough to hug her.

"Hey, Laila!" Lexi said. "Let me get you a glass of wine." Laila slid onto the stool next to mine, while it appeared that Lexi was going to continue standing.

"What happened to your ring, Lexi?" Laila called out

immediately. "Did you lose it?" I stiffened. *Shit. Laila still doesn't know.*

Lexi turned around slowly. "Rob and I are separated." Laila looked from Lexi to me and back.

"Damn, did you know?" Laila asked me. She didn't even wait for a response. "Of course you did. How come neither one of you told me?!" I kept silent to let Lexi answer.

"It wasn't the kind of news that you just text somebody with," Lexi said.

"I would have," Laila said. "Or called."

"I figured I'd see you soon enough and tell you then," Lexi said, attempting levity. But Laila wasn't letting it go. She turned her attention to me. I had been watching the two of them like a volleyball match, just knowing that the tension would soon dissipate. Instead, it was rising.

"And you knew when we were at the gym?" Laila looked at me with extreme intensity. I felt frozen and tight-lipped. "Tabby," she warned.

"Yes," I said, feeling caught. "But, you know, I didn't want to say anything until Lexi had a chance to tell you herself."

"This shit is *crazy*," Laila said, shaking her head. I watched Lexi tense up.

"Rob was cheating," Lexi offered quickly.

"How did you find out?" Laila asked. Lexi was silent. *Come on, Lexi, just answer,* I silently prayed. I'd seen Laila mad before and she could go from zero to sixty in a heartbeat. Right now, we were already heading toward the thirty-mph zone with the needle steadily moving toward the red.

"How did she find out?" Laila turned to me. *Shit.* I froze. It wasn't mine to tell.

"Are you fucking *kidding* me right now?" Laila said. Lexi still didn't say anything. "What is this, the fucking house of secrets?" Laila's voice started to escalate. "HOW DID YOU FIND OUT, ALEXIS?" Laila asked again. I saw tears well up in Lexi's eyes, but she still didn't speak. I figured she must have been embarrassed, but I couldn't understand why she wouldn't speak up.

Laila turned to me with fire in her eyes. Her head turned so fast that her dreads made a thwack against her back. "You fucking told her, didn't you?" Laila said to me, nearly growling through her clenched teeth. I was completely thrown off.

"Told her what?" I asked.

"Did you tell her?" she said, standing up out of her seat.

"I didn't tell anybody anything," I said, clueless about how to stop what was happening.

"Bullshit!" Laila said. She turned to Lexi and spat the words out at her. "So now you're judging me?! You always think you're better than somebody, Alexis, and I'm *sick* of your *shit!*" Laila was yelling now.

"Laila . . . that's not what . . ." I didn't know how to even start to explain without betraying the confidence of either of my friends. I kept searching for words.

"You're always defending her ass, Tabby!" Laila said.

"What the fuck are you talking about, Laila?" Lexi said. "The only person I've ever *judged* is Rob's whore. Are *you* a whore?" Lexi asked rhetorically. *Oh no.*

"Maybe I am, Lexi! Maybe that's what *you would* say!" Laila grabbed her bag. "You know what, fuck *both* of you! I knew I shouldn't have even come here tonight!" As Laila turned to walk back toward the door, I could see that her eyes were already red, even though the fresh tears that gathered only just began to stream down her face.

"Laila!" I said as I rushed over to her to try to grab her arm. She covered ground so fast that I almost had to jog for any hope of catching her before she reached the door.

"Don't fucking touch me, Tabby!" she yelled as she opened the door and then slammed it so hard behind her the walls shook. Lexi and I looked at each other with wide eyes and mouths dropped open, frozen. For moments, neither of us moved or spoke.

"What the *fuck* just happened?" Lexi said finally, breaking the silence. She steadied herself with both hands atop the kitchen island to take a deep breath. "Tab, maybe you should go see if she's still outside." I knew Lexi was right, but I wanted no part of Laila in that moment. Her crazy was on a thousand, and I figured it was better to just let her cool off alone than to run after her and say something that could push her even further into the red. I still had no idea how any of what either Lexi or I just said would have set her off like that. In spite of my reluctance, I slowly made my way to the door, pushed my way outside, and looked for any sign of her or her car on either side of the street. She was gone. Feeling slightly relieved, I stepped back in to rejoin Lexi in the kitchen.

When I came back in, Lexi had a quizzical look on her face and was staring at me. "What was she talking about?" Lexi asked. "What was she talking about when she said, 'Did you *tell* her?'" Lexi looked at me, her face contorted, showing a mixture of confusion and suspicion.

"I have no idea . . ." I said honestly. And then, my mind

clicked. *Oh . . . my God. Oh no. How could I have been so stupid?* The realization must have registered on my face, because Lexi asked me again.

"What?" she said, searching my face. "You have to have some idea."

"Nope," I lied. "I have no idea." I was in a catch-22. Laila already thought I had told Lexi about her situation, but I hadn't. I would never violate that trust. So even now, I held the line, in spite of the conflict that I felt.

"Why don't I believe you, Tabby? Laila is crazy, but she's not *that* crazy. What do you know?"

I hesitated. I didn't want to lie to Lexi's face, but Laila's business wasn't mine to tell either—even if she was convinced that I already told. I tried to stop the flooding in my mind of prior conversations with Laila, swallowing the memories so that I could process it all in private. Without Alexis trying to pry me open. I was being a good friend—to both of them. Except, in the reality of this moment, being a good friend to both was impossible. I headed over to get my wineglass, trying to pretend like I was still searching my mind for Laila's truth.

"You know Laila," I said taking a sip. "It could be anything."

"Why would she think I'd call her a whore, though, Tabby?"

"How should I know? You know her just as well as I do," I said, thinking about their secret sisterhood at Post & Beam.

"I know her?"

"Well, it seems like the two of you have gotten extra close. She knows stuff about you that I don't. Remember, 'Ask

Alexis?'" I said, reminding Alexis of the moment. I didn't mean to go there, but I couldn't help it.

"You can't be serious, Tabby," Lexi said, looking annoyed. "Laila and I had some random conversation one day waiting for you! This is *hella* petty."

"Oh, so you're from the Bay now too, Alexis?" I said. I *was* feeling petty now anyway. It was that kind of day. Plus, Alexis had zero appreciation that I had just gotten in a fight with my other best friend because of her—trying to keep *her* information private.

"Get a life, Tab. Grow up." *Me? Grow up? Coming from Mrs. Thing?*

"You know what? You *are* a judgmental bitch, Lexi. Always have been. I'm leaving." I picked up my keys and headed toward the door.

"And you're a lying bitch!" Lexi yelled. I flipped around and looked at her, blinking slowly to make sure the moment was real.

"Oh really, Alexis?" I said. "Fuck you!" All I saw was red as I reached for the door. I could not get into my car soon enough.

I heard Alexis shout after me. "Fuck you too, Tabitha!" My oldest and best friend spat my name out like rancid wine.

I walked so quickly to my car I thought my stiletto heels were going to splinter. If I could have made it to Crestmire then, I would have, but I could barely see far enough through the tears to drive the ten minutes back to downtown.

I had already lost my eggs, my boyfriend, my friends, my house, and my savings. On this night, I felt like I was also losing my mind. I called Laila on the way home. Six times I let it ring through all the way to voice mail. She didn't even send me so much as a text back. When I got home I texted her.

> Me:
>
> Laila, call me. I didn't tell Lexi anything.
>
> Me:
>
> Please?
>
> Me:
>
> Are you OK?
>
> Me:
>
> I just left you a message. Call me back.

Nothing.

27

A COUPLE OF DAYS WITHOUT YOUR FRIENDS TELLS YOU A LOT about who they are to you. As much as I missed him, not talking to Marc had rolled off me like water. But not talking to either Alexis or Laila felt like walking into work every single morning like I forgot something important at home. I carried the feeling around all the time, like the forecast called for rain and realizing, once you already left the house, that gray clouds were actually beginning to gather and you had no umbrella. It was that kind of missing—the kind that you fix. You fix it not because you should, but because you have to, or it ruins you.

Every day I texted Laila, and like never before in our friendship, she didn't respond. I followed up with a call, just to be sure, and she didn't answer. Laila had a hot temper, but only rarely was it ever directed at me. I decided to give it a full week before I resorted to going to her apartment. Alexis, on the other hand, I had been in so many fights with since childhood that I knew exactly what to expect. Eventually, time would suffocate the flames of anger, much like baking soda on a stove fire. Soon enough, it would become perfectly safe to reenter our friendship with no visible damage. I wasn't worried about Lexi, but I missed her something awful.

I sat in my office contemplating sending her a text when I heard Chris's voice in my doorway. I put the phone down and immediately tried to look busy.

"Hey, Tabby, you have a second for me?" Chris said, already walking toward one of my guest seats.

"Hey, Chris, I was just finishing up some scheduling, come on in," I said, gesturing to the empty chairs facing my desk even as he was lowering his frame between the armrests. "Okay to leave the door open?" I asked, motioning to get up.

"Yes, door open is fine. Actually, I prefer it," he said as I sat back down. He leaned forward in his chair to rest his elbows on his knees. "Scott Stone gave notice today."

"As you predicted."

"Yes, as predicted," Chris said. "I've had some time to think about it, as you can imagine, and I've decided I want to do something different, to switch things up a bit." I braced myself for what would come next.

"Tabitha, I want you to hire Scott's replacement. That person is going to become part of your permanently assigned reporting team." I hoped that Chris would continue speaking because I needed time to process his words. "This is part of a larger change I'm making. All of the senior reporters are going to have their own reporting teams." I couldn't tell if this was a good or bad thing. My skepticism must have shown on my face, because Chris answered my thought as a follow-up. "This is going to allow for more thorough investigative reporting, more complex stories, more depth!" Chris said excitedly. "It's what our viewers want. They're tired of being told what to think—they want to think for themselves. They want us to present all angles, all sides, to do the work, uncover the facts, give the complete picture and let the viewer use her own mind!" Chris said with the energy of a stump speech. I sat there wondering if I should clap.

"Sounds like big changes."

"Very big. And it's going to be a big opportunity for you also. For all of the senior reporters. I want you each to take more responsibility for the ratings. Your compensation, your success, your trajectory here will depend on it. You'll have a real chance to make an impact."

I started to feel a slight tinge of nervous anxiety rise. Sure, what Chris was describing was a huge opportunity, but it also meant more responsibility, more work, and more time. Strangely, all I could think about was my egg-freezing appointment. *I'm not going to be able to do this now*, I thought. But I had to. Somehow, I was going to have to do both—do everything, even though deep down, I felt like I was already failing miserably at the things that mattered most. How could I start an egg-freezing cycle in two weeks, with this news? And how would I find the time I'd need for not one cycle, but three? I made a mental note to call Dr. Young's office.

"I'm excited about this, Chris," I said with as much enthusiasm as I could muster. "I've got some great ideas for the next newsroom meeting."

"Great! Just great!" he said as he worked to squeeze himself out of his chair. "I've got parent-teacher conferences today. I think I missed the damn appointment, but guess it can't hurt to try to show up anyway." I looked at Chris's bare left hand. I was sure he was divorced. He lived and breathed the news station. It was starting to become clear that he wanted me to do the same. At least I had no marriage on the horizon to screw up.

Once Chris was safely out of eyesight, I pulled out my phone again. I pulled up the message I had been contemplating to send to Lexi and changed it to current news.

Me:
OMG, Scott Stone quit today.

Lexi:
What? Because of you?

Me:
Basically. Now I'm hiring his replacement.

Lexi:
You're hiring?

Me:
Yeah, Chris is giving me a permanent team.

Lexi:
Big time!

Lexi:
I'm sorry, btw.

Me:
Me too.

Me:
Have you heard from Laila?

Lexi:
No. I haven't reached out yet, though. Have you?

Me:
Yeah, she won't respond. I'm starting to worry.

Lexi:
Don't worry. She'll come around.

Lexi:

Rob and I started therapy. Dr. says that you can't own what isn't yours.

Me:

Sounds wise.

Lexi:

Should have done this years ago.

Lexi:

He finds new ways to apologize every week.

Lexi:

Maybe I'll keep him, lol.

Me:

Yeah, maybe he's the rare type.

Lexi:

What's that?

Me:

Granny Tab says the rare type is the guy who keeps trying.

Lexi:

Yeah, maybe so. I don't know if I am, though. Still deciding.

Me:

I understand. Gotta run. Work is cray now.

Lexi:

See you Sat if not before! <3 <3

Lexi and I always fought and made up the exact same way. That's also because we never fought about much. And I guess, like my dad said, one day, you just know that you're gonna make it. Lexi and I had a friendship like that for certain. What worried me was that I still hadn't heard from Laila and, to the contrary, we had never had a fight like that before.

As I had been doing every day, I pulled out my phone and tried again.

Me:

Laila, can you call me?

Me:

It was a misunderstanding with Lexi. Easy to explain.

Me:

Are you OK?

Still, nothing.

28

BY THE END OF THE WEEK, I STILL HAD NOT SPOKEN TO OR GOTTEN any kind of response from Laila, which evolved my concern to escalating worry. Marc still hadn't reached out and neither had Todd to "remind" me to reschedule our date. This meant that I was still down one bestie, one boyfriend, and one potential. Although, I'll admit the Todd thing was totally my fault, and it was probably too late to fix it. Granny Tab had called me twice in the past week, once just to chat and a second time to let me know that Ms. Gretchen had gone on a weeklong road trip with one of her seniors traveling groups. She also asked if I was definitely coming this week, which I had done nearly every Saturday without fail over the past six months that she'd lived at Crestmire, so I assumed that she was just really lonely without saying it. Even if it's just a week, it's a special kind of missing someone when your best friend is away.

When I arrived at Crestmire to see Granny Tab, I was surprised to find her in the common area, sitting off to herself in one of the rocking chairs near the window, in front of the willow tree. I smiled to myself, wondering whom she had to contend with to secure this kind of prime seating. I walked over to her and pulled an open chair with me the last few feet to sit next to her.

"Hey, Granny Tab. Looks like you're missing your left arm!" I said, laughing. Granny Tab laughed too. She used to say that about Lexi and me when we were younger on the rare occasions when we could be found apart, especially when we lived down the street from each other in View Park.

"Oh yes, Gretchen is on her road trip!" she said in a tone that sounded like sadness covered with a thin wrapping of forced enthusiasm.

"I can only imagine what kind of trouble she's getting into!" I said, hoping to make my grandmother smile again. From the look on her face, I would have to try harder, much harder.

"That Gretchen is a load of trouble, that's for sure. I bet she's having a great time." My grandmother adjusted her feet beneath her.

"Looks like that swelling has gone down for you," I said.

"Oh . . . yes, for the most part. Doctor says I should still have my feet up most of the time if I'm sitting, but I just wanted to be here for a bit. No sense being in a rocking chair with your feet up," Granny Tab said.

"I was surprised to see you over here, Granny Tab! You doing some thinking?"

"I reckon I am," she said pensively. "I was just . . . remembering some things . . ." Her voice trailed off.

"Like what?"

She paused to look over at my face and take my hand, like she usually did when she had something important to say. The interface of our skin was a perfect juxtaposition of dark and light, wrinkled and smooth, old and young. Some part of me loved knowing we could be so different and still have the same blood coursing through our veins, and the same love shared in both of our hearts. I never doubted Granny Tab's love and never had reason to, no matter what else in life was happening.

"Two, ever since you told me about Marc, and what he said to you about his family," my grandmother said, turning to me with a look of deep concern on her face, "I've been thinking. I have something I need to tell you—and I guess I should . . . even though it's not completely my story to tell."

"What is it, Granny Tab?" I said, starting to feel some alarm.

"I need to tell you about your grandfather." For reasons I didn't know, the word *grandfather* brought a pang to my abdomen. We almost never spoke of him, except in capsule memories that highlighted his dancing skills or his and Granny Tab's early romance.

"What about him?"

"The truth," she said. "The truth about . . . what he was."

"What he was?" I asked, bracing myself.

"Tabby," my grandmother said, motioning for me to pull my chair closer. Once I did, she continued quietly, "Your grandfather . . . was . . . also an alcoholic." She stopped to let the information register.

"He was?" I said rhetorically, trying to imagine what that meant. "Is that why you guys separated?"

"Yes . . . and no," she said. "Your grandfather, he was really a great man. He wanted to be greater than the times would allow. The years in the military were hard on him. Having a young wife and child . . . it wasn't always easy . . .

and he let it all get to him sometimes . . . a lot of the time." I stayed silent, letting her have the pauses to regroup and continue. "He drank. When he got out of the service, there still weren't that many places that would have us, being a mixed family and all. But mostly on account of the fact that *he* was Black. He couldn't find steady work very easily, so times got pretty tough. He found his ways to . . ." Granny Tab turned away to face the tree, and turned back when she had words to continue with. "Manage, is what I guess I'd say. Having a family, needing to provide back then, and with all the nastiness of racism, discrimination, even in California, it was a lot to bear."

"Did he ever get help?" I asked. Granny Tab smiled a weak smile at me.

"Two, we didn't have those kinds of resources back then. And even if we had, we didn't have the wherewithal to think about any kind of help. It was just something that you bore in private and tried to hide signs of in public." She dabbed the crumbled tissue in her hand to her eyes and continued, "Just after he left the service, it got real bad. Real, real bad."

"Granny Tab," I interrupted, alarmed, "did he . . . did he . . . hit you?"

My question brought a look of panic to her face, and then her head dropped a bit. Again, I saw the wad of tissue go back to her eye.

"I wish I had a different answer," she finally replied, almost so quietly I couldn't hear her. "Most of the time, it wasn't in front of your father, though. I thought, if he just hit me, he wouldn't hit Paul. And for a long time, it worked that way."

"And then it got bad?" I studied my grandmother's face.

Her tears felt like they were etching into my own soul. I hated seeing her cry, but I knew I needed to hear her story.

"One day, he got very drunk. He came home in the middle of the day looking for a fight. Your dad was usually at school at that time, but on this day, he stayed home with a cold. Your grandfather was yelling, pushing me. I tried to get him to stop, tried to remind him that Paul was in the house. But he slapped me down, hard. Paul saw."

I couldn't believe what I was hearing. The tissue that Granny Tab held in her hand was starting to disintegrate.

"He tried to defend me, but Grandpa Walker was in a rage by then. He hit Paul, knocked him down hard to the ground. I didn't know what else to do, I was young. I ran into the kitchen and got the biggest knife I could find. I told your grandfather to get away from my son." Granny Tab's tears were flowing heavy now. "I said, 'Get away from my son!'" she repeated through tears. "And then I told him to get out. I didn't care where he went, but go. The next day, I took what money I could find and got on the bus with your father back to West Virginia. We never went back to that house."

"He did that to my dad?" I asked.

"Yes, Two, and I didn't have the good sense to leave sooner. But West Virginia wasn't any better. I went back to my daddy's house with your father. Times weren't good then for a brown child like him. My baby." She turned away again. "My family, they didn't treat us right. Seemed like everybody was so much more concerned with what they thought was appropriate than with what was *right*. No responsibility for thinking back then—actions didn't come from the heart, or the head either. They all just did what they were told they were supposed to. And they were told that they had the right to treat my baby boy like he wasn't their family, like he didn't deserve to be there. So we left. And my daddy, he knew everything that happened with Grandpa Walker, and he just said, 'Well, I reckon there were worse things about him than just the color of his skin.' That was the closest to any apology I ever got."

"Where did you go after you left there, Granny Tab?"

"West Virginia was no place for a little colored boy. So I came back to Los Angeles. Your grandfather knew that if he didn't stop drinking, he couldn't live with us. It wasn't safe. But he couldn't stop, it had gotten so bad . . . So he gave us, your father and me, money to get a place of our own, and I had to sign up for assistance for a while. I enrolled myself in community college and then finished my degree on my own. The first good job I could get was as a teacher, so that's what I did. That part of the story you know."

"Granny Tab, what happened to Grandpa Walker?" I asked.

"He died, not long after. He drank himself right into the ground. I won't say that how he got treated is what killed him exactly, because that would be giving him excuses, and what he did to us, and to himself, had no excuse. But there were reasons, Tabby—I saw it with my own eyes. I felt it with my own family. I just wish he had gotten a chance to be the man who I knew he could have been. I would have loved to see him in different times. I know you think that we divorced, but we stayed married all the way up until he died. I never loved anyone else."

"Granny Tab . . . I . . . how . . . how did you manage?" I asked. It was all I could muster through my own tears, which had started to fall.

"Two," she said, following a deep breath, "I just learned that *life*, no matter what kind of bad happens . . . it's all about finding some bit of optimism, some kind of hope that the next moment, or even the moment after that"—Granny Tab looked away as her eyes glazed wistfully in the direction of the willow tree, before she continued—"is going to be all that you had originally wished for, and that your good is still on the way."

She blinked away the tears in her eyes, which today were almost the color of periwinkle flowers. She looked like my grandmother, but in that moment, different to me somehow. Like the release of all that she had been holding inside, the sharing of it with me, had given her back some of the girlish qualities of her youth. She looked beautiful, in the light from the window, like a goddess bathing in her own resplendence. Who knew that those aged hands, showing blue veins and resting on the rocking chair, had once held the weight of the world? For a while, we just sat there—quietly, holding the space between us. Sometimes, there is just nothing more to be said. *No matter what kinda bad happens* . . . I let her words replay in my mind.

My phone ringing broke us out of our thoughts, and I would have ignored it, but I thought it might be Laila, finally getting back to me and, secretly, I was hoping it was Marc. I looked at the screen, which showed an unfamiliar local number. I held it through another ring, debating whether or not to answer. Something in my gut told me I should.

"Hello?" I said.

"Hello, is this . . . is this Tabby?" The woman's voice on the other end sounded familiar, but I couldn't quite place it.

"Yes, this—"

"Tabby, this is Naima Joon, Laila's mom. Do you remember me?" Of course I did, but the familiarity didn't bring me any feeling of comfort. *Why was Laila's mother calling me?*

"Yes, Mrs. Joon, I remember you—is everything all right with Laila?" The pause was too long for the answer to be yes.

"Tabby, I'm sorry for this to be the reason that I'm calling you. I know it must be strange. It's just that . . . Laila, she's in the hospital." I could feel the tears that were already in my eyes cross the threshold of my lashes and begin to roll down my face anew. Before I could pick a question to ask, Mrs. Joon continued. "She, um . . . there's no good way to say this, I guess . . . she made an attempt . . . some pills. I don't even know where she got them. I found her unconscious in the bathroom, on the floor." Mrs. Joon spoke in a carefully measured way. "The ambulance came and got her to the hospital in time. She's been here a few days." *A few days? Oh my God. I knew something was wrong. Why didn't I just go to her place?*

"Mrs. Joon," I said, "I don't know what to say—thank God you went to her place."

"Her place?" Mrs. Joon said with surprise. "She was at home with her father and me. Laila has been living with us for the past four months! She didn't tell you?"

"I . . . guess . . . it never came up," I said, trying to hide my shock. My grandmother was looking at me with concern. I wished she didn't have to hear this. I wished that I didn't either.

"She got laid off and needed to just reset for a bit. We had been trying to make it work with her back home temporarily until she got something new going. Thank God, because I don't know how I would have . . ." Mrs. Joon's voice filled with emotion and stopped abruptly. I could hear her sobbing in the background. I was afraid to ask the next question, but I needed to.

"Mrs. Joon, is Laila okay?" I could hear Mrs. Joon's quiet sobbing slow into a couple of muffled nose blows into what I guessed was tissue. I heard her take a staggered inhale before continuing.

"She's better. Stabilized now. The doctors want to keep her a little longer, and she still can't have her phone. I think it would be good if you could come to see her. So far it's just been her father and me at the hospital."

"When can I come?"

"You're familiar with USC Medical Center, right? There're limited visitor hours for . . . this . . . for psych. But you can come today until eight p.m. I already put you on her visitors list, just in case."

"Mrs. Joon, I will be there. I'm just with my grandmother right now in Glendale, but I'm on my way soon. Tell her I'm coming. Please. Please tell her I love her. I'm on my way."

"I'll tell her, Tabby. She'll be glad to see you." *Would she?* I felt a clammy sweat come to my hands as I hung up. My grandmother was looking at me. I'm sure she heard the entire thing. I couldn't think clearly, especially as the warm mud of guilt started to fill my insides. *This was all my fault.*

"Is everything okay?" Granny Tab asked with a look of concern that had now fully replaced the nostalgia of moments prior. *No matter what kind of bad happens . . .* My mind kept running my grandmother's words.

"I guess you heard that . . ." I said.

"I only heard what you wanted me to hear, sweetheart," my grandmother said. "What did I hear?"

"You heard that my friend Laila is in the hospital. She . . .

got hurt," I said. "Her mom wants me to come and see her tonight, well, like now. Are you going to be okay? I was going to stay a little longer since Ms. Gretchen isn't here."

"Don't worry about me, Two," Granny Tab said. "I'm tired now, anyway." She yawned, as if on cue. "I'll probably just take a nap for a bit, and then your dad will be here soon enough to pick me up."

"Tell him hi," I said. "And the girls too," I added, thinking mostly of Dixie. "He and I had a chance to talk last week. And Dixie. I didn't realize how long it had been since I'd seen the girls. Danielle is almost as tall as me now."

"Yes, Danielle is going to be tall. And a real beauty once she gets her braces off," Granny Tab said, smiling. "Dixie, she's something else. She reminds me of you at that age." I tried to mask the feeling of jealousy that hit as she spoke of my *little sister.* "I can't claim favorites, but you'll always be my first grandchild," she said with a wink and a small pinch to my arm. For now, I had to be satisfied with her little concession. "I'm proud of you, Two—I'm glad you went." It would probably take me forever to admit it, but I also was glad that I had gone.

"You get some rest, Granny Tab!" I said with overdone cheer, found and forced from somewhere else in my body. "You'll need it for Senior Prom! That's next week, right?" I used the promise of better times to come in the hopes that I wouldn't cause her to worry. I tried not to rush my goodbye, but the rising panic in my gut was difficult to fight. I grabbed my belongings, attempting not to appear as rushed as I actually was.

"It is!" She perked up entirely. "You're still coming, right? To help me get ready?"

"Of course!" I said. "Wouldn't miss it."

I managed to say my goodbye to Granny Tab even though my mind had been outpaced with the information of that evening. I couldn't even think about what I'd learned about my grandfather, or how it related to Marc. I was too busy thinking about Laila and the last time we saw each other. *Just days after, she tried to kill herself?* I spent every minute of my drive to USC hospital replaying the events of that night—*how could I have just let her leave like that?* The rational part of me said that there was no way that one thing could have made my strongest friend take such an extreme action. But my heart knew better. *Did her mother say she was living at home?* Why didn't Laila tell me any of this—even that she got laid off? *Did Laila lie to me, or was I just not paying attention?* I couldn't remember. All I knew was that I had to get there—I had to see her. Laila was lucky, but so was I. She was still here—still alive. So, thank God, I had the mercy of a second chance—to ask all the questions that I didn't know to ask. I couldn't get to the hospital fast enough—I needed to lay eyes on Laila.

29

PULLING UP AT THE HOSPITAL WAS A SLIGHT RELIEF FROM MY rushing thoughts. It brought me closer to knowing that I'd be able to see, speak to, talk to, and touch my friend while her body was still warm and her brilliant mind still capable, competent, and governing. *She made an attempt . . .* Mrs. Joon's words played in my mind almost like a foreign language that I was just learning—vocabulary words for unfamiliar rituals.

I called Mrs. Joon, and she gave me the instructions to find Laila's room. She told me she and Mr. Joon would use the time I was there to take a break in the cafeteria and asked me to text her when I was leaving. Walking down the hall to Laila's room felt surreal and out of place. I started to think of our freshman year dorm at the USC undergraduate campus not even that far away. I counted down the numbers next to the doors as I made my way to where I was told I could find her. *She made . . . an attempt.* I thought about all the things that Laila had accomplished since college. She was even more headstrong and determined than I was. She landed her first newspaper column while I was still in grad school. Whatever she set her mind to, she achieved. *Except this.* I found myself grateful for whatever miscalculation, or intervention of fate, kept Laila from . . . the unthinkable. My mind signaled a match to the number I was looking for. I was there, at her open door.

The first thing I noticed about Laila took my breath briefly and made me glad that I saw her before she saw me. She had cut off all of her hair. The lovely, long, well-kept, hard-come-by locs that I had never known her without were replaced with a halo of ringlets. The much shorter hair made Laila look kind of like a small child in the bed, a visual rein-forced by the too-large hospital gown that she wore. She was watching something on television but turned quickly to me when I gave a slight rap of my knuckles against the doorframe. She looked at me, but didn't say anything, and at first, her face registered neither happiness nor sadness in particular. Seeing her expression change to a slight smile was the reas-surance I needed to enter.

"Can I come in?" I asked. Laila nodded. We'd never shared so much silence in the entire length of our friend-ship. I walked into the room and waited for the right words to follow. *How are you?* That seemed inappropriate. It was a question that I should have asked in earnest a long time ago. It was Laila who spoke first.

"Hey."

"Hey. You . . . cut . . . your locs?" Laila brought her hand up to her head as if to confirm that they were in fact gone. As if my words were news to her. She looked nervous and uncertain as she ran her fingers through one side of curls.

"Yeah . . . I needed to start fresh . . . cut off all the deadweight . . . I guess I shouldn't say *dead*," Laila said with a slight smile. "I mean, given these circumstances." She laughed a little, indicating the room with her hands. I made a small awkward laugh in return. It was a good reminder that Laila was still in there.

"It looks . . . good." *I was lying.* But I could see how her new look would be pretty, in a different place and time, without sunken eyes, wires, drip tubes, and hospital gowns.

"Tabby, I look . . . like shit," Laila said. "You can be honest. I prefer it."

"Okay," I said with a smile. "You do . . . look . . . kinda bad. But you're still the most beautiful thing I've seen all day." I walked over to the chair next to her bed.

"Then you must have had a pretty fucked-up day," Laila said.

"Could have been worse," I replied softly. At this, Laila's face changed. It clouded over with seriousness. She looked down for a moment and then looked at me.

"I'm really embarrassed, Tab," she said. "I just need to be able to say that."

"You don't have to be embarrassed. You shouldn't be. Not with me."

"This just isn't something I want anyone to know about me. It's not something I want to know about myself. I wish I could undo it," she said, reaching for a tissue from the box on the stand next to her.

"I'm just glad you're still here, Laila. And I'm glad I could be here with you . . . for you," I said, also reaching for the same box.

"Tabby, I'm so sorry. I feel like I owe everyone a million apologies. What I did . . ." She paused, dabbing at her eyes. "As soon as I swallowed the first pill, I knew it was wrong; by the last one, I regretted everything. I decided even then that

I should try to throw up, but I passed out." She paused again, shaking her head and looking away. "And then my mom had to see that . . . She shouldn't have had to see that. All my hair on the floor and me on the floor—God only knows what else. I'm just so sorry. So sorry." She whimpered into her tissue.

I could only obey my compulsion to sit on the bed and hold her in the tightest hug I could make. She allowed her head to rest on my shoulder. I still had trouble finding words, but I was hoping she could hear how much I loved her from everything unspoken, from my own tears that fell onto her hair, to my heartbeat that thumped against her own chest, to the warmth of my embrace. I gave everything in my body to that moment, to try to lift her up, to be the friend that I had failed to be when it seemed like she needed me most and I was too caught up in my own shit to notice. I held on to her like a mother who had found her lost child, understanding the miracle of second chances.

"I think I finally managed to embarrass my parents," Laila said in a halfhearted joke.

"Hardly. They'll get over it."

"Will you?" Laila looked up at me. Her question brought a sharp feeling to the innermost center of my body. I could only imagine how vulnerable and exposed she must have been feeling.

"Laila, there's nothing to—" I attempted to reassure her, but she cut me off.

"Tabby," she whispered. *"I'm* ashamed." She pulled herself back to look me in my eyes. "I lost my baby." She managed to push out the words, and then collapsed again against me.

"Wait, you *were* pregnant?"

"At the gym . . . I knew then. I didn't want to say anything because it was so early and I had such a bad feeling about it all. What kind of person would bring a baby into my situation?" Laila said.

"What did . . . your Mr. Big say? Did he know?"

"I told him—he wanted me to . . . 'fix the situation,' as he put it."

"Asshole!" Somehow, I managed to hold back the other words that I wanted to say.

"When I wouldn't agree, he just stopped responding. He didn't even text me back when I told him . . . what happened."

"Oh my God. Oh my God. Laila," I said. I didn't know how one body could hold so much pain, hers or mine. I squeezed her harder, as if she were crumbling and somehow I could hold us both together.

"Everything was going wrong—my job, everything. And then there was this little ray of light—this idea, that things could be better, this little bit of hope growing inside of me . . . and then, all of a sudden, it was gone. And I just couldn't stop hurting, Tabby. I had no way to stop hurting."

"Why didn't you say something?"

"I don't know. I couldn't? I was embarrassed? I thought I had it handled—I was so used to having all the answers. The whole time, I was running from the darkness, Tabby, and I got good at it. Maybe I felt like talking about it made it real, so I kept running and hiding. I stayed one step ahead, you know?" I nodded. "But then everything started closing in on me. It caught up to me. I should have reached out, but I didn't know that I was already in trouble—that I was so close to breaking. I should have known, when we got in that fight . . . I felt so stupid, right away, before I even got home. I knew you hadn't told Alexis anything. You reached out that night, and I wasn't feeling well, and didn't feel like talking. Then it"—Laila used her eyes to quickly motion downward along her body—"happened just after. The . . . miscarriage . . . and . . . then the pills. I woke up in an ambulance, on the way here . . . They took my phone." She looked back up at me. "I'm so sorry about that fight with Alexis. I was just so stressed out—I know I overreacted. You two probably thought I was crazy—maybe I am crazy. I don't know."

"We're probably all crazy, Laila. All crazy, with our own good reasons to be crazy," I said. "Can I ask you something?" I studied Laila, meeting her eyes in the center of her glance. She nodded. "Can you tell me now, I mean are you able to— that this won't happen again?" I asked.

"This won't happen again, Tabby. I promise." I just looked at her, searching her face for some way to know that this was true. "It *won't*," she repeated, looking at me. I took a deep breath, and so did Laila, never breaking our eye contact.

"Are you okay staying at your parents?" I asked. "Do you want to stay with me?"

"I'm okay there," Laila said. "It's just temporary. I've had a lot of time to think. Being in here has taken a lot of the pressure off—of everything I thought I was *supposed* to be. I didn't even realize how much I was trying to live up to other people's expectations. And all this time I thought that I didn't give a fuck. But it turns out, I was giving lots of fucks. Way too many." She gave a weak smile, and I couldn't help but laugh. "Tab, I've been thinking about what I really want to do. When I get out of here, I'm going to have a plan—a real one and stop BS-ing. I realized there's a lot more that I could be doing—it sounds silly, but all I can think about is starting a blog—my own publication. Just my thoughts, my words, and no filter. Is that silly?"

I wasn't used to being the one to reassure Laila, but with the roles reversed, I was happy for once to be the one who encouraged *her*, like she had done for me so many times before.

"No, not at all. Laila, I bet it'd be hilarious," I said, "and wildly successful."

She smiled weakly and then continued. "And, I started a journal—I mean, I haven't written much yet, but it's something," she said, looking over at a large-size leather-covered notebook on the stand next to her bed. "My mom brought it for me on my first day here."

"The world has a lot more to hear from you, Laila Joon," I said, trying to hold back the tears that the thought of my next words brought. "I don't have . . . a lot of family." The tears dropped as I spoke. "You . . . and Lexi . . ." My words caught in my throat. Laila covered my hand with hers. I managed to continue. What I had to say was important. "Sometimes we don't say what we *need* to say to each other."

Laila looked at me and handed me one of her tissues. "I understand," she said. And there we sat as minutes passed, saying nothing, learning together how to find the words unspoken in silent space.

"What can I do to support you?" I asked eventually. "I feel like such a *bad* friend, Laila. Like I missed something somewhere—like I wasn't paying attention. But I was, I just . . ." *How did I miss this?* is what I wanted to say—what my mind kept thinking. I thought about the fact that Laila had no visitors other than her parents and me, and made my best suggestion. "Do you want me to bring Alexis? I know that she'd want to see you."

"*You* came to see me. That's enough." She paused, and it seemed like she was looking for her next words. "I'm not ready to see Alexis. I don't want her to know just yet. I need a little more time." I nodded. "I'll tell her, though," Laila said. "I'll tell her myself."

"I understand."

"But there is something else you can do . . ." Laila said.

"What? Anything."

"Help me figure out what to do with this hair!" With this, she gave a big smile.

"Now, that I can *definitely* do," I said, so grateful for the laughter.

I stayed right up until the near end of visitors' hours, sending Mrs. Joon a text at a quarter past seven to give her parents a chance to finish up the evening with their daughter. For some reason, I thought of my father. As imperfect as he may have been, I was starting to understand what my grandmother meant about him being "the rare type." Even when I pushed him away, he never stopped trying to reach me, even in spite of his faults. And, just like Laila, didn't we all need the space to fall short and keep fighting? Isn't that what we're all asking from one another? For the space to try again with the hope that one day, somehow, we could earn that type of forgiveness—the getting over it type, *all* of it. Laila's secret weighed heavily on me, but there was no one to share it with. It would be my burden for now, my thought to process, my guilt to weigh, my mind to heal. All I could think of was the bottle of wine waiting for me at home. My phone rang, interrupting the cascade of thinking. I figured I forgot something and perhaps Mrs. Joon was calling me back to remind me. But it wasn't Mrs. Joon. Of course it wasn't—it was Marc.

30

AT THE MOMENT HE CALLED, I WANTED TO TALK TO MARC MORE than I wanted air. I wanted comfort to suffocate and quench the raging brush fires burning in my mind. Lightning had struck twice on that day in the already vulnerable territory of my consciousness. Laila was a wake-up call, forcing me to become aware of my own fragility and to recognize my limitations. Based on the explosiveness of our last encounter, even though this was everything I'd been waiting for, I let Marc's call go through to voice mail. I considered it self-preservation. I knew I was drinking too much lately, but it was only the better part of a bottle of wine that allowed me any kind of sleep that night, and even that was restless. I found myself awake, again, at three a.m.

I kept thinking about my dad. I found myself stuck imagining the scene Granny Tab had described. The one in which the little-boy version of my dad tried to defend her with his lanky body and wound up broken and bruised by my grandfather. My grandfather, who, because of his own actions, I'd never get to meet. I thought of Granny Tab, and her eternal softness, picking up the handle of a knife, much like my mother did that spatula in our kitchen, in the defense of her child. I thought about Marc's summary of chaos and abandonment, and wondered how that could be so different from my dad's experience, or even if it was different. Maybe it was similar. And if it was, how did I wind up repeating a cycle that I didn't even know about? *Was Marc like my dad in some way?* I thought of Laila's small frame, with her short hair and all of the wires and tubes draping from her too-thin hands and wrists. *Laila made an "attempt"?* My friend Laila, with her acerbic wit and tough-as-balls humor, tried to kill herself, and I had missed all the signs. I knew I needed to talk to someone, but at three a.m., those options were limited. That's when I decided to call my mom. With the East Coast time difference and the general's early rising habits, I presumed she'd be awake, and I was right.

"Tabby Cat? Is everything okay?" My mom picked up the phone on the first ring.

No, Mom, I thought, *it's not okay. It's not okay, and I'm not sure that it will ever be okay again. But I need it to be okay. But nothing is what I thought it was. I need answers.*

"Hi, Mom, sure everything is fine. I'm just . . . awake. I had a few things on my mind, and I thought I'd call . . . just . . . just to talk."

"Oh, calling at three a.m. just to talk? My Tabitha? Something must be *very* wrong, then," my mother said. "How is your grandmother? Is she okay?"

"She's fine, Mom."

"Alexis?"

"Fine."

"Laila?" I froze. *Laila.*

"Laila is . . . recovering. She . . . had an accident."

"Is she okay, Tabby?" *How did my mom always manage to figure me out? Or was I that transparent?*

"She will be. I think it's going to take some time, but I saw her earlier and she was fine." I tried to bring my mother enough satisfaction to drop the topic.

"Well, what about your dad?" she said.

"He's okay. You know, I went to dinner over there last week."

"Oh? You did?" My mom said, only thinly veiling the edge that came into her voice.

"I did," I said. "Granny Tab asked me to go—and they didn't even have me on the list at the guard station, but I managed to make it through the gates," I said, surprised at myself for including those details.

"Uhm, uhm, uhm. Diane should *know* better. I've never liked how she's treated you, Tabby, I—"

"I *know*, Mom," I said, interrupting. I had a point to reach, so I pushed to continue. "It was fine, because I really just wanted to talk to my dad, you know, about some work things, and some life things, about Marc."

"And what did *your dad* say?" my mom asked, saying "your dad" in largely the same way that someone else might say "the village idiot."

"He said a lot of things. He said . . . that what you needed from him was on the other side of damage that you didn't create." I let that sit in the air. "Did you know that?"

"Hmph." My mother made only that noise, but really said nothing. She was silent for a while. I guessed she was letting the words absorb and roll around in her mind until they developed some kind of meaning to her. I imagined a batter, words mixing together with old memories, sadness, and a whole history lived with another person, until it became a smooth and uniform consistency—enough to speak on, which she finally did. "I guess, that's about true," she said. "But people decide what damage they're going to fix, and whom they're gonna fix it for."

And that was just it, wasn't it? The root of the question I'd never known I needed to ask when it hurt the most—*why was I the one you gave up on?*

"Would you have changed anything, Mom? Anything at all?"

"I don't suppose I would change much. Well, if anything, I'd have just kept what was mine, and given back what wasn't." *Kept what was hers? What had she taken that wasn't hers?* I started to ask her what she meant, but my own feelings started to push through.

"Mom, I . . . I just feel like sometimes I'm trying so hard. And no matter how hard, I'm always missing something— like everything I've been told to stand on is some kind of quicksand."

"Tabby, you sound like there's more that you're not saying."

"Rob and Lexi are separated. She's not wearing her ring."

"Oh no! What happened, did Rob get someone pregnant?" I loved how my mom skipped over the obvious, because, with Rob's history, it was *so* obvious.

"No, he cheated."

"Well now, that's not new. I feel like I might have dried some of Lexi's 'Rob cheated' tears myself," my mom said with full cynicism. "Well, the most important question is, does he want to leave or to stay?"

"He says he wants to stay."

"Lexi needs to figure out if he means it, and then decide what she wants to do. If he wants to stay, she's got options. If he doesn't, well . . . there are only so many decisions as a woman that you're really able to make. There is no way to make a man stay if he's intent on leaving. And no way to make a man leave who is intent on staying." I thought about my grandfather. I wondered which one of my mother's examples he would have been.

"He says he wants to work it out—they're in therapy."

"Then Lexi has options that I didn't. Not with your father . . . if that's what you're asking."

"I'm not sure what I'm asking, Mom, honestly. I'm just trying to figure some things out."

"Are you sure you're okay, Tabby? You don't sound like yourself . . . why don't you come out here to visit with me in DC? Take a break?"

"I'll think about it, Mom," I said. "Right now, I just need to sleep. It's been a long day."

"Okay. I didn't get to ask you about Marc," she said, not taking my cue.

"Oh, Marc. Maybe it's better to have a burrito," I said. "Or a book."

"Okay, Tabby, you're talking nonsense, go back to sleep. I love you." I told her I loved her too and hung up, still very much awake.

31

I WAS GLAD TO FINALLY BE IN DENISHA'S CHAIR, READY FOR THE last and most complex element of my styling ritual. For once, Denisha was running ahead, rather than behind, since I had managed to get there early. Instead of going to the gym that morning, Laila and I had coffee together. It was a relief to see her looking better, and I agreed to help brainstorm on some ideas for her blog. It had been a long time since I'd seen her that excited. It made me believe that I could count on *all* of her commitments toward moving forward. Later that afternoon, I planned to keep my own commitment and head to Crestmire to help Granny Tab get ready for Senior Prom. Ms. Gretchen was still out of town, so I'd be Granny Tab's prep partner and her date for the evening's events.

Denisha's hand floated just above my head as she started to fill me in on the local events as if she were the afternoon anchor for the hood's very own live-action production of the news. I swear I did not trust an animated Denisha with a hot comb. It was a perfect recipe for grill marks across my forehead.

"Girl, did you hear about the shooting that happened in View Park?" Denisha said.

"You mean the boy who was shot by an off-duty police officer? He's okay, though, right? Still in the hospital?" I had heard about the shooting. We covered it briefly on the news the day before, but didn't spend much time on it because, unfortunately, among the things we hate to admit, if the shooting victim didn't die, it holds much less interest. Thankfully, the nineteen-year-old college student was only shot in the arm and received timely emergency treatment at the local hospital.

"Yeah, he still in the hospital, but he shouldn't be," Denisha said in her usual shorthand English. "It ain't even right what happened to that boy. All 'cause *people* keep moving into View Park and don't even know who their neighbors are!" Hearing the elaboration piqued my attention. I hadn't heard any of this from our own reporting of the story. At the expense of my forehead, and my ear, which had only just finally healed from a small burn mark from last week, I asked for further details.

"Wait, what do you mean?"

"Well, this is the part that they didn't say on the little news coverage that I did hear about it. But you know my cousin Tre and them stay in View Park, so they know exactly what had happened. And it ain't what the police said happened, that's for sure."

"Oh really?" My reporter's ear perked up. *Perspective.*

"Yeah, girl, Tre told me that what really happened, the boy, Daequan, it was his grandmomma house. And she had just sold it. 'Cause, you know how everybody tryin' to move into View Park right now. Like they done discovered it or somethin'. Well anyway, his grandmomma was selling the house because Daequan was having to work two jobs and go to school. He over at UCLA trying to be a doctor."

"Oh, he's premed?"

"Yeah, his momma a nurse, and his grandmomma retired. So, he had decided that he was gonna be a surgeon. But meanwhile, he was struggling paying for school, right? So the grandmomma decided she would sell the house while white folks were driving the prices up, and get that check to help her grandson out with the costs for school. She and the momma got a new house together out in Palmdale."

"So, what does this all have to do with the shooting?"

"Y'all didn't know this?" Denisha said, waving the curling iron. Instinctively, I reached for my ear and held it down. "You good. You can let your ear go, I already got that part." Reluctantly, I brought my hand back down to my lap. She continued, "See, y'all be missin' important stuff on the news."

"What wasn't reported?" I asked.

"See, what had happened was, the momma and grandmomma was supposed to move the next day. The moving truck was coming and everything. The momma and grandmomma had already taken a car full of stuff out to the new house earlier in the day. Daequan came after work to help with another load to take out there. You know, to help. So, he was packing up the car with stuff from the house. One of the new nosy-ass neighbors saw him moving stuff out, didn't ask *no* questions and straight called the po-lice." *Called the police.* I felt an immediate pang in my gut.

"What?"

"Yeah, called the police and said specifically that a *Black man* or *group of Black men* was committing a burglary down the street from their house, and that they didn't know if the burglars—the *Black* burglars—were armed or not. Meanwhile, it was just Daequan, movin' stuff out his grandmomma house. No one else."

"So, there was a false report?" I asked.

"I didn't even know you could call something like that no false report. I wish someone would. Seems like it happens all the time. Calling the police on Black people. It doesn't have to be *true*, it just has to be *said*."

"Ain't that the truth," some older church lady said from across the salon.

"Um-hum," Denisha said. "So, the call went out over the police radio, and the closest to report was this new cop—just like his second day, and he was off duty down the street. Just so happened that his friends, his white friends, had moved in on the same block. They had been at the block club meeting complaining about the neighborhood and how the 'gangs,'" Denisha said, using air quotes with the curling iron still in her hand, "were setting up all these break-ins."

"What?" I was mesmerized.

"Yup. And so that cop, the new one, the off-duty one, was the first to respond," Denisha said, continuing the story with more animation. "Girl, hold your other ear, I'm going to get your edges real quick." Nervously, I complied. "So, you can imagine, this . . . I mean, basically he's a *boy*, right? He's trying to help his momma and grandmomma move out, after school, after work, tired as hell, and then has some off-duty cop roll up on him outside the house in the dark? That's crazy!"

"So, how did the shooting happen?" I asked, already starting to type notes on my phone.

"The cop pulled out his gun on Daequan, like right away as he was coming out of the house. Daequan put his hands up and was trying to explain to the cop that it was his grandmomma's house and he was just helping move. But the cop didn't believe him. So, Daequan was like, 'Look, I'mma just call my momma real quick, she'll explain,' and reached to get his cell phone. The cop immediately thought the phone was a gun and shot him in the arm. On some *bullshit*." I couldn't believe what I was hearing. None of this backstory had been reported yesterday.

"So, did you hear anything about Daequan? Is he going to be okay?" I asked, still trying to type notes.

"He all right. He lucky, though. Tre said that there was blood all over the sidewalk after the ambulance left. He could have lost his arm or something. Then he'd have a hard time being a surgeon. Already gonna have a hard time 'cause he starting off Black. Too bad they can't shoot the Black off you instead, since they're just going around shooting Black people for no reason."

"Sure would be easier that way!" the same lady from across the room injected into our conversation. *Would it be?* It was hard to make sense of Daequan's shooting. It wasn't fair, and worse, nobody knew the truth. Anyone who heard about the story would think that he was just another thug-in-training shot under questionable circumstances.

"Does anybody know how bad the wound was?" I asked.

"Tre said that Daequan's cousin told him that the bullet went straight through and he'll be discharged this afternoon. The family is doing a little thing on Facebook Live as they leave the hospital. That's just for the neighborhood folks who wanna know that Daequan is all right. Me personally, I don't know why this isn't the biggest news story out there," Denisha said emphatically.

"Why do you say that?" I asked.

"Because Daequan ain't die!" Denisha said. "He's a rare one who can still tell his own story. He can tell the truth about exactly what happened. With them other boys, the ones who got shot dead, you don't get to hear the twelve-year-old ask for his mommy. Think about Tamir Rice. Let the media tell it, he was some seven-foot-tall monster with a Glock, instead of what he really was, a *baby* playing with a plastic toy. About time the *real* victim gets to tell his *own* story and people can see for themselves how ridiculous this shit is that we got to live with."

"Denisha, you're a genius," I said, the wheels already turning fast in my mind. "I'll be right back to pay you. I need to step out and make a call."

There was no way I was going to phone Chris inside that noisy salon. So, just outside the door, I was relieved for the minimal street noise when he picked up on the first ring.

"Chris, sorry to disturb you on a Saturday, but I have a story I think we need to pick up today."

"Wait, Tabby, are you implying that there is such a thing as a *weekend*?" Chris said. "That might be the only thing that actually is fake news . . . although I hate that term. What's up?"

"You know that officer-involved shooting in View Park yesterday?"

"Yep, we covered it. The officer responded to a burglary-in-progress call, mistook the kid's cell for a gun, shot him in the arm to disarm him, and the kid's doing all right, recovering fine with no lasting damage in the hospital. Where's the story?" he asked curtly.

"There is definitely a story," I said. "Much more to it than that. The kid was helping his grandmother move. She sold her house to take advantage of the rising prices due to gentrification of the View Park neighborhood. Remember my piece on Los Angeles real estate trends?" I asked.

"Oh yeah, that was a great piece, really well done—and got great ratings for us."

"Well, this is a story of another one of the effects of gentrification. One of the white neighbors called the police. They identified the supposed burglar in their call *by race*. The kid is a premed college student working two jobs studying to be a *surgeon*. Came over to help Grandma move out of her house that she sold to help with college expenses."

"This *is* getting interesting. Tell me more," Chris said.

"It was an off-duty officer who responded to the call. It's not black-and-white, so to speak, about whether the shooting was justified. He mistook the boy's phone for a gun and shot. The kid was just trying to call his mom to give an explanation of why he was there moving. He wants to be a surgeon, Chris. What if he had lost his arm?"

"So, what are you proposing?"

"The kid gets discharged this afternoon. The family is doing a Q&A on Facebook Live leaving the hospital. No press conference was scheduled. I don't think anybody even asked for one. They were just planning on answering questions for concerned people from the neighborhood and the family's church. I say we need to be there. If you assign a team now, can't this make the evening news?"

"Assign a team? Tabby, this is *your* story. You cover it."
Shit. I was supposed to be at Crestmire. I couldn't cancel on
Granny Tab.

"Oh no, Chris, I'm not . . . ready . . . I was just pitching the
story because—"

"Tabby, you're a senior reporter. You don't pitch, you
cover. Scramble your team. You get me the package, you're a
go for the news at six p.m." I tried to find the words to protest.
I knew I should have told him I had plans with family. But
I couldn't. My mouth opened a few times, but the words I
could have said failed to exit.

Oh shit. Granny Tab. Shit. Shit. Shit.

32

"HI, TWO! ARE YOU ON YOUR WAY?" MY GRANDMOTHER'S VOICE sang out of my cell phone after the first ring. Guilt wrapped its clammy fingers around my windpipe, making it hard to speak. It took me a few seconds to push the words out that I struggled earlier to find.

"Hi, Granny Tab!" I finally managed to say. "I . . . I . . . hate to disappoint you, and you know I wouldn't in a million years if I could help it, but I'm actually on my way to an emergency work assignment that I have to cover. I don't think that I'm going to be able to finish in time to make it today, and I know that it's the Senior Prom tonight. I'm so sorry." Once the words did break free, they became a deluge that was almost impossible to stop. If I could say enough of them, perhaps that would somehow drown out the fact that I was choosing work over my grandmother, and without even having Ms. Gretchen there to take my place. Lately, all I'd been faced with was a series of decisions with no clear right choice. On this afternoon, I hoped that I was making the correct one, one that could possibly save a life in the future.

"Oh?" was all that Granny Tab said, with innocent curiosity.

I could hear her sigh in the pause. I knew that she was thinking, resetting, reclaiming her disappointment, and swallowing it whole like a pill. All this so that she could hold on to it herself, sparing me with her willing sacrifice. Sparing me so I could feel like my decision had no consequences of hurt. It was a process that I, and perhaps every woman, knew well, the contorting of oneself around failed expectations, the twisting and turning to hide your pain from others, so that they might walk free of it, believing that we're always all right. We call that love.

"Well, sweetheart, I understand you have to work!" Granny Tab continued cheerfully. "And this was just something to do if you had nothing else to do. Us old biddies here, we've got nothing but time."

"Granny Tab, are you sure? I really was looking forward to being there! Thank you so much for understanding . . . my boss said I . . . I have to do this—you know the boy who got shot by the police in View Park, the nineteen-year-old, did you hear about that?"

"Yes! I saw it on the news! But they didn't say too much about it, though. The boy is gonna be fine, they said. Is that right?"

"Granny Tab, there's so much more to the story. At first, none of the news stations were interested. Why would they be, right? The boy is gonna live, seems like there's no controversy. But while I was at the hair salon my stylist told me the background. He was just an innocent kid trying to help his grandmother move in the evening after work, and the neighbors called the police on him."

"Well, any grandmother could relate to that," Granny Tab said. "What a nice boy to help her, even after he had been working all day! And who would call the police on a kid?"

"It's worse than that—the neighbor identified him as Black when they called. As if that made him *more* dangerous, or even more suspicious. Like they hadn't moved into a Black neighborhood . . ."

"Well, even if they hadn't moved into a Black neighborhood, it shouldn't be suspicious just to see a Black person, and definitely not in View Park. I just don't have a lot of sympathy for this kinda stuff. I used to worry for your father all of the time—that because of his skin color people wouldn't see his *innocence*."

"I know. I know, Granny Tab. And the officer shot the boy in the arm when he was trying to call his mom to get her to explain. I can only imagine how scared he was. Luckily, the bullet went through—but he's studying to be a surgeon! Just one millimeter off and . . . can you imagine?"

"You're going to cover this, Two? Is that what you've been assigned?"

"Yes, Granny Tab. I have to go to the hospital to interview him and his family as he gets discharged this afternoon. No other news crew is scheduled to be there. So, long story short, that's why I can't come today."

"Well then, don't you *dare* worry about me, Tabby. This is exactly what you're supposed to do. This is *your* story—I just know it. I'll do my own makeup, and I will be fine. What's for you is for *you*. Will it be on the news tonight?"

"Six p.m.—that's what Chris said. If I can get the interview package done and in, they'll put it on at six p.m."

"Well, I'll be watching!"

"Thanks so much, Granny Tab! I'll come by to visit with you tomorrow."

"Okay, sweetheart! I love you, and knock 'em dead!" I imagined my grandmother's pale knuckles balled up, punching at the air in front of her, like she would always do when she said that to me. Her hands might have changed over time, skin thinned and wrinkled by age into near-translucence, but she had used that saying many times before, on my most important occasions—from my first day of high school, to when I left for grad school, to my first day on my first job. And now.

"Thanks, Granny Tab. I love you too. I'll do my best—see you, well . . . you'll see me at six p.m.!"

While this, by far, was my most important call of the day, there was one other that ran a close second. I managed to scramble my reporting team and hold a brief planning session in the van on the way to cover Daequan's hospital discharge. We talked through the questions that needed to be asked, and I put my research team on pulling all the pertinent background facts. Thankfully, Scott Stone stealing my Rams assignment worked out to my benefit, because I already had much of the data on gentrification and Los Angeles real estate trends to reference. I started to feel comfortable that this was going to shape into a great story for our viewers. But still, one element remained open, missing, and it happened to be part of my particular perspective. I needed to reach someone who I hadn't thought about in quite some time.

"Tina, Jim," I said, "I need you guys to find an Officer Mallory. M-A-L-L-O-R-Y."

33

JIM AND TINA JUMPED ON THE LITTLE BIT OF INFORMATION I COULD give them without a badge number. They stood in front of me with notepads in hand hanging on my every word.

"When you find Officer Mallory, tell him that Tabitha Walker, senior reporter at KVTV, wants to interview him about an officer-involved shooting. He should remember who I am. He stopped me once . . . and let me go." If all went as I wanted, before the end of my interview with Daequan and his family, I'd have a contact on Officer Mallory so that I could interview him as well.

We pulled up to the hospital just in time to set up the camera and for me to scribble some final notes on the questions I would ask. No matter how much reporting I'd done in the past, I never failed to get a little nervous before a big moment, and especially an interview. A properly worded question could make the story, but a wrongly worded question could ruin it.

Coming out of the hospital door, Daequan and his family were not what I expected. I found a five-foot-eight gangly boy, who looked no older than sixteen, maybe seventeen, with the hair in his juvenile mustache looking like darkened peach fuzz. He was neatly dressed, in jeans and a baggy black T-shirt, wearing clunky gym shoes that didn't seem at all fashionable. His right arm was in a sling, the bandages and cast evident and in obvious contrast to the black cotton short sleeve of his clothing. The woman to Daequan's right, who I presumed to be his mother, was still wearing her nurse's scrubs. The other woman, who I assumed was his grand-mother, had her arm protectively around his waist on the left side, even as he had her slightly beat on height. A teenager walked in front of them with a cell phone, giving instructions for how they would go live on Facebook. I approached them, alone, to introduce myself and to request the interview. We were the only news team.

"Hi!" I said, holding my hand out. "I'm Tabitha Walker, I'm a reporter with KVTV." They all looked at me with surprise. "Are you familiar with our station?"

It was the mother who spoke first. "Yes! We watch you all the time. Ma!" She turned to her mother. "This is Tabitha Walker—you've seen her, right?"

"Yes, I think I have," the older woman said. "But I usually turn on KTLA for my news," she said dismissively. *Well, it's KVTV covering your grandson today,* I thought to myself.

"I've been following the story of what happened with Daequan," I continued. "I thought that it was important to cover this moment of him leaving the hospital, and to have the opportunity for him to tell his story to our viewers. Would that be okay?"

"Yes, that would be fine. Daequan, you okay with that?" His mother turned to face him to ask.

His voice was surprisingly soft for his height. He was

well-spoken and exceedingly well mannered. "Yes, ma'am," he said.

"May I ask your last name? Ms. . . . ?" I asked.

"Jenkins," Daequan's mother said.

"And?" I pointed to Daequan's grandmother.

"Wilson. Gloria Wilson, and that's my daughter, Felicia Jenkins, and grandson, Daequan Jenkins—he's a straight-A student, by the way. Gonna be a doctor. Thank God we can say, *still* gonna be a doctor," she said proudly.

Grandmothers, I thought with a slight smile.

"Nice to meet all of you," I said. "Daequan, I'm just going to ask you a few questions about what happened that night, is that okay?"

"Yes, ma'am," he said.

"Great. And then, I'm just going to ask you a few more questions to give our viewers a sense of who you are, is that okay?" He nodded. "Excellent. I heard that you want to be a surgeon, is that right?"

"Yes, ma'am." And then he paused like he had something else to say. I gave him the moment to let him finish the thought. "I do want to be a doctor. I *will* be, I mean. Especially after this . . . Dr. Wesley, he took real good care of me. Saved my arm. So, I know I want to be a vascular surgeon."

"Excellent, Daequan. We're going to give you a chance to tell all of our viewers that as part of your story. Is everybody ready?" I motioned for my reporting team to come up and join us. Barry was manning the camera and already behind me to start taping. Tina was on the phone, and Jim ran up behind Barry with his notepad ready for show notes.

"Hold up!" said the kid with the camera phone. "We're

supposed to be doing a Facebook Live session for the folks in the neighborhood. How we gonna . . ."

"Boy, if you don't get your silly behind out of the way . . . Excuse me . . ." said Mrs. Wilson, finally realizing that she was in mixed company. "If you don't go over there with that phone. You best just record us being on television," she said in the way that you know you'd better comply.

"Okay, Auntie," the boy said, defeated. He left the group to go stand behind Barry and our television camera. I watched as he started talking to the screen in front of him, explaining the situation, I presumed.

With my handheld mic in order, and the tape rolling, I started the interview with a walking introduction to lead the camera to Daequan and his family, who were standing in a group to my left. I steadied myself, summoned my most professional and polished reporter voice, and began.

"Hello, I'm Tabitha Walker, reporting for KVTV LA. Yesterday evening there was an officer-involved shooting in the View Park neighborhood of Los Angeles. A young man, nineteen-year-old Daequan Jenkins, was identified as an African American burglary suspect by a white neighbor to police. In reality, Daequan was simply trying to help his grandmother move out of her newly sold home." I moved in closer to the family as I spoke, trying to minimize the sound of my heels clacking on the sidewalk. Barry followed me with the camera. "First to arrive on the scene was an off-duty officer who was in the neighborhood, apparently visiting with friends who had recently moved in. What happened next landed Daequan here at Lynwood's St. Francis Medical Center Trauma Unit. Daequan was admitted yesterday with a bullet wound. He had been shot by the officer, who has now been placed on administrative leave." I arrived in front of the family and allowed Barry some time to align all of us in the camera's view.

"I am ·here now, with Daequan and his family—his mother and grandmother—as they prepare to leave St. Francis, thankfully with Daequan's arm intact, but I'm sure still healing from the impact of what must have been an incredibly traumatic police confrontation."

I turned to Daequan. "Daequan, we've all heard the official reports of yesterday's events. Could you please tell me and the KVTV viewers what happened in your own words?" I pivoted the microphone in Daequan's direction as he shifted uncomfortably and leaned down slightly to speak, like a thin reed bending in the breeze.

"Yes, ma'am. I went to my grandmother's house after work to help her move. She told me that she needed to get some things out of the way before the moving truck came in the morning. I had to work that evening, but I got there just after. I was tired, so I was moving kind of slow, getting things into the car that she asked me to bring over to the new place. Next thing I know, somebody rolled up on me, said he was a police officer, pointing his gun at me. I got real scared and tried to tell him I was gonna call my mom to explain everything." As he spoke, Daequan pointed to his mother with his unencumbered left hand. "She was at work. So, I tried to get my phone out of my pocket, and next thing I know, I heard the gunshot and I was on the ground bleeding. I thought I was going to lose my arm. That's all I could think about. That, and calling my mother."

Hearing his words brought tears to my eyes. I thought of my father, my cousins, little Lexington and Rob Jr.; I even thought of Rob and Marc. I had to force the tears back and compose myself to continue in my best professional tone.

"Unbelievable to think that this would be what resulted from that night," I said, looking at him. "Tell me, had you met any of the neighbors on your grandmother's street?"

Daequan started to speak, but his grandmother stepped in front of him, to address the mic. "What *I* will say about *that* is that *none* of those people that moved in ever bothered to speak to me with so much as a hello before they called the police on my grandson. Never. I don't even know if they know what I look like, let alone Daequan, who was in school . . . getting straight A's. I just have to say that—straight-A student right here. Always has been."

I didn't want to cut her off, but I had to move the mic back to Daequan.

"Thank you, Mrs.—"

She pulled the mic back in her direction. "Mrs. Wilson. Mrs. Gloria Wilson . . . Daequan Jenkins's grandmother," she said proudly.

I smiled at her. *Grandmothers.*

"Daequan, do you have anything that you want to say to the neighbors who called the police, or to the officer who shot you?"

Daequan scratched his head with his left hand and made a brief scrunched-up face, which released just as he began to speak again. "Yes, ma'am. I guess I would say to the officer and the neighbors the same thing. You can't always judge a book by its cover. I learned that a long time ago in school.

I understand that you think you're trying to protect somebody's house, my grandmother's house—so actually, I thank you for looking out. I have to assume that you *thought* you were doing the right thing. But *I* could have *died. I* could have lost everything I've been working for my whole life to become a surgeon."

"I could have lost my *son!*" Ms. Jenkins said, now in tears. I wanted so badly to comfort her, but I needed to finish the interview and make sure that Daequan had the full opportunity to say his piece. Daequan tried to move his arm to put it around his mom, but the cast and sling made that impossible. Instead, Mrs. Wilson came around to the other side and put her arms around her sobbing daughter, moving them off camera. Now it was only Daequan in the frame. He bent himself back down to the microphone to finish.

"I was a part of PAL when I was younger. I'm not holding a grudge and, honestly, I still look up to a lot of police officers. But, I guess, all I have to say is, what would you want an officer to do if it was *your* son? That's how I wish I could have been treated."

"Thank you, Daequan. You certainly deserved better. Thank God that you're here to tell your story and, on behalf of our viewers and the entire KVTV news team, I'd like to thank you for sharing it with us. We wish you a speedy recovery."

Daequan nodded and walked off to join his mother and grandmother, still in a sobbing huddle, leaving me to close things out with Barry and the camera.

"I'm Tabitha Walker, reporting for KVTV Los Angeles. Now, back to you in the newsroom."

Barry gave me the signal that the recording had stopped. All that was left was to thank Daequan and his family and then rush to get the package ready for the news. We would have to head straight to the newsroom. We all piled quickly into the van. Tina was still on the phone, but once we got seated, she handed me a sheet of paper with scribbled writing on it. I saw the phone number first and then the name, *Officer James Mallory.*

34

ONCE WE ARRIVED AT THE STATION, WE ONLY HAD TIME TO GIVE the interview a quick edit and format the segment for the six p.m. news. It aired successfully, so all there was left to do was wait. Chris liked the piece so much that he wanted to continue with a follow-up, which meant that I had to get Officer Mallory on the record. Our strange encounter had never fully left my mind, but on this day, if perspective was going to be what mattered, there was enough of a reason to try to contact him. I made a note to work the call with him into my swelling to-do list for the story. I already had a paper-ream worth of notes to review from my research team, and if the ratings were good, Chris would want the follow-up ready for Monday. If the other stations caught on to the news, then there would be even more pressure to stay ahead with the leading developments. We'd have to follow up on all angles—on the surgeon, Dr. Jonathan Wesley, who saved Daequan's arm, inspiring the evolution of his career plans to become a surgeon. It made the perfect human-interest angle, a shooting victim following in the steps of the man who treated him. We'd also have to follow up on the responding officer, the department's response, the changing landscape of the neighborhood, and interviews with any of the neighbors who would be willing. My work was cut out for me.

Even before I left the station that evening, my phone was busier than a beehive—buzzing, chirping, ringing, and making all kinds of indications that people were trying to get in touch. I saw a few text messages of congratulations and people letting me know they had seen my segment. There was even a text from Marc saying that he was proud of me. As soon as I got home, I decided to try Officer Mallory and see if I could make arrangements for an interview. It was strange to be calling him, and I wasn't sure that he'd answer. I pushed myself past the nervousness not to hang up prematurely. I *needed* to talk to him. The story required it. Sure enough, he finally picked up.

"Hello, this is James," I heard his still recognizable voice say.

"Um, hi, Officer Mallory? This is Tabitha, Tabitha Walker from KVTV LA. Tina from my research team reached out to you?"

"Hi, yes, Tabitha. I've been expecting your call." *He had been expecting my call?*

"Oh, good thing I didn't wait, then," I said awkwardly, with an even more uncomfortable laugh.

"Yes, it's somewhat strange to be speaking to you, I have to admit. I'm not accustomed to speaking to the media."

"Yes, I understand. Our first encounter was . . . certainly memorable," I said, trying to be diplomatic. "I remembered what you said, and I thought that you might be interested in providing an officer's perspective on the officer-involved shooting that occurred in View Park this past week. Have you been following the story?"

"Yes, after Tina contacted me, I made it a point to watch the six p.m. airing of KVTV news. I thought that you did a good job with the interview." *He did?*

"Excellent. Well I always look to provide as much of a story as I possibly can. It's my job to lend perspective."

"Ms. Walker, how can I help you?"

"Well, I was wondering if you'd be interested in doing an interview—on the record, providing your particular perspective on the shooting." To this, Officer Mallory was silent, other than the sound of clearing his throat.

"Tabitha . . . Ms. Walker . . ."

"Tabitha is fine."

"Okay, Tabitha, can we speak *off* the record?"

"Of course. You have my word," I said.

"As much as I do have my own thoughts about what happened between that young man and the responding officer, there's no way that I can speak on record as an individual or in my official capacity as a police officer. We have strict rules as a precinct and as a force—with a designated spokesperson for each matter."

"I see . . ." I said, trying to hide my disappointment.

"That said, what I want *you* to know is that as officers, we do get scared, just like anybody else; and angry, just like anybody else; and can be in need of resources and training, just like anybody else. There are ways to manage all of this. It's just that everything that needs to be done doesn't always get done." He paused abruptly. His voice became much more tentative as he continued. "Even with that . . . I'm probably saying too much."

"Officer Mallory, don't worry, I promise that we're off record."

"Still, I don't have any business talking to a reporter, you know? Not if I want to keep my job. Listen, Tabitha, I'll just say this, okay? If, with your reporting, you can somehow help the department, alongside everybody else, it would be welcome. In our world, everybody just wants to get home to their family at the end of their shift. And, believe me, there is no good and decent officer on the force who wants to go home on any night knowing that he shot a nineteen-year-old kid."

I thanked Officer Mallory for his candor and reassured him I would keep our conversation off record. It was left up to me to figure out what could be done with the information that he gave. Sure enough, he did provide perspective, but unfortunately it was nothing that I could use publicly—for now.

As I worked through the evening, my phone continued to ring and buzz with what I'd assumed were more congratulations and messages. Around ten p.m., I finally had a free moment and decided to take a look; there were messages from my mom, my dad, and Crestmire. I figured that Granny Tab must have watched the six p.m. news, and cued up the voice mail message.

"Ms. Walker, this is Dr. Johnson at Crestmire. The message is fairly urgent. I am also calling your father, Mr. Paul Walker. Please call us back as soon as you get this." *What?* I was confused hearing her voice. *Dr. Johnson would never call me . . . unless . . .* I cued up the next message from my dad.

"Tabby, it's Dad . . . um . . . I need to speak to you,

sweetheart. Call me right away, okay? Okay, it's Dad." *This isn't good. This cannot be good.* I called Granny Tab's direct number. The phone rang, and rang, and rang, and eventually went to voice mail. I started to feel the drop of panic in my gut and the quickening of my pulse. My hands felt clammy and started to shake as I dialed back the main number to Crestmire.

"Hello, this is Tabitha Walker calling. Tabitha Walker, my grandmother, I'm named after her, she is a resident there. Dr. Johnson called me. She called me and left a message. An urgent message. Can I please speak to her? Or, can you get my grandmother? Tabitha Walker. She's not answering her phone." *Please God, please don't let this be what I think this is.* I held the phone in silence, praying, waiting for the doctor to tell me not to worry. Finally, she came to the phone.

"Tabitha?" she said softly.

"Yes, Dr. Johnson, this is Tabitha, Tabby. Is my grand-mother all right? Please tell me she's all right. She's not an-swering her phone. Is she all right?" I begged.

"Tabitha, I called earlier and left a message. An aide went to perform our usual night checks on the residents and your grandmother was . . . she was nonresponsive." *Nonresponsive?*

"I'm sorry, Dr. Johnson, what does that mean?"

"I'm sorry, Tabby." *Why is she apologizing? People don't just apologize like this. Unless . . .*

"What? What?" I was having trouble breathing. *Please don't let this be what I think it is, please don't let this be what I think this is.* I silently and desperately prayed against what I already knew.

"I'm so very sorry, Tabby. We did everything we could to revive her, but we could not. We believe she had already passed in her sleep."

"Passed? What do you mean? What does that mean? I . . . I . . ." I knew what it meant. I couldn't breathe anymore. I was having trouble formulating words, and thoughts, within the surreal reality that had begun to swirl around me.

"She's gone, Tabitha, I'm so sorry." Gone. I lost control of my body. My hands dropped the phone. I could hear my own voice, but not feel where it was coming from.

"WAAIIT!! WAAAAIIIIIT!! WAAAAIIIIIT!! WAAAAAIIIT!" I heard myself wailing. My own sounds grew until that was all I heard, all I could hear—my own voice wailing, screaming "wait" until it turned into a small whimper. I had no idea how long Dr. Johnson stayed on the line. I slid down the wall with my body, dropping softly to the floor. My bones and my muscles had turned to mush. The energy I had left drained into the ground beneath me, and what remained of the many tears I had cried fell in puddles just under my face. I have no idea how long I stayed there.

It was only a text from Marc that stirred me. Out of the corner of my eye, I saw "WYD?" flash on the screen of my phone as it lay on the floor next to me. Compulsively, I reached for it.

Me:

Come over.

Marc:

Now?

Marc:

What for?

Me:

Sex.

Marc:

U sure?

I was not sure. But I let my text stand. My life these past months had been just one long run-on sentence of bad decisions. My hand, along with the phone in my palm, fell to the ground. *If I don't call my parents, they're going to barge in here*, I thought, realizing I still had unreturned messages from earlier. I found the energy to dial my father.

"Tabby, I've been trying to reach you." He sounded distraught, his voice hoarse, as if he'd been crying. Other than when I was a child, I couldn't remember ever seeing my father cry.

"I heard . . . what happened . . . to my grandmother," I whispered, through my own brand of hoarseness.

"Oh, Tabby, I asked them not to call you. I wanted to tell you myself."

"They told me. Dad, I can't really talk right now. I need to hang up, okay?" It was taking everything in me to form these basic words. I hoped that I would wake up from this terrible dream tomorrow, if I could just get to sleep.

"I understand, Tabby. This is rough on everybody. I'm going to Crestmire in the morning to try to collect some of her things. If you're able, you can meet me there. I know it's early, but we should start planning . . ." *Oh, her funeral. Of course, because that's what happens when people die. Granny Tab . . . died.* My mind continued on its spiral.

"Okay, Dad, see you tomorrow. I'll try, okay? I'm saying I'll try to be there. I'm sorry, I really need to hang up now."

"Good night, Tabby . . . I love you."

"I love you too."

I picked myself up off the floor and poured myself as much of a bottle of wine as would fit into my largest glass, not caring in the least if the deep red juice spilled on my neutral-tone leather sofa under me, or on me, for that matter. I didn't care other than it was that much less I'd be drinking, and I wanted to drink as much as possible. I had been drinking a lot lately. But I didn't care about that either. I had made it nearly to the bottom of the glass when I heard the knock on my door. I had almost forgotten that I asked Marc to come over. With foggy thinking and uncoordinated, heavy limbs, I picked myself up and answered. He stood there looking good, deliberately dressed, holding a bottle of wine.

"Hey," he said in what I had come to recognize as his sexy voice.

"My grandmother jussdied," I slurred. I opened the door wider to let him in and turned my back to him to walk toward the sofa and my waiting wineglass. Marc stood there stunned for a minute, looking around my apartment, and then stepped inside, closing the door behind him. He walked toward me and put the bottle in his hand down on a side table.

"I'm sorry, did you just say that your grandmother . . . died?" I was drinking, so I didn't answer. "Tabby! Are you talking about your grandmother that you're named after? When? Are you okay?"

"Marc, I . . . donwanna talk." I got up from the sofa with my wineglass in one hand and used the other to unbutton my blouse, letting it drop to the floor as I walked over to him. In that moment, I understood what Laila meant by just needing to stop hurting. The wine had anesthetized the bulk of my pain, and the rest, I just needed to replace with something else. Topless, in just my bra, I kissed him full and heavy on his lips. For a second, he kissed me back . . . and then, he pushed me away.

"Tabby!" he said, holding me at half arm's-length distance. "You're drunk."

"Immnot," I said. "I tolyou want I wanted, din'I?"

"How can you . . ." he tried to ask, but I cut him off with another full kiss. This time, grabbing him in a way that I knew he wouldn't resist. In response, he kissed me back, full and heavy. He took the wineglass out of my hands and placed it down on the nearest surface. To the bed, we moved as a single organism, shedding clothing along our path in a wake of textiles, underwear, bra, and socks until we were naked on the bed. My head swirled. I felt him enter me. I pushed back. Like this we continued as I searched for the intensity that continually felt just beyond my reach.

I lost control of myself in the ways I needed to. It was all too much. Flashes of everything ripped through my mind: Dr. Ellis, Dr. Young, Scott, Chris, Officer Mallory, Laila, Rob, Alexis, and Daequan's mother's tears. I thought of my grandmother and the choices that I'd made, trying to save everyone else and I couldn't even save myself. *If only I could stop all this thinking*, my mind cycled back to me. But I couldn't still my thoughts. "Harder!" I yelled. "Marc, harder!" Marc pushed against me harder. But it still wasn't enough. "Harder! Harder! Harder!" It started to hurt. I knew we needed to stop, but I couldn't.

"I don't want to hurt you."

"Yes you do." The words came out on their own. I started to cry.

"Whoa, Tabby, I don't . . ." I cut him off again, with a kiss, another kiss, and a tightening of myself around him. I didn't want him to stop. I needed him . . . right now, I needed *something*. Maybe it was this. If this was all Marc could give me, I would take it all. On this night, Marc would be my refuge and my punishment. Like a thousand other tiny deaths before, I wanted to expire by consumption and be reborn perhaps as somebody else. Somebody who didn't make all the mistakes that I had. Somebody who didn't miss seeing a friend in trouble . . . somebody who didn't let her grandmother die alone . . . somebody who was worthy of being chosen for love . . . somebody worth staying for. I let my tears flow, hoping that Marc would leave me extinguished, exhausted, fully. At the least, so I could find the slightest comfort in a few hours of sleep.

I don't remember how or when we fell asleep, but I woke just before dawn groggy with a throbbing headache. I sat up and turned slightly to see a naked and sleeping Marc in my bed. A feeling of disgust rose in me, and the memories of the evening flooded forward into my consciousness. Maybe like the darkness that Laila described, exhaustion could also creep up on you too, like a silent thief, at your throat before you know it for all your valuables. I had let so much build up, pushed through it all, and for what? Chasing everything I thought I was supposed to have was costing me everything that mattered most. *My grandmother, my Granny Tab, was dead. I missed the last chance to spend time with her. She was counting on me . . . I let her down, just like Laila.*

I watched Marc sleep. I remembered his words, his rejection, his denial of interest in any of my most sacred gifts, preferring instead to make use of my time, my body, and my pleasant company. I felt a slight satisfaction in knowing what it felt like to use him similarly. I felt him stir beside me. I wondered if he'd open his eyes and see me watching him. I wondered if he knew I was watching him because I was ready for him to leave. I cleared my throat. His eyelids lifted halfway.

"Hey . . ." he said groggily.

"Good morning."

"That was quite a night."

"Was it?"

"Tab, everything happened so . . . so fast, we didn't get to talk. I'm sorry about—"

"My dead grandmother?" I said flatly.

"Whoa." Marc sat up quickly. "Tab, are you okay?" He tried to put his arms around me, but I pulled away.

"Does it matter?"

"Tabby, what's wrong with you?" *Everything. Everything is wrong, can't you see that, Marc?*

"Nothing, Marc. Absolutely nothing. I'm fine."

"You're *fine*? So, you're not going to talk to me? What am I—just some good dick to you now?"

"Relatively speaking." I knew I needed Marc to leave. I realized I was being cruel in a way he didn't deserve, but I couldn't help it. The prior night just confirmed what I already knew in my deepest parts, and the disappointment made me bitter. He thought that somehow the magic from his penis would fix everything. Well, I tried it, and there was no magic in it. I was still just as broken.

"What the *fuck*, Tab? What is *wrong* with you?"

At that very moment, so much of me wanted to collapse in his arms and just let go. The other part remembered how he hurt me and wanted to hurt him right back. And yet another part wanted to build a barrier between us to protect the deep wounds still fresh underneath. My body shook as

I felt the tears come. But I couldn't allow myself to cry, not with him. He couldn't be trusted. I forced it all back inside.

"I don't understand, Marc, why are *you* getting upset?" I asked. "I thought *you* wanted to be single purpose." Almost instantly, I regretted those words. In the very moment I needed him desperately, I couldn't even trust him enough to take the comfort that he offered. And I couldn't figure out if it was his fault or if it was mine. *Look what he did when you needed him before,* my thoughts reminded me. Marc got up and jumped out of my bed, snatching what clothing he could find in front of him.

"I think I should go," he said, bending over to replace his underwear.

"That's probably a good idea." *Keep running, Marc. Keep running. And I'll keep building walls so you can't hurt me.* Marc disappeared from the bedroom. Finally, I heard the door close. And then I lowered my head back onto the pillow, wrapped my own arms around my torso, and finally let the tears come.

3 5

FOR THE SECOND TIME ON SUNDAY, I WOKE UP WITH A START. I had been dreaming of my grandmother. It was almost a replay of our last conversation, but the only specific thing I could remember was of her with tears in her eyes, yet smiling and saying, "Be optimistic." *Optimistic.* That was quite a word for today's circumstances. And a better challenge for another day. Admittedly, under questionable judgment, I poured what remained of the wine from the previous night into an empty coffee mug and gulped it down before leaving for Crestmire. To my credit, considering how much of the bottle I had actually consumed in the prior night's mega-serving, there really wasn't much left to finish off. Deep down somewhere, I worried in some way what my drinking had become. All I knew was that it allowed the flood of memories from the prior day and evening to be metered by my brain, slowing the rush to something I could process. I cringed just slightly, recalling that Marc left in a huff after our morning in the bedroom. It was something I didn't have the energy to fix.

By the time I picked up my phone, Chris had already sent an email to discuss the follow-up on our interview with

Daequan and his family. As it turned out, *both* of our competitors in the local market picked up on the story during their eleven p.m. news hour, which meant we must have hit pay dirt with our exclusive. On any other occasion, this would have been an incredible development. Not today. I sent Chris a note back to let him know of my circumstances and that I wasn't available. Yesterday I had the option of focusing on my grandmother or work. Today, I had fewer choices. At Crestmire, my dad was waiting on me to make one final visit.

On the car ride, I called my mother and then Lexi to tell her the news. I tried my best to keep things brief. The attempted comforts around death are sometimes the worst part of the experience—the heaviness of the conversations, the expectations of sadness, and the careful word choices. All that inevitably trended toward depressing, rather than uplifting. Thankfully, my arrival at Crestmire provided the perfect excuse to end the rolling of obligatory outreach.

My dad was standing in the middle of Granny Tab's living room when I walked into her apartment. He was holding a faded family picture of her with him as a little boy from her cluttered menagerie shelf and seemed absorbed in a memory. I hesitated to disturb him, but felt uncomfortable as an observer. I let the door close behind me with enough noise to announce my presence. My dad turned to me, startled, with the picture still in his hand.

"Hey, Two," he said softly. I couldn't help but notice the slight hesitation before he addressed me as "Two." I guessed because there weren't two anymore. Now I was the *only* Tabitha Walker.

"Hey, Dad, whatcha got there?" I said.

"Just a picture of me and your grandmother . . ." he said

wistfully. The moment felt more awkward than it should have. I realized that, presently, my dad and I were operating at the far limits of our relationship. We found ourselves in the grip of an emotional tide that was rivaled only by that fateful day in the kitchen, when my mother broke the news of his departure. And other than my father's wedding, this would be the most significant day of loss that I had ever felt.

"She looks . . . *looked* so young and happy," I said.

"Those were good times . . . and not so good times . . . but mostly good times," he said. I thought back to what Granny Tab told me about my father's history with his own father. I wondered if I would have ever known if she hadn't chosen to tell me that day.

"I . . . miss her," I mused, as much to myself as to my dad.

"I miss her too. It feels like she's *right here*, but just barely out of reach. It's like this picture. We had gone to the beach. I almost drowned." He let out a little laugh. "Well, I *thought* I was going to. Mom took me out in the ocean, and the tide swept me away from her—just enough that my feet couldn't touch the bottom and I couldn't reach her hands. For the few seconds until she stepped out to pull me back to her, I panicked. I just knew that I would wash away, lost forever. That's kind of how . . ."

"You feel now . . ." I said, finishing his sentence as he trailed off. He nodded, taking a dab at his eyes. I didn't know how, or if, to comfort him, so I just stood frozen in the uncomfortable silence. My dad seemed to catch the wave of a thought and brought himself back into the moment with renewed attention.

"I guess we need to talk about the funeral program."

"I'm not sure I know how to plan one, but anything I can do, you know I will," I said.

"Your focus should probably be on giving the eulogy, and I and Diane will handle the rest. I think I have a pretty good idea of what she'd have wanted." What? *Me, the screwup? No way I could be trusted with the eulogy.*

"Oh, Dad, I can't. I can't give the eulogy. You . . . need to find someone else—what about you?"

"Me? Oh no, Tabby—this is what your grandmother would have wanted." *Are you sure? I couldn't even keep my word to her. I'm not anyone to rely on.*

"Dad, really, I can't. I'm not the right person."

"Tabby, you *are*. Will you just think about it? I'll understand if you need some time to consider things. You have some days to decide." This was exactly what I did not want to do. I didn't want to consider anything. I just wanted to be numb.

36

ON SUNDAY EVENING, ALEXIS CAME OVER TO MY PLACE TO SIT with me. We talked and cried, reminiscing over memories of my grandmother. We cried until we laughed. We laughed until we got tired. Eventually, I was able to sleep.

I wasn't able to take a day off of work because of the Daequan Jenkins story, so I forced myself into the gym on Monday morning for rapid self-care. The question of my grandmother's eulogy roiled through my mind like a tornado. The idea of standing in front of the entire church, like I was this dutiful granddaughter, felt like a heinous lie. *What kind of person picks an assignment for work over the last moments with their grandmother?* In my mind, it was almost as if the turn of events was instant judge and jury, the ultimate condemnation for yet another one of my wrong decisions. No, I couldn't stand up there and pretend like I deserved to be there, or that it might have been anything Granny Tab would have wanted, especially now. Still, as much as the punishment of my thoughts seemed to fit my "crime," in the deepest part of me, not doing the eulogy didn't feel like the right resolution either.

On my phone, I noticed a missed call from Ms. Gretchen, who I presumed was calling for the funeral details. She was still on her road trip, but was going to arrange to come back early, "whenever she needed to," she said, for Granny Tab's funeral. She said, at her age, friends' funerals were like the weddings of her late twenties. According to Ms. Gretchen, both events took place in a church and both eventually put you in the hole. Of course, after two divorces, she would think that. Walking back home from the gym, I returned the call.

"Hey, Tabby! How're you doin'?" Ms. Gretchen said with her usual cheer.

"I'm hanging in there, Ms. Gretchen."

"Hanging in there?" Ms. Gretchen said. "At your age, nothing should be hanging except your hair, honey!" *Did she not realize my grandmother just died?* "Now, when are Tabitha's arrangements? I'm about ready to head back, anyway. Mr. Harper brought these pills—he's a frisky somebody. Just after me. I tell you, I had to find those pills—little blue things—and hide them! Vinaga, Vegara, somethin'—anyway they had to go, or Mr. Harper was gonna have to have an early meeting with *his* maker!"

"Viagra, Ms. Gretchen?"

"Yes! Now, that sounds like it. He was telling me he had this Vinagra, and I said, Mr. Harper, if you don't get your old ass away from me!" She broke out in laughter. "What do I look like messin' with a man *older* than me?"

It felt good to laugh.

"I'm glad you got him told, Ms. Gretchen!" I said.

"I sure did! Okay, so now, give me the news. When will we celebrate my friend?"

"The funeral will be on Wednesday," I said. "We just need

to find someone to give the eulogy," I mumbled more to my-self, than to her.

"What do you mean, find *someone*? You're not going to do it?" Ms. Gretchen said.

"I don't think so, Ms. Gretchen. I just don't feel right . . . you know, I missed Senior Prom with Granny Tab. I wasn't even there to help her get ready."

"I'm sure you had a good reason!"

Did I? How could she be so sure? "I don't know about that, Ms. Gretchen. I didn't have to do that interview."

"Then who woulda done it? The way you kids think these days, I swear I will never understand it. You were *always* your grandmother's pride and joy. She'd watch the news ev-ery day—wouldn't miss it and would make me watch too—just on the *chance* that you were on," Ms. Gretchen said with a small laugh. "She would have *wanted* you to be your *best*, Tabby, always. Including that interview. You have the chance to have a career and a life that Tabitha and I could only dream of. I'm sure it wasn't some *Senior Prom* that was the highlight of your grandmother's evening. It was watching *you* do your interview. She was proud of you and happy for you. I know it as sure as I know my own name."

"I don't know about that, Ms. Gretchen."

"Well you *should* know it. Listen, people can't control what happens from one moment to another. I can count on one hand all the times I've seen Tabitha dance, in all the years I've known her, but I know she loved it. If she had a heart attack, it wasn't 'cause her makeup wasn't on right or her updo was missing a bobby pin. Some things are just gonna happen, sweetheart. Nothing we can do about them one way or another. We just have to focus on what choices we have in front of us, not the ones behind. I know you'll make the right decision about that eulogy. Now I've gotta go—I have to figure out how to get back there before Wednesday. And keep Mr. Harper off my tailfeather till then!" Laughter forced its way upward and carried a smile to my face. Her wisdom was a welcome anesthetic for that portion of my mind that lived to rub salt in my wounds of guilt and self-doubt. And maybe she was right.

37

I MADE IT TO THE OFFICE, BROKEN, UNCERTAIN, HURTING—WELL, aching really, but focused and with my so-called game face on for the workday. Chris already knew the events of the weekend and had asked me to meet with him first thing to discuss my "certainly understandable" needs for time off. In the meantime, my Daequan Jenkins interview began to spiral upward and outward to take on a life of its own. I was leaning heavily on my reporting team to chase after leads and angles while I contemplated the most important question facing me for the week: Would I, and really, should I, be the one to deliver Granny Tab's eulogy?

Coming off the elevator, the same one I had shared just weeks ago with Scott Stone challenging my "limited" *perspective*, I took a breath into the center of my being. I knew my emotions were running too hot and too raw for me to be there, but I had no choice. Plus, all I really needed to do on this day was make it through my meeting with Chris, set the direction for my reporting team on next steps for the Jenkins story, and get the hell out of there . . . to start planning my *grandmother's funeral*. *Granny Tab is dead*, my mind echoed. As I walked to Chris's office, the mental reminder of my grandmother's passing operated like a snooze button that I kept pushing, pushing off, pushing away, to stave off the looming breakdown that I felt threatening my professional demeanor. *Just make it through this meeting with Chris,* I told myself. *Just this one meeting.*

Chris's door was slightly ajar when I got there, and I knocked and pushed it open when I heard his voice call out for me to enter. I headed for the open seating in front of his desk.

"Tabby! Please, have a seat. I'm *so* sorry about your grandmother. I know the two of you were close."

"Thanks, Chris."

"I hate to jump right into business, but Tabby, your Daequan Jenkins interview is on fire! Three local stations now covering, two cable nationals, and I just got a request this morning for footage licensing from corporate. You're going national broadcast! Tabby, dammit, it only took you a month, and you proved me right. Congratulations, this is your first major win." *Ask me what I lost, though, Chris.*

"I'm sorry, I wish I could be more excited."

"Tabby, this is not the time to go falling apart. You hit major pay dirt. This is the once-in-a-lifetime career opportunity that people would *kill* their own grandmother for. Sorry, that was probably insensitive."

You think? I just sat there and blinked at him in stunned silence. I couldn't believe that Chris had kids—in that moment, he seemed like he would eat them himself if he happened to get hungry enough. Although I felt the anger rising in my gut, I said nothing. Sometimes, silence speaks for you.

"Sorry, honestly, Tabby, that was probably, most definitely, inappropriate . . . What I'm trying to say to you is, take the time that you need. Take these two days off, mourn with your family. Tina and Jim will cover for you. But don't take your eye off the ball—you *have* to run this play. It's *your* story. Make sure it's *your* win. This is the kind of stuff that makes a whole career."

I had to count backward from ten to keep myself from exploding. I took a deep breath and closed my eyes, managing to find a measured tone to respond.

"Thanks, Chris, I understand what you're trying to say. I think I'm going to need more than two days off, I think I need at lea—"

"No—Tabby, don't do this," Chris said, interrupting. "You don't want to do that. Look, if you insist, I have to find a way to give you the days off. That means someone else gets your spot. Do you want me to give your spotlight to another reporter?"

I sat fuming but forced myself to think about his question. The honest answer was no. But my soul screamed inside, *You need some time to heal!* I just couldn't afford to take any. Chris was right. I could manage with the two days through the funeral; if I counted half of today, that was almost three. Somehow, I'd make it to the weekend. If I could just make it to the weekend.

"No," I said softly.

"No what? Which no?" Chris said quickly, in a near panic.

"No, I don't want another reporter on my story," I said firmly. "The funeral is Wednesday. I'll find availability out of the office as I can. I'll be back in the office on Thursday," I said, getting up. I was *done* talking to Chris.

"Tabby, I know it doesn't feel like it now, but this is a good decision!" Chris called out to my back as I walked out the door.

I walked double time to my office, picked up all my things and the paperwork that I would need for the two days off I did have. I sent quick emails to Tina and Jim that I would call them later from home. Jacket on my arm, with a bag full of papers and a mind full of raging thoughts, I walked as quickly as I could with my head down to the elevator. Although not quickly enough, because steps before the doors to safety, I ran into Lisa, who started talking before I had a chance to make a clean getaway.

"Tabby, hey! Amazing story over the weekend! Just amazing. *That* is the kind of interview that we need to be doing, and you got the exclusive! Wow. Listen, we missed you at the women's issues meeting—your voice is going to be so powerful . . ."

I stopped hearing anything after that. It's a funny thing about losing control. Perhaps like exhaustion, perhaps like darkness even, it's another thing that just creeps up on you— it's there before you know it, and when you do know it, you're already in trouble. And it's a funny thing about breaking points—all at once, everything is so clear, yet nothing is clear at all.

"*Every* problem can't be *my* problem, *Lisa*!" I heard myself say a little too loudly as I moved toward the opening elevator doors to make my escape. "I'm sorry, I just . . . *can't*. I have to go—I have to go write a eulogy!" I could feel Lisa's eyes on my back as I walked past her into the closing elevator, not stopping until I could support myself against the wall. I'd need it, because I was near collapse. The doors closed, and all the energy that I'd summoned to make it into the office that day drained from my body. I leaned against the wall, and although I tried to stop them, the tears came again, carving their familiar path through my makeup down my cheeks.

I was tired of crying, so, so tired of crying.

38

THERE IS ONLY SO LONG THAT A PERSON CAN STARE AT A BLANK computer screen before certain madness starts to set in. My right mind I lost somewhere between Saturday and Sunday, so whatever was left was operating on generator power, and the gas was running low.

I squeezed my eyes shut with my fingers for a brief massage and took another sip from my wineglass. Thankfully, the calls and text messages of condolence had died down and I could focus on the gargantuan task at hand—to look at my grandmother's eighty-five years of life, find the high points and perhaps a lesson in it all. My memory served as her voice, reminding me of all the patches of stories she told me about her journey. I imagined what an interview with her would cover, what she would want the world to know, and what I needed the audience to hear . . . and to remember.

There were the things I couldn't, or shouldn't, talk about. The things that hide within a family, between the lines of generations—alcoholism, rifts, lack of educational opportunity, racism. Granny Tab had ended so much of the iniquity, yet not all of it. My dad had been fighting battles that I was unaware of. Perhaps I was, as well. My mind went to Marc, his words floating in across the waves of other thoughts. "My father is an alcoholic," I could hear him say again. *An alcoholic.* My father and Marc were equally yoked by the common sins of their fathers' burdens. "Your father, he is the rare type," I heard Granny Tab say in my mind. I wondered if it was she who made him that way. Losing her best friend to segregation and racism at eighteen, and then her whole family to the same affliction years later when she dared to love a Black man—I imagined the same set of circumstances would have been enough to destroy a different woman.

I couldn't talk about how she managed to survive abuse at the hands of a persecuted Black man, who, by the laws of his own country, was denied the basic rights of where he could own a home and send their little brown baby to school; who, by the rules of society, was denied employment and a fair shot at making a way for his family—the fundamental ability to provide and protect. I also couldn't mention the family I didn't know. So, I wouldn't discuss my grandmother's white relatives in West Virginia, who forgot that the ties of blood were stronger than tribe. I would have to leave all of these things out, to focus on the life that my grandmother lived in spite of it all. Instead, I would talk about *courage*, my grandmother's courage to continue alone and to make her own family, by her own definition, through her own love, according to her own vision.

I couldn't talk about how she died, or what ultimately took her last breath away. I could only talk about how she lived. Not the adversity, and the hardships and the worry and pain—these were only the seeds that were planted in the fertile soil of her spirit, watered by tears and blood. I would speak only of the fruit—the flowering rewards of transmuted hardships, evolved and metamorphosed into beauty that undeniably radiated from within. My grandmother's grace could not be obfuscated by the curtains of wrinkles that time pulled into her skin, or dulled by the thinning of her hair and lips and the skin on her face. She taught me important lessons of the strength of vulnerability and power in simply holding space. She left a thousand pieces of herself everywhere like the fluffs of a dandelion, carried by the wind—in the students she taught, in the hearts of her friends, in the spirits of her progeny—in me.

I knew what I needed to say. Not just to people who would come to pay their respects on Wednesday, but to one person who had recently borne the brunt of my worst. As a tribute to my grandmother, I remembered the strength in my own vulnerability. I pulled out my phone to text Marc.

Me:
Sorry about the other night/day.
Me:
My grandmother's funeral is on Weds. Will send you the details.
Me:
You don't have to come, of course.
Me:
Just would be nice to see you there.

39

FOR THE FIRST TIME EVER, I SPENT THE NIGHT VOLUNTARILY IN Calabasas. On Wednesday morning, we would wake up, get dressed, and as a clumsy version of a family, travel together to lay my grandmother to rest.

My mother called me early to let me know that she and the general had arrived from DC. I was impressed she made no mention of the fact that I would be arriving with my dad and said only she would see me at the funeral. For her, that was unprecedented restraint. Alexis, who had called me faithfully every day since Sunday, said she would be there also. It was Laila who I still hadn't told about my grandmother. I didn't know how. It seemed too soon. My grandmother's funeral was an unfair burden to ask Laila to bear, so even though I would have loved to have her as support, I wanted to allow her space for her own healing. I hoped she'd understand later why I didn't ask her to be there this one time.

I got to the house late in the evening, after a phone conference with my research team. I would return to broadcast just one day after Granny Tab's funeral, with a follow-up interview and report on the Jenkins shooting. As it turned out, the family was considering filing charges against the city, and the DA was considering pressing charges against the officer. No decisions had been made, but since my coverage on the steps of the hospital, it had bubbled forward to the biggest local story of the week. I couldn't ignore it entirely, so I worked as late as I could to keep Wednesday sacred and set aside to observe and honor Granny Tab.

The morning of, I was in the middle of running through my mental notes and curling my hair in the en suite attached to the guest bedroom when Danielle and Dixie appeared in my sight line, hovering around the bathroom door.

"Can we come in?" Danielle asked.

"Of course," I said to both of them.

"I . . . wanted to ask . . . if you could help me with my hair," Danielle said, not fully looking me in my eyes.

"Sure I will," I said, trying to sound reassuring. "How do you want it?"

"I want it to look . . . like yours," Danielle said, now half looking up at me. For some reason, those words delivered a sharp pang to my gut. *Like mine?*

"Can you make mine look like yours too?" Dixie interjected.

"Dixie, she doesn't have time to help us both. She's speaking for Nana. I'll do yours after," Danielle turned and said with loving firmness to her sister. Dixie turned to her signature doe-eyed pout, which worked miracles on my dad but got nowhere with Danielle. I laughed lightly to myself at both of them and brought Danielle closer to start working on her frizzy curls with my flat iron. Thankfully, her hair responded quite easily to the heat after a couple of passes. "We saw your interview on Saturday, of that kid who got shot," Danielle said.

"Yeah, it was really good!" Dixie added.

"You guys watch me on the news?" I asked.

"Oh, yeah, every day pretty much," Danielle said. "Our mom turns it on at every news hour, just in case you're reporting. Sometimes you're not even on, and we still watch it."

"Yep, KVTV!" Dixie said.

"Is he still going to be able to be a surgeon? I mean, after he got shot in the arm like that?" Danielle asked.

"The doctors all think so," I said. "Thank God the officer's bullet just passed through and didn't destroy anything major. He was really lucky."

"We didn't understand why he got shot," Danielle said, half turning around to look at me. I gently pushed her head back to the forward-facing position so that I could finish the curl that I was working on. She sighed and then continued, gesturing with her hands, "I mean, he didn't do anything wrong, did he? It seemed like he was just helping his grandmother move."

"That's right, that's what happened. He wasn't doing anything wrong," I said, still working the flat iron around Danielle's head.

"I bet the officer who shot him feels really bad," Danielle said. "And the people who called the police on him when he was just helping his grandma. I couldn't imagine that happening to me. I'd be so scared."

Officer Mallory's words echoed through my mind. *No good and decent officer wants to go home at night knowing that he shot a nineteen-year-old kid* . . . I hoped that was the truth.

"I don't think he *wanted* to shoot the boy, so the officer probably does feel bad in some way," I said. "But, no question, it should not have happened."

"Should we be afraid of the police too?" Dixie asked. I felt another strange pang. I looked down at little Dixie, with her huge version of Granny Tab's blue eyes and her sun-streaked, straight, glossy brown hair, cascading down across her only lightly toasted beige shoulders, and I knew words that I couldn't speak. I wish that I could have told her that the answer to her question was no. If all she meant by "we" was her and Danielle, then perhaps the answer would be no. But if "we" meant all kids, then there was no way for me to tell her how to distinguish the good cops from the bad cops, the well trained from the underequipped, and that it wouldn't be just a factor of luck that determined who any kid, or any person, would come across on any given day. I wish I could have told her that anything I ever saw in my reporting, or in life in general, could assure me of my safety, or her of her own. Perhaps she would be protected by her straight hair and fair skin, and those beautiful blue eyes that she could make doe-like at will. Perhaps she'd be protected by the fact that she didn't look like a Black girl, that no one would ever think to see her as a "color"—but it didn't mean that she wouldn't be *affected*. I thought of Officer Mallory and the pain in his eyes and the pleading in his voice, the honesty and sincerity . . . *No good and decent officer wants to go home at night knowing that he shot a nineteen-year-old kid* . . . I remembered the feeling of fear that must have been reflected in my own eyes in our original confrontation. Maybe we could all be part of a different future. I gave the best answer that I could, the one that reflected all of the truth that I knew and all of the hope that I could muster. I looked directly at my little sister to speak.

"You shouldn't *have to* be afraid of the police, Dixie. No kid should have to be."

40

DIXIE, WHO UNFORTUNATELY I DIDN'T KNOW WELL ENOUGH TO distinguish her usual cheeriness from unusual nervousness, insisted on holding my hand along the entire car ride and into the church for Granny Tab's funeral. Our being joined in this way held the same feeling of mild awkwardness as being made to introduce yourself to a stranger at a networking function. It occurred to me this might be Dixie's first-ever funeral, so I bore out the unease. I figured she wouldn't be doing it if she didn't feel that she needed to in some way. Danielle had attached herself to our dad, and similar to Dixie with me, she didn't let go. Diane had his other side, and I wasn't sure if it was as support for him, or for her own shoulder to lean on.

While I rode in the limousine, wearing my black sunglasses, I was able to steal a few glances at Diane. It surprised me that she watched me on the news, even when my father wasn't around, and that she involved the girls in this attenuated way of connecting us all. I guess, all these years, it was the most of myself that I had offered to them. Different from the woman threaded through some of my worst memories, this Diane looked older, much older than the version of her in my mind, like a more run-down and road-weary version of my tormentor. She looked tired, and blue-black puffed-out bags sat beneath her eyes. I was almost relieved when she put her own sunglasses on just as we arrived at the church.

Our group walked in and up the aisle to the front section, reserved for family members. I looked briefly to the right and left and could see my mother and the general seated discreetly a few rows back. I wondered who else would come. I also saw Ms. Gretchen, wearing a very interesting hat, sitting in the third row of pews. The front of the church was decorated with flowers of all sorts and colors, from planters on the floor to beautiful rose sprays on stands. For a moment, I wondered where they all could have possibly come from. Granny Tab didn't have much family to claim, and her friends were mostly at Crestmire, as I knew it. I also couldn't imagine how the pews could be so full of just people that she knew. I leaned over to whisper to my dad.

"Dad, who are all those people?" My dad seemed startled that someone was actually speaking to him. He seemed lost in a world of his own thoughts. He turned to look at me and leaned down to speak to me over Diane and Dixie, who still had not let go of my hand.

"What people?"

"All those people in the pews. I've never seen any of them before," I said, slightly looking back. My dad joined me in looking back as well. He let his glance linger and took his time turning back around.

"You don't know?" he said to me with surprise.

"No idea. Who are they?"

"They're all her students," he said. "And their families,

looks like." I turned back around with a profound under-standing. In front of me lay my grandmother in death. But in the rows and rows of full pews behind me, in the people at my sides, and even in the memories inside me, there I could find her life.

When it came time for me to give Granny Tab's eulogy, I was asked by the church pastor to come up to the front of the church, to the podium, to deliver my remarks. For this, I wouldn't have minded having Dixie's hand to hold on to, rather than to walk alone across the front of the church and up the stairs to the pulpit, a place I had not been since my baptism over twenty years prior. I tried to walk steady in my heels, channeling my anxiety into determination and resolve to honor my grandmother in the best way I knew how.

From an elevated position, facing everyone in attendance, I could see much more than before. Not only was I looking out at Granny Tab's life, I was looking at mine as well. I took a moment to absorb as much as I could before I started. I got a good look at my mom and the general, sitting off to themselves, on the opposite side of my dad and Diane, at a very respectful distance from the front. My mother still looked beautiful, but also appeared slightly worn down—perhaps by grief. The general looked as I remembered him, clean-shaven and handsome with brown skin, strong, as-sured features, and a full head of low-clipped salt-and-pepper hair. His posture was as precise as a Pilates advertisement. I saw Ms. Gretchen, who of course wasn't wearing black, but some kind of lilac-colored ensemble, *with* matching nails. I remember her telling me once that she didn't wear black to funerals—"Because the ones I go to, we're lucky to live this long!" she'd said. "Somebody's got to be the timekeeper!

When I die, folks better walk by my casket and say, 'Congratulations!'" I was grateful for that balancing memory in the effort to maintain my composure. I also saw Lexi, sitting with Rob Jr., Lexington . . . and Rob. And then, to my surprise, directly in front of her, sat Laila. *Laila.* As I looked at them, they both connected eyes with me. Lexi had her still-ringless left hand on Laila's shoulder in front of her and I watched as Laila raised her hand to cover Lexi's with her own. Their eyes glimmered with wetness, visible even from the distance. I looked away quickly to the back of the room to make sure that my own eyes stayed dry. And there, focused on the back, they connected with Marc, sitting in the last row of pews, in the seat closest to the aisle, leaning toward it. I presumed it was to make sure that I saw him. We locked eyes for only a moment. But it was enough. On the way back to my notes, I let my eyes linger slowly over all the faces of the people I didn't know. People of all colors, all ages. Some were holding kids in their laps—some were nicely dressed, some had on jeans and looked like they came this day without much knowledge of the dress code for the occasion. But still, they were *here.*

"Friends, family, colleagues . . . and . . . *former students,*" I began, emphasizing the newly added words at the end. "I welcome you to a celebration of life for Mrs. Tabitha Abigail Holland Walker, my namesake, and my grandmother."

41

I DELIVERED MY GRANDMOTHER'S EULOGY IN A HAZE OF EMOTION and adrenaline. If I hadn't written the words before I gave them, I'd have no recollection of what I said at all. For this, I gave myself over entirely to the moment. She deserved the best of everything I had to give.

For the end of the service, we scheduled a modest reception at the church hall to greet those who would not be attending the much smaller program later at the burial site. Not everyone was capable of devoting a full Wednesday to a funeral. This meant, ready or not, *we*, meaning Granny Tab's immediate family, would need to transition into socializing mode, almost as if it had been a very sad wedding that had just taken place, rather than a funeral.

The first wave of people who approached me, I very much did not know. True to my father's words, they were my grandmother's former students and their families. Most shared compliments on the eulogy I delivered and kind thoughts about their time in Mrs. Walker's classroom. The children she had taught to read, write, and do algebra, just like she did me at her kitchen table, had turned into adults with real lives and still-lingering fond memories. I was surprised to hear that Granny Tab was also a much-beloved counselor—not in the official type of capacity, but the kind who always had an open door, open ears, and an open heart for a kid in crisis. My mother rushed over to me, pushing her way through the growing throng of people, to give me her own big hug. She squeezed me tightly, in protective mama-bear fashion, and I let myself be held, grateful for the connection.

"Tabby Cat!!" my mother exclaimed while still holding me close. "You did an incredible job today. Your speech was perfect . . . It was moving and excellent, it was such an honor to your grandmother. I'm so proud of you," she said, stepping back, but still holding me at my shoulders. "We are so proud of you." She motioned with her head to the general, standing just behind her.

"Excellent job, young lady," he said. He reminded me of Colin Powell in the way that everything he said sounded like an official decree of the government. My mother beamed through her own weight of sadness. I was just starting to ask her how their trip in from DC was when I saw a head poking up behind her, trying to get my attention by pretending that she wasn't. It was Lisa, from KVTV. I looked past my mother, straight at her. *What's she doing here? Please, not to bother me about work. Not today, Lord, I don't think I have the patience.*

"Lisa?" I said to her, loud enough to ensure she heard me. She pretended to be surprised.

"Oh!" she said looking around, as if I could have been calling out to some other Lisa in the vicinity. "I'm so sorry, I don't mean to disturb," she said tentatively and looking apologetically at me, my mother, and the general.

"Oh, no, don't worry!" my mom said, taking the general

by the arm. "You two talk—we'll have plenty of time to catch up." She turned to Lisa and extended her hand to shake for an introduction. "Hi, I'm Jeanie Williams, Jeanie Walker Williams. I'm Tabby's mom."

"Oh, so nice to meet you!" Lisa said effusively. "Lisa Sinclair, I'm Tabby's colleague at KVTV." My mom also briefly introduced the general as my stepdad and then excused the both of them to move to a different part of the reception, leaving just Lisa and me to talk.

"I hope you don't mind that I came. I promise I'm not stalking you," she said with a forced smile.

"I actually probably owe you an apology."

"No, no, don't apologize. Really, I owe *you* an apology. When you left the office on Monday, they announced right after that your grandmother had passed, and I felt just awful. I mean, imagine me bringing up something so small in relation to everything you were dealing with in that moment."

"Really, you had no way of knowing, I—"

"Still, I just get total tunnel vision about things sometimes," she said. "I'm so caught up in how things could and should be, sometimes I miss seeing . . . what I need to see, that's right in front of me."

"Don't worry, it happens to everyone," I said, immediately thinking of myself with Laila.

"Well, I asked at the station if I could be the one to represent your work family at your grandmother's funeral." Lisa smiled at me earnestly. "And wow, I just have to say that was a beautiful service your family had for her—so moving. And to see all those people . . . She must have really been an incredible person . . . and obviously the apple does not fall far . . ." I managed to summon a smile; I could tell that Lisa was really trying. "Anyway, there's a flower arrangement up front, on behalf of all of us and, you know, sometimes they aren't as nice in real life as they seem when you order online, so you really have to just go and see for yourself, and I . . ." I shifted on my feet and gathered my patience. It didn't take much to recognize that she was nervous. Lisa noticed and caught herself. "Sorry, I'm rambling," she said, suddenly looking down. "You don't need to know all that. Just . . . the flowers are there—they're beautiful—so, there's that."

"Thank you, Lisa. Really, I appreciate it." I still felt the need to apologize, to let her know that I was just overwhelmed, with *everything*, but was too exhausted to search for the words to say. I tried to make the gesture, but Lisa cut me off before I could begin.

"And most of all, I really did want to apologize to you, *personally*. I was badgering you about the women's issues group at every possible occasion, and never gave you a minute to catch your breath. I mean, first the promotion battle with Scott, then getting settled into your new role, and then all of Chris's changes, and pressure . . . I'm just saying, you were right. You are so *strong*, Tabby. I can see it—I can see myself in you. But I had to realize, strong doesn't mean invincible . . . and that *you*, Tabitha Walker, don't have to take up *every* battle." She reached for my hand and searched to meet my eyes most directly. I allowed the connection. "You *don't*," she emphasized, bringing water to my eyes again, as she gently pulled my hand for further emphasis. "And you can't. It's not possible . . . So, I just wanted you to know, that even if you never show up for a single meeting, even if you pick other battles, I'm still going to keep fighting this one for you . . . for *us*." She hugged me and whispered, "I got your back, girlfriend." And she pulled herself apart from me, smiled, and walked away.

After my conversation with Lisa, I stood still for a window of lost time, stunned into statue-like contemplation. I think my mouth was still slightly open from the shock of it all when Alexis and Laila walked up to me, followed closely by Rob Jr., Lexington, and Rob pulling up the rear. I couldn't help but notice that while Lexi still wasn't wearing her wedding ring, Rob *was* wearing his. I didn't have long to be confused by this because it dawned on me that I hadn't told Laila, or invited her to the funeral. I prepared myself for awkward.

"Hey, girl!" Lexi said, and ushered Laila and me into a three-way hug. "You did a great job, you really did."

"Thank you," I said to Lexi, and then turned to Laila. By this time, Lexington was wrapped around my legs, his crisp white shirt completely untucked, with chocolate handprints on it. Lexi pushed Rob Jr. forward as well, and he gave a slightly higher hug around my waist. They both told me they loved me and moved away, to stand closer to their father.

"Hey, Tab," Rob said as he reached over for a tentative one-armed hug around my shoulders. "I know this can't be easy, but you did a great job up there, fam." He moved to corral the two boys. "Anything you need, okay? Just let us know." Then he turned to Lexi. "Babe, I'm going to take the boys outside and get them some air. We'll be out there when you're done. Take your time." Once he was safely out of earshot, Lexi turned to me with a *what did you expect?* kind of look on her face.

"Okay—Rob?" I said to Lexi with a raised eyebrow. She smiled.

"I mean, it's nothing definite. I'm giving him a chance to *show* me what he keeps trying to *tell* me. That's all. And I'm not putting a damn thing back on this hand until I know for sure." We all laughed, until Laila spoke up.

"Tabby, Alexis and I, um, we had a chance to talk. I wanted you to know that. We came here together." I noticed her fidgeting. "And I wanted to be here . . . because . . ." Laila looked up and smiled slowly. "I had to bring you this . . . for any emergencies." She pulled back the sleeve of her blouse and showed me a thick chunky bracelet she was wearing. Seeing the confusion on my face, she twisted the bracelet around, showing a small knob on the top that looked like a screw top. "It's a flask," she whispered. "Just for you. I'm not drinking, right now."

I examined her wrist more closely, "Wait, you have a *Bat-Signal* bracelet?"

"Bat-Signal!" Both Alexis and Laila affirmed in concert, nodding their heads yes.

I laughed. "Oh my God . . . now you *know* I'll be coming to find you later."

Wrapping up my conversation with the two of them, I knew who I did need to find—Ms. Gretchen. With her soft lavender in a sea of black fabric, it wasn't difficult. She was standing talking to a group of women and a man I recognized from Crestmire. I tapped her lightly on the shoulder. She turned.

"Tabby!" she said happily. "Now see, I told you I'd get here."

"Yes, Ms. Gretchen, you did."

"And you know I don't wear black."

"The lavender is lovely. I'm sure Granny Tab would have

loved it." Upon mention of my grandmother, Ms. Gretchen's eyes softened.

"I . . . miss my friend," she said, quietly, as if it was a secret that only the two of us were meant to share.

"I know, Ms. Gretchen, I miss her too . . ."

She paused and looked at me, taking my hand. "You come and see me sometimes, okay?"

"I will, Ms. Gretchen. You know I'll be there."

Ms. Gretchen smiled, and then looked as if a good idea had just occurred to her. "You know, I've got my *good* dress on. I always meet the nicest men at funerals. Mr. Harper just about wore me out on that trip, but I realized that I'm gonna need some new . . . company." She gave me a wink and turned and started to walk in the direction of another group of older men I also recognized from Crestmire. And I noticed she started to put an exaggerated sway in her hips the closer that she got to them. She turned around and looked back at me one more time with a smile, and joined the group talking. Alone again momentarily, I looked around for Marc—I'd seen him at the funeral, but there was no sign of him anywhere so far. I wanted to at least thank him for coming. At least now I knew he really did care. It was a place to start. Two laps around, at least fifty hugs and a hundred *I'm so sorry*s later, I still hadn't found him—only my dad, standing off to himself in a corner, looking somewhat shell-shocked. There was no Diane, Danielle, or Dixie in sight. I abandoned my search for Marc and went directly to my father.

"Dad, how's it going?" I asked. He turned in my direction and appeared to relax just slightly.

"I needed a little breather," he said. When he looked at

me, I saw a fleeting trace of the small boy that I had imagined so often from Granny Tab's stories.

"Where's Diane and the girls?"

"They went to grab a bite and pick Tanner up from the airport."

"Tanner's coming?"

"He wanted to be here, so he flew back from school. He'll make it for the burial."

"You doing all right?" I asked, giving him a pat on the arm.

"I suppose I should be asking you that."

"I don't know that rules applied to these sorts of things," I said.

"Then let's go get some ice cream," he said.

"Seriously?"

"Don't I look serious?"

In all honesty, he looked sad, and a little spent. But I understood what he meant. So, for the first time since I was a little girl, I took my father's hand. And out the door we went without a single word to anybody else.

EPILOGUE

ALMOST EXACTLY A YEAR FOLLOWING GRANNY TAB'S FUNERAL, I was at home on a Saturday afternoon, singing along to music in my bathroom, hovering close to the mirror while getting myself ready for a *very* important date.

For once, I wasn't running late. Denisha and I reached a compromise on my hair, and she agreed to cut it into a short tapered natural with a well-placed side part. I agreed to let her place those highlights that she always insisted would look so good on camera. She was right. And I was right too—my natural hair did look good, and became much more manageable as a "wash and go," with some slight application of product. Denisha had also been right about chasing the Daequan Jenkins story, and I chased it all the way to the end. The DA declined to press criminal charges, but the officer who shot Daequan was suspended indefinitely and a departmental investigation was launched into training protocols. As the investigation continued, I reported on any new developments. The story was picked up by every local news station and became national news for quite some time. My original interview segment on the steps even ran internationally. Daequan and the Jenkins family hired an attorney and successfully sued the city, reaching a settlement that more than funded Daequan's education, all the way through what remained of undergrad for him, along with medical school, residency, fellowship, postdoc, and even business school, if he wanted. The irony was lost on no one, as it was the need to fund his education that precipitated the entire incident. The story won an Emmy Award for me as a reporter and another for my entire reporting team. It was a good year for KVTV. Now I was up for a promotion again, to weekend anchor. This time, there was no competition. I had not one, but two excellent mentors—Chris *and* Lisa.

True to her word, Lisa took on the challenge of pushing the women's issues group forward. Once I recovered from the loss of my grandmother, the heavy demands of the most intense period of the Jenkins shooting story, and the physical experience of freezing my eggs, I was finally able to make time to attend a meeting. By then, they had already successfully lobbied for a change to our healthcare coverage, which not only included birth control, but also infertility treatment for women and families. This was a landmark development for our industry and catapulted KVTV to the very top of the local news stations in the Southland. In addition to her being a mentor, Lisa and I became pretty good friends, meeting at least once a month for our spa day and tea party, which allowed us to let off some steam just between the two of us.

Finishing my makeup in the mirror, the last bit of mascara applied to precision, with the extra time I decided to pour myself a glass of iced tea and relax in my backyard for a bit before I put my dress on. The change to our insurance allowed me to preserve my down payment, and Granny Tab left me with a little bit more to afford the house that I *really* wanted. The room that I always had in mind for her was here, but now it was littered with random artifacts left from time to time by my *little sisters*, Danielle and Dixie. I'm still learning how to say that—"little sisters"—and I'm still learning how to be a big sister. There was never an official decision of *let's all try to be a family*. I just started accepting a few more dinner invitations in Calabasas, and started extending a few of my own. Diane and I still aren't close, but we have a respectful orbit that she usually doesn't cross. Last time I hosted dinner, I served wine from a vineyard that Laila, Alexis, and I visited on our girls' trip to Napa, just a few months after Granny Tab's funeral.

Alexis and Rob were still working their way back to a marriage, but without a final decision between them she continued her own policy of not wearing her ring. He still wore his faithfully and still lived outside the home, now in his own apartment. It's been no easy road for Laila either, but she found a great life coach and eventually included Alexis and me in a few group sessions. Once we realized that we were talking about everything to one another except for what really mattered, we each realized we needed to do better— for one another, and for ourselves. The counselor gave us a short affirmation to say when we didn't quite know what to say or how to ask for what we needed. It felt awkward to say to one another at first, but it eventually become second nature. I started practicing it in the mirror on myself every morning:

I see you.

I love you.

I acknowledge your struggle.

I think you're beautiful.

Sitting outside on my patio, I pulled up a chair to enjoy a few minutes with the sun, a gentle breeze, and a refreshing glass of tea already covered with the light coating of sweat from condensation. I was looking forward to this evening. My date, I hadn't seen in over two weeks. Relaxing into my chair, I reached over to my phone to check for any work messages and saw that I had a missed call from Marc. I sent him a quick text back to let him know I'd call him tomorrow. Tonight I would be busy—it was Senior Prom at Crestmire again, and Ms. Gretchen was waiting on me. Marc's appearance at Granny Tab's funeral had been the entry point to a new kind of relationship between us. It wasn't lost on me what my father taught me about the kind of damage a person carries, or what my mother taught me about claiming only what's yours and leaving the rest behind. In spite of perhaps his evolving intentions, I realized that Marc was what I called *limited*. He was limited in his capacity to commit, to love, to support, and to show up for me in the ways that I couldn't always name but, well, knew I needed. So, for now, we're friends. *Just* friends—at least, *most* of the time. Sometimes, our chemistry could still get the best of us. Was he the rare type? Maybe. Only time could tell me that. It did take me a very long time to tell anyone about what happened after Marc and I broke up, the confrontation in the car, and the episode after Granny Tab died. For a while, I was really ashamed. In retrospect, perhaps that was *my* breaking point, and I just happened to break wide on him, spilling my guts. Eventually, I told Lexi, and then Laila, and they both said they were shocked that he hadn't ghosted me entirely, after either time. "Guys ghost women now if they do anything that makes them even slightly uncomfortable," Laila said. "And look at what the fuck you did, Tabby, you went full frontal with *your* crazy. I'm shocked he even reached out to you with that 'WYD?' text." But Marc did reach out, he *always* did. Sometimes it would take him a while, but sure enough, something would pop up on my phone. I was learning my own way of trusting him.

Before it got too late and I got too relaxed and too tired, I headed back into my house and into my bedroom to slip into my dress for the evening's festivities. I offered to help Ms. Gretchen get ready, but she refused, saying that she'd let one of the girls at the salon do her makeup after she got her nails done. Ms. Gretchen said to me, "Now, what you need to learn is if you *stay* ready, you don't have to get ready. You know I stay *sittin'* on ready." True to form, Ms. Gretchen was still taking rideshares, watching makeup tutorials, and maintaining that dye job in her particular shade of blond that drove all the men at Crestmire crazy.

WHEN I PULLED UP AT CRESTMIRE, THE VISITORS PARKING LOT was almost empty. I was thankful for the proximity to the door this time, as I clacked my kitten heels through the entrance. Usually, on Saturdays during my regular visits, the spaces were packed. I continued to keep almost the exact same schedule with Ms. Gretchen as I had with Granny Tab. It was another unspoken thing between us. After the funeral, she'd never asked me again to come visit her, but I made sure that she'd never need to. I showed up every week on Saturdays, just as usual, unless I had an emergency work assignment, which did happen sometimes.

I met Ms. Gretchen at her apartment and handed off the

flowers that I brought. She looked radiant in a bright magenta fitted mermaid-style dress, with an off-the-shoulder top and a flare at the bottom, just below the knee. She even had on her two-inch "high heels" that were black-and-white polka dot. Her hair was curled perfectly into a just slightly elevated, more polished version of her regular style, and her makeup was subtle but immaculate. Today, she had chosen metallic magenta polish to match the color of her dress.

Standing in her kitchenette, I said to Ms. Gretchen, "Clearly I have the hottest date at Crestmire!" She smiled in a big way, dropped the flowers on the counter along with my purse and keys, and pulled my hand to usher us out the door.

"Now, you know I had to show these old biddies how it's supposed to be done!" We shuffled quickly down the hallway to the reappropriated activity room, where the Senior Prom would be. "I have Mr. Parker holding some seats for us at the good table, the one near the dance floor," she said.

"Mr. Parker, Ms. Gretchen? Is he somebody special?" I asked, teasing.

"No more special than lunch meat!" she said quickly. We both laughed. "Although," she continued in a playful tone, "this *is* a special night . . . and on special nights, special things can happen." She winked.

Walking into the event space, I was surprised to see that Crestmire had been decorated true to theme. The activity room, which was normally reserved for bingo, crafts, and rocking chairs in front of the willow tree, had been transformed with gold and black balloons, streamers, confetti, tablecloths, and floral centerpieces. One of the aides I recognized from my regular visits even wore a black suit and crisp white shirt as he manned a makeshift DJ station that was already playing music. I took a seat at the table that Ms. Gretchen had indicated for us, and she went directly to the dance floor, led by Mr. Parker's shuffling yet confident steps. Their departure gave me the opportunity to sink into my own thoughts. I placed Granny Tab here in my mind and wondered if she'd be drinking the punch or eating one of the hard candies that were scattered across each table. Maybe she would have even been up dancing with Ms. Gretchen, enjoying herself with a gigantic smile, similar to what I could observe tonight on so many of the other residents' faces. I imagined that I could feel her presence there with me, and maybe she'd be observing in her own quiet way, taking in everything around her and seeing magic in places that other people missed. I thought of the sea of former students at her funeral and, for some reason, my sister Dixie's eyes. In fact, sometimes I imagined if you put the three of us together, Danielle, Dixie, and me, you'd almost have a version of Granny Tab. Danielle had her quiet strength, Dixie her eyes and fearless ability to connect, and as for me, I liked to believe that I shared her passion for the spirit of humanity—that part of her that could see past the color of my grandfather's skin to find a great dancer with a brilliant smile; the part of her that could hold a space for the tears of a friend and keep a door open for redemption, even for those who had hurt you the most. The thought made me realize that somehow, in everything I'd lost, as imperfect as it was, I'd gained a family.

As the evening continued, from my seat across the dance floor, I watched Ms. Gretchen shake it to every song, including the most disorganized version of the Wobble line dance I had ever seen. It literally looked like the slow-motion version of a cage match, with walkers and stepped-on toes and cracking knees—everything colliding everywhere. But still, even in the midst of the chaos, I couldn't help but notice the joy that still streamed in all directions. People seemed to forget their limitations, even if just for a moment. Even crotchety Mr. Lim was up, turning around in offbeat circles. And, to my further amusement, in the rolling sea of many-colored dresses, lace and ruffles, neatly coiffed gray hair and gleaming tops of bald heads atop time-rounded shoulders, Ms. Gretchen stood out almost as if she had her own spotlight. Her face lit up from the inside like a bright flame, as I watched Mr. Parker steal a swat at her ample behind. She pretended to be offended, but giggled when she caught my eye and realized that I had seen it.

Ms. Gretchen made a big gesture for me to come and join her on the dance floor. My feet were hurting, even from just sitting, but there was no way I could say no. As I headed in Ms. Gretchen's direction I envisioned what Granny Tab would have been doing out there dancing, and for the first time I felt a true sense of ease in knowing that my presence was not required for a good time on this kind of night. I thought of the light sparkling in her faded blue eyes, the smile that stretched wide across her face, and her hands waving in the air as she might also have been trying to catch the rhythm of whatever song she danced to. I imagined that Granny Tab's heart quit that night because it had been overfilled with joy—and that she had died exhausted in the best way, that the fullness of her life had finally overflowed and that happiness burst through her at the seams, like an explosion of vibrant, expansive light. In that moment, I was certain that

Ms. Gretchen would also one day die exhausted, and when my time came, when I finished filling out the corners of my own life's adventure, so would I.

And as for my little secret, there were only a few more weeks to go before I could let everybody know . . . that, soon enough, a baby would make two.

ACKNOWLEDGMENTS

I WAS TOLD THIS BOOK WAS IMPOSSIBLE, AND YET IT EXISTS. AND so I must give thanks to all those who played a role in making this most unlikely dream a reality.

Thank you to my agent, Lucinda Halpern, who is a force of nature and unwavering belief. You saw not only what *BGMDE* was, but also what it could be. You made sure that was what it would be. Merci beaucoup.

To my editors, Sarah Ried and Amy Baker, your vision and diligence have continually inspired and encouraged me. Thank you for pushing me to higher levels as a writer and for not only seeing this book for all of its potential but elevating it further to serve readers in the excellence of its best and highest form.

To the Harper Perennial team whose enthusiasm is contagious, thank you, Heather Drucker, Lisa Erickson, Kristin Cipolla, and each and every person whose time and effort touched this book. You are appreciated beyond measure.

To the gorgeously generous *BGMDE* community—thank you to each reader for your incredible support, for all of the reviews, word-of-mouth endorsements, discussion groups, social media posts, and for the energy of "bookstagram." You have given meaning to this work and inspire me every day in my journey as an artist. I do this for you. Also, a special thanks to Dawn Michelle Hardy—your passion and commitment is such a gift. You helped turn *BGMDE* from a one-woman show into a community effort.

Thank you to each and every member of every single book club that made *BGMDE* a selection. It has been my greatest pleasure to have the opportunity to get to know you and for you to know me through your gracious invitations into your intimate spaces and discussions. To Ashley Bernardi, who through an act of kindness connected me with my agent, thank you for showing up as a friend to a stranger. I'm so glad to have you in my life.

Thank you to the bookstores, and especially the independent bookstores that provided my first shelves and first venues to connect with readers in person. Thank you for believing in me when I was an independent author, for opening your doors and hearts and joining me on this incredible journey.

To my parents, Shermane Sealey and John Sealey, for all of the tremendous sacrifices, foresight, advice, and encouragement—thank you for showing me very early that it's pretty hard to beat the combination of education, hard work, and excellence and that I can achieve anything as long as I refuse to give up. I love and appreciate you endlessly.

My grandmothers, Flossie Dixon Sealey and Ailleen Evelyn Holland Townsend, gave me my earliest examples of what a woman's strength and audacity looks like in a life well lived. They also provided key inspiration for character names (as did other of my family and friends). I will continue to live out my gratitude.

To my aunties (including the Howard University D.I.V.A.s), uncles, cousins, and friends, thank you for celebrating my wins, supporting my whims, and encouraging my attempts. I especially want to thank Danielle Gray, my sister-by-choice, for being my first editor, sounding board, and cheerleader, and Bernice Grant, for being my patient reader when I was first shaping the ideas and words of this book.

To the incredible people past, present, and future, whose irreplaceable contributions have made this journey one of hope, faith, and love, thank you for being everything that dreams are made of.

ABOUT THE AUTHOR

JAYNE ALLEN is the pen name of Jaunique Sealey, a graduate of Duke University and Harvard Law School. An avid traveler, she speaks three languages and has visited five continents. Drawing from her unique experiences as an attorney and entrepreneur, she crafts transcultural stories that touch upon contemporary women's issues such as workplace and career dynamics, race, fertility, modern relationships, and mental health awareness. Her writing echoes her desire to bring both multiculturalism and multidimensionality to a rich and colorful cast of characters inspired by the magic uncovered in everyday life. *Black Girls Must Die Exhausted* is her first novel, which she calls "the epitaph of my thirties." A proud native of Detroit, she lives in Los Angeles.